STRANGER THAN FAN FICTION

UNLUCKY IN LOVE, #1

PIPER SHELDON

QUERQUE PRESS

To J.R., always

And to the writers of fan fiction — for that story that hits like nothing else can.

1

Two Years Ago
Charlie

I gestured to let my new housekeeper lead the way out of the dining room. Not *just* out of a sense of chivalry, but because I didn't trust her behind my back.

"The kitchen is right through here," I explained.

The older woman's sensible trainers hardly made a sound on the worn hall carpeting. *The better for sneaking around ...*

Agata had been so quiet since she arrived. Normally, I relished silence, but this felt like a form of torture. Did she have misgivings about my scandalous past? Or was she simply wondering how I'd managed this long alone?

Based on how she eyed the stack of dishes near the sink, I suspected the latter.

It had been years since I had people working for me, and as it turned out, I still found the whole experience of managing people when I couldn't manage myself incredibly uncomfortable, if not hypocritical. If Emma hadn't insisted that I hire someone to keep the ancient estate from crumbling, I might have just gone on alone forever. After all, the whole point of disappearing from a life of celebrity and into the English countryside was to avoid uncomfortable interactions at all costs.

"No dishwasher?" She sniffed, looking down her nose even though she barely reached my chest.

Did she scare me? Absolutely. I didn't like it, but dammit, I respected it.

An inoffensive light lemon smell clung to her gray frock. Her blond hair was tight in a low bun, and she had a tiny, pinched mouth.

"I plan on doing some renovations and additions over time. But for now, it's a bit rustic," I said.

I glanced away when she scrutinized me. The thing with sobriety was, as fast as everything goes to shite, it takes a hell of a lot longer to work back up to any sense of normalcy. I had intended on updating the Vicarage ages ago, but some days simply existing was chore enough.

She nodded; hands clasped in front of her. "Okay," she settled on.

The small reassurance unclenched my jaw.

"The Vicarage is a bit of a drive from the nearest town. But you can have groceries delivered. I'm assuming the agency told you about ..." I scratched the back of my neck.

"No booze," she said in her soft Polish accent.

"Right. Except in your cottage, of course. I just ask not in the main house."

She nodded firmly. "I don't drink. It's no problem."

Straight to the point and no nonsense, Agata was beginning to grow on me. Emma likely had these traits in mind when she set up this appointment with the agency's recommendation.

"I guess that's everything. Do you have any questions?" I asked.

She looked me up and down. "What you want for lunch?"

"You just got here. You don't have to—"

A hand snaked out and pinched my abdomen sharply. "Too skinny."

I flinched. That's something I'd never been accused of. "I just—"

"You don't pick. You have sausage soup." Her mouth hardly moved when she spoke, but the words felt as threatening as a yell.

Feeling more than a little frightened, I acquiesced. "Ah, that's good. Thank you."

She turned her back to me and got to moving in the small kitchen.

I looked around, feeling useless. I'd already brought her single worn suitcase to the small guest house. I knocked once on the counter. "Welp, I'll let you get settled. It's been nice meeting you. Welcome to the Vicarage, Agata."

I moved to walk away.

"It smells like boy feets in here," she said as she set a large pot on the hob.

"Ah. Right." Honesty was an admirable quality in a home-maker. "I suppose you got here in the nick of time."

She sniffed again. "My children watched you when they grow up. That space show." She looked me up and down. "You were chubby funny one."

Her kids must be grown now too. Probably close to my age. That space show she referred to was *TerraFormative*, part of a multi-billion-dollar franchise based on the science fiction books written by G.S. Sedar. The series followed three children through adolescence upon a spaceship adrift in space, looking for a new Earth. Eight solid years of my adolescence I was Freddy Finks, chubby comic relief of the Intrepid Trio. My real-life best friends Emma Flynn and Harrison Evans played my two closest comrades in trouble, Lucy Lennon and Adam Abbott, respectively.

Almost twenty years ago, over in the blink of an eye to most, and yet the thing that would always define me. I was used to these types of conversations. I kept my face blank.

"Freddy." I dropped my arm before I could scratch the back of my neck again. "Yep. That was me."

"Skinny Charlie is not so funny. You eat more. You be funny. Funny man gets wife. Or husband," she added. "I'm modern woman. I understand."

"Good. Right. I'll keep that in mind." I was hardly skinny. As I'd aged, my notable baby fat had melted off my face, but I would always be described as sturdily built—now with defined cheekbones.

Her gaze narrowed on me. "Soup will be ready in one hour. Come back. Have bread too."

"I try not to eat carbs—"

"You eat the bread."

I swallowed before I nodded, afraid to do anything but agree.

"Well, I better get back to my office to ..."

To pretend to work. I finished in my head.

She paused from taking inventory of my cabinets to give me another sharp nod.

I slunk off to my unused office. I didn't really work. Hadn't really needed to in the ten years since the show wrapped. I'd been sober three of those years thanks to therapy and rehab. My only job now was to ensure I stayed on track and didn't put the people who cared about me at risk for bystander humiliation. Each day, I spent about an hour responding to fan mail, but even that had dwindled down considerably over the years. That, reading, and working out occupied most of my time.

Maybe it wasn't an exciting existence, but it was a safe one.

It was Emma who insisted I bring in help now that I had

gotten most of my life back in order. Emma was all about goals and motivations and life purpose. I didn't have the heart to tell her that simply making it day to day took so much emotional toll, there wasn't much room for anything else. I would get back there eventually, but right now, I lived tucked away safely at my home in Devon.

After rehab, I moved away from the temptations of London and bought a former vicarage. The plan was to eventually modernize the estate, but I hadn't gotten around to it yet. AA didn't recommend too many major life changes once sober, so I'd been waiting until I felt secure. Sobriety had taken more focus than I had anticipated. Employing Agata felt like a step in the right direction, another level of accountability.

It was almost time for my monthly meeting with Emma and Harrison. Their schedules were far more packed than mine, but we at least tried to arrange monthly video chats. I had dubbed those first few meetings as "proof of life," but I think seeing my face reassured Emma as much as it did me.

It was five minutes until our appointed time when they both texted to say they couldn't make the call today. Emma had got caught up in the details of arranging clean water for a town in a developing country and Harrison was working on a film bound to land him another Oscar nod. And here I was, doing absolutely nothing except getting bullied by my new homemaker.

I let out a long sigh. They weren't my keepers; they had busy lives, but this wasn't the first time I felt stuck in limbo because of my actions as the world blurred by.

I opened a tab on the internet when a wave of something crashed over me. Boredom? Listlessness? Loneliness? I fought hard to keep the indescribable emotion from pulling me under. One thing about sobriety that I wasn't prepared for was how both crucial and yet mind-numbingly boring routine would be in my life. It was better than the alternative: waking up without knowing whose bed I was in ... or what country, for that matter. This was a slow and tedious process to feel secure in myself, but how many months of monotony stretched ahead? Every day safe, but uneventful?

Agata hit the mark when she made the comment about my getting a wife. At least, she recognized my restlessness. I was lonely, but that was a whole other aspect of moderation I wasn't ready to tackle yet. Without my two best friends, who I was lucky to still have, I didn't really have anybody else to talk to. I could call my sponsor, but I didn't want a drink. I just wanted ... I didn't know, someone to talk to.

God, how pathetic.

Poor rich child star, all alone in his big country house with all his money.

I sighed again loudly and did the thing I told myself I wouldn't do any more. *One* of the things. Because what else does a retired child star do when amid a pity party? They googled themselves.

The articles about me had slowed down in the years since rehab. My publicity team had done a great job of keeping press to a minimum. The top results were old articles about England's biggest "glow up," whatever that meant. All the links led to "articles" that included countless GIFs and JPEGs of shirtless photos taken in the past few years, side by side with chubby Freddy bulging out of his *TerraFormative* flight suit.

I rested my chin in my palm as I lazily scrolled. Bored. This was pathetic. I should just close out the browser to go workout or something.

A clickbait article at the bottom of the screen caught my eye. "Top Ten Freddy Fanfics—Can't get enough of the UK's hottest former child star Charles Downing? Check out these Freddy fan favorites that take this heavenly body out of this world."

"Oh lord," I said out loud to the pun-tastic title even as I clicked the link.

I'd heard about all the fanfic that *TerraFormative* had manifested over the years. Emma, Harrison, and I had been paired in every possible combination. It was an unavoidable product of being part of one of the world's largest franchises. I'd always stayed away, feeling a new level of skeezy hearing about the various scenarios people had placed my character in. Especially with Harrison and Emma. We'd grown up together and were closer than siblings. Anything romantic was ... icky.

The headline took me to a website called FanFavz. The interface was not terribly user-friendly, but after clicking around a bit, I got the gist. You could search by franchise, author, story popularity, etc. I sorted by author popularity within the *TerraFormative* world since I'd already committed to spending time in the gutter. The very first result was the story that had been mentioned in the article. In fact, the author had a few dozen "fics" under their name. The article dubbed this particular story, "Fresh Stars," "the top Freddy post-grad fantasy." It had been favorited an astounding forty *thousand* times, and comments were a never-ending gushfest, consisting mostly of emojis and lines of repeated vowels. Post-grad referred to the time after the show ended, when Freddy had graduated from the flight academy.

"Bloody hell," I mumbled. So many people out there reading a version of myself far more interesting than the one that existed. The top author on each list was someone called FreddyStan4Life.

"Regrettable username." My face contorted, leaning closer to the screen. "Who the bloody hell is Stan?"

I read the first sentence.

Then the next.

Then several chapters. The story focused on my—er, Freddy's post-flight academy life, as he worked up the ranks to become a captain of his own vessel and featured a particularly strong romance with a cyborg named Nix, who had been in the show but only briefly in season four. I'd loved that subplot when it had debuted in the show. I had approached the writers about stretching out their love story over a few more episodes but had been shot down. The writers had reminded me that Freddy's character only existed to relieve the tension when things got too heavy. But this "Fresh Stars" I read now was ... *good*. Really good.

I also couldn't help but notice that FreddyStan4Life's description of Freddy resembled me as I looked now, instead of the child I was in the series. Interesting.

It felt like only a minute had passed when a loud rap on the closed door caused me to jump in my seat.

"You come eat, Mr. Downing." Agata's soft voice was a deceptive ruse, like calling the shake of a rattlesnake as soothing as a child's rattle.

"You can call me Charlie," I shouted through the door.

"Mister Charlie, come eat."

"Can you bring me a bowl in here?" I asked.

"No. Break from computer better for your eyes." Her footsteps retreated back to the kitchen.

I sighed loudly but pushed away from my desk.

At the kitchen island, Agata shoved two warm crusty rolls on my plate and wouldn't stop staring at me until I ate them along with the soup.

The whole meal was delicious, but she side-eyed me as I shoveled bites into my mouth. I couldn't focus on anything but getting back to my computer.

"Thank you. It was fantastic," I said.

She nodded knowingly as I rushed out of the room.

I thought I knew what fan fiction was—admittedly, I thought it was primarily an excuse to make characters have sex—but this was unlike anything I expected. The writing was compelling and thought-provoking from the first line. The world was as familiar as sliding into a worn jumper, but the new scenarios were intriguing and the additional settings captivating. It felt so familiar and yet unlike anything I'd ever read. My eyes couldn't read fast enough. My heart raced, desperate to get back to it. I missed feeling ... *excited*. About anything.

I would just read a few more chapters, just to see what happened next, and then I'd stop.

2

———

Twenty Months Ago
Kate

"Kate, do you have a second?"

My head snapped up at my boss's voice like I'd been caught playing solitaire on the company computer.

Mrs. Jennings, or Gail as she preferred to be called, stuck her head out from her office a second later. I was supposed to have been organizing her meetings for next week, when really I'd been totally zoned out thinking about a plot hole I'd gotten myself into. I never technically wrote at work, but I never could keep myself from daydreaming. Story of my life.

The chances that my boss would suddenly be able to read my mind and fire me for misuse of company time were low, but never zero.

"Yes," I answered with a sinking feeling.

Apparently, my trepidation was written all over my face.

"It's nothing bad," she added with a patient smile. Her eyes crinkled softly at their edges, the only indication she was ten years my senior. "I just need you in the conference room in ten."

"Of course. Do I need my laptop for meeting minutes?" I asked, feeling slightly deflated. It was almost time to pack up and leave for the weekend. If a meeting was starting, that meant another hour at least. It was lame enough working on my birthday, but meeting minutes was a disappointment akin to being gifted the special movie edition of my favorite book.

"Not this time. It shouldn't take long." She smiled reassuringly again before sauntering in the direction of the conference room.

I let out a slow breath before standing up and heading to the bathroom. After washing my hands, I pulled my phone out and typed a quick note. I didn't want to lose the thread of what I had been thinking about for my current story, but already it was fraying away as concerns of what Mrs. Jennings needed grew heavier.

Rationally, there was no need to worry. In the years I'd been working for her, she'd only ever been fair and pleasant. Still, if my mind wasn't jumping to conclusions, it would never get any exercise.

I wasn't ashamed of my writing. In fact, I linked my social media to my FanFavz account and had a good number of followers. But I understood that no one outside the *TerraFormative* bubble would ever take my writing seriously. And I didn't exactly want that twitchy guy from our multimedia team to start asking questions about "the dirty stories" I wrote. It didn't matter how in-depth and nuanced the stories were, once people found out sex was involved, that's all they cared to talk about. It was more indicative of their issues than mine, but still pretty creepy.

I wouldn't ever be a Real Author until I had a publishing contract. That had been the plan since I graduated college and took this administrative assistant job—temporarily—while I finished my book. I continued to write TF fan fiction because it made me happy, but I never expected it to blow up like it did. As my popularity grew, so did my passion for story telling in that world. Readers would tag me in prompts I couldn't turn down. Gorgeous fan art would inspire a short story and vice versa. It was a whole world that I was happy to get lost in.

I gave myself a silent pep talk in the bathroom mirror to kill a few minutes. Finally, the anticipation got the best of me and I made my way to the conference room.

The door was shut, and I debated between knocking and interrupting the meeting or silently sneaking in to sit in the back. I waited until it had been exactly ten minutes since Mrs. Jennings first asked me to join her and turned the door handle. Rather than meet the eyes of everyone glancing up at me, I kept my back to the room as I silently closed the door behind me.

The door clicked like a clap in the quiet, announcing my arrival. I winced and turned around, an apology already on my lips.

"Happy Birthday!" the whole room shouted.

I jumped, causing my back to bump into the door handle. "Oh my god!" *This is my nightmare.* "What a surprise!" *I want to crawl under my desk and hide.* "Thank you all so much." My lips pulled into a tight smile.

The room was filled with at least a dozen of my coworkers. A large cake sat on the table and Mrs. Jennings came forward to hand me a bouquet.

"Wow. This is so nice. You didn't have to do this." I hid my face in the flowers, pretending to examine the blooms.

The gesture was incredibly thoughtful. I was so grateful they remembered me, but to my poor introverted mind, this was only slightly better than having a middle-aged man ask me about my sex scenes as he licked his lips.

No. Never mind. I definitely preferred this.

"It's not much, but we wanted you to know we appreciate all that you do around here," Mrs. Jennings said, a teasing smile playing on her mouth. "Should we sing to you?"

"No!" I snapped and quickly covered up my rudeness. "No, thank you. You're so kind. Let's just get to the cake!"

She winked at me, and I let out a breath.

The cake was cut and passed around.

"I'm sorry. I know this isn't really your thing," Mrs. Jennings said softly to me a few minutes later. She came up to me where I stood in the corner, hiding like a little coward. "It was Kline's idea from HR. And I couldn't really think of a reason to say no."

I frowned at my cake, feeling bad for being so ungrateful and so completely obvious in my awkwardness. "It's really sweet. I appreciate it."

"And we appreciate *you*. It's been almost five years and you've done so much for our firm. I would be lost without you."

What was a normal response to direct praise? Ridiculously specific internet memes were more my love language. "Of course. I love working for you."

My smile stayed firmly in place even as I did the math. It was not possible that it had been five years since graduating college and taking this admin position until I launched my writing career.

That couldn't be right.

But ... it was.

A few of my coworkers drifted past to say their birthday wishes, including the cute guy, Pete, from sales, so that was nice. Several people invited me to join them for happy hour and graciously pretended to believe me when I said I had plans. Maybe someday I would join them to chat and gossip about office stuff, but today I had been walloped upside the head by unexpected birthday blues. After just a few minutes of being social, I was ready to leave for the day. I excused myself with as little fanfare as possible without being rude.

I had a good job. I liked my boss. I made enough money for everything I needed. I chose to major in business over creative writing. I earned the degree and the secure job with benefits. I did everything right. I should be grateful. I *was* grateful.

I guess I just thought I would have a literary agent and several books already published by now ... or even a finished novel to pitch.

But that was me: romanticizing life with my head permanently in the clouds.

Writing *TerraFormative* fan fiction brought so much joy and distraction, but it was only ever that, a distraction. It would never be taken seriously. *I* would never be taken seriously as a writer until I got that book deal. I could hear my mom's voice mentioning "those silly little stories." And yet even now I wanted to get lost in the TF world I knew so well. Maybe I'd just write a quick one-shot. That would make my fifty thousand plus subscribers happy. And of course, it would make me happy. A little stress relief.

At home, I dropped my keys on the side table by the door, immediately changed out of my business clothes and into sweatpants, and shot my bra off like a slingshot.

I had stopped at my post office box and found it filled with several cards and gifts from readers. I scanned through them now, causing my eyes to well with tears. Readers were really just the best people. I poured myself a glass of milk to have with my dinner—a to-go piece of birthday cake from the office—and opened my laptop.

My social media was filled with birthday wishes from online readers and friends. I smiled as I sifted through the messages and GIFs, many of them featuring a shirtless Charles Downing holding a birthday cake. I should feel bad about ogling the guy. He was, after all, just a person, but the man was beautiful, and my crush was not new. It had all started when I was eleven and I watched my first episode of *TerraFormative*, or TF, as I would soon begin to refer to it. I understood why all the girls went crazy over Harrison. He was obviously the cute one with the damaged soul eyes that appealed to so many. But I always preferred Freddy Finks, with his sweet dimples and silly jokes. As time went on, my crush morphed from not just infatuation with the fictional character but to the real-life Charles Downing. Embarrassing. We were basically the same age but had lived completely different lives. I wondered what he was doing now. I wondered if he ever felt lonely.

I should write a fan fiction based on those GIFs of him showing up at the door holding a cake for my birthday. I would be sitting here writing; he would walk in with my piece of cake …

I blushed. "Jesus, Kate," I muttered and stuffed a bite of rich frosting into my mouth.

Tonight, I would let myself indulge in my fan fiction writing. Then I would focus in earnest on my novel.

A message from a new user popped into my inbox just as I was about to close out and get to writing. User78767645 looked like the default log ins they gave to new members. Usually those messages were spam, but the glimpse of the first line, "I swear I'm not a nutter," had me clicking on it out of curiosity.

I read the thank you note, feeling a grin grow on my face. Then I read it again. The words were vulnerable yet light and funny enough to make me snort out loud. Maybe because of the birthday blues or maybe because I was high on sugar and feeling adventurous, I responded to the message. And not the polite canned answer I sent to the many people who reached out to me. This user78767645 required a personal touch. And there was a sense of humor and surprising vulnerability that stuck out to me.

But there I went making a mountain out of a molehill again and romanticizing an innocent message. I would send a simple thank you, nothing more.

3

———————

DRAFT UNSENT

From: user78767645

To: FreddyStan4Life

Hi. My name is Charlie Downing. That likely seems hard to believe, but it's true. I came across your stories by accident a few weeks ago. (I swear I'm not some nutter who searches out stories about himself for an ego boost.) I've since read every story you've written. I imagine people must reach out to you all the time to compliment you. Your stories are so rich and intricate and captivating. I didn't even mean to read, no offense. I saw an article that linked to an article about fanfics ... Anyway. It doesn't matter how I got there.

I just wanted to write to say thank you. I can't tell you how much your words have meant to me. I've been struggling all these years since we finished filming. I'm sure you've seen much of it in the tabloids. Nothing has made me feel as grounded as being back in the TerraFormative world. You've managed to take a beloved story and improve upon it. I am in absolute awe of you. Every time I struggle and want to find a way to numb myself, I let myself read your stories and manage to get through another day sober.

It's ridiculous that I'm reaching out to you like this. I never even created a FanFavz account to read your stories. I had to create one just to message you. Thank you for taking Freddy's character and making him something more than a chubby sidekick who exists only to break the tension. I've always thought he had untapped potential.

Undoubtedly you already think I'm some creep on the internet and probably won't even read this letter. I just need you to know how important your words have been to me. But you'd never believe I'm actually Charlie Downing. Not to mention it's bloody embarrassing that I'm reading fan fiction about my own character.

Fuck. I can't send this.

———

From: USER78767645

To: FreddyStan4Life

I swear I'm not a nutter. Of course, that's likely exactly what a nutter *would* say ... I guess you'll have to take my word on it.

I've never written fan mail before. Just know this feels deeply uncomfortable. (But thankfully, as a British man, that's my typical state of being.)

Alas, I am compelled to say thank you. In the last couple weeks, I have read everything you've written. You've helped me during a tough transition in my life. Every time I feel particularly sorry for myself, I open one of your stories. I tell myself just one chapter, then proceed to get lost. The hours slip by, and I have made it through another night.

So, thanks.

Cheers,

user78767645

PS: Also, thank you for making Freddy more than a bumbling idiot.

———

From: FreddyStan4Life

To: user78767645

Dear user78767645,

Thank you for your letter and for powering through centuries of English pride to pay me a compliment. My American ancestors are cackling in triumph.

In all sincerity, I'm touched that these stories have meant something to you. Though they aren't my characters and *Terra-Formative* isn't my world, it's an honor to write in it. Letters like this are part of the reason I enjoy it so much.

Since we're both already oversharing, I'll be honest and tell you that your note was perfectly timed, as I was in the midst of my own pity party about having completed another full rotation around the sun. Also, I realized today I've been working at a "temporary" job for almost five years. Recently, I've been feeling like making some changes in my life and was inspired by your words.

Sincerely,

FreddyStan4life

PS: Freddy has hidden depths that weren't properly conveyed in the show. I've always had a bit of a soft spot for him.

———

From: GodSaveTheQueen

To: FreddyStan4Life

Dear FreddyStan4life,

Americans don't have ancestors. They have traitorous bloodlines.

Freddy is grossly misunderstood.

I'm sorry to hear you're American. I honestly just assumed you were from the right side of the pond based on your writing.

Unfortunately, Her Majesty the Queen has reached out and asked that we cease all communications.

Happy Birthday. Sorry, it was less than exciting.

Don't fret about time passing quickly, it has a habit of doing that, and I'm afraid it only gets worse with age. You have plenty of time to make changes. Life is short. Still, I do recommend that you start now. Don't wait for the right time because there is no such thing.

Just ask the house in disrepair all around me.

I have spent the last few years in a blur. But in part, thanks to your stories and my therapist, I have now been sober for over three years. Lord, look at me oversharing. I'm a shame to my countrymen. I don't usually talk about these sorts of things with anybody. I don't usually talk to people at all if I can help it. But since I've already shared all my darkest secrets with you, there it is. I feel weary most days. Stuck, but too young to give up. Too old to have youthful optimism. Christ, I was much more fun when I drank ...

Cheers (with fizzy water),
GodSaveTheQueen

———

From: FreddyStan4Life

To: GodSaveTheQueen

Dear GodSaveTheQueen,

Congrats on the sobriety. I'm incredibly honored that you think that I had anything to do with that. But that's all you, my teetotaler friend.

I like your new username. Reminds me of how terribly embarrassed I am about my own. In my defense, this account is over fifteen years old, and teenagers cannot be held accountable for their actions. At this point, I can't change it because of how many subscribers I have. That sounded braggy, but I didn't mean it that way.

You have inspired me. After our last message, I continued work on a novel I started years ago. No more wasting time. I'm finishing this baby!

Humbly yours,
FreddyStan4Life

———

FROM: BEFUDDLEDBRIT

To: FreddyStan4Life

I'm thrilled to hear you're writing a novel. I look forward to reading it. You should brag. It's impressive. As is your writing.

Plus, isn't boasting a requirement as an American? I picture you as wearing a ten-gallon cowboy hat and snakeskin boots, driving your massive truck. That's what you all do, right?

I most certainly would not like to be compared to my sixteen-year-old self.

Speaking of usernames, who is Stan?

BefuddledBrit

———

FROM: FREDDYSTAN4LIFE

To: BefuddledBrit

Sweet, sweet summer child,

WHEN I TELL YOU I AM CACKLING. Have you not heard of Google? Maybe the technology hasn't reached your neck of the woods. I'll save you the trouble. "Stan" is not a specific person but rather "an extremely or excessively enthusiastic and devoted fan."

My mocking has backfired. I'm even more embarrassed now.

Remember, I WAS SIXTEEN. (Have I just aged myself?) Thankfully, he (the actor, Charles Downing) hasn't been outed as a perv like so many of my childhood idols. And actually, as the years pass, I respect him more than the character he played. Sorry for laughing at (with?) you. I forget that you're relatively new to this whole world of obsessive fandoms. But where *have* you been? Did you watch *TerraFormative*? I imagine you did, if you happened upon my stories and found them the least bit interesting.

Hey, not all Americans! But maybe all Texans. I'm in Minnesota, Land of 10,000 Lakes, baby! Also, perpetually freezing. It's March, so we've had six(?) straight months of snow now, and I'm absolutely OVER IT.

Hiding in shame,

FreddyStan4life (ugh. I hate this username now)

PS: I just decided that you can call me Kate. It's not a big secret because my social media accounts are linked. And I would feel better if you'd picture me accurately and not dressed in that deplorable American uniform.

PPS: That doesn't mean you have to tell me your name. And you certainly don't need to picture me. That didn't come out right. I should probably stop typing now.

PPPS: Okay, last thing. Here's my email (KateDubois@geemail.com) if you ever want to try talking that way. FanFavz is known to crash randomly and is not very user-friendly.

4

Charlie

I STARED AT THE SCREEN. IT WAS AFTER TWO IN THE MORNING, AND I needed to get sleep.

And yet ...

I wiped a hand over my mouth. My smile was embarrassing enough, but this jittery anticipation was worse. I hadn't expected FreddyStan4Life, or *Kate* as she said I could call her, to respond. I definitely hadn't expected her to be so funny and charming. And why not? Her stories were smartly written and had pockets of humor delicately woven in. Of course, she would be as equally charming in her conversation.

Her conversation with *me*.

She'd responded, and then I had, and then like normal humans, we were conversing. Wild. Was I so starved for simple company that Kate's emails felt like a gift?

I laughed out loud thinking of her teasing. My humor sometimes accidentally offended people, but she gave as good as she got.

I stared at the email address she provided.

My heart raced like she'd asked me out. This didn't mean anything. Maybe she talked to all of her fans like this. She could just be friendly like most Americans. Maybe this wasn't typical for her. Or maybe I was hopeful and projecting. This was more invigorating than foreplay.

Lord, I needed a life.

Kate must get dozens of messages a day like mine. I still got fan emails, and I hadn't played Freddy in over ten years. It wasn't like I deserved the praise, not like she had with her writing. I had been hired at eleven to play Freddy Finks because I *was* him. We were the same age, we had similar personalities, and my round face and rotund build slipped me perfectly into the role. I was the obnoxious kid who found making people laugh preferable to having them laugh at me first.

Based on what she shared, Kate was only a few years younger than me. That made sense. It was more surprising when I discovered new generations of devoted fans that hadn't even been born when the show was still filming.

It was the maturity of her writing that had me imagining her as an older woman, maybe with a gaggle of children around her. Or maybe that'd been wishful thinking. Because truthfully, I had a crush on her before I even sent that first message. With every exchange, the weight of those feelings grew. Soon I'd be flattened.

I was flustered. Like I was a teenager and had just made eye contact with someone across the hall at a dance. At least that's how I assumed teenagers did it. I wouldn't know what a normal childhood felt like. The first time I kissed a girl, there were thirty people standing around, a camera in my face, and the director pointing out how awkward I looked.

Anyway.

She wrote back. She had said I could reach out any time. Had the offer been out of politeness? But if she offered ...

I should send her an email.

No, play it cool. I didn't want to appear as abysmally depressing and lonely as I was. She deserved more than blatant lies ... but she couldn't learn who I was now, could she? Our exchanges had already gone on longer than I had meant.

Whatever this was should end before things got too out of control. She probably wasn't sitting around debating all this.

I forced myself to bed. I slept a whole four hours before getting up and hitting the home gym. Agata had a spinach smoothie and a cuppa ready for me after.

I sniffed the tea when she wasn't looking and thanked her.

My resolve lasted eight hours. Eight measly hours before I was back in front of my laptop.

I couldn't leave Kate hanging like that. I couldn't let her think she had done anything wrong. Maybe just one more message. Just to make a clean break.

Now. How to respond? I wouldn't ever lie to her. I made that promise to myself before I ever even sent the first message. But I couldn't tell her many personal details without giving too much away.

I reread her last message. Kate had essentially told me to go look at her social media accounts. She told me to picture her.

I swallowed. My lonely mind filled in gaps that I wasn't proud of.

No. It would be good. I would look at her pictures and find some reason to end this fascination. Maybe she had a partner? She'd have to be with someone else for me to stop daydreaming.

I followed the links and my heart stopped.

"Bloody hell," I groaned.

She hadn't posted a ton of pictures of herself, mostly fan art that readers had made based on her stories. Lots of sketches of me, hand-drawn and brooding.

"Regrettable." The fan art, not her. Kate was breathtaking. I was already half in love with her from her stories. This wasn't good.

Dated a fortnight ago, she'd posted an exquisite photo of herself sitting in front of a window with buttery light illuminating a round face with big brown eyes behind large circular framed glasses. Her light brown hair was short in a chic-looking bob with fringe that matured her otherwise innocently cute features. The sun made her eyes look as speckled as the freckles on her pert nose. Her full lips softly curved into a contented smile. It was as though she'd been lost in a book, and someone had walked in and taken a photo of her in her most natural habitat.

"Enjoying the sun from the safety of my apartment," she'd captioned it.

With every image, warmth spread through me. But also a sort of niggling fear. She was more than I hoped for. She must be with someone. There was no way people passed her in the street, worked with her, and said hello at cafes without instantly falling for her. It was unfathomable.

More and more photos and yet no mention of a partner. It was better to have not known, let myself keep imagining her as a housewife happily married with a slew of children. Or better yet, a man living in his mother's basement. Now I had a gorgeous face to put to my growing infatuation. I was a total nob.

I needed to get my head on straight.

"Very pretty," Agata said from right behind me.

I jerked so hard my knee slammed into my desk. "Christ!" I clutched a hand to my chest. The sneaky little ninja.

"So jumpy, Mister Charlie." She set down a fresh cup of tea. I hadn't even noticed mine had gone cold.

"Thank you," I told her.

"You spend too long on that computer."

"Good morning, Agata. Why yes, I'm fine this lovely day. And how are you?"

She clicked her tongue at my sarcasm and walked to the window behind me. Without asking, she tugged the curtains open and let the light pour in. I fought to keep from hissing like a vampire.

"How you know it's lovely? Or morning?" She snorted. "You are getting pasty," she added.

"I'm British."

"Is no excuse."

Maybe I had been spending too much time online reading Kate's stories and our email exchanges. But I lived to see the little message indicator. I couldn't remember the last time I felt this excited about anything.

"Pretty girl," Agata said again from directly over my shoulder, blatantly looking at my screen. "Girlfriend?"

I snapped my laptop closed. "No. She's an American."

"So? You can do the face screen calls. You can do the camera phone sex."

"I ... don't think ..." A thousand images popped into my brain that I really didn't want to have with a tiny Polish woman standing right behind me. "Is there something you needed?"

"I need you to get out of house more. You are always here."

I stared at her. "You want me to leave my own house?"

"Go outside. Get a dog. A girlfriend. Go meet American woman. You are always here. Always underfoot looking sad. I need to get things done."

I opened my mouth to respond, but she was right. I was supposed to be moving forward with my life. Not replacing one obsession with another. I was falling for a woman I didn't even know. A woman I could never know because I could never reveal the truth of who I was without risking her going to the press, or worse, thinking I was a perv. A relationship would never work, especially since I'd shared almost nothing about myself, and she had been so open and giving from the start.

I sighed and pushed back out of the chair. A response to her last message could wait.

The weather in Devon was pretty mild for England this time of year, and so even though it was overcast, it wasn't too chilly. I tugged on my wellies and mac and decided to stroll around the countryside looking for inspiration. I was moving forward, getting healthy, and staying steady.

It was decided. No more messages.

5

———————

FROM: TheRealFreddyStan4Life@geemail.com

SUBJECT: CALL ME DADDY

Kate,

You would not believe the morning I've had. I was unceremoniously kicked out of the Vicarage this morning by Agata after being told I needed a life. (She isn't entirely wrong.) I had wandered past the grounds of my estate when the heavens opened up and drenched me. Typical English karma.

I was sprinting home to get out of the rain, looking rather like a drowned rat, when I passed the neighbour's. A small cardboard box was sat at the end of his drive, slowly dissolving in the rain. As I got closer, the box made sad little chirps and peeps. Inside were the most pitiful looking creatures I'd ever seen.

Chickens.

Three of them. Wet and blinking up at me in utter confusion. Can you believe it? They are older than little baby chicks; they have coarse feathers mixed in with their fluff and are a bit gangly looking. They are in that awkward teenage phase if I had to guess.

I took the box home, if only to keep them from drowning. I may be a grumpy bugger, but nobody with half a heart could just leave them there. Imagine my surprise when I called my neighbour and he told me this happened a lot after Easter. It was common for *monsters* to purchase baby chicks for cute photos and then, as they grow, dispose of them. It's a travesty. I cannot imagine. I hate humans.

If you could hear them even now ... their sad little noises.

Christ, becoming a parent—however temporary—has made me a sad sop.

Now, obviously, I shouldn't be taking care of anybody else when I can hardly care for myself, but I could not rightly just abandon them after what they've been through.

No. It's my duty to make sure they're okay, just until I know they have a good home to go to.

I cannot wait until Agata gets back to show her. Bet she didn't have this in mind when she booted me. I was so excited to tell you that I haven't actually come up with a solid plan yet.

One has escaped, so I need to rush off. Sneaky little buggers.

Yours,

DUKE of CHICKENSTON

PS: I hope you like my email address. Can you believe it wasn't taken? I was inspired by one of my favorite writers.

PPS: You probably give your email to all your fans, but I appreciate it, nonetheless. I will try not to abuse the privilege.

TO: TheRealFreddyStan4Life@geemail.com

FROM: KateDubois@geemail.com

SUBJECT: So you're the reason they crossed the road ...

Congratulations! I will not be calling you daddy. Nice try.

It was very kind of you to save those poor babies. Hopefully, you will be able to find them a good home. (You're one of those gruff on the outside, squishy on the inside people, aren't you?)

So. Not that I'm trying to change the topic from your most happy news but are you a daddy, er, a father, that is? Is Agata your partner? I feel like I know so little about you. I can't help but notice you didn't actually answer the questions in my last message. No pressure to answer any of these questions, BTW. (That means "by the way.")

Also, the Vicarage? GROUNDS OF YOUR ESTATE?!?

I'm sorry, but if you tell me you're a rich duke looking for a duchess, I will have to end this email exchange because I KNOW the next question will be you asking me to wire money.

It's funny, thanks to your email address, I've decided to picture you only as Charles Downing. Because real celebrity accounts always say "real" before their name. Did you know that? Are you being cheeky? But then again, you didn't know about "Stan," so I'm still very unclear on your age.

I'm sorry if I pried too much in my last message. Obviously, you don't have to talk about anything you don't want to.

And truthfully, I've never shared this personal email with anybody. So now you know all *my* secrets.

Best of luck with your chicky teenagers,

Kate

———

TO: KateDubois@geemail.com
FROM: TheRealFreddyStan4Life@geemail.com
SUBJECT: O Ye of Little Faith
Attachment: IntrepidTrio.jpeg
Kate,

Tsk. You Americans are so skeptical.

I didn't mean to avoid your super personal questions,

random stranger on the internet; I was genuinely flustered about my unexpected fostering. I have named them, BTW (I know what that means, I'm not *that* old). They are Adam, Lucy, and Freddy, my own little Intrepid Trio. (I attached a pic—I know they look the same, but Adam is the best-looking one, of course, Lucy has a tint of red to her head, and Freddy is the chubby one. Yes, a little on the nose, I know.)

They will not stop eating. I've had to go into the nearest town twice to get them feed already. And I won't bore you with the atrocities coming out of them because I am a proper English gentleman, and quite frankly, it's appalling. Adam seems to be the boldest of the three. He pecks at my ankle, but I think he— uh, she actually, now that I think about it. Perhaps this wasn't the best naming convention. Lucy stays tucked next to her brother, Freddy. Christ, I mean *sister*. But I suspect they will warm up with time.

They are all lady chickens, hens. Apparently, Farmer John from next door (that is actually how he introduced himself—I'm never cheeky and mystified why you would even suggest that) came over to tell me that he would take them if I wanted. But he mentioned splitting them up and I just didn't think that was a good idea. They're siblings and should be kept together. Plus, I know for a fact that there is a fox that roams these parts.

Farmer John mentioned that they are Gingernut Ranger chickens (I could not have invented that breed if I tried) and they will produce many eggs. For now, I'm going to build them a little pen with a heat lamp and a dry bed. They can't be outside just yet. I have had to do a lot more research than I want because these are the first creatures I've ever cared for. That's how I'm telling you I have no children, Nosy Nelly.

Agata had a fit when I brought them home. It was almost worth the tiny little messes and the total lack of sleep just to see her face. She threatened to make chicken noodle soup if she finds them anywhere but my office. She'll warm up to them yet ...

For now, I will have to keep them safe from her clutches. At least until I can find them a good home. Currently, they're peeping away in a shoe box in my closet. Agata, by the way, is the tiny, terrifying Polish woman ruining my life. Technically, her title is housekeeper and cook.

I am not married. Nor am I a duke. Sadly. (If I were, would you call me daddy?) The Vicarage is the name of my house. It's my attempt at humor because the house is a former vicarage originally built in the 1850s. Alas, I have no plans to scam you out of your riches. I know writers must scrape together every penny. Oh wait, you said you had a "temporary" day job. How is that going? How goes the novel? What genre is it?

It would appear I have still avoided your questions about *TerraFormative*.

Yes. I was very close to the show. The fact of the matter is, I was (am?) so absurdly obsessed with it I don't really like to talk about it with very many people. It was such a big part of my life for so long that I've had a bit of a hard time moving on from it. Another reason I connect so deeply to your words. Other people don't really sympathize. I don't understand my inability to move on. I'm a grown man and shouldn't still think about "a kid's show" so much.

Anyway. You really do know all my secrets now. You have a way of prying information out of me I don't share. Reminds me of one of my best mates—you'd give her a run for her money.

Since we are doing this whole ... sharing thing, *ew*, I've been reading through all your stories again. Yes, I know I have a problem. I have tried other authors, but they just don't do it for me. Don't let it go to your already large head.

I hope it doesn't go against fanboy etiquette, but I was wondering about one of your stories. The short story "Mobius

Strips and Shooting Stars," isn't like any of your others (as you know). It's the only one still set during within the timeline of the show. Why didn't you write more of when the characters were still in the youth space program? It felt like I'd stumbled upon the script for a missing episode—a better written (shh, don't tell anyone I said that) and more intriguing episode.

Yours Truly,

RealCharlie

PS: I'm fine with you picturing me as the actor. However, you see me in your head (or in your fan art) is probably much better than reality anyway. You can call me the Real Charlie. ;p (that's a winky tongue face—see, I'm hip with the youths).

TO: THEREALFREDDYSTAN4LIFE@GEEMAIL.COM
FROM: KateDubois@geemail.com
SUBJECT: Real Life is Lame
RC (for Real Charlie),

Anytime you say "youths," immediately you've aged yourself. Sorry, Gramps.

I don't want to alarm you, but it sounds like you may be getting attached to your feathered children. What if maybe, instead of trying to find them a home, you kept them for yourself? You know, so they don't get separated. At least until they're grown and can handle farm life. Just throwing that out there.

As far as *TerraFormative* (TF) goes, I get it. I'm the same way. Especially writing in that world. I feel like I can't really tell anybody about how deep my feelings go without ridicule or judgment. Especially not at my work. I sometimes feel like I'm living two different identities or like I have this big secret. So I understand. In some ways, it's a way to instantly bond with someone. Like you and me :) (I'm still laughing about you telling me the meaning of your emoticon. Dork.)

I'm still at the same job. Sadly. I know we don't do details, but it's just your run-of-the-mill corporate job where I dress professionally and answer calls. I can't complain, my boss is lovely, and the pay is good. I wouldn't say I'm passionate about it, but how many people are about their day jobs? I'm thankful for what I have.

The novel is actually going well. I've written more in these last few weeks than I have in years! It's a space opera, of sorts. I already know you're asking, "What the bloody hell is space opera? Chuff chuff, cheerio!" (Or whatever you say when you're confounded.) Just google it, Gramps.

Hmm. I still feel like I have shared much more about myself than you have with me, but I suppose I could answer your deeply personal question about "Mobius Strips and Shooting Stars."

I usually find writing the Intrepid Trio as adults, Freddy primarily, much easier. I can put them in whatever scenarios I like and not feel weird about it. (Not just the ... er, romantic aspects but how they process their emotions and handle stuff). It's been so long since I was a teenager, I wouldn't even know how to write one anymore.

That being said ... that episode was a passion project. I guess all these stories are. But that one, in particular, I remember it being the first time I was fully obsessed. I was about thirteen, I think (I have edited it a lot since then, but that was when I first wrote it), and I would sit and write for hours in that world. My mom thought I was wasting my time. She always told me that I needed to get my head out of the clouds. I tended to be fantastical as a kid. The episodes with Nix felt so unfinished. The show writers set up this perfect opportunity to give Freddy more depth and become more than just comic relief, but they totally pulled the punch. I know it's all so silly to people outside the TF bubble, but it felt like he was robbed. I couldn't move on until I wrote it. That story is basically canon to me at this point. I forget sometimes that the show never dealt with his trauma.

Anyway, that's why I wrote it. I wanted Freddy to be a fully formed adult and get the happy ending he deserved.

That was probably more than you wanted to know, but there you go. Thank you for saying that the writing was as good as the show. I promise not to tell them whenever we hang out. ;p

Best,

Kate

———

TO: KateDubois@geemail.com

FROM: TheRealFreddyStan4Life@geemail.com

SUBJECT: RE: Real Life is Lame

Attachment: TemporaryHome.jpeg

Kate,

On your advice, I have decided to keep the chickens for now. You're right, it's just too risky. I need to ensure they aren't separated, or heaven forbid *whispering* made into chicken nuggets. Actually, they remind me a bit of my two best mates and me sometimes. Adam seems to be running the show. Lucy has already started to warm up to me. She wobbles up to me anytime I walk in the room and lets me scratch her tiny little head. Freddy ... Freddy keeps running into the wall. I think she may have knocked her head once or twice, but she's very affectionate and even now is sleeping in my lap. Poor little lady.

Hard to believe these descended from terrifying dinosaurs, especially when they have trouble finding their way out of an open shoe box. They have been upgraded to a homemade pen with heat lamp and a little bed made of cozy wood chips. Eventually, I will move them to the outside coop I'm building.

Thank you for sharing about your first story ever. I can just picture tiny little Kate, journaling away, tongue sticking out in concentration as she wrote. I'm glad you grew up with your head "in the clouds." I suspect that's exactly why you're so good at what you do. There's nothing wrong with wanting to be a writer. A lot of perfectly respectable people are authors. It's not so fantastical. That story was perfect and hard to fathom you originally wrote it at such a young age. Even more evidence that you were destined to be an author. I wish we could go back in time and have you write for the show. (Even though I do very much enjoy the grown-up stories you tell too. I think "Little Black Dresses and Little White Lies" may be my favorite.)

So, tell me about this space opera novel of yours. And yes, I did have to look up what that was.

RC (I am sticking with this name for now.)

6

Sixteen Months Ago
Kate

"Is he flirting?" I paced my small apartment, mumbling to myself. "Am I flirting?" I looked in the mirror, cheeks flushed and eyes glinting in excitement. Was it just me or did I look prettier, lighter? I would not start singing bits of *West Side Story* just because he complimented me. Tons of strangers compliment me and my writing online all the time, but none of them seemed to impact me like RC does.

I hummed as I got ready for work. *I do feel pretty*. Dammit, I earwormed myself.

RC said that one of my most popular, and probably not a coincidence, the most erotic pieces I have ever written was his favorite. He wouldn't have mentioned that if he wasn't trying to flirt, right?

It was times like these I was noticeably lacking in friendships I could discuss romantic sort of things with. I purposely closed myself off from work relationships because I had never thought I would last there. My friends from college were at different stages in life and very busy. I had friends online, but none of them I talked to regularly enough to warrant the level of deep dive that I needed to analyze these exchanges.

What did friends get you anyway? Just look at Julius Caesar.

My exchanges with RC had quickly become my favorite part of my day.

There was a voice in my head, sounding suspiciously like my mother, that warned me I was moving too fast. Making something from nothing. Had I come on too strong, too soon, sharing my real name and social media? But those details weren't a secret, and RC absolutely emailed me back all the time. Nothing felt one-sided. We had a repartee going. It felt like this was the start of something.

This was why I wasn't on any dating apps. It was too hard to read people on a screen.

Not that this was even ... not that he even ...

I groaned out loud again. But I felt like the flirting was there. What I needed was some sort of forensic expert to analyze it.

From the first message, there was an instant connection. I was compelled to click on it, and then we were chatting. And now, his messages were the most important part of my day.

What if it was a scam and he was just waiting to ask me to wire him money? What if I had just made it easier for him to lure me in? I was lonely and gullible, and he probably already knew exactly who I was before he even read my stories.

Oh my god, what if he never read my stories?

Calm down, Kate. I heard my mother's exasperated voice. Maybe I should call her. She'd knock me down to reality in the way that only she could.

But I was enjoying RC. We talked most days and once several times. I loved hearing about the chickens he was so clearly in love with. My god, it was adorable.

RC seemed so genuine. Vulnerable and lonely. Was he actually an older man who didn't want to be alone? Did that matter? It didn't feel like it did. Sure, I didn't even know his name or what he looked like, but I knew some inherent truth about him. I wasn't being played. Our connection was real.

Just as I grabbed my purse to leave, I realized there was one obvious solution to my problem. An easy way to understand where he stood.

I could ask him.

I *would* ask him if he wanted to take our relationship to the next level.

A face-to-face call. It was a modern world with a dozen different ways to communicate. Email was honestly a little dated, even if I did find it romantic.

I groaned. I really was blowing things out of proportion.

I would ask him directly, and then I would have my answer.

No big deal. I was a grown woman, and I could handle it.

———

Charlie

WELL, I HADN'T EXACTLY ENDED THINGS WITH KATE. BUT I wouldn't let myself cross any more lines.

No more flirty banter. No more asking personal details. I would keep things simple. I'd let myself get too comfortable with her. I just felt so much, so fast. She was so easy to talk to. But it would be easy with so much hidden still, wouldn't it? No. I needed to pare down my emails and focus on our friendship.

No more having strong feelings.

I could do that. I could keep our exchanges friendly.

Unless. Maybe I should finally tell her the truth? Ugh.

So what if we'd gotten in the habit of talking every single day? That was fine. Plenty of friends talked every day.

Or so I've heard.

Speaking of …

My computer lit up with an incoming video call from Emma.

"Hello," I said. "I've met someone."

Well, shit. That was not what I meant to say.

"What?" She leaned forward to scrutinize me. "Where are you? Why's it so dark?"

"I'm in my office. And keep your voice down. I'm hiding from Agata."

"Oh, so that's going well." Her jaw dropped. "Oh my god, is she who you met?"

"What? No." I clicked on the lamp next to me.

"Just because she's older, you know women don't lose value just because society says they have no worth after the age of—"

"Emma." I rubbed my eyes, adjusting to the brightness. "Agata is a grandmother and married. I'm sure that she's a lovely woman but that was not who I was referring to. Also, what the hell?"

"Sorry. I—" She waved away whatever she'd been about to say. "All right. Out with it. Who's the new lady? Wait. Can Harrison join in?"

"Yeah."

A moment later, Harrison's stupid handsome mug filled up the screen.

"Heya, mates." He had to yell to be heard over the din. In the background, attractive people stood around laughing and chatting.

Emma and I said "hi" in unison.

"What's going on? Everything okay?" he asked.

I rolled my eyes.

"Oh shit, is it the end of the month already? Hang on." The phone rustled as he juggled some papers and left the loud area of wherever he had been. "Sorry about that."

"Need us to ring later?" Emma asked.

Harrison stood on a quiet patio, produced an e-cig, and took a pull. "It's just a party." He shook his head and blew out the e-smoke.

I didn't blame Harrison for forgetting our monthly call, but once again, the sting of feeling like I was the only one who'd not been able to move on got me.

Distantly, I heard Emma nag him about his smoking, but I was lost in regret for having mentioned Kate. She felt ... like my secret. My safe thing. Like if I shared her, somehow, the delicate balance of our friendship would vanish into thin air. It would end just like that. She was a good thing, and I knew better than most that all good things must come to an end.

"Right, Charlie?" Emma asked, bringing me back to the present. "You said you met someone?"

In for a penny ...

"Yeah. Online," I said.

"Oh yeah? Congrats, mate. Serious then?" Harrison assumed.

I never brought up women. Ever. I'd stopped the random hookups with fangirls along with the excessive drinking.

"We're just talking." I shrugged. *But I can't stop thinking about her, and I flirt with her, and I fancy the bloody hell out of her.*

"Well, what's her name? What's she like?" Harrison prompted.

"She's a writer. She's talented and hilarious and thoughtful and gorgeous. We talk every day ..." Their eyebrows shot up with every word. I cleared my throat and finished with, "So. Right."

"She sounds lovely." Emma took pity on me and stopped me from talking anymore. "When do we get to meet her?" Emma asked.

"About that." I looked toward the window. "She's American."

"Oh lord, so it's terminal then?" Harrison said, dryly. "Christ, mate, you said it like you're dying. It's America, not the moon."

I shot him a look. "And, I haven't exactly told her who I am."

Harrison winced and Emma's jaw dropped.

"How?" Emma asked, shaking her head in confusion. "How can you talk every day and her not know?"

"We've kept things anonymous." I groaned. "Well, I have. She's shared her email and I've looked her up. She told me I could," I added before it got too creepy.

If that revelation was bad, wait until they found out how I met her. *No.* That would forever remain my secret. I absolutely would not share that embarrassing factoid.

"Let me see her!" Emma practically hopped up and down.

"Yeah, let's have a look," Harrison said.

"Okay but don't make it a whole thing." I ran a hand over my face even as I pulled up her account. "God, I shouldn't have told you guys about her. It's not anything like that. We're just friends."

I dropped the link in the chat for the call. "Right. That's why she was the first thing you mentioned," Emma said.

"Bloody hell, Brits are a sarcastic lot," I grumbled, then quickly added, "Don't use your professional accounts to look at her. I don't want you accidentally liking her photos or some shit. I don't want the super fans who stalk your activity harassing her."

"Duh," Emma said. "Oh, she's lovely. Really, cheers. Oh, and single ..."

"Nice," Harrison said, his screen grayed out as he presumably scrolled.

"Okay, enough," I said.

They brought their attention back to the call.

"I was thinking I should tell her who I am," I said cautiously.

My tiny face in the camera window was twisted in an unattractive wince.

My heart hammered even as I thought of how I would go about confessing the truth to her.

"You have to tell her who you are," Emma said at the same time Harrison said, "Definitely do *not* tell her."

"Bloody helpful. Thank you, both."

Emma looked aghast at Harrison. "Why should he continue to lie?" she asked.

Harrison ignored her and looked at me. "Listen, mate, what's the plan? Where do you see this going? You trust her to find out who you are and not immediately send all your exchanges directly to the tabloids?"

"Harrison! Not everybody is evil and looking for their fifteen minutes," Emma said, high-pitched.

"I didn't say that they were, I'm just saying, they've been chatting online, what, a few months? How well does he know this bird?" He flicked his focus back to me. "Give it more time. Learn more about her. If things progress naturally and you really trust her, then go for it."

"The longer he goes without telling her, the worse it will be." Emma worried her lip. "Although." She let out a sigh. "Is there anything in your exchanges that would be bad if the press got hold of it?"

The trickle of doubt at the idea of sharing my identity turned into a deluge. I hadn't shared specific details, but I had poured out more of my soul to her than anybody other than these two. More so, if I was being honest. Not even Emma and Harrison knew how adrift I still felt. They'd want to interfere, and I wanted to figure things out on my own. I didn't need them dropping everything in their epic lives to help their already screwed-up friend. They'd done enough when I went to rehab. I was lucky to have not totally destroyed that relationship.

"Well, there's your answer." Harrison tapped a finger over his pursed mouth. "Tell me you didn't send any prick pics."

"Oh, Charlie, no," Emma gasped.

"I didn't! Bloody hell, you two. I'm not a total muppet." I scratched at the back of my neck. "But I did talk about my drinking and ... stuff."

Emma made a sound of contemplation. "I hate to change my stance, but maybe Harrison's right. It's pretty soon to know if you can trust her."

Harrison nodded. "Sorry, mate."

"I don't like being paranoid, but we've all been burned," Emma said.

Each of us had at least one experience of being used for our fame. When I was still drinking, I woke up to find pictures of myself completely pissed and passed out in bed all over the internet. The woman I'd been hooking up with for three months decided it was time to cash in. And that was just one example out of countless others. It took time in this industry to know who you could trust with intimate details. A thousand friends and no allies.

"A few more months won't change anything. If she's the real deal, a little more time won't matter," Emma said.

"Yeah," I said. "You're right."

"How did you meet to begin with? You just said online," Emma asked.

I made a show of looking up to the door. "What's up? Oh sure, be right there." Turning back to the call, I said, "I gotta run."

"He forgets we worked with him for eight years and have known him all our lives—" Emma started, her voice growing louder with every word.

"Agata needs me. Chat later. Cheers." I smiled and waved.

"We know when you're lying," Emma finished, practically yelling.

Harrison asked, "Who's Agata?"

I closed out of the call and sat in the silence, ears ringing.

I did trust Kate. I knew without a doubt that she wouldn't leak anything to the press. That wasn't what scared me anymore.

What I couldn't risk was that she'd stop talking to me. Not yet. I didn't want her to think I was some nutter with nefarious reasons for talking to her. I couldn't risk any change. These daily chats meant too much to me, and I looked forward to things. Before Kate, it was all the same day blurring on forever.

Just a little while longer, to ensure she got to know the real me, then I would tell her everything.

7

―――――

DRAFT UNSENT

TO: KateDubois@geemail.com

FROM: TheRealFreddyStan4Life@geemail.com

SUBJECT: What are we doing?

I told my best friends about you last night. I wanted to tell you who I am, but they convinced me I should wait. Honestly, I was being a coward when I asked them. Part of me knew they'd advise me against it in order to protect me. We've all been screwed before by people claiming to be our friends.

You're not like that. I could tell from the first time we spoke ... maybe just from your stories. But I do worry about telling you, nonetheless. I worry you won't believe me. I worry that you will think that this means I want things to change. I don't want things to change. Or maybe I do. Talking to you is the only thing I have to look forward to.

But maybe ... what if we tried a video call? And then I'd—what? Sit with a blanket over my face? Or hide behind a mustache filter?

Christ, I'm pathetic.

I can't send this ...

―――――

TO: KateDubois@geemail.com

FROM: TheRealFreddyStan4Life@geemail.com

SUBJECT: I was right...

Attachment: AllGrownUp.jpeg

Kate,

Agata is officially in love with the kids. Ever since I moved them out to the hut and they started laying eggs, you'd have thought it was her idea from the beginning. The feeling is mostly mutual. Freddy sometimes pecks at her when Agata takes her eggs. She's taken to replacing them with rocks. Poor sweet, stupid Freddy.

They've all really flourished. The picture attached shows how big they are already. Just a few months and they're fully grown. My little kiddos, all grown up. Their confidence is, at times, a little much. They strut around the yard pecking and gossiping ... well, like hens. I'm told that getting a rooster might help keep them in line.

Which is how they get you. You rescue funny-looking teenaged chicks, then you're building them a house and collecting eggs, and now I am going to have to get a cock.

That ... did not sound right.

I can't believe how fast my babies have grown. Soon I'll be a grandpappy. Or at least I will be if I get that rooster. Hmm, now that I think about that, I'd have to be careful to keep him away from the ladies ...

Best,

Gramps RC

PS: That podcast about the spooky lakes was really interesting, thanks for suggesting it. I also learned that thalassophobia is a thing. Have you started that show I suggested?

———

TO: TheRealFreddyStan4Life@geemail.com

FROM: KateDubois@geemail.com

SUBJECT: You were RIGHT again!

RC,

Yeah, that lake with the bodies ... *shudders* It's nighttime here, and I'm getting creeped out. No more talk of that.

The kids are so grown! We can't even call them kids anymore, I suppose. But they will always be your babies.

I DID finally binge-watch that show you were telling me about. YEP. So good. I cried like a little baby at the final episode. It left me in a funk. You know that restless sort of ennui that reading a good book leaves you with? It was like that.

Hey! I just realized I don't know what genre you like to read. I like romance, sci-fi (obviously), some fantasy. Honestly, I'll read pretty much anything if it comes recommended enough.

I thought about writing something to help ease the pain of my show hangover, but that's a can of worms I do not want to open. Between you and me, I haven't felt the desire to write *TerraFormative* stuff in a while. I mostly just want to write my novel. And our emails. That's half my word count every day ;p (still laughing at you).

The chickens are looking so great. I'm excited for your future cock. Hahahahaha

And with that, I have to call it a night.

Loopy and exhausted,

Kate

———

TO: KateDubois@geemail.com

FROM: TheRealFreddyStan4Life@geemail.com

SUBJECT: Good morning

Kate,

You're probably reading this before work. Hope you have a good day. Make sure you take your lunch. Don't make me call Gail to confirm that you're eating.

HAR. HAR. I set myself up for the cock joke, didn't I? Well, at least we can laugh about these things. There is a total lack of action in my life aside from my chickens. Also, that didn't sound right. I'm okay with that though ... MOVING ON.

Why'd you cry when watching the show?

RC

———

TO: TheRealFreddyStan4Life@geemail.com

FROM: KateDubois@geemail.com

SUBJECT: I will be late for work...

... but this is way more important.

Why did I cry?! Are you seriously asking me that?! BECAUSE I AM NOT A HEARTLESS MONSTER!

Are you honestly telling me you didn't cry when Jane was talking about taking her son to school and daydreaming about their pretend future?? Because tears. Just pouring out of my eyes.

Worried for your soul,

Kate

———

TO: KateDubois@geemail.com

FROM: TheRealFreddyStan4Life@geemail.com

SUBJECT: IT IS NOT REAL

Fiction just doesn't get to me like that.

RC

———

TO: THEREALFREDDYSTAN4LIFE@GEEMAIL.COM

    FROM: KateDubois@geemail.com

    SUBJECT: and now I am SUPER LATE

I don't even care if I'm late. Gail will understand (I told her to watch it too).

Fiction doesn't get to you?? I'm sorry, who am I speaking to?? I don't understand. We have spent many days discussing our mutual obsession of TF and the hole it left in our hearts. How, *HOW* can you say "it's not real." LORD. Well, no kidding, it's not real, but IT IS REAL. And it is so sad and beautiful and tragic and heart-wrenching and hopeful ... GAH. I'm crying again just thinking about it.

This conversation is *not* over. I really have to go now. But this is NOT OVER.

You think you know somebody ...

Kate

———

TO: KATEDUBOIS@GEEMAIL.COM

    FROM: TheRealFreddyStan4Life@geemail.com

    SUBJECT: CALM YOURSELF

Kate,

I have never gotten very emotional over fiction. I know it's not real. But as you pointed out, I am mostly heartless. I never cried over TF either. It was a huge part of my childhood, but it wasn't entirely about the show ... exactly. It was more about where I was and who I was around at that time. It's difficult to explain. Maybe you're right though. Maybe, I do need a good cry to get on with my life ...

You better not get me in trouble with Gail. There's nothing more to discuss, but we can continue to debate and I can continue to be right later. Get to work!

Heartless Monster

————

TO: TheRealFreddyStan4Life@geemail.com
FROM: KateDubois@geemail.com
SUBJECT: sorry I yelled
RC,

I hadn't had breakfast. I've had the day to cool down, and while I still don't understand how you weren't in a puddle crying, I don't actually think you're heartless. You were the one that suggested the show, so you obviously understand the beauty of it.

What exactly do you mean about TF? About it not being about the show entirely? Are you able to elaborate?

I wanted to ask you about something. I have been wondering if maybe you'd like to video chat sometime? It would be easier than these back-and-forths (which I do enjoy). I inevitably forget something I want to tell you when I'm writing you emails because I get so distracted about the next line.

No pressure. I know writing is easier for some people than face-to-face conversation. Some people being me. And I suspect, based on the fact that you have said that you definitely avoid talking to people at all costs, that maybe you aren't up for it either, so I totally understand.

At the risk of total humiliation, I have come to see you as one of my closest friends. I haven't really kept up with anybody from college. I have online friends, but I don't really know them (and somehow, that feels different than what we have). I've purposely kept people at a distance at my "temporary." And so, talking to you is the highlight of my day, even when you're arguing with me (especially?).

Anyway, just throwing it out there. Again, no pressure.

Kate

———

TO: KATEDUBOIS@GEEMAIL.COM
FROM: TheRealFreddyStan4Life@geemail.com
SUBJECT: RE: sorry I yelled
Kate,

I feel the same way about our exchanges. I look forward to these conversations more than just about anything. Besides Agata and the children, I don't have people to talk to either. My two best mates are off leading exciting and active lives, and often I feel a little left behind. But I also know that lifestyle is just not who I am. I'm a fan of privacy and solitude.

When I tell you that I hope to meet one day, please don't think I'm trying to be trite. But right now, I just don't think that the time is right. I am still trying to stay focused on my health and avoiding major life changes, but I do hope to meet face-to-face one day. I'm just not quite ready yet.

I don't want anything to change between us. I still hope you'll consider me a dear friend because I certainly feel that way too.

Sincerely,
RC

———

TO: THEREALFREDDYSTAN4LIFE@GEEMAIL.COM
FROM: KateDubois@geemail.com
SUBJECT: RE: Re: sorry I yelled
Of course! No reason to even apologize. I shouldn't have ... You have your privacy, and I respect that. I'm sorry if I made you uncomfortable. All is good here. <3

Best,
Kate

———

DRAFT UNSENT

TO: KateDubois@geemail.com
FROM: TheRealFreddyStan4Life@geemail.com
SUBJECT: I'm a bloody idiot
Darling Kate,

How appropriate that I am a father to chickens because there is no bigger chicken than me.

I want you too bad. I don't want anything to change. I'm so afraid of what you will do when you discover who I am.

I am the biggest of chickens.

Please don't let this change things. I like you so much. I won't be able to handle not talking to you every day. I want to tell you all my secrets. I want you to know everything about me. I just keep picturing your face when you learn the truth ...

I just couldn't take it if knowing who I was changed things between us. I would rather have this friendship than nothing at all.

I can't send this ...

8

———————

Ten Months Ago
Kate

I MOVED MY MOUSE, JUST BARELY KEEPING MY SCREEN AWAKE SO Gail wouldn't notice I'd been completely zoned out the last ten minutes.

This time I wasn't sidetracked by things in a fictional world. I had been replaying a recent conversation with RealCharlie, or RC as I referred to him in my head. I wish he'd tell me his name. Maybe I should persist. It'd been over a year of talking every day now, and while I felt like I knew so much about him, I didn't know anything important.

Well, nothing that would help me to cyberstalk him online, and that was probably the point.

Somewhere over these months, he'd transformed in my head from a lonely man hobbling around in a bowler on his grand estate into a silver fox, the likes of which I compared to the current Bond. And yet he'd never crossed any lines. Never made me uncomfortable. Never felt pushy; if anything, he seemed shy. He'd never asked about my relationship status.

Because he probably didn't care. At least not in any way that I secretly hoped for.

He had gently declined video chat. I understood his reasoning, but it was impossible not to feel disappointed. We still talked every day. He still knew more about my life than any other person. Tiny details that wouldn't make sense to anybody else. We had inside jokes and we teased and bantered.

"Hey, Kate," Gail said, and I jumped so hard she gasped in response.

"Oh, sorry," I said, a hand pressed to my chest.

"You were really out there, weren't you?" She smiled, arms crossed.

There was no denying it. I had been fully lost in thoughts of RC and our exchanges.

"Sorry," I repeated.

She laughed and waved me away. "Wanna have lunch while we go over the schedule for the week? I'll order some sandwiches from Zullo's?"

"Sounds good."

An hour later, I sat on the couch in Gail's office, eating lunch with my laptop open on my lap.

"Kate, I hope you don't mind my saying so but you seem happier lately."

I flushed and pretended to type something on the computer. "Oh?"

"Yes. More relaxed, if not a little more distracted." Her tone was gentle.

"I'm sorry. If it's impacting my performance—"

She held up her hand. "No. No. It's a good thing. You seem lighter."

I couldn't fight the smile. "I am."

"And the reason for this? Maybe a new special someone?" she asked.

I hesitated. "Technically no. But I'm talking to someone. He lives in England and I don't think it's like that. Not for him anyway. Not that it's like that for me." I fumbled for words, feeling myself flush. "But we are close. I don't even know why I said any of that." I shook my head to clear it. "I have a friend and it's been nice to chat with him."

Why had I said that? RC was just a friend. It was probably weird that he was the first person who popped into my head. I wasn't actually *seeing* him at all.

But obviously, we had a connection; we'd always been comfortable with each other. There was an ease of conversation.

"That sounds nice," Gail said. "What does he do?"

"I think he's retired. He has chickens and a little farm. It's just a friendship right now," I added. Unnecessarily.

"Because he's older?" she asked.

"No." I shook my head. "I don't know how old he is, I haven't seen him."

I instantly regretted saying that. This was partly why I hated sharing about my personal life. A flash of worry crossed her features.

"Have you heard of catfishing?" Gail asked delicately.

I couldn't tell her about his gentle refusal to see him face-to-face. With all the facts laid out, this one-sided friendship was pretty damning.

I picked at the remaining crust of my sandwich and answered deliberately. "I have. But it's really not like that. If he was trying to play me, I feel like he would want something from me. But it's more that he likes chatting with me because he's lonely." *Just like I'm lonely.* "He has a home caretaker and I wonder if maybe he can't get around so easily because he doesn't seem to leave his house much?"

As I spoke, I realized it was true. Maybe that was why he didn't want me to see him? Was it possible he was ashamed of a disability? I hoped he knew I wouldn't be bothered about something like that.

"Well. That's sweet that you're there for him." She gave me a gentle smile before her eyebrow quirked and her smile changed entirely. "So then, you aren't dating Pete?"

I scoffed and looked at her in surprise. "Pete from sales?"

"He's young and cute and single?" She shrugged innocently. "He does seem to find a lot of excuses to stop by your desk considering I hardly have any reason to work with him."

"Yeah, but ..." I tucked my hair behind my ear.

In shape with short brown hair and appealing symmetrical features, Pete was an office favorite. He was even attractive by normal standards, not the skewed standards of an office that made even an average-looking person better looking with time and familiarity. Plus, Pete was charming and a wiz at his job.

"How could he be single?" I thought out loud.

"How are you single?" she asked with a frown. "You're far more of a catch, in my opinion, you just don't let many people see it." I pretended to focus on my sandwich at her compliment. "You keep yourself isolated. And that's fine," she said quickly when I worried it was a criticism. "Obviously this is none of my business and don't feel like you even need to consider this because I brought it up, but maybe you could go talk to him, just to see if there are sparks."

"Sparks?" I asked.

"Chemistry. Just because you two look good together on paper, doesn't mean you're the right fit. But you won't know until you try."

Chemistry. That's what RC and I had. It made no sense, but we totally had chemistry through just our words. But ... what were we even doing with these back-and-forth messages? I had tried to push our relationship forward and it was a mistake. We had a good thing going with our friendship and it didn't need to be any more than that. It clearly wasn't any more than that for RC. Maybe he was gently trying to keep me firmly in the friend zone without hurting my feelings. That was fine. I was being silly anyway with this crush.

Pete was right in front of me. And maybe I should have noticed him more. These feelings I'd developed for RC weren't healthy. It wasn't even real. It was just me—once again—projecting my fantasies onto someone that wasn't available.

It was time for me to stop putting my hopes on RC. That was a pressure he didn't deserve and may lead to us both being disappointed. Time I move forward with my life. I would go have a chat with Pete and see what happens.

9

———

Eight Months Ago

TO: THEREALFREDDYSTAN4LIFE@GEEMAIL.COM
FROM: KateDubois@geemail.com
SUBJECT: Gutted
Hey RC,

I'm sure you saw the news about Robert Galloway from TF passing. Maybe it's silly to feel so sad about the loss of a person I didn't even know. But I felt like I knew him? He always seemed so warm and like he really cared about the kids on the set.

I watched a TF behind the scenes a long time ago—gosh, I don't even remember when or where. But there was footage of him interacting with the Intrepid Trio between takes. He was so friendly, and I just feel so sad.

Pete said that Robert Galloway would want people to remember who he was at his best, not crying over him on social media in order to get likes. I have seen some virtue signaling, but I hope you know that's not what I'm doing. I just thought that if anybody understood how sad I was feeling, it would be you. Does that make sense?

How are you doing?

Hugs,

Kate

————

DRAFT UNSENT

TO: KateDubois@geemail.com

FROM: TheRealFreddyStan4Life@geemail.com

SUBJECT: RE: Gutted

Tell Pete that he can go get fucked. I can't believe you are still seeing that tosser. Rob Galloway was a goddamn angel of a man. You're allowed to feel however the hell you want. And your intuition was right, Rob meant so much to all three of us. All the kids on set, really.

I just got the call from Emma. She was crying so hard I could hardly hear her. I'm glad I found out from her though, and not online. I'm absolutely shattered. I loved that man like a father. He often treated us better than our own parents. There were years we spent more time with him than with our own families. Fuck. I'm so bloody sad.

I promised Emma I would go to the funeral for her. I really don't know how I'll stomach it. Everybody standing around simpering and posturing about who loved him best. You think it's bad online, you should see the people who crawl out of the woodwork at these things.

But I'm no better. I should have been talking to him still. More than just a few chats a year. The man meant so much to me for so long, and I just pushed him away like I did with every fucking person in my life.

I wish I could bloody send this ...

————

TO: KateDubois@geemail.com
    FROM: TheRealFreddyStan4Life@geemail.com
    SUBJECT: yeah
I did hear about Robert Galloway. I think it's okay if people post about him. People are allowed to grieve in any way they want, even if that means getting upset about somebody that they didn't know personally. I think that's quite lovely. I don't think anybody would mind being remembered after they pass.

I'm struggling tonight. I just found out I'm going to have to take a trip in the next few days to attend a funeral for a former coworker, and I'm desperate for a drink. To mourn Galloway. And to mourn the loss of a friend I should have reached out to more often. And then another during the flight. And another before I see people I haven't spoken to in a decade. And most of all, I want one because I have to leave the kids with Agata.

I'm a bit of a wreck right now. You know it's bad when even Agata isn't yelling at me as much …

I should call my sponsor.

RC

———

TO: TheRealFreddyStan4Life@geemail.com
    FROM: KateDubois@geemail.com
    SUBJECT: CALL HIM NOW
And don't respond until you've talked to your sponsor. (Sorry if that was pushy. But seriously, go!)

I'm so incredibly sorry about your friend. I can't believe I was going on about someone I didn't know, and you were … it doesn't matter. Call your sponsor. Take care of yourself.

Hugs,

Kate

———

TO: THEREALFREDDYSTAN4LIFE@GEEMAIL.COM
FROM: KateDubois@geemail.com
SUBJECT: Just checking in
Hey RC,

You don't have to respond. I just want you to know that I'm thinking about you. Good luck on your flight and being around people. I hope the funeral is a lovely celebration of your friend's life.

Please call your sponsor any time on your trip. I know you know that, but I had to say it. I'm around too if you want to chat.

Thinking of you.

Hugs and kisses,

Kate

———

TO: THEREALFREDDYSTAN4LIFE@GEEMAIL.COM
FROM: KateDubois@geemail.com
SUBJECT: Hey
RC,

It's been a couple days, and I'm torn over whether or not I should even be writing you. I don't want to add anything to your plate, but I'm really starting to worry. This is the longest we've gone without talking in almost two years.

You don't have to do anything. I know you are busy, but please take care of yourself.

Maybe just drop a line so I don't worry?

Love,

Kate

———

TO: THEREALFREDDYSTAN4LIFE@GEEMAIL.COM

FROM: KateDubois@geemail.com

SUBJECT: NOT freaking out

RC,

It's been a week. I know I have a habit of catastrophizing. Rationally, I know you're probably just grieving and have NOT been in a plane accident (also, I checked and there haven't been any in the UK). I understand if you can't write me back. I am still thinking of you. Every day.

Lots of love,

Kate

———

TO: KATEDUBOIS@GEEMAIL.COM

FROM: TheRealFreddyStan4Life@geemail.com

SUBJECT: I'm here

Kate,

I fucked up. I fucked up big time. I'm a bloody fucking idiot. I'm sorry it's been almost two weeks since you heard from me, but the funeral took more out of me than I thought. I made the stupid fucking mistake of taking some pills to help me get through the flight. Then some more pills to get me through the funeral. Then some more pills to get me through every moment of every day away from my house. Because I'm a bloody pathetic loser.

I didn't drink alcohol, but technically my sobriety has been restarted. I confessed to my sponsor that I was using again and that I needed help to stop. He told me it was normal, it happens all the time, and that he was proud of me for letting him know so quickly. Between him and the help of my two other best friends (besides you), I was able to get a handle on things pretty quickly. Even though I derailed everybody's plans ... Will I ever stop being the fuckup?

I'm humiliated. I feel weak and pathetic and wish I could just be like everybody else and not have to feel every fucking thing so deeply. And everybody is being so damn nice about it and that's somehow making it worse.

I've been clean a week now. Seven fucking days. All those years down the drain. What a fucking waste.

I'm such a loser.

I can't send this ...

———

TO: KateDubois@geemail.com
FROM: TheRealFreddyStan4Life@geemail.com
SUBJECT: FUCKITY FUCK FUCK
Shit. Shit. Shit! I didn't mean to send that last email. Shit. I'm sorry for unloading on you. By any chance you see this one first, please don't read that last email.

Also, sorry for all the cursing.

RC

———

TO: TheRealFreddyStan4Life@geemail.com
FROM: KateDubois@geemail.com
SUBJECT: OH THANK GOD
Hey! It's okay! It's just me: your friend, dare I say, one of your best (I can because you said it first). I'm immensely relieved to hear from you. Nothing else matters. You emailed me back and that's truly all I care about. Because *you* are alive. Not that I was worried you decided to totally ghost me or literally were a ghost —too soon? Sorry. I'm a little giddy right now. I really need to

stop making jokes about death in light of everything. I think your corrupt British humor is rubbing off on me.

Full disclosure: I read both emails. I was just so thrilled to hear from you, I didn't have time to stop myself. I may have turned my ringer up the last two weeks just in case and read it as soon as I got the notification. NOT TO ADD TO YOUR GUILT.

Please don't be ashamed to have shared your feelings with me. I'm honestly honored to be a person you trust. Except ... I guess you didn't mean to send it ... do you often write emails you don't send me (color me intrigued)?

But seriously, your sponsor is right. It's normal. I'm sure you've seen others experience what you're going through, and you didn't think the worst of them. You're battling a disease. You're still strong, okay? You had to deal with a ton of stress and outside factors all at once. You were strong enough to recognize you had a problem. You were strong enough to ask for help. I am *incredibly* proud of you.

Also, who the hell is the jerk who gave you pills?? What is wrong with people?

BUT if you're tired of people being kind to you, I can try being mean. DAMN YOU FOR NOT LETTING ME KNOW YOU WERE OKAY SOONER.

Ugh, I can't do it. I tried. I'm still just too damn pleased you're safe and sound.

XOXO,

Kate

TO: KateDubois@geemail.com

FROM: TheRealFreddyStan4Life@geemail.com

SUBJECT: Tied for first

Between you and the chickens, you're moving to the top slot of that friend's list.

I'm so sorry I scared you.

I promise to never "ghost" you, whatever the hell that means. The only way I would ever stop talking to you was if I was actually a ghost. And even then, I'd probably still haunt you just to annoy you. (And Agata. That would be fun.)

Thank you for understanding and somehow not thinking the worst of me. It wasn't that I hadn't meant to send you that message, I just meant to clean it up a bit before I did. I was ... at a very emotional point. I'd been traveling and not feeling well, and I saw all your emails, and it only made me feel worse.

Your attempt to be mean was very cute.

I didn't know the person who gave me the pills. Some friend of a friend. They probably didn't know about my issues. I used to hang around a different sort of crowd. Not bad people, just people who didn't care about me as a person, more as a means to an end. They aren't at fault. I could have said no. Which is another reason I find it difficult to leave the house. It was a test, and I failed.

Now. Can we please never talk about this again? There have been a lot of *feelings* going around lately and it's becoming unbearable.

Agata and the kids say hello.

RC

———

TO: TheRealFreddyStan4Life@geemail.com
FROM: KateDubois@geemail.com
SUBJECT: A distraction
RC,

Ew. Feelings. How American. Maybe I'm rubbing off on you just a little too?

Say hi back to the fam from me <3 I bet they were all so happy to see you.

So. I promise to move on but if you ever want to talk about the funeral or anything else from that trip, just know I am here to listen. You never have to sensor yourself with me, okay? Also, it wasn't a test, and you didn't fail anything. You literally did exactly what you should have when things started to get out of control. So stop beating yourself up. It's not going to change anything.

Now, I'm done.

MOVING ON.

This feels gauche in light of everything you've been struggling with, but I finished my book. I mean, it still needs to go to an editor but ... if you want to read it? God, I'm so sorry if this is completely out of line. I'm sure it's terrible. Not that I'm fishing. I don't want you to lie to me just because you think you have to be nice. I want you to be honest. If you even want to read it. You totally don't have to.

THIS IS SO UNCOMFORTABLE. Worse than feelings.

GAH.

XOXO,

Kate

———

TO: KateDubois@geemail.com

FROM: TheRealFreddyStan4Life@geemail.com

SUBJECT: SEND IT NOW

I can't believe you even had to ask me that.

RC

10

Six Months Ago
Charlie

"WHAT SORT OF STUPID NAME IS PETE ANYWAY?"

Adam tilted her head and pecked at my boot.

"Yes. I am aware I waited too long and have nobody to blame but myself."

She pecked again.

"I wanted to tell her. I will tell her. Eventually. The timing wasn't right."

Lucy joined her sister and flapped on a hop kicking up dust and feathers.

"Ah, what do you two even know?"

I tossed another handful of feed into the patch of dirt.

Adam and Lucy waddled over to peck at it. Freddy's head was stuck in the chicken wire fence.

I bent to gently let her free. Not for the first time. Their yard time had to be closely supervised even with the rooster, Nugget, dutifully patrolling the scene.

Summer rain had poured down on the rolling green hills

surrounding the Vicarage earlier in the day, but now the sun shone, and the air smelled clean and a little bit like chickens.

"Of course, somebody snatched her up. How was she ever single?" I grumbled.

I hadn't stopped thinking about her manuscript since she sent it. It had captivated me from the first line, not that I was surprised. I'd see something that would remind me of her characters, and I'd forget for a moment that they aren't real. A particularly clever bit of dialogue would pop into my head and I'd find myself smiling. She was amazing. Pete had better appreciate her massive talent.

Pete.

What a stupid dumb name for a stupid nob. He had better appreciate what he had in her. Kate's first few mentions of him had been subtle. A line here or there. *Pete got me flowers. Pete loved that movie too. Pete blah blah blah.*

She'd even posted a picture of the two of them together on her social media account. Just the one, thank god. He was painfully average-looking with an out of fashion goatee and short brown hair. He looked like every average white guy in a commercial for herpes medication. He likely had a picture of himself holding a fish on his dating app profile and said he was an "outdoorsman." He was probably still active on dating apps ... I should check.

"That may be crossing a line," I said.

Freddy responded by pecking a stone.

I hadn't expected their *relationship* to have lasted so long. But why not? If Kate were mine, I would never let her go. She was charming and gorgeous and talented. Compassionate and kind. Patient and loving. Of course, this shark would swoop in and scoop her up.

And it was all my fault. The first mention of him was shortly after I turned down her offer of a video call. Then the funeral and the relapse ...

The last few weeks were a blur of shame spiraling and therapy. And her constant reassuring messages.

God, I'd been so stupid. And now she was taken. Officially. If I could go back in time, I'd say yes to that cursed video call; just let the truth come out and deal with the consequences.

But no. It was still better to have these emails with her than nothing at all. Those at least remained consistent. We talked about everything and anything—save my aversion to details. She was accepting of my flaws and weaknesses and never seemed to think I could do more or be better. She accepted me as I was. At least the bits I allowed her to see.

There was one noticeable change that had come with Kate's new relationship status: the time stamps of our emails. Less random and more predictable. We used to email back and forth all night. Now I only heard from her primarily during what must be her lunch hour. Not that my brain automatically calculated the time difference between Devon and Minneapolis on reflex or anything so sad.

"Christ, what a nob." I wasn't sure if I meant him or me. No. Definitely me. I waited too long. And I'd wasted my shot.

I put the ladies away and headed back to the house to wash up. After I showered, I stood at the back window, watching another storm blow in and making sure the kids were okay.

I was also silently regretting every life choice I ever made.

"You're in my way," Agata said from beside me.

I didn't jump as high as I used to. I'd become accustomed to her sneaky ninja ways. Now Agata only startled me slightly.

"Go mope somewhere else," she said.

"I'm not moping," I said. Just because I was staring out the window and watching the rain, thinking of Kate, didn't mean I was moping.

"Your forehead grease is all over my clean window."

"Sorry." I sighed and stepped back.

"This about your pretty American you always write to?"

I nodded. "She's seeing someone." I wasn't sure why I mentioned it. Maybe I was looking for a little extra company at this pity party. A little extra coddling.

"Ah. You stupid man," Agata said.

I blinked at her. I should have seen that coming. Seeking sympathy from Agata was like going to the freezer to warm your hands.

"No frowning," she said. "If you wanted to date her, you should have wooed. Did you woo?"

"No." I thought about all the times I debated mailing her gifts to the PO box she had listed on her website. It would have been so easy to send her something related to Freddy Finks or even Charles Downing, but it felt too risky. Too ... underhanded somehow. Sending gifts was another line neither of us had crossed. Same with me asking about stupid Pete.

"I didn't woo," I finished gruffly.

She shrugged before aggressively wiping a rag across the glass where my forehead had just been. "There you go. Women like her, they don't wait for you to get your head out of your dupa."

This wasn't the first time Agata had used that particular Polish term in association with me.

"I know. It doesn't matter anyway. I don't know what I expected."

Agata muttered more Polish under her breath.

"What?" I asked.

"You waste so much time. Young are so stupid. You like her, you tell her. It's easy." She stretched on her tiptoes to try and wipe the top of the window.

I took the rag and wiped the area she couldn't reach. "It

wouldn't have mattered. She's too far away. She wouldn't have ... It doesn't matter."

"You make it harder than it needs to be. You have time and money." She waited for me to finish before reaching up to slap my cheek in a somewhat affectionate, somewhat painful manner. "You are strong and good looking. You have money," she repeated.

Like money was some tool that solved all problems. My money meant nothing. It was a symptom of the disease that is fame. It wasn't like I earned it. Kate wouldn't be impressed by it. Kate was a woman who deserved a man who would move mountains for her. A man who had worth, who would make her proud to be seen with.

I had nothing to offer. I was a lump on a log and a coward too afraid to show his face.

"It doesn't matter," I said.

I should have told Kate everything from the beginning. Now, it was too late. I'd waited too long. It was better this way. There was no chance for our relationship from the start. Things were best as they were with me safely tucked away in Devon and her with ... well, so long as she was happy. That was all I could hope for.

Agata sighed and strolled away. Before she was out of the room, she pointed out the window. "Your cock is out again." I stilled in horror before spotting Nugget. She added, "Go get him."

"If only that I could," I mumbled.

11

———

Three months ago
Kate

"Hello, Mom," I said, pitching my voice to sound happy but not too excited.

Thank god my mother never insisted on monthly video chats. As it was, she was almost always traveling for work anyway, and a phone call was the most she could manage.

"Hi, darling. How's things?" she asked, her keyboard clacking away as she spoke.

"All's well here. You? Where are you today?" I asked, following our safe script.

"Prague. No. that was last week. Nuremberg," she amended. The clattering increased in aggression. "Sorry, hang on." She muttered about someone having their head so far up their ass they could see their own tonsils.

I winced. She sighed loudly. "Okay. Sorry. I'm all yours. How's the guy—Peter?"

"Pete. Um, he's good." I glanced up from my window seat to

look out into the living room where Pete sat sprawled on my couch.

Again. Lately, it felt like he was always here. Today he was watching some sports game that caused him to yell out from time to time. That, along with the blaring commercials, was stimulation overload. I quietly crept to the door and closed it, my ears relaxing in the quiet of my room. It was an adjustment having company so often. I was so used to being alone.

"Hmm," my mother said. "Well, it's the longest I've seen you in a relationship."

That was a neutrally safe comment if I ever heard one. I needed to talk to somebody about this. I couldn't exactly ask RC about it. The idea of me seeking relationship advice from him made me cringe. We didn't talk about that. Plus, as far as I had deduced in the last almost two years, RC wasn't close to anybody but Agata, and that was reluctant cohabitation at best.

"Pete is very sweet and kind. He's exactly what anybody could want." I was trying too hard to sell it. My mother brought that out in me, this compulsion to justify my actions. Like I wasn't a grown adult.

Though truthfully, the more time I spent with Pete, the less I was sure about our relationship. It was like he'd been so eager to get to the comfortable stage of our relationship that the courting phase had been painfully brief. But, again, I had nothing to compare it to. Maybe this stifling feeling was typical. Was it normal to feel drained by your partner and not refueled by their presence? Logically, entering a serious relationship was the next step. Get a degree, a job, and finally, a partner. Wasn't that what I should want?

My conversations with RC never felt forced or awkward. They flowed so easily, sometimes, we had multiple threads going at once. They were also only in email, and he lived in another country. It wasn't even worth comparing the two. Why did my brain keep doing that?

"He sounds nice. Is something wrong?" she asked.

"No. Nothing. Things are moving along. He's over a lot. Sometimes I wish I had a little more space. But him being around a lot is the next step, right? The natural progression of a relationship?"

Almost as soon as I asked, I knew it was a mistake. I'd be better off talking to Gail, but I still felt weird chatting about dating with my boss.

"I guess," my mother said after a moment. "But if it were me, I'd cut and run. Life's too short, darling."

"Mom."

"I'm serious. If you aren't putting yourself first and he's taking all the attention, it's not worth it. If it feels like work, then move on. Relationships should be full of the fun stuff, not another job."

There wasn't a ton of "fun stuff" happening either, but I was most definitely not about to discuss that with my mother. Pete and I had been intimate a few times, and it had been ... nice. He was sweet, but I wasn't very sexual by nature.

Except in my fantasies. I pushed away the conflicting thoughts.

"But aren't relationships about compromise?" I asked.

"No. That's what men say to slowly grind out your spirit," she answered swiftly. "Put yourself first. Nobody else will. If he doesn't like it, he's free to leave. That's all I can offer," she said.

Why had I thought to ask a woman who's never in a country long enough to commit to a phone carrier, let alone a relationship? My mother always chose herself first, it worked great for her career, but Rose Dubois wasn't exactly a stellar example of #RelationshipGoals.

"Yeah." I pretended to agree and swiftly changed the topic back to her career. A safe topic for both of us.

Talking about my love life with my mother was as helpful as googling symptoms when feeling sick. I'd only end up feeling worse. If I had thought she would be pleased just to see me committed to someone, I was so wrong. But it wasn't about her. It was about me and my idealistic version of what I thought love would feel like. Just because Pete wasn't living up to that fantasy, it wasn't his fault. Pete was kind and particular and, yes, maybe a little overly involved (I would not think smothering), but wasn't that better than the opposite? Wasn't it good that he wanted to know where I was all the time and what I was doing? It meant he cared. He was here.

And he showed me his face.

I quickly pushed the doubt aside.

I had enough one-sided relationships. Talking with my mother reaffirmed that I needed to calm down. This was just normal relationship stuff that I would adjust to.

After wrapping up the call, I went out to the living room to find Pete with his feet on the coffee table and a beer in his hand. When I walked into the room, he held up the empty bottle.

"How was the call with Mom?" he asked.

I was glad I had my back to him as I headed to the kitchen because there was no hiding the wince. Were we to the point where he could call her that? It felt a little too soon.

I let out a breath. I was doing the thing again, looking for problems.

"It was good. Same as always," I called through the opening between the kitchen and the living room.

I grabbed chips, anticipating his next need, and dumped them in a bowl. I brought his beer and snack and joined him on the couch. I rested my head on his shoulder and took simple pleasure in his presence.

Pete was *here*. I didn't have to get all in my own head about it. I was done overromanticizing things. I was committed to this.

I munched away, thinking about my book as he yelled at the people on the screen.

"Not too many," he said after I took another handful of the chips.

I sat up and frowned at him.

"What? Don't want to spoil your appetite, right?" He kissed my nose.

This wasn't the first time he'd made a comment about what I was eating, but he was right, I would fill up on junk food if I wasn't paying attention. I put the chips back.

My phone swooshed with an incoming email notification. My heart raced. There was a chance that it was just junk mail, but the anticipation of hearing from RC never diminished. That sound was the electronic equivalent of unwrapping a piece of chocolate. Instead of my mouth watering, a small smile formed before I even opened the message.

The subject read "COCK PIC" and attached was a file named *RoosterontheRun.jpeg*.

I snorted so loudly Pete looked up.

"Something funny?" Pete asked, glancing at me with a frown.

"It's just RC," I said, reading the message. "I guess the rooster snuck into the house and is wreaking havoc." I cackled loudly reading RC's account of Agata chasing Nugget around with a broom. "Oh no. Agata—" I couldn't even talk I was laughing so hard. The picture was of the rooster standing proudly on what looked like a dining room table and a tiny woman waving her arms wildly at it.

Pete looked over my shoulder. "Cock pic?"

"It's a joke, it's his rooster," I explained, wiping away tears.

He brought the beer to his lips and shrugged. "Doesn't seem funny to me."

I turned fully toward him, tucking my phone away. "Wait, are you mad?"

He didn't take his eyes from the screen, but his jaw was tight with tension. "How would you feel if I got an email from some chick saying, 'tit pic'?"

"I—It's hardly the same. It's just RC. He's … harmless."

"Yeah. Yeah. You're just friends. I'm sure he doesn't want to sleep with you."

I gasped at his vulgarity. I'd never seen Pete's anger so sharp like this. My stomach soured at his tone. Worse, I found myself feeling guilty. I had only been laughing a moment ago, and now I went shaky with nerves.

"That's uncalled for," I said.

The muscles of his jaw clenched, and he glared at the TV, not looking at me.

"Sorry." He spat the words. "This game is just pissing me off." He gestured toward the TV with his beer. "And maybe don't flirt with the guy right in front of me."

I had to force my mouth closed. I was always open about my friendship with RC. As far as I was concerned, there was nothing to hide. We were just friends. Pete was just mad about the game. He'd had some beers and he was jealous. It wasn't okay, but if he was buzzed, I wasn't going to pick a fight. RC was my friend and that wasn't changing any time soon.

Pete never seemed to mind, but lately, he'd been making more and more of these comments. Maybe he was picking up on the fact that at one point, I'd had a fanciful crush on RC? Or maybe it was plain jealousy. Regardless, I tried to picture how I'd feel in his shoes. My emails with RC had slowed down a bit since Pete and I started dating, and though Pete always insisted it was "fine," I felt a little weird about emailing him back in front of Pete.

I put my phone away.

Later, when Pete mentioned spending the night, I asked if he could go back to his place tonight so I could get some work done. It was true, but I also needed some space. Between the call with my mom and his weird outburst earlier, I was emotionally drained.

Pete froze and turned to me. I had my arms wrapped tight around my middle.

"Hey." He stepped forward and cupped my chin. "I'm sorry I acted like a dick earlier. I know you two are just friends. Isn't he some old retired guy? I don't know why I got so jealous. I just like you so much." He threaded his fingers into my hair and pulled me close. "I'm sorry, okay?"

I nodded. I had needed to hear his apology more than I thought. Tension melted out of me.

"Let me cook for you tonight, okay? No more football, it's just pissing me off anyway. Just a nice dinner, you and me? Okay?"

I relaxed and let my arms go around him. It had just been a weird moment. Nothing to worry about. He was here and he wanted to take care of me. "That sounds nice. I really do have to go work a little."

"Yeah, of course. What work does an admin need to do on a Sunday?" he asked.

"I want to get some more revision done."

"Oh, I thought you meant your real job. Okay, sure, baby. You go *work* and I'll let you know when food is ready."

I leaned back. I heard the condescension in his tone, but he was watching me with warm, hopeful eyes. He'd just apologized. I didn't want to pick a fight about whether my writing was "real" work or not.

In the spare room I used as an office, I opened my WIP. I was working on incorporating the comments RC gave me. He'd loved the book and offered some tweaks that were super helpful. Soon, I could start querying the book. I felt a tremble of anxiety but pushed it down. I would work on it, but first, I wanted to quickly reread his latest message and reply. He might still be up.

I checked that my door was closed and locked before reading through his adventures again. RC had been in the shower when he heard the screams of Agata. After making sure she was okay, he couldn't resist snapping a picture of the scene unfolding. "*I was going to come to her rescue, but she's scared me enough times I thought a quick pic for you wouldn't hurt.*"

I smiled into my palm as I opened the attached picture and studied it without the prying eyes of Pete. Agata was exactly how I pictured her. Petite but threatening. Zooming in, I took in every detail of his home that I could. Relishing in this glimpse into his life. The dining room was quaint and much smaller than I'd expected. There was an ancient-looking buffet off to one side and a china cabinet on the other. The walls were a warm yellow and covered in small frames filled with art and photos. I couldn't make out any people in the pictures as the action had blurred the background. His home was absolutely as charming as I imagined it would be.

I was just about to close the image when my eyes snagged on something in the corner of the picture. The china cabinet's back panel was a mirror. The angle of the photo was such that I could just make out the photographer.

I swallowed.

I glanced toward the door again. Pete clanged about in the kitchen. My heart thundered in my chest as I zoomed in on the picture.

The image was grainy, yet the figure was clear enough. It was RC. My RC. He was holding the phone in one hand; the flash going off obscured his face completely, but his other hand held a towel secure around a very fit and very *not* old body. The arm holding the phone was perfectly formed, leading to sculpted shoulders that connected to a trim waist and tightly flexed abs, like he was laughing. He'd mentioned spending time in his home gym as part of his rehabilitation, so I assumed it was some sort of physical therapy for the condition that left him stuck at home and in need of assistance.

What did this mean?

There was no way he meant to capture himself. There was no way this was anything than an oversight in a rushed email. And yet a tingling sensation covered me head to toe.

RC was gorgeous.

I didn't realize I was biting my lip until I tasted blood.

This was not good. I'd just gotten over this crush. I'd happily settled into the friend zone. I was not so vain that seeing grainy footage of a beautiful body would immediately change my feelings. But all the desires and dreams I'd been pushing down and avoiding came springing back up. My overexcitable brain took this image and ran with it. I had a body to match to a name. A beautiful body.

I stared at the picture for much longer than I would ever admit. I eventually turned to revising my novel, but my brain kept going back to the picture of RC. It wasn't just his figure; it really wasn't. I'd been handed another clue to the mystery person who consumed so many of my thoughts, and this time my brain wasn't about to let the puzzle go unsolved.

12

—————

Present Day
Charlie

I CLICKED MY MOUSE, REFRESHING MY EMAIL UNNECESSARILY. IT was Kate's birthday today, and when she woke, she'd finally open the parcel I'd shipped her. She checked her post office box earlier in the week, and when she got my gift, she begged me to let her open it. I hadn't relented and enjoyed her pouty impatience.

I anxiously waited to hear if she'd enjoyed the present. It was the first time I felt comfortable sending her something, a new frontier for us, but now I questioned every choice. All the time and thought I'd put into my choices for her now seemed ridiculous and not nearly enough for what she deserved.

Kate had been there for me during my relapse. She'd sent me her book. She'd helped me research how to raise chickens. She'd been my person for so long and she didn't even know. The amount of trust she had in me, and I couldn't even tell her who I was. I had to fix this. I had to be better. Could I tell her?

If I explained that I never meant for things to get this serious

... but then what if I implied it was serious on my end, and she freaked out? I never meant to fall for her through her writing, emails, and stories. Not that I was in love with her. I just had extremely strong feelings for her. And couldn't stop thinking about her. And wanted to explore every inch of her body ...

"Hello, Kate, so you know how I've been purposely vague and changed the subject every time you ask about me ..."

I groaned at hearing the words out loud.

I never meant to lie to her. Well, I didn't ever lie, but I did withhold a pretty large piece of information. That was on me. I get that. It didn't matter what my intentions were, it was time.

I scratched at my neck, hesitating.

But why tell her, really? It didn't matter. She had a boyfriend. We were just friends, *best* friends. Why mess with perfection? Maybe this was selfish to change things at this point. On her birthday. Maybe I only wanted to tell her in the hope that she'd ... what? Leave her boyfriend for some guy online she's never even met? Who knowingly withheld crucial information from her for the last two years?

My heart sank.

I stood and paced in front of my laptop.

When she found out the truth about me, everything would change. All the deep conversations and raw honesty ... It would no longer be us. It would be her talking to the Charlie of her fantasies. And what did I even want by telling her?

Nothing. I wanted to keep our friendship the same. Everything needed to stay exactly the same.

The doorbell rang loudly, causing me to jump.

"Bullocks."

At the front door, the security camera showed Emma. I sighed loudly. I'd expected her sooner or later.

I pressed the talk button. "Go away."

"Let me in, Charlie." Her voice was high and whiny,

reminding me of the time I hid a frog in her makeup chair on set.

"You're wasting your time," I said.

"It's cold and wet out here. I really have to use the loo, come on."

I sighed when she shot her patented puppy dog look right into the camera. The heavy door clicked open, and I turned to walk away.

"You're a real saint, you know that." She zipped past me and toward the toilet.

"You chose to drive out here," I called after her.

"Maybe if you didn't live ninety minutes from the closest town," she yelled through the shut door.

I went to the kitchen to wait for her, fingers itching for a drink with the inevitable conversation I was about to endure. Instead, I put on the kettle and grabbed two mugs.

Agata was off today, so at least the two of them wouldn't gang up on me.

A few minutes later, Emma sighed as she sat at the large island, slapping down an over-sized tote that said SAVE THE PLANET. I gave the bag a pointed look.

"What? You expected Prada or Gucci?" she asked at my curled lip.

"What's wrong with treating yourself to a new bag, Em?" I asked. "You've had that since season two."

She rolled her eyes at me. "It's not that old."

"Oh, so it only looks like a relic," I teased.

"Do you have any idea how bad the fashion industry is for the environment? If you knew—"

I held up a hand and she stopped. "You have time for one speech with this cuppa. Is this really the hill you came to die on?"

She frowned but stopped talking.

"Didn't think so." I slid a steaming mug to her, and she wrapped her hands around it, sighing as she warmed herself.

"Alright. Out with it," I prompted, watching the steam swirl off my tea. "Who sent you? Harrison? The studio?"

"Nobody *sent* me. I came to check on my reclusive friend and make sure you haven't started collecting your fingernails in jars."

I held out my arms and gestured to the spotless kitchen. "No jars. Now the people locked in the basement, you can't see them."

She rolled her eyes but softened her tone. "I've just missed you." She shrugged innocently. "I've not even talked to you since the funeral."

Good lord, she was good at that. Even if she was still planning to push me, my shoulders relaxed.

"I've missed you too," I said. "And sorry about missing the last few chats. Haven't felt up for it."

We smiled softly at each other, passing two decades of feelings in a glance as only long-time friends can. Emma was more like family than my own flesh and blood.

She took a dainty sip and said, "That being the primary reason for my visit, I do also—"

"Ah, there it is."

"—think that you should consider the reunion special," she finished.

"And why's that?"

"Twenty years since the first episode. It's a big deal. I know you already told your agent and publicist no."

"And the director and the producer," I interrupted.

"It would be good for you to get out. The funeral was awful, and you had a small hiccup."

"Understatement, Emma." I gave her a flat look.

She had been there. Of course, I hadn't done anything

humiliating. I caught myself in time. But it had been a close call. Too close.

She went on, "This can be the last thing related to TF. A final high note to end on. The cast and crew were our family for so long. I know how much they meant to you especially. And the fans ..."

As she rambled on, I felt my eyebrows contorting into a grimace. I hated that while she knew me so well, she couldn't understand everything. I was tired of needing sympathy and understanding. It was easier if I was just left alone.

"... there's going to be a lovely segment in memoriam of Robbie and a few others who have passed ..."

My frown deepened, and my hands shook as I gripped my mug tighter.

She didn't seem to understand that seeing everybody again only worsened the loneliness. That it would rip off the Band-Aid that was barely holding together the gaping wound in my chest. I couldn't even handle the funeral; how would I handle a trip across the pond and on a set in LA? It would be too much.

Instead of conveying all these complicated emotions, I said, "I'm done with the show. It's time to move on."

She held my focus, eyes narrowing. She didn't buy my half-truth for a moment. "I just want you to be happy."

"I am happy." *Mostly*. I am safe. I sighed and gently explained, "I did the ten-year anniversary reunion. I did the theme park opening. I did the behind the scenes for the extended edition box sets. I've endured twenty years of interviews and I'm done. I'm not trying to be difficult. I'm just tired."

"And the fans?" she asked. "It wouldn't be the same without you there."

Ugh, her forever trump card. "Twenty years of putting the fans first, I'm putting myself first for once."

"I know the fans mean more to you than the rest of us. If

they didn't you wouldn't respond to every single letter you've ever received."

"Well, I don't get nearly as many as you and Harrison, so it's not that hard," I said, sounding pathetically petulant.

She chewed her lip, contemplating a new tactic.

"Would you do it for me?" And there came the puppy dog eyes again, the look that got billionaire tech giants to sign blank checks for her charities.

"Don't play dirty," I said.

I scrubbed a hand over my face. Emma thought showing up at my house to ask me personally would break down my defenses. In the past, it would have worked. I told myself time and time again that I wanted to move on, but there was always something more. But not this time. I was serious. I was sober. I had chickens. Things were simple and I was fine. It's why I wouldn't tell Kate the truth and why I wouldn't go to LA. The balance of my life was too precarious. One major change and I fell off the tightrope.

She continued like she was winning me over. "A few days of filming. Couple of convos. And you're back in your big, lonely home by the end of the week."

I rubbed my eyes so hard black spots danced across my eyelids. She made it sound so easy. But it wasn't. It was hours of forced conversation about something incredibly personal to people who don't know the first thing about what it had been like for Em, Harrison, and me. It was exhausting finding the right amount of giving the information they wanted to pry out of me, while keeping the important things to myself. The other two managed well enough but I'd never been able to.

I cleared my throat and braced myself. I held her gaze. "I'm sorry, Em. Of everybody, you'd know I'd do it for you. But I just can't. I'm sorry you drove all the way out here." The coy smile melted off her face as I spoke.

Her delicate features pinched, but she knew me well enough to know when she'd lost.

"Okay." She reached out her hand and squeezed mine. "Okay, I understand." Her easy smile was back in place. "But you're not getting rid of me yet. Let's play a few rounds?"

I smiled into my teacup. "Yep. Fine. I'll set up the board."

"Oh, real quick." She glanced at her phone, tapping the screen. "Let me get on your Wi-Fi. There's no damn reception out here—"

She reached for my laptop, which still had all the incriminating tabs of fan fiction and email exchanges wide open for her nosy eyes to see.

I snatched it away from her quickly. I held the computer tightly to my body, causing her to arch an eyebrow at me. She looked at the laptop clutched to my chest, then up to my face, and then back to the laptop.

Her lip pulled in disgust, and she gestured to the computer. "Tell me I didn't interrupt you ..."

"Yep," I answered instantly. Whatever she thought was much less embarrassing than the truth. Not that I thought there was anything wrong with reading fan fiction. But reading fan fiction about one's self most definitely did not pass any sort of weird vibe check. "Yep. Loads of porn. Weird shit too."

"You're deeply disgusting." She stood with the shake of her head.

"Wi-Fi password is in my office. I haven't changed it since the company set it up."

"Lord, you're worse than my grandfather." She grabbed her phone off the counter and headed to the office.

"On the Post-it on my desk," I said to her retreating form.

"Got your passwords for all your bank accounts there too?"

I frowned. "Maybe."

"You're hopeless."

The second she was out of the room, I opened my laptop and closed out the FanFavz tabs. I had been rereading one of Kate's earliest stories when my unexpected visitor showed up. I was just closing out my email, getting ready to shut it down completely, when I saw an email from Kate. As always, my heart beat faster at the sight of an unread email from her.

Her subject was all caps "AHH BEST BIRTHDAY EVER" followed by countless exclamation points.

The side of my mouth lifted into a smirk as I opened it. How was it possible for someone to show so much of their sweet personality through a single subject line?

Selfishly I hoped that her declaration had nothing to do with the boyfriend and everything to do with the box of treats I'd sent her.

My eyes were so greedy for her words, as always, I had to force myself to slow down and focus on one line at a time.

I heard myself gasp.

She'd been invited to the *TerraFormative* reunion fan segment.

My eyes moved so fast my brain couldn't process.

She was invited because *obviously*. Kate had more subscribers for her TF fan fiction than any other author on the entire site. She had artists begging to create fan art for her stories, just to be close to her greatness. She was an amazing storyteller. None of this surprised me. Her effervescent joy bubbled off the page so much I couldn't fight back a grin. My chest ached with pride and hope and excitement for her.

Then the implications hit me. She would be going to LA. She had been invited to the same special I had just turned down. She was going to the twentieth-anniversary reunion.

My mind began to whirl on every possible door opening to a different future. I could see her in person. After all this time talking with her. I could just be in the same room as her. I wouldn't do anything. I didn't want anything to change. I couldn't tell her the truth, especially not now, but I could see her in person. I could be near her.

It could be enough. It had to be enough. I could *see* her. One year and ten months of talking.

I quickly wrote out a reply. I wanted to take more time, convey my pride and joy for her, but I wasn't skilled with words. Not like her.

"You look like you've seen a ghost," Em said, causing me to jump for the second time today.

I shut my laptop with a loud snap.

"I'll go. I'll do the reunion," I said.

Her eyebrows jumped, and her mouth fell open. "Oh. Okay. Brilliant!"

13

Kate

I was still vibrating with energy by the time Pete got to my apartment. There was a hop in my step as I ran to greet him at the door.

"You're never going to guess what just happened!" I shouted as I let him in.

"Okay, calm down, calm down. I just walked in." He sniffed the air. "No dinner?"

I shifted on my feet. "Not yet. I've been distracted. I'll order some takeout or something."

He sighed. "Okay. You're lucky I love you so much."

He'd said the "L" word first, when we'd only been dating a couple weeks. I'd still not returned the sentiment. I wasn't ready, but he said he was patient.

"It's just that—" I started, but he held up a hand.

"Kate. Come on. Let me sit down for a minute. Work was insane. I need a drink," he said.

I quelled my excitement. "Sure." And ran to the fridge to get things moving along.

I reminded myself that Pete had to work late, and I assumed he had forgotten my birthday judging from the lack of flowers or a gift. I'd honestly forgotten too, even though I'd taken the day off. Gail sent flowers, and RC sent a huge box of funky British snacks that had me smiling. But nothing compared to the adrenaline pumping through my veins from the email I'd received this morning.

Pete was easily overwhelmed if I showed a lot of emotion. More and more lately it felt like I acted too loud or said the wrong thing. Was it too much to ask that he be excited about my interests?

A little voice warned that I was unconsciously comparing Pete to RC, and that wasn't fair. Of course, online friendships were easier to maintain. If I was around RC all the time, I'd probably wear on his nerves just the same as I did Pete's. I wondered if RC had gotten my email yet. What had he thought of the invitation? I realized I'd zoned out thinking of RC again. Not the first time that'd happened lately. In fact, it'd been happening with greater frequency. Another slither of guilt. I pushed away thoughts of RC.

I waited for Pete to get settled in front of the TV when I brought him a beer.

He glanced up to me and smiled. "Okay. Out with it. You look ready to burst. Someone in your shows get married or something?"

I fought a flash of hurt but smiled. I was so deep in the fan fiction world that I sometimes forgot that not everybody took the characters as seriously as I did. "I've been invited to LA."

The beer stilled in front of his mouth.

"The producers of *TerraFormative* are filming a twentieth anniversary special. They invited me." It came out on a rush of words. I took a steadying breath and perched on the arm of the couch next to his chair. "They've asked me to be part of a segment about people whose lives have been impacted by the show. They're going to film me. I'm going to be on actual TV! They're paying for the flight and hotel and everything."

His eyebrows shot up. "Wow. That's a big deal."

I leaned forward excitedly. "I know. What if I meet the cast and people who worked on the show?" I pressed my fingers to my cheeks. "I can't even think about that. I'll probably make such a fool out of myself. I can talk about my writing. Oh my god!" I gasped. "What if a literary agent sees it and wants to represent me?"

My deepest fantasies were pouring out without thought, and it was the wrong thing to say. I saw the moment Pete's face went from tentative excitement and disbelief to full-on pity. Becoming an author was a silly pipe dream. But I'd completed my first full-length novel outside the fan fiction world and wasn't sure what to do next. This invitation felt like kismet.

I couldn't help it, the words tumbled out excitedly as I tried to clarify. "Many writers of fanfic end up getting publishing deals. What if I get a book deal out of this? I mean, I have so many subscribers—"

"Whoa, whoa." He held up his hand and reached for mine. He squeezed it softly. "Let's not get ahead of ourselves."

"No. I know." I stared down at our hands. "I'm just saying. It would be cool, right?"

His brows furrowed before he tilted his head in thought. "When's the special?"

"Not until June. Months away."

"Okay. We'll need to plan some things," he said seriously.

"Of course." Pete was a planner.

"We can't just drop everything, you know. What about work? And you know my mom needs help."

My heart stuttered. The invite had been for me. Not for me

and a plus one. Anxiety burned down the back of my neck and coiled into my gut. I hadn't even thought about him going with me.

"Oh, you don't have to go," I said lightly.

It was the worst thing to say.

"You don't want me to go? Embarrassed of me?" he asked lightly, but his eyes pierced me as his head tilted.

"Of course, I want you to." My heart raced. I didn't want to hurt his feelings. But when I had daydreamed about the trip, I imagined flying alone and getting the aisle seat. Wearing what I wanted to wear in the LA sun, even if it was a crop top. Eating where I wanted to eat and when without worrying about upsetting him and his routine. He'd just gotten so particular about things lately. I was looking forward to the space. "It's just a silly thing for my writing. I don't want to impact your schedule."

He sighed and squeezed me tighter. "If it's important to you, I want to be there with you."

I smiled back. Technically, it was the nice boyfriend thing to say, but my mind was reeling. I could save up the next few months. It was only March. I had enough in savings that I could buy him a flight. Hopefully. He wouldn't need to know. A niggling feeling whispered that if I told him he wasn't invited, then he wouldn't want me to go. I swallowed carefully. Pete wasn't one for surprises. I should have tampered down my excitement a little before I told him. He didn't like to be blindsided.

Thankfully oblivious to my internal panic, he said, "You'd think they'd be weird about it, since you basically took the author's writing and said 'nah, I can do better.'"

I blinked. "No. My stories are more like a continuation. It's still his world and characters."

"Obviously, I know that. But do you think that Sedar will be there? How would that introduction go? 'Hi, I took your beloved characters and make them have freaky sex.'" Pete laughed, and his focus moved to the TV behind me.

My stories were about so much more than sex. But maybe he was right? That was how so many people saw fan fiction. *No.* Those stories meant something real to thousands of people. I'd received so many comments and letters over the years. RC understood the power of the TF world …

"I've helped people. You know that," I said.

"Of course, I do. I think it's amazing. I'm just saying from their point of view, it seems odd."

A crush of sadness and anxiety dampened my excitement until it almost extinguished. Ever since I was little, I'd gotten too excited about things only to hear from my mother how everything would probably go wrong. *I don't want you to be disappointed. The real world doesn't care.*

I shut my emotions down. I made my face blank. Pretended I didn't care. "If you don't want me to go, I can decline the invite." Even as I said it, my insides rebelled. I wanted to go. I had been excited about it, hadn't I? But maybe he was right? It would be a lot of preparation and planning. Even though they were paying for most of it, there would be additional costs, and I'd have to take off work. Maybe it was a silly idea.

This would expose me to the wider world outside the hardcore fans. People would know I was the owner of the cringey FreddyStan4Life and there would be no going back. My stomach twisted tighter. I wanted to be a real writer. What if my route to publishing through fan fiction made me a laughingstock?

Accepting the invitation was a bad idea. I hadn't thought this through at all. God, I wish I hadn't written RC. He probably thought I was an idiot. My fingers itched with the need to go check my email and unsend the message or backtrack. He probably thought I was overreacting too.

"Sweetie, come here." Pete pulled me into his lap. "I just know how you are." I frowned and he lifted my chin to kiss my forehead. "It's what makes you so good at the writing thing. You can take one little idea and spin up it into a whole world. I just don't want you to build it up too much in your head."

"I know."

"I hate seeing you disappointed. Best to go into events like this with no expectations."

I took a deep breath in. He was right. I was sure my mother would say the same thing. I shouldn't get my hopes up. He just wanted to protect me.

I snuggled into Pete, focusing on the familiarity of his arms. He was my grounding force when I spun out. He was here. I just needed to sit with the idea for a little bit, but the more I thought about the invitation, the more I understood that maybe I'd rushed into things.

"You know I'm the rational one. You tend to romanticize things and then when it doesn't go the way you want, you're disappointed. Remember the time you wanted to try that new sushi place and it ended up being terrible?"

It had been unpleasant because Pete complained loudly about the food and service, and I was mortified. I thought the food was great.

"I promise I have no expectations. I'm not getting my hopes up," I said.

"Let's just put a pin in it for a while. We can talk about it more later, okay, babe?" he said.

I nodded against his chest. I was all muddled up.

This was for the best. I had gotten ahead of myself.

As soon as I could, I would email RC and hope he hadn't read my last message.

"And hey," he said lifting my chin to look at him. "Happy birthday."

"Thank you."

"Why don't you order whatever you want for dinner."

I tried not to let my smile falter. If I accidentally hurt his feelings when he was trying to be nice, he'd throw a fit about it.

"Great," I said with a forced smile, all the while my brain somersaulting. "Thanks."

TO: KATEDUBOIS@GEEMAIL.COM
    FROM: TheRealFreddyStan4Life@geemail.com
    SUBJECT: RE: AHHH!!!!!!!!!!
Kate,

This is amazing news. I'm so happy for you. You're going to be bloody amazing. This could be your big break for the book. An agent might take note of you, and you will be ready to go. This could be how you get your book published.

Also, let's not glaze over the fact that it's your birthday. Hopefully, no surprise songs at the office? Oh wait, you took the day off from work, right? Did you like my goodies? Start with the caramel bits, they're the best.

Seriously happy for you. You deserve every bit of good news.
RC

TO: THEREALFREDDYSTAN4LIFE@GEEMAIL.COM
    FROM: KateDubois@geemail.com

SUBJECT: THANK YOU!

RC,

Thank you for the delicious treats and the birthday wishes. Pete got to the caramel ones before I could snag one, but he said they were delicious! I had a great birthday, but I think I was a little overly worked up on birthday adrenaline when I emailed you earlier.

I feel silly. I should have waited to tell you about the offer. The more I think about it, the more I'm not sure I can just pick up and go to LA. The timing is a little tough. They didn't technically invite Pete, and I don't think I could just leave him behind. We don't have a lot of extra cash for a second flight. Also, his mom needs him around a lot, I think I told you that. He's not a great traveler. We have work. I just shouldn't have rushed into making a decision. I got carried away (what else is new, right?).

Thanks for being happy for me, but I don't think this is the right time.

Kate

PS: Did you also know that it's the second anniversary of our first exchange? Happy anniversary, bestie ;p

———

DRAFT UNSENT

TO: KateDubois@geemail.com
FROM: TheRealFreddyStan4Life@geemail.com
SUBJECT: YOU HAVE TO GO

Kate,

First of all, that wanker is not allowed to touch your treats. I picked every single thing out specifically for you. That is absolute rubbish. And to take the best ones. I swear to bloody hell ...

Secondly, Kate, do NOT let that man rain on your parade. You

deserve happiness and excitement. You deserve all the best bloody things in the world. How that man wasn't dropping everything to figure out a way to make it work ... And on your bloody birthday. For fuck's sake. He doesn't deserve you.

Thirdly, of course, I knew it was the anniversary of our first email exchange. I almost mentioned it ten different times but didn't want to seem as pathetic as I actually am. I sent you a gift to mark the occasion. Thankfully, your birthday coincides so I don't look completely mental.

Lastly, I'm getting you to that reunion come hell or high water. Even if it means seeing your stupid bloody boyfriend. I can't be responsible if I punch him in the face. Fair warning.

Fuck. I can't send this.

———

TO: KateDubois@geemail.com
    FROM: TheRealFreddyStan4Life@geemail.com
    SUBJECT: YOU HAVE TO GO
    Kate,
    It's okay to be excited. It's a big deal. If you don't, you might always regret it. Don't respond to the invite yet. Give yourself a few days to think about it. You can find a way to make it work. It's important enough.
    RC
    PS: Happy anniversary to us.

———

TO: TheRealFreddyStan4Life@geemail.com
    FROM: KateDubois@geemail.com
    SUBJECT: OMGEEEEE!

RC,

You aren't going to believe this! The producers just emailed me. I was just figuring out how to decline the offer (thankfully, I waited a few days like you suggested). Apparently, they forgot to mention my plus one for the trip. They're even providing a per diem for food and stuff. This doesn't even feel real! And I just looked up the hotel and it's amazing! I was expecting this tiny little motel, but this is a legit fancy-schmancy place!

Maybe they really do want me to go?

I have to find a way to make this work, right? I would be crazy to pass on this opportunity. And it feels like I should go especially now.

GAH! I AM FULLY FREAKING OUT NOW!

But you know, there's this voice in my head that is worried that they're just inviting me to make fun of me. Or that I don't deserve to go because my stories aren't "real" writing. Why do I do this?

Sigh,

Kate

———

TO: KateDubois@geemail.com

FROM: TheRealFreddyStan4Life@geemail.com

SUBJECT: Own it.

Kate,

That's the fear talking. Tell it to piss off. You never know what could happen. This could change everything. You're an amazing writer, Kate. Your stories are as real as anything else. Let yourself enjoy this.

You have earned this.

RC

TO: THEREALFREDDYSTAN4LIFE@GEEMAIL.COM
FROM: KateDubois@geemail.com
SUBJECT: RE: Own it.
You're right. I'm doing this. AHHH!!!
Kate
PS: Can you hear me screaming across the pond? Because this still doesn't feel real. Now the countdown begins. THREE MONTHS.

TO: THEREALFREDDYSTAN4LIFE@GEEMAIL.COM
FROM: KateDubois@geemail.com
SUBJECT: Two-month meltdown
Attachment: option1.jpeg, option2.jpeg
RC,
HELP!
I need advice. The producers said that it's a business casual recording. But I can't decide between the two outfits I attached pics for. The first one (the dress) is more pretty but maybe not professional enough? The second one is typical for what I wear to work but maybe not dressy enough?
I have no idea what I'm doing.
Thanks in advance and totally not starting to panic,
Kate

DRAFT UNSENT
TO: KateDubois@geemail.com
FROM: TheRealFreddyStan4Life@geemail.com

SUBJECT: are you trying to kill me …

It's bad enough that I have to imagine you in my mind, to see you in those outfits … I am in actual pain. You are so incredibly beautiful, either will look perfect. My god, you are gorgeous.

I'm so bloody glad that we are friends but giving fashion advice while that prat gets to touch you is a travesty …

Fuck. I can't send this.

———

TO: KateDubois@geemail.com
FROM: TheRealFreddyStan4Life@geemail.com
SUBJECT: uh …
Kate,

I honestly know nothing about fashion. I've been wearing the same jumper and jeans for years. The only reason I bought more clothes is because Agata "accidentally" threw away my last hole-filled set.

Speaking of. Agata said dress for dinner and skirt suit for filming. So there ya go.

She, uh, also said you are beautiful. She's standing over this as I type this, flicking the back of my head. Send help.

Ouch

RC

———

TO: TheRealFreddyStan4Life@geemail.com
FROM: KateDubois@geemail.com
SUBJECT: ONE month
RC,

I feel sick. It's hitting me just how fast time is flying. Doesn't it feel like it's just flying?

Hey. You know what, I haven't even asked if there is anything you want on my trip. I have no idea what to expect, but if I end up talking to some of the cast, I could ask them something for you …

Oh.

Emm.

GEEE.

I just realized that I might not only see the actors but what if I TALK TO ONE. I might actually meet Harrison, Emma, and the *real* real Charlie. *Mind blown emoji*

What if I bump into Emma over bagels and lox? What would I even say?

What do you think they're like in real life? I mean, I know everything in the media is manufactured to be interpreted a certain way, but I always felt like the main three, the Intrepid Trio, had good heads on their shoulders. They seem kind. But still, how do I even talk to them??

WHAT DO I DO WITH MY HANDS? Gosh, I just have no idea what to expect. What if I just verbal vomit and embarrass myself? What if I fall or say something offensive in British English? Tell me every offensive British word. Ever. Go.

Do you know what? I probably won't even meet them. They probably won't let the riffraff hang around with the elite. Heh.

Look at me freaking out for nothing.

This is all fine. I am totally fine.

Kate

———

TO: KateDubois@geemail.com
FROM: TheRealFreddyStan4Life@geemail.com
SUBJECT: take a breath

You've been writing British English for years. You're probably more well-versed in it than I am at this point.

When in doubt, just ask to see their pants. ;p

RC

TO: TheRealFreddyStan4Life@geemail.com

FROM: KateDubois@geemail.com

SUBJECT: I AM BREATHING

HAR. HAR.

How can you make jokes at a time like this?

Kate

TO: TheRealFreddyStan4Life@geemail.com

FROM: KateDubois@geemail.com

SUBJECT: ONE WEEK!!

RC!

HOLY FREAKING BALLS. I just got the schedule for recording. The first night is a meet and greet gala with EVERYBODY. Everybody. Even the cast. That means I will be breathing the same air as them.

I think I just passed out for a second.

You've been awfully nonchalant about all this. It's very frustrating. Tell me you wouldn't be freaking out if you were me! You lie.

Okay. But seriously. What if I meet them? What if I meet the *real* real Charlie and I just turn bright red? Can you imagine if he knew some of the scenes I'd put him in. Oh *god,* I need to wear sunglasses because there is no way I'll be able to make eye contact. I AM FREAKING OUT. HALP!

Not so subtly losing it,
Kate

————

TO: KATEDUBOIS@GEEMAIL.COM
FROM: TheRealFreddyStan4Life@geemail.com
SUBJECT: Did you forget to breathe again?
Just be yourself and they'll love you.
They're just people.
RC

————

TO: THEREALFREDDYSTAN4LIFE@GEEMAIL.COM
FROM: KateDubois@geemail.com
SUBJECT: whatevs
Just people?! PFFT. What help are you?!

————

TO: THEREALFREDDYSTAN4LIFE@GEEMAIL.COM
FROM: KateDubois@geemail.com
SUBJECT: what was that about breathing?
RC.
RC? RC!!!

I'm about to leave for the airport. I didn't sleep. This time tomorrow, I could have met the Intrepid Trio. But also, uh, I'm going to be on TV.

I think I've been blocking that out. Living in a state of denial. Focusing on the wrong things. I can't do this. Talk about my stories? Most people think fan fiction is ridiculous. What am I thinking? I'm just going to hide under my covers. Until forever. I've had a good run.

Probably dying and should go to a doctor,
Kate

————

TO: KateDubois@geemail.com
FROM: TheRealFreddyStan4Life@geemail.com
SUBJECT: GO.
Kate,

Your stories are so much more than that. I will not let you talk poorly about your writing. Get your arse on that plane. One step at a time. You're doing this. It's going to be fantastic because *you* are fantastic. I don't want to hear another word about it. Don't make me come down there and drag you to the studio.

Do as I say, not as I do,
RC

————

TO: TheRealFreddyStan4Life@geemail.com
FROM: KateDubois@geemail.com
SUBJECT: fine.
RC,

Threatening to come down here is not as scary as you think it is. I wish you were here. I don't know if I'm allowed to say that, but you make me braver. Thank you for helping me do this.

On the plane, about to take off.
Kate

————

TO: KateDubois@geemail.com
FROM: TheRealFreddyStan4Life@geemail.com
SUBJECT: Me too.

Kate,

You don't need me to be brave. You're braver than I will ever be, trust me.

RC

(I wish I was there too.)

15

Kate

THE FLIGHT TO LA HAD BEEN SMOOTH, BUT IT WAS LIKE PETE AND I had totally different travel experiences. I interacted with friendly staff and smiled at grinning toddlers. Pete forgot his neck pillow. The air was too stuffy. A child made a sound.

I was already so anxious about the event I didn't have the bandwidth to try and appease him. It was best just to nod and go along with him. If I tried to point out anything positive, it only upset him more.

Lately, it felt like his words were at odds with his body language. He told me he was fine but then sighed loudly when I checked my phone. I asked to leave for the airport three hours before boarding and he went along with it but then made comments about how long we had to wait at the gate. It made me feel unbalanced.

I checked my email the second the plane touched ground. It took everything not to react to the message I had waiting.

RC said he wished he was here with me. He said that. That was the most he'd ever admitted about wanting to meet me.

Then I went into the bathroom to read it again where Pete couldn't look over my shoulder and I could smile freely. It felt shady to me too. But Pete was just so ... He'd already been in a mood all day. Maybe it was a guilty conscious that kept me from sharing any more about RC, but I no longer brought him up around Pete. Ever since I saw that picture of RC I hadn't been able to stop myself from wondering if ...

He wished he was here.

Did he mean at the recording? Did he want to meet the cast, or did he want to see me?

It hardly mattered. It *couldn't* matter. But lately, our friendship, or rather my developing reliance on his messages, was making me question our relationship again.

I tucked my phone away along with my smile, washed my hands, and met Pete outside the bathroom.

There was a driver with a sign with my name on it waiting for us at baggage claim. It was the coolest thing I'd ever experienced. I had to remember to tell RC about that. He seemed very unaffected by all things fame and fortune, but come on, a limo? Even that had to impress him a little bit. Pete thought the driver had taken a bad route after we sat in traffic for an hour, but I didn't care. I was in a limo!

Not for the first time, I've found myself narrating my experiences as I would later recount them in an email to RC. I wished I could talk to RC about the growing doubts about Pete. But there were certain topics that we never touched. My relationship and/or the troubles that came with it topped that list. It would feel like a betrayal to him, and I wasn't sure which "him" I meant

...

The hotel was amazing; the lobby glittered with marble and gold accents. The staff jumped to help us with our bags at check-in and made me feel like a VIP. It was easily one of the fanciest places I ever stayed. Pete said he'd stayed at nicer hotels when he came here for work.

"I'm going to shower," I said once Pete and I were settled in the room. "I want to leave in about an hour, so we aren't late for the meet and greet, okay?"

"Sure. I'm lying down. That food at the airport made me feel weird."

I ground my teeth. "Okay," I said.

He didn't have time for rest. I couldn't be late. But if I rushed him, he would drag his feet more. Better to let him do what he needed.

The shower was refreshing after traveling all day, and I took my time luxuriating in the water pressure. I shaved my legs and exfoliated. I dried and styled my hair carefully. I did my makeup just right, and by the time I walked out fully dressed and ready to go, we had to leave in ten minutes.

Pete was still in bed pretending to sleep.

"Hey, Pete. Time to get up and get ready." I gently shook his shoulder.

He groaned and rubbed his eyes. "How much longer?"

"About ten minutes." Which was more than he ever needed at home when we went out.

He sat up quickly, then pressed the heel of his hand to his forehead, groaning. "Why didn't you wake me sooner? I hope you left me hot water."

I took a deep, steadying breath. "You'll be fine. Please hurry."

"Don't rush me," he snapped. "You know I hate that."

He went into the bathroom and slammed the door behind him. Hot tears burned my eyes. I squeezed my nails into my palms to keep from crying and ruining all my hard work. I had been looking forward to tonight for months. It meant so much to me, and yet he couldn't be bothered to try at all. He made it seem like he was doing me a huge favor by being here, but he had done nothing but add to my anxiety. And now we were going to be late and ...

The tears started to fall.

"Crap." I sniffed them back and checked my makeup.

I fixed my mascara and examined myself in the mirror. *Who was this person?* I lifted my chin and glared at my reflection until I reminded myself of my mother preparing for a meeting.

My mom may seem like an unfeeling hard-ass at times, but she had instilled in me a strong work ethic and moral code. The producers had invited me, and I wouldn't be late. I wanted to be here. This was important to me. I would have a good night. I would enjoy myself. How had it gotten to this point? Why had I let a man have so much influence over me to the point that I was crying on what should be an amazing evening? His easy charm made it so easy to slip right into dating, but with every week, I slid further away from myself.

No. I wasn't this person.

I imagined RC shaking his head at me. Making a sarcastic comment about being a chicken and me teasing him back with a "takes one to know one" comment. Not that I really imagined *him*. Not really. RC was sort of this ambiguous masculine shape when I picture him. Kind eyes and an amazing figure that vaguely resembled Charles Downing.

I debated responding to his last email, but I was already so jittery with nerves, it would be rushed and probably too revealing. I would respond to him after the meet and greet and could catalog all the night's events for both of us, once my nerves were more settled.

I'd dressed in a simple lavender wrap dress that worked nicely with my petite figure and coloring. RC said that Agata said I looked beautiful.

I looked at the clock. The water was still running, and I had to leave.

I left Pete his pass and a note explicitly detailing where to go. I couldn't wait any longer. I wouldn't.

I came here for my writing and wouldn't miss this opportunity.

—————

Charlie

EMMA AND HARRISON WERE WAITING FOR ME IN THE LIVING ROOM when I came out of one of several guest bedrooms in Harrison's massive LA home. Emma and I could have stayed at the fancy-schmancy hotel, as Kate called it. But the three of us had made a pact long ago that when we were in town together, we'd stay together. At least until we had partners and it got weird.

Lucky for us, all three of us were shite at romance.

"Ready?" I asked my two best friends.

I flicked out my wrists to fuss with the cuffs of the dress black jumper I wore. I had done well on the flight out here. Maybe it was the promise of seeing Kate that distracted me, but I hadn't been nearly as itchy to numb myself this time.

"Damn, Charlie." Harrison let out a low whistle.

I glanced down over the dark jeans and shoes, worried I'd forgotten something crucial. Like trousers. I hadn't slept well since ... well, since I found out I'd be meeting Kate tonight. At least seeing her. Around three months?

I wish I hadn't said that last line in the email. The stupid comment about wishing I were there too. Not only was it too close to revealing my feelings for her, but it was also the closest to a lie I'd come in our chats because I would, in fact, be there. But I had been jet-lagged and anxious, and I had wanted to soothe her. Her anxious energy was palpable throughout her last several emails. Every single time she was excited about something, that prat would find a way to diminish her light. God, I hoped he would be there tonight so I could punch him in the face. I'm sure my publicist would love that.

Former Child Star Punches Stranger at Dinner for No Apparent Reason.

I wouldn't touch him. It wasn't my business. Kate's relationship was her own. All I could do was show her support as a friend would. But still. I shouldn't have said that. That must have crossed one of those unspoken boundaries we'd been so great at skirting. I needed to reel myself back in. Being this close to meeting her had made me sloppy. I wouldn't do it again.

I checked my phone to see if she had responded to my last message. She hadn't. But she was probably already at the hotel.

She was *here*. I couldn't think about that right now.

Harrison and Emma were looking at me.

"What is it?" I asked, pushing my sleeves up after debating if they looked better down. Pushed up, definitely.

"I think he's referring to your ..." Emma gestured up and down with a casual wave of her hand. "Physique."

"Oh." I turned to grab my wallet off the table, hating that my ears burned like I was twelve again.

I had beefed up a bit more since I last saw him at the funeral. Only because I had a lot of free time. And a *lot* of pent-up energy.

"You've gained a stone of muscles easily, mate." He poked my bicep and pretended it hurt his fingers. "You're about to bust through this shirt."

"So dramatic," I grumbled.

"Stop talking about his body. You're making him blush," Emma chastised Harrison before coming in for a hug from me.

"It's fine," I grumbled and squeezed her tight.

She wore a sleek silver romper thing that made her look even more lithe than normal. Her red hair was done in perfect waves, and her green eyes were piercing under sharp flicks of eyeliner.

"You do seem a bit bigger since January," she whispered with only a hint of concern.

"Emma," I warned.

She held her hands up in surrender after releasing me.

Admittedly, my body always was a sore spot. Since being dubbed the glow-up of the last century, I was a bit cheesed off to even have it brought up. Every magazine or online news rag had run at least one article about my transformation from chubby child star to pumped-up beefcake or whatever charming vernacular they used. At first, it had just been due to puberty, sharpening my jawline and filling out my muscles. Then after I quit drinking, I really started to take pride in my health. But it wasn't anybody else's damn business.

Harrison walked close to me, eyes narrowed. "You're not using anything are you?"

"Bloody hell, Harrison, are you trying to get a black eye before we even go?" Emma cried.

Harrison arched an eyebrow at Emma. "Why? 'Roid rage?"

He winked at me. Ever the charmer. Harrison could joke about these things as he'd always been glamorized in the magazines. He'd been a hauntingly attractive child and only grew into his looks over the years. Now, he was always at the top of every good-looking list with his piercing blue eyes lined with dark lashes that gave him that sort of pretty hot guy thing that all the thirsty birds adored.

"Well, if you can't joke about substance abuse among friends, what can you joke about?" Harrison swung an arm around me, pulling me in for a genuine hug. "It really is good to see you."

I patted him firmly, and some of the tension melted out of me. "Yeah. You too."

These two. Just seeing them again. It felt like a little bit of my world was back in order. The three of us bickering, well, them two mostly, could be recorded and played on a sleep sounds app and I'd be the only subscriber. I missed them so bloody much when we weren't all together. But I couldn't tell them that, could I? Emma with her world-saving and Harrison with his constant filming schedule. They'd moved on. I felt like the last sibling left at home as his brother and sister went off to college.

I cleared my throat. "Well, let's get this over with, shall we?"

Emma clicked her tongue in disapproval and Harrison chuckled. I wiped my palms on my trousers and took a deep but quiet breath to steady myself.

Not quiet enough, though, because Emma was watching me closely as we stepped out the door. "Nervous? There are no cameras tonight. It's just a casual thing."

"I'm not nervous," I said even as my Adam's apple bobbed to betray me. "Just knackered."

"This whole event is pretty random. Not that I care, but what's the point if it's not for publicity?" Harrison asked, smoothing his eyebrows in the reflection of the waiting car. "Happy to schmooze with the fans though."

I shifted on my feet.

"The producers told me it was a way for us all to get comfortable before we started filming tomorrow," Emma said. "I guess they're mixing up how they do the interviews and stuff."

My head shot up. "What do you mean?"

She shrugged. "I'm not exactly sure. We'll know when we see the new filming schedule."

"Don't worry, dear, I'll be there to hold your hand. I won't leave you alone with the big scary reporters," Harrison teased.

I shoved him off me. "Prat."

We chatted about various things as the town car drove through the city and to the hotel where the meet and greet was taking place. The closer we got, the more my nerves started to thrum. My heartbeat ticked like the countdown on a bomb.

I wished I could take the edge off.

But then I pictured the sloppy tabloid shots of me stumbling out of bars. If there was any chance in hell I'd been meeting Kate tonight, I didn't want her to see that side of me. That Charlie was long gone.

The second the car doors opened, all worries about tomorrow were pushed away. People were milling about in the hotel lobby, making their way toward the banquet room for the meet and greet. Never since we began our correspondence had I been this close to Kate.

Kate.

She was somewhere in this hotel, and I would finally get to meet her. I needed a minute to collect myself.

Emma and Harrison moved toward the banquet hall.

"You guys, go ahead. I just want to check in with Agata," I said, my voice contained a slight shake that I worried would give too much away.

Emma squeezed my arm with a nod and pulled Harrison away.

"Who's Agata again?" he asked as they made their way in.

I stepped to a quiet cove in the hotel lobby, head tucked to remain unnoticed, and took out my phone to check on the kids. It was late enough here that she might be up for the day.

I would just hear how life back home was. See Kate. Record the reunion. And then go home. Everything was fine. Everything was under control.

16

Kate

I smoothed my features with a steadying breath as I stepped out of the elevator and into the lobby. It had been a mistake to bring Pete to LA. From the beginning, my gut told me it was a bad idea, and I should have trusted it. Now, here I was, plotting ways to give myself some space from him when I should only be focused on the amazing experience I was here for.

My hands still shook, so I decided to double-check my face to make sure I wasn't splotchy with stress. A long corridor led off to the left that might lead to bathrooms. Past a business center where people could fax things, in case they were communicating with someone from 1998, there were several semi-closed off booths lined up and separated by short opaque partitions, providing a bit of privacy. What I didn't see were any signs of a bathroom. As I passed one of the booths, a man speaking into his cell phone stopped me in my tracks.

It was a voice I instantly recognized. Deep and rich, somewhere between posh BBC and cockney London accent. Instant chills traveled down my arms as he continued in a low, soft tone.

Charles Downing. Feet away from me. I swayed slightly. Okay. What would RC say? Just breathe. Don't lose your mind.

I moved to a booth across and one over from him. I couldn't be responsible for my actions. I was not in control of my body. The partition partially blocked me, so he wouldn't see me creeping on him but gave me an entire slice of him. My god, he was even larger in person.

He sat forward on the seat, one hand rubbing at his eyebrows as the other held his phone to his ear. The bicep muscles of the arm that held the phone were all but bulging out of his black sweater. His light brown hair was cropped short as always, looking fuzzy without any product. Had I mentioned the shoulders yet? Because they were also asking a *lot* out of the soft fabric of his shirt.

"If he continues to act out ..." he said.

I couldn't keep the thread of what he was saying. He was just so soft-spoken, exactly like in the dozens of interviews I'd watched over the years. Especially when he was clearly not using or drinking. It made me sad to watch the videos of Charles when he was at his worst, so I avoided them, preferring the ones where his eyes were bright and his speech wasn't slurred. He was focused and gentle, if not a little agitated. And he was. Right. There.

"No. He won't bite you." He sat back, head leaning against the back of the booth, legs spreading wide. His *thighs*. They were easily as wide as my waist, and that was saying something. "Well, he might," he added with a grin.

I sucked in my lips to keep from smiling.

"You have to have a firm hand with him, or he'll walk all over you. Would you—"

He was cut off by the person on the other line. Who was he talking to? His partner, perhaps? And was he referencing a kid?

He didn't have any children unless he was amazing at keeping them out of the limelight.

"No. I know."

Another pause. He chuckled softly.

After the many videos I'd watched, the sight of Charles Downing should have felt so familiar. And yet watching him in easy conversation with someone he was obviously comfortable with was like seeing an entirely different person than that man I saw online. It made me truly understand just how uncomfortable he had been behind the camera. Not in TF, but in interviews. He was a good actor, even though he hadn't been asked to do that much for the character of Freddy, but he held his own. But this was a totally different side. A soft smile tugged what was usually the hard line of his flat mouth. His famous square jaw was dimpled as he rolled his eyes good-naturedly at the speaker on the other side of the line.

He was ... adorable.

But he also very much seemed the type that would adamantly refuse to admit he was anything but a hard-ass. He'd tell you he was just trying to protect his own shoes as he held an umbrella over you. The type that would rock a baby to sleep only because the crying was too loud.

And then I pictured a tiny little baby cradled in his massive forearms.

Boy, look at me projecting all my fantasies. How utterly unlike me.

I needed to stop staring but found it impossible. More than half my life, I had looked at images of this man and had fantasies that I wouldn't even write in my fan fiction. Fantasies I wouldn't ever even admit out loud.

"Yes. I didn't—" he continued.

Sigh and pause.

"Yes. I know. I will."

His voice lowered, and I started to feel weirder about listening to his private call.

Overhearing these easy bits of conversation—perhaps with his mother, not at all wishful thinking—should have put me at ease. He really was just a person. Rationally, I understood this.

A powerfully handsome person. In normal circumstances, that alone would likely keep me from being able to make direct eye contact. Tack on the disarming smile and gentle countenance, and I was absolutely hopeless.

But the thought of trying to strike up a conversation? What does even one say? Wow, how about that weather? Please.

An embarrassingly audible sigh escaped from my lips just as I took a step to move away.

His gaze snapped up and I swore he looked directly at me through the small crack. I froze in place. He couldn't see me, could he?

"I have to go." He ended the call and stood up so that he now towered over the short partition.

He was definitely looking directly at me. Or behind me? I checked. There was nobody else. I was in a cubicle with my back to the wall. Well, crapola.

His mouth gently parted as though he was about to speak. Why was he looking at me like he recognized me? Or was this me projecting my hopes onto a man who definitely just found an obsessive fan eavesdropping on his personal conversation? Was I about to be escorted out of the hotel before I even made it to the meet and greet?

I needed to leave. I needed to explain.

I opened my mouth to speak.

You know what, on second thought, I should definitely go.

I turned and smacked right into Pete. He grabbed my arm. "There you are."

Pete looked up and saw Charles Downing, who was now playing on his phone, before turning back to frown at me. So maybe I had imagined all that?

"Is that why you left early? To come gawk at celebrities? Really, Kate. Have some self-respect."

"Pete," I hissed. "This is unacceptable—"

"Come on," he interrupted. "Let's get you to your party. That's why you dragged me all the way here, isn't it?"

I was humiliated. Ashamed. There was no defending what Pete saw because what had I been doing? Trying to ease my nerves? Or just trying to play out some secret fantasy where Charles would see me and fall instantly in love with me.

I really was hopeless.

When I looked up again, Charles Downing was gone, and I wondered if I had imagined the whole exchange.

Pete put his arm through mine. "Let's go."

I nodded but turned back one time to see the actor about to turn the corner, watching us with clenched fists.

Great. He definitely thought I was some weirdo fan. So much for a solid first impression.

———

Charlie

Emma, Harrison, and I were stationed in the middle of the crowded banquet hall in a slow-moving processional. A couple other cast members were lined up too, but Intrepid Trio was clearly the bride and grooms of the event. It seemed as if the whole party was lined up to meet us while munching on snacks and sipping drinks from the open bar.

Kate hadn't come in yet.

I was still shaken from my first sighting of her. I had a plan for how I would act. Well, sort of. Really, my only plan was to say something witty and have her taken aback by my utter charm. I hadn't exactly worked through the details yet. But even that miserable plan immediately went out the window the second I spotted her. It was so unexpected. I'd felt someone watching me as I talked Agata down from making Nugget into soup. I'd been preparing to growl at the interloper to bugger off, only to find Kate standing just a few feet away. She stood with hands clasped and her mouth rounded in surprise. Her beautiful full cupid's bow mouth pursed like she'd wanted to say something. Had she heard my conversation? Had I given something away? Then that bloody arsehole showed up and the moment was stolen from me. It all happened too fast. Almost like I had imagined her.

Pete had looked pissed, and she was surprisingly cowed by his unexpected arrival. But when he tried to loudly shame her, I was two seconds from punching him in the face. Yes, I was aware of my anger issues. I *didn't* punch him in the face, so that was progress. My therapist would be proud.

No matter how hard I tried to focus on the guest I was being introduced to my eyes lifted to scan the room every ten seconds like a paranoid bodyguard.

Would she decide not to come tonight after Pete had embarrassed her? He seemed so irritated; I was worried. I would give it five more minutes before I went to make sure she was okay. I really hated that nob she was with.

Emma had seen my desperate glances and had placed a glass of sparkling water with a lime wedge in my hand before a server could come by with champagne or anything else tempting. I'd found it was easier to look like you were drinking than to explain why you weren't. Or telling people to piss off.

Time blurred in casual conversation with strangers and former cast members. So far, the evening hadn't been as hard as the funeral. Maybe because Emma and Harrison were here but probably because the run-in with Kate had overrun every other fear or emotion.

All at once, I glanced up just as she entered the room. Like I had a preternatural awareness of her.

Her eyes were shining, and her cheeks were splotchy with a red flush. I glared daggers at the man currently directing her toward the bar. He had made her cry, and for that alone, he should be catapulted into space. My jaw clenched so hard, my teeth ground.

Emma laughed at my side, breaking my rage glare, and I managed to get a hold of myself. I shook a few more hands and said polite words I couldn't remember until I looked up and found Kate still at the bar.

She was glancing anxiously at the dwindling line of people waiting to meet us. The boyfriend was leaning casually across the bar, completely ignoring her as he cackled at something the bartender said.

She was breathtaking.

Far more stunning in reality than I could have possibly imagined.

Her short bob with bangs—her signature look, though she wasn't wearing her round glasses—was pinned back with sparking clips showing off the elegant length of her neck. Her petite figure was wrapped in a clinging purple fabric that made me long to run my hands over it. I yearned to get closer to her. To shake her hand. To grab her and tell her to run away with me.

Whoa.

Where had that come from?

No. She was here with her boyfriend, no matter how big a prat he was. It wasn't my place. I promised myself it would be enough to just see her. To possibly shake her hand. And if there was a god, maybe have an actual conversation with her.

The line to meet us had dissolved, and now the three of us were free to wander to our seats and eat our dinners.

A glance to Kate found her looking absolutely crestfallen. Well, she hadn't missed her chance to meet us. I would ensure it. Her boyfriend pointed to the tables where other guests were getting settled.

"Hey." Emma nudged my ribs. Her gaze followed mine to the bar and I tensed. "Are you okay? Need to step out and call your sponsor?" she whispered it quietly, her back to the rest of the room so it would look like she was just making chitchat.

My fists unclenched. I raised a stern eyebrow at her in question.

"You're staring at the bar like you've been crawling through the desert and it's the last glass of water on earth."

Haha, no, no, my oldest friend. That look of desperate longing is directed at the woman I could never hope to have.

"I'm fine," I said gruffly.

"I'm worried about you tonight," she said softly. "You seem ... off?"

I brought my focus back to her and flashed a reassuring smile. "I promise I'm okay. Just, you know. It's been a bit since I've been out and around this many people. I'm trying not to embarrass you."

"You're doing just fine," she said. "And remember, the less you talk the more mysterious you seem." She poked me teasingly.

"That's me. Man of mystery."

She gave me a soft smile before raising on her tiptoes, and I bent to let her kiss my forehead. My eyes flicked up to find Kate watching us. Her eyes widened fractionally before glancing away and back at the table in front of her.

A camera flashed right as Emma's lips brushed me. "So much for no pictures tonight," I grumbled.

I sighed as Emma pulled away with a wince.

"Well, that'll be all over the internet in five minutes. And thus fueling the rumor fire for another year. Sorry." She put her arm through mine.

"Don't be," I said. "Better than most of the shite they post about me."

Harrison broke away and joined us. "I'm starved."

"Come on, fellas, let's eat." She looped her other arm through Harrison's and dragged us to our assigned seats at the center of the room.

As the food was passed around, I only allowed myself to check in with Kate two more times. The air returned to my lungs when I saw her eating. My jaw unclenched when she laughed genuinely at something her neighbour said.

Her stupid prat boyfriend looked absolutely miserable and was on his third or fourth drink at least. His posture continued to slip in the chair, eyes turning glassy.

After dinner, the DJ brought up the tempo, and guests flocked to the dance floor. It really was like a wedding.

I was trying to contrive a way to meet Kate when the opportunity presented itself naturally.

Whether Emma believed that I was actually nervous or she was worried I'd sneak a drink when she wasn't watching, she hadn't left my side for more than a few minutes the entire night. I'd be annoyed if I wasn't secretly relieved to have her close like a security blanket. I was a huge baby.

Harrison had wandered to the bar to get a drink. Kate slipped off to the restroom, and the second she was gone, the boyfriend slithered back to the bar. He noticed Harrison and started chatting him up. Harrison, used to oily suck-ups, placated him accordingly but had the look of wanting to be saved.

"Harrison needs us," I whispered to Emma.

She followed my gaze to where Pete was crowding Harrison, imparting some deep knowledge only he was privy to. Harrison was basically bent backward, avoiding the close talker.

"Let's go save our boy." She stood up and smoothed her outfit. "Who is that guy?" she asked as we made our way across the room.

I shrugged. "Some wanker."

"And that's the thing that most people don't get. The artistic craft of what you do." Pete slurred his words, his whiskey breath potent from several steps away.

What a piece of work. Two minutes ago, he was looking down his nose at everyone in this room. Harrison scratched at his neck, nodding politely, looking desperate for an out. His eyes widened in relief when he saw us approach.

"Hey, mates," Harrison said. He moved to slide between Emma and me. At least I wasn't the only big baby using Emma as a shield. "This is, uh, sorry, what was your name?"

"Pete Klester." He extended his hand to me.

I grabbed it and gripped it as hard as I could. He hid his wince well enough, but his blurry gaze held mine a moment too long in curious disbelief. He clenched and released his fist at his side. *Oops.* It felt wrong to shake his hand before Kate's. I wanted to scrub my hand clean.

"Charles," I said shortly.

"Emma Flynn," Emma said. Pete flicked a glance up and down her body without offering to shake her hand.

She must have felt me tense because she casually brushed a calming palm down my arm.

I was just about to make an excuse to pull us away when I felt her arrive.

Kate.

Her mouth was parted softly in surprise to find her boyfriend talking to her three childhood idols. Her eyes widened minutely as she took in Pete with his fresh drink, leaning sloppily against the bar. I studied as she swallowed down her irritation and plastered a sweet smile in place.

My body rioted against an impulse to pull her into a hug.

It's me. It's me. It's me.

Finally, her gaze made its way to me. I was completely unaware of anything else in the world. It was as cliché as a scene in a film, where the world around faded to black and melted into white noise. I was sure, on some level, I was too stiff. I gave too much away.

Eye contact was such a peculiar thing. It wasn't even something I thought about until a moment like this. The countless random eyes that met mine in my life. Strangers stared at me, wondering if they recognized me. Thousands of people at this point, probably. Fame made eye contact much more confusing. So many people looked at me for one reason only. It was hard to know when it was genuine interest or just the allure of celebrity.

This moment was nothing like any of that. The second Kate's eyes clashed with mine a zing of awareness shot through my body quickly, followed by the realization that I'd held her gaze just a fraction too long. I hadn't looked away but neither had she. We were both frozen. My brain screamed to STOP STARING, but my body refused to comply. And in that fraction of a moment, so much was conveyed. My heart jolted with adrenaline. My whole vision narrowed down to a singular point. Her.

Look away. NOW.

An elbow jabbed into my side.

Emma said, "This is Kate Dubois."

I hadn't even realized Kate had spoken. I reached for Kate as she extended her hand. Electricity shot through me. I felt everything, everywhere. Her skin was so soft. My entire rough hand encompassed hers as gently as I could. I was touching Kate. I couldn't look at her. I could only focus on how small and pale her dainty little hand looked in my massive freckled mitt.

My eyes tracked up her arm and shoulders. Soft dark hair against alabaster skin. A freckle or a birthmark just above her wrist. I tucked the new detail away. These were the things that I never knew as her pen pal.

Jealousy flared, thinking of how this drunken fool got to paw at her when he didn't deserve to even breathe her air.

I tugged my hand back and tucked it into my pocket. I needed to get a grip. I was acting like a barbarian.

"Cheers," I said.

My voice was too rough. I was looking at her too much. I was giving everything away. I glared at a point on the horizon.

"And this is Charles Downing," Emma politely joked to cover my faux pas.

Harrison shot an arched eyebrow my way.

Great. Now I looked like a tool who assumed everybody knew who I was.

Emma asked about Kate's affiliation with the franchise, but their voices faded away as I tried to collect myself. I assumed it would be hard to see her. I assumed it would be challenging to hold all my feelings at bay. But I had no idea I would react to her so physically. It didn't seem fair.

I needed to say something more. How does one not act like a total wanker?

My throat locked up. With every passing second, I didn't speak, I felt my face contort in anger with myself. I was a grown man and couldn't string together a few polite sentences. But this woman deserved to hear the right thing. I needed to give the right first impression and every wasted second was too late.

I allowed myself one more look at Kate.

Her dark brown hair tucked behind the soft shell of her ear.

Look away. Count to ten.

Her sweet heart-shaped face framed by fringe.

Look away. Count to ten.

Her full mouth, dangerously seductive in contrast to her innocent round face.

The conversation whizzed on around me, and I was stuck in slow motion.

It was too much. I was mucking all this up. I needed to clear my head. I needed to get away from her and the sweet scent that clung to the air around her. I needed to stop myself from punching Pete in his stupid face.

Kate looked directly at me. Her mouth moved. Her gaze flicked to mine and away. She was asking me something. I couldn't hear her. What was she saying? The blood pumped too loudly in my ears.

I couldn't take it anymore.

"Excuse me." I pushed away and rushed to the loo.

I gripped the basin, taking deep breaths.

I'd made a complete arse out of myself. I'd only had one shot to meet her and make her see I was more than some random celebrity and I ruined it.

"Bloody fucking hell," I swore at my reflection.

My eyes were narrowed in frustration. Anger made my neck red. I took a deep breath in and out. What the hell was I doing?

I wouldn't waste this chance. I splashed my face with water and patted myself dry as I collected myself.

I knew how to talk to her. We'd been talking for two years. I knew her better than anybody else, *goddammit*. Definitely better than that Klester-fuck.

I walked back out, determined to start up a conversation. Anything.

Searching the room for a purple dress and sparkling eyes,

Emma found my gaze and raised an eyebrow. I waved off her concern.

They were gone. Kate must have left after I acted so unfathomably rude. I ran a hand down my face.

Just like that, it was all over. All these months of buildup. Us. Finally meeting. I blew it.

17

Kate

As I stared at Charles Downing's retreating form, a wave of mortification crashed over me. All these years daydreaming of a time I'd get to meet him, and I managed to ruin it all in a single conversation.

"What'd you say to him?" Pete slurred at me.

"I-I just asked if he was glad to see everyone," I said softly.

Embarrassment burned my cheeks as I felt Harrison and Emma's eyes on me. I frowned at the place where Charles had just been standing. Had I assumed too much closeness? I had thought ... I don't know what exactly. Maybe I'd subconsciously conflated years of *thinking* about him with actually knowing him. Maybe I'd talked to him like we were friends when I had no right to. I thought it was a safe question, but the second I'd found Pete talking to the Intrepid Trio, I hadn't felt anything but anger radiating off Charles. Had he recognized me from when I'd been listening to him earlier and thought I was a weird obsessive fan? Was I a weird obsessive fan? Probably.

I had naively thought that maybe Pete had said something

off-color in his drunken state, but the way Charles refused to look at me said the angry vibes were more about me than anybody else. No matter the reason, I blew it with Charles.

"He just had to take a call," Emma lied smoothly.

I blinked up at her. She smiled sweetly at me, but I felt like the floor had been tugged away, and I was at risk of falling through.

I plastered a smile on my face but it twitched at the corners. I was close to tears.

Harrison and Emma exchanged a look, and Harrison said, "Excuse me."

Emma made a polite excuse too, leaving Pete and me alone.

Pete sighed loudly. "They're shorter than I expected. Don't see what all the fuss is about really."

He threw back the rest of his drink until the ice fell and hit his teeth.

"I want to go back to the room," I said numbly. I was too close to crying and that realization caused another wave of humiliation.

"Yeah, this *party* is lame." He exaggerated the word party.

I was numb as we made our way back up to the room. Distantly, I heard Pete going on about his conversation with Harrison. "... I think I made an impression. Maybe I can put in a good word for you ..."

I slipped out of the dress I had put on only a few hours earlier. Back when I had been so filled with hope and naïveté.

Pete went into the bathroom and locked the door behind him. Not knowing what else to do, I grabbed my computer and sent a quick email to RC. It was the most inauthentic email I'd ever sent him but just writing helped soothe my nerves.

When Pete came out, I closed my laptop and went into the bathroom to wash up.

I slowly removed the makeup from my face and that's when

the tears came. I'd done exactly what I'd told RC that I wouldn't do. I built up tonight in my head. What had I thought? Charles would be so blown away by my amazing conversational skill that he would just … What?

I scoffed and rolled my eyes at my reflection. "You're pathetic." I sniffed, and my face crumpled.

Running the water, I bent to splash my face clean. The image of Emma kissing Charles's forehead appeared behind my eyelids. The surge of jealousy I'd felt at that moment had shocked me. The media had always paired them up, but I'd always felt they were just friends. Honestly, the media had connected Emma with all the members of the cast at some point. Even the actor Wesley Cole who played Max Malachi, the mortal enemy of the Intrepid Trio. And Wesley Cole was married.

I stared at my reflection as water dripped from my nose and eyelashes. Why did I even care? I didn't actually know any of these people. I was creating entire fantasies in my head. I shook my head into the towel, growling at myself.

I needed to get my perspective in check. I had been invited to a party with the cast and crew of my favorite TV show ever. I got to meet my childhood idols. I got to ride in a limo and eat free food. That was all amazing, and really, how many people could say that? After all this, I would go home, and I would focus on what really mattered. I would continue writing and tonight would make a great story for a cocktail party one day.

So, I had made a total ass of myself? Who cared? Charles probably forgot about my existence the second he walked away. He met people all the time. I was nobody. My jaw clenched as I thought of his face again when he finally looked at me.

It was almost tortured. Like looking at my face caused him actual pain. Maybe he had heard about some of my fan fiction and was one of those people who thought it was trash. I didn't know why that thought cut to the quick when I didn't even know the man.

Pete knocked loudly on the door. "Kate?"

His voice jarred me, almost aggressive with its high-pitched nasal tones. I closed my eyes and gathered my strength. The issue here wasn't Charles at all. It was Pete. Even if the evening had gone as planned, one thing was cemented solidly in my mind. Bringing Pete had been a mistake, and I needed space.

I took a gathering breath and opened the door to find Pete standing with arms crossed.

"What's this about?" he asked before I could even open my mouth. He gestured to *my* laptop, sitting open on the bed, my latest sent email on the screen.

"Did you go through my computer?" I asked in disbelief and stormed over to it. I grabbed it from the bed and quickly shut it down with shaking hands. I couldn't wrap my mind around such a betrayal. It didn't seem possible that this was the same man who had been so charming at first.

"You shouldn't be hiding things from me." He leaned against the corner of the wall; his tone thick with condescension.

"You had no right," I said.

"You just couldn't wait to tell your bestie all about it, could you?" He glared at me, that little bit of his goatee poking up as he chewed on his bottom lip.

"Pete," I said, and my throat cracked with nerves.

I had actually been feeling bad for Pete. I'd been worried dragging him here was a mistake when I never felt sure of my feelings for him. But all that sympathy was long gone.

"I can't do this anymore," I said.

I didn't realize until I said the words just how true they were. I could not carry on in this pseudo-relationship anymore.

"Do what exactly?" He stepped forward, and I moved around him, positioning myself closer to the door. I'd never seen Pete violent, but I'd also never thought he'd sink so low as to snoop either.

I had been studying my slipper socks but forced myself to look up and meet his gaze. "Us." I smoothed my hair behind my ear. "I was having doubts before we came. I shouldn't have brought you with me on this trip." My breath shook as I sucked it in. "I want to break up."

I was shocked at how sure I sounded even as I waited for Pete to snap into an even more sour version of himself. He would accuse me of being a flirt with all the men in my life and disrespecting him. He would somehow twist this all to be my fault.

He dropped to his knees in front of me and hugged my legs. "Kate. Please no."

I had not expected that.

I lifted my arms in the air, unsure of what to do, and floored by his reaction. "Pete—"

"I know I've been a mess lately." He rubbed his face into my thighs. "I just love you so much. I'm so scared to lose you. I see you with other men, and I just lose my mind. You're the most wonderful woman I've ever known."

Where was this fervor coming from? These feelings? I had always felt like I annoyed Pete and never quite met his expectations. He certainly never acted like a man obsessed.

"We aren't compatible," I said, the first of many truths.

"No. We are," he answered, looking up at me. His stubble poked into my thigh. "You just keep so much of yourself closed off from me. It drives me crazy. You seem so free with fucking RC online but never with me. You're always so distant from me. Cold."

I couldn't believe this. Had I kept myself closed off from him? I thought I had been the one trying to make this relationship work, trying to match his instant enthusiasm. It had been like trying to break in an expensive pair of high heels; I wanted them to fit so bad, to validate the commitment, but all they did was blister. They turned me into someone that I was never supposed to be.

"The closer I tried to get to you, the more you pushed me away," he added.

I blinked in surprise. Is that what had been happening? Hadn't I thought my reaction to his closeness abnormal? But every time he tried to progress our relationship, I felt smothered.

"You went through my computer. You can't have a relationship that's not built on trust," I said even as the doubt crept in. I took a breath. I had made up my mind. "I don't like how you acted tonight and how you treated me all day."

There were so many things that felt off in our relationship. But they were hard to pin down, to define. Just feelings that didn't seem right, but if I tried to explain, Pete would have an argument for those too.

Pete rocked back on his heels and grabbed my hands. "You're right. You're so right. I'll be better, I swear. I never meant to be like this. I just love you so much. It makes me crazy."

"I-I—" I just couldn't say it. He deserved someone to say it back, didn't he? But the only thing I felt when I looked at him was a curl of disgust. And maybe pity.

"It's okay. You can say it when you're ready. Look." He ran a hand over his face. "I was going to wait until after the trip, but I can't wait anymore."

My body grew still with cold foreboding. "What are you—"

He fumbled in his pocket and pulled out a small box. "Kate. I love you. I love you so much, I can't go another day not being married to you."

"Pete." My hands covered my mouth. I looked only in his eyes. I didn't even want to see the ring.

"We can go to Vegas. Right now. Let's throw caution to the wind and get out of here."

"You want to go to Vegas?" I asked numbly.

"Yes. For you. I can mix it up."

"I have to film tomorrow. I made a commitment." I don't know why I bothered to give him one last chance to show me he took anything I cared about seriously.

His jaw ground for a moment before a smile was back in place. "I'm literally on my knees begging you to run away with me and you're talking about your hobby?"

"Getting published has been my dream ..."

"I thought I was your dream. Getting married, settling down. I would make it so you could quit that job you hate and have my babies. Then, if you still wanted to, you could write. We could build a whole life together. Don't you see? It's perfect."

An entire alternate timeline flashed before my eyes. Me pregnant with a toddler on my hip, haggard, and lonely. Pete coming home from work late, demanding dinner. My writing forgotten. Any other friendships long gone.

I said calmly, "You don't care about any of my dreams. You only care that you have me."

I stepped back.

"That's not true." He stood and the anger from only a few moments ago was back. My response had clearly not been part of his plan.

"You could have made that proposal to anybody. I don't think you even know me at all." The words dawned on me as I spoke them. I was literally just an available woman to him. He wanted the plan, and he thought I would slide perfectly into that role.

"And who knows you, huh? Who do you show yourself to at all?" he snapped.

RC. I didn't voice it, but it must have shown on my face.

"Right. Your little online buddy. I fucking knew something was going on there." He slammed the ring box on the dresser.

"It's not that at all—"

"Like hell it's not. He's probably just sitting there waiting for your next message so he can say, 'Haha, I have this guy's girlfriend and he's so clueless.' You made an idiot out of me."

Pete's anger really wasn't about my rejection at all. This was his fragile male ego talking. I could not get him out of this room fast enough.

"Listen. I'm sorry I brought you here. But you need to go. You can't stay here with me. I can help pay for another hotel room, but you cannot stay here." I'd figure out the money. I'd dip into my savings if I had to. I could not and would not be with this man for another moment. I'd been so stupid. So desperate to just not be alone. I felt rejected and vulnerable when I met him. If my mom taught me anything, it's that I did not give men control of my value. I had been the only one bending to make our relationship work. Both parties should be doing that. Not just one person. I had goals and plans. If Pete didn't take me seriously, how could I be with him? How would I ever be able to look myself in the mirror?

"You think I want to be here now? With all your crushes wandering around? I saw how you flirted with Harrison. How you were stalking Charles."

I started to pack his suitcase. "You need to leave. You and I are done. When I get back, I'll box up the stuff you've left at my place."

Thankfully, I'd never given him a key. How had he integrated himself so fully into my life when I had hardly given him permission?

"Kate. You're going to regret this." His dark vehemence was back. He ripped the suitcase from my hands and finished throwing his stuff in there. Maybe I should have waited until he was more sober to have this conversation, but a nagging voice told me this was just the beginning of his dark side. The sooner he was out of my life, the better.

"You won't get another shot with a guy like me. Not the way you hide yourself away from everyone living in that fantasy world. Not with the way you are obsessed with that stupid old TV show. You're lucky I found you." He paused on his way out the door to grip my upper arms.

"Let go of me now," I said calmly.

He looked at his hands as if he was confused as to how they even got there.

"What about my mom? What am I supposed to say to her? I told her I was marrying you. She's sick." He frantically searched my face, his pitch whiny now. His mother never even warmed to me. She'd always been so icy the times we'd gone to her house. I never felt good enough for her boy.

I scoffed in utter disbelief. "You'll figure it out."

"You're making a mistake." It was a threat.

"Maybe," I said. "But I'm okay with that."

With that, he was out the door, and I locked it behind him.

No more of this. How quickly I had almost lost sight of my dreams for a man who didn't trust or care about me.

My mother raised me better than that, and I wouldn't do it again.

18

TO: KateDubois@geemail.com
   FROM: TheRealFreddyStan4Life@geemail.com
   SUBJECT: Well? Etc.

TO: TheRealFreddyStan4Life@geemail.com
   FROM: KateDubois@geemail.com
   SUBJECT: RE: Well? Etc.
RC.
RC! RC!!!

It was amazing. I'm still flying. I can't believe my life. Pinch me. No. Don't. I don't want to wake up if it's all a dream.

Well, first, the flight was great, and when I got to the airport there was A DRIVER holding a sign with my NAME! I basically had to act like it wasn't the coolest thing that's ever happened, but basically, the whole time in the limo, I was screaming on the inside.

Hi, I'm Kate. I take limos now. No big deal. But also bow before me, peon!

So then the hotel is amazing. Like fancy-schmancy. Some of the cast is staying here. In the penthouse, obviously, but WE ARE SHARING THE SAME BUILDING.

(Okay, I promise I will stop yelling now. No. I cannot promise that.)

Speaking of the cast. I met them! I actually MET THEM!

Wait, but first, do you care about how the room looked and stuff? I can give the details if you want, but you never seem to care about that stuff. I will say, it was all very swanky with a DJ and gourmet food on real china and everything. (Haha, I sound like such a doofus, don't I? I swear I've been in public before!)

I still can't wrap my mind around it. Emma was amazingly nice, as you'd expect. Harrison was scary good-looking (but it's true about celebrities being shorter in person). Except Charles. He was huge. Like massive and muscular. I always worried that I exaggerated his looks for the fans, but now I think I may have been selling him short ...

The only thing ... ugh, never mind. It was fine. I'm just doing my overthinking thing. Actually, I need to get it off my chest, and I know you will give it to me straight. I feel like I may have annoyed Charles. Am I crazy? I asked him a question, and he walked away. And he was like *glaring* at me before that. I'm just projecting, right? I'm sure he was being totally normal, and I just built things up in my head.

Pete says never meet your idols. I suppose he's right. Well, anyway. It was amazing. I'm so glad I came. Thank you for pushing me to do so. I would have regretted it, you were right.

Thank god I didn't trip or dribble spit all over myself. Can you imagine?

Can't wait to see what tomorrow brings. On that note, I better hit the hay and get my beauty rest. I can hardly keep my eyes open after the nonstop adrenaline of the day.

Love,

Kate

PS: This is NOT gossip. You know that I don't do that. But I saw Charles and Emma kiss. Maybe I was wrong all these years thinking they were just friends. But it was a forehead kiss. As a man, do you think that's brotherly affection or "I've secretly been in love with you for most of my life?"

PPS: Not that it matters. Obviously. I'm happy for them if they are in love.

PPPS: Not that my opinion even matters. OKAY, I AM GOING TO BED NOW.

DRAFT UNSENT

TO: KateDubois@geemail.com
FROM: TheRealFreddyStan4Life@geemail.com
SUBJECT: I was an idiot

Are you sure you're okay? You sound ... off? Was it because of how I acted? I'm sorry I was such an idiot tonight. I saw you, and I couldn't take it. I wanted to scoop you up in my arms and hold you and tell you everything. I hate your boyfriend. I know we don't talk about him. I know he's important to you, but you are such a bright light in this world, and every time you are near him, he's like this black hole that sucks away everything. He doesn't deserve you. Fuck. I've messed things up so bad. I want to tell you the truth. I want to stay away from you so I won't tarnish you.

I botched it up again. One day, I will say what I mean when I speak to you.

Also. RE: Emma and me. Please. We are brother and sister, far as I'm concerned. The media has a field day with us but my feelings for her have never been more than protective older brother.

Lastly, did you mean to close your email with "LOVE" or were you falling asleep?

I wish I would just send this ...

TO: KateDubois@geemail.com
FROM: TheRealFreddyStan4Life@geemail.com
SUBJECT: I was right again

Kate,

Glad you had a great time. You can thank me later for encouraging you to go.

Charlie sounds like a prat for not being charmed by you.

I saw the picture of said kiss on the internet, definitely just friends.

Get some sleep.

Xoxo

19

———

Charlie

I SLID MY PHONE AWAY WITH A FROWN. KATE SOUNDED OFF. Forced glee. I hadn't liked how Pete and his stupid mouth mullet treated her all night. My annoyance at his presence was turning into a different sort of worry.

If I could just know that she was okay.

"Wanna head out?" Harrison asked, appearing at my side. "There's a pub round the corner, with some good greasy food."

"Yeah, sounds good." I had too much anxious energy to go back to his house at this point anyway. It's not like I was worried about having a drink around these two. If I stayed in, I'd just keep staring at my inbox until I did something stupid like email her again.

The line between truth and fact was blurring with every exchange. I would need to stop responding soon. Or reveal the truth.

The bar was a quaint attempt at a real British pub, complete with union jacks plastered over everything.

"This feels like going to a Taco Bell in Mexico," Emma said

as we sat at the table. Then her eyebrows furrowed, and she added, "Wait. That doesn't make sense. But something about it feels weird."

"Like Disney branded 'authentic British pub experience,'" I said with air quotes.

"Yeah, but the food is pretty good. Try the fish and chips," Harrison said. "It's the closest thing out here to home and it's never crowded. Most of the regulars hardly give two shits about who I am." He waved over a waitress. Maybe because it was LA, but she hardly reacted to seeing the three of us. That was good enough in my book.

"It wasn't too bad, was it?" Emma asked me with an elbow nudge once their drinks and my food arrived. "The meet and greet?"

It took me a moment to register her question.

Yes. It was. I had a terrible time, and I wished I could both completely forget about it or have a re-do in which I actually talk to the woman I've been daydreaming about for two years.

"It was fine," I said.

"I'm glad you came." Harrison held up his pint, and we clinked our glasses with his. "I honestly thought it was a lost cause."

We all took a drink and set down our glasses.

Harrison wiped some foam off his lip. "Should have known Emma would get you. She could convince the Queen to twerk."

"It's true." Emma sipped her wine with a self-assured smile. "But this wasn't on me. I'd given up when he did a one-eighty."

She shot me a look, and I swore under my breath.

"Oh really?" Harrison said drawing out the words. "What changed your mind?"

"I knew nobody would watch if it was only you two," I said dryly, tossing a chip into my mouth.

They laughed, and I used the opportunity to shift focus from myself.

"I thought we'd see Wesley there tonight," I said innocently.

Harrison's eyes widened, and he took a long drink watching Emma's reaction.

Emma shrugged coolly. "I thought he was on the schedule to record this week, but I haven't seen him, and I don't care to."

Harrison winced. "Ouch."

"It's not like that," she defended, her voice rising in pitch. "There's no bad blood. I just don't care what he does."

Harrison scoffed. "You were obsessed with him for our entire TF career. You checked the call sheets every day to see if you'd have a scene with him."

Emma lifted her chin and rolled her eyes. "I was a child. I got over it. It's been twenty years, for crying out loud."

Not for you, I thought but knew better than to say. She'd not stopped loving him until the last few years, and even that I wasn't entirely convinced of. When he got married, she spent a year in a developing country, completely devoting her life to making potable water available to a single community.

"Anyway, he only ever saw me as a sister," she added, flicking a crumb off the table.

"I thought you two took each other's virginities?" Harrison said as if he didn't fully know.

"Jesus, Harrison, say it louder for the people in the back," Emma swore, leaning closer.

"It's sweet," I said. Then wished I hadn't.

She scoffed. "You're such a softy. It was just sex. We wanted to make sure we wouldn't totally fumble it when we finally did it with other people. Plus, we couldn't really trust strangers at that point. Our fame was so new. It was just sex," she added again, and it almost seemed like she was reminding herself.

"I'm just saying, if he really saw you as a sister, that would have never happened. Not in a million years," Harrison said.

Emma finished her wine in one gulp.

"I heard he's getting a divorce," Harrison added casually.

Emma's head snapped to him. She coughed and wiped at her mouth. "What?"

I scratched at my jaw. "You know. I think I did hear they were separated last year. I can't remember who told me," I said.

A blatant lie. It was Kate who told me. It was all the rage on the fansite rumor mill. I hadn't told Emma because, well, because of the look right there on her face.

A flash of hope before she schooled her features. If Wesley hadn't made a move in the last ten years, he wouldn't now. It made me want to find the guy and shake him. I hated to see her heart start to heal and then get all mashed up again. Now I felt bad for moving the focus off me and onto her and Wesley.

"I didn't see Sedar tonight either," I said, hoping to pull Emma back from where she was lost in thought.

Emma blinked and said, "The producers said he turned down the invite."

"He told me he's not writing anymore," Harrison said.

"Why?" I asked, surprised. "His last two books were a hit."

"And surprisingly good," Emma said. Then amended her thought. "Not that they haven't always been good. But Freddy and Lucy's characters seemed to have a lot more depth to them. And it was very clever."

Kate had said the same thing. My fingers itched to check my phone.

Harrison's face was shadowed with new worry. "George's not responded to my last few messages." He tapped at his glass, thinking out loud. "I think I might go pay him a visit and check on him."

Harrison and Sedar had been close for many years. Even

when Hollywood threatened to take us all under, the three of us would spend summers at his Northern California home. We felt like surrogate grandchildren alongside his real ones.

"I hope he's okay," Emma said.

"Me too." Harrison let out a long breath. Though we'd all gone to his house during filming breaks, it was clear that Harrison had always been closest to him. Maybe because his character was based on a childhood Sedar always wished he had. He'd talked openly about being a loner, always wishing he had two best friends. I think Harrison saw himself in the character too. We all did.

He shook off his worry like sliding a mask in place and smiled. "Off to the loo. Order another round?" he asked Emma and she nodded.

Not three steps, and he was stopped for an autograph. So not total anonymity. I pulled my hat lower and slumped in the chair. People were mostly decent about not coming up when we were eating, but I made my body language clear that I wasn't in the mood. Plus, most people only cared about Harrison and Emma.

I felt Emma's focus before I turned back to her. She was dewy with her glass of wine and grinned as she watched me with an arched eyebrow.

"What?" I asked suspiciously.

She shrugged. "Nothing. Just missed you. Missed this."

My heart tugged. I glared at my fizzy drink. "Yeah. Missed you too."

She flicked a glance to Harrison. "It'll be an hour before he's back, huh?"

"Likely."

"What did you *really* think of tonight?" she asked, watching me closely.

Instantly, I thought of Kate again. Her giant grin, her

gleaming eyes. I cleared my throat and kept my face passive. "It was fine. More of the usual."

The server came to bring more drinks for them. I did not care for how closely Emma studied me. I shifted in my chair when it was just us again. "That little guy with cancer was very touching," I said.

She smiled sadly. "Stuff like that ... it feels ..." Her gaze went cloudy. When she came back to herself, she finished with, "That was very special."

She'd always taken her success as a burden that she needed to prove herself worthy of. I worried about her.

"What about that one woman?" she asked, not to be deterred.

I stilled. "You're going to have to be more specific. We met at least fifty people today."

"The pretty brunette. Chic French bob? The writer with big, earnest eyes."

I cleared my throat and performed some of my best acting since TF. "Yeah. She seems nice. Those fanfic people. That's another world, eh?"

She rolled her eyes. "Why can't you just admit you fancied her?"

There was no point in denying it. She'd only make more of a big deal about it. "Yeah, so. She was a pretty bird. And there with her boyfriend." I couldn't help the grumbled "prat" under my breath.

She, thankfully, didn't comment on that.

"She seemed in awe of you," she said.

I fought back a growl. "*Freddy* has that effect on people."

Emma was wrong. Kate hadn't fancied *me*. She may have been attracted to the character I played all those years ago. She may have thought she was meeting with the version of Charles

Downing or Freddy Finks in her head. Not me. It soured my mood instantly.

"I still think she was into you," Emma said. "You could have probably gotten her number."

"Again. Boyfriend."

"That didn't used to matter. With all the TF groupies."

I winced. Another wave of shame over the action of my young self who loved the fame and attention. Thirsty birds threw themselves at me. I was done with all that.

"Not for a long time," I mumbled. The heat under my collar grew.

"That's good. That never suited you."

I shrugged, willing Harrison to hurry. "Wait. What does that mean?"

"The whole player vibe. You're way too much a romantic."

I scoffed. "Hardly."

"Please. Of all of us ..." She hesitated. "I know you struggle the most with life after the show. You're sensitive and romantic. You'll never admit it, but you loved that world as much as the fans."

Damn Emma. I ground my jaw.

"I was just tired of worrying about becoming a baby daddy," I said.

She rolled her eyes. "Okay, we will go with that."

"What'd I miss?" Harrison asked, plopping down next to me.

"We're discussing our dismal love lives," Emma said, thankfully not mentioning the Kate nonsense.

"Then I'm just in time," Harrison said. "Hey, speaking of. What happened with the American girl you were talking to?"

I winced, hoping they'd forgotten about that.

I shrugged and suddenly wished I had a drink. I took a long pull of the fizzy drink. "She got a boyfriend. It didn't work out."

"Oh, sorry, mate," Harrison said.

Emma was looking so close at me now I felt my skin itching.

"I don't understand why the media is so obsessed with our love life. Even after all these years," I grumbled.

Emma scoffed. "Trust me, as the girl who has been dealing with it since we were ten. It's disgusting."

Harrison and I exchanged a look but didn't comment. It probably was worse for her but that only ever made us feel like shite. Like we should have protected her more when we were all younger.

"We're barely thirty," Harrison said. "There are plenty of people single at our age. There's nothing wrong with us."

I clinked my mug against his. "Exactly."

"I don't know that I'll ever get married. It's too hard to get close to people when you're this famous." Harrison's honesty surprised me. I thought he loved everything about his fame.

"It is a bit weird that none of us have ever been in a serious relationship," Emma hedged.

I thought again of Kate. Not that we were in a relationship. Obviously. But it was the longest I'd talked to any single person outside these two.

"Maybe that's the exchange," I said softly.

"Fame and fortune," Harrison said. "Shite personal lives."

"That's us. Fortunate in life. Unlucky in love," Emma said.

"To the Intrepid Trio," I said and held up my drink.

"Not so intrepid lately. Aging trio, more like," Emma said.

"Has-been trio," I said.

"Speak for yourself," Harrison feigned affront.

"To the loveless trio. At least we have each other," Emma said.

"Always," I said and flicked my gaze to my two best friends on the planet.

20

———————

Charlie

She said love.

She clearly wrote. "Love, Kate."

I'd reread her last email again before going to bed last night. And I signed with bloody *hugs and kisses.*

I came to the studio earlier than needed the next morning because sleep was impossible. Partly because of jet lag but mostly because visions of Kate danced through my head. We'd never signed off like that before. The lines had always been clear. She had a boyfriend. We were friends. I knew so much about her. She knew everything about me. Everything real. Except for the small detail of who I was.

"Bloody fucking hell," I swore, and the driver looked up at me in the rearview mirror.

"Sorry." Held up my phone as a way of explanation.

I was overthinking it. The L-word hadn't meant anything. She was exhausted. She was overwrought and had an exciting day. She had just signed off as she would with anyone. She probably throws around the "love" to everyone.

Good god, man. Get it together.

I rubbed at my temples. My eyes felt like sandpaper from lack of sleep, but the caffeine from this American coffee was giving me the shakes.

She's mentioned a few times that she had a bad habit of building things up too much, but that was what I had done last night. I had imagined our first meeting so many times there was no way I could have acted in any appropriate manner that lived up to what I'd pictured in my mind. I should have told her the truth of who I was the first time we ever spoke. She wouldn't have believed me, she would have never even responded to me, but maybe that would have been better than this.

Whatever *this* was. But even picturing Kate not part of my daily life cut me through with sharp panic.

I would make it up to her. If I saw her over the next few days of filming, I would just make polite conversation and rectify my rudeness. I would put a distance between us because the actor she saw me as was a stranger. It was image control so I wouldn't wind up reading about what a rude prick I was on the internet later. Not that she would ever do that. I wasn't worried about her ever selling any information about me to the press. She wasn't like that.

I spent a lot of time thinking about how she might respond to the truth of who I was. I actually didn't think she would be all that concerned about it after the initial shock. The media, on the other hand, would destroy her. They'd look into every detail of her life. Nothing would be kept private. They'd tear apart her stories, take the beauty of her storytelling and turn it into something lurid and dirty.

The driver got us through the lot gate and dropped me off at the studio. It wasn't the same cluster of buildings that were used for TF back in the day, but when I walked in, my breath came out in a gasp.

It was the same set. The main mess hall of the ship where so many of our scenes were filmed over the years. I swallowed back the tightness squeezing my throat. I ran my hand over the tables. Were these the actual set pieces they had used during filming? Every detail was perfect, down to the uncomfortable metal chairs that made my arse go numb after long scenes. So many memories, pushed down over the years, bubbled to the surface instantly.

Overwhelmed with emotion, the shaking in my hands worsened.

Get a grip, get a grip.

I wanted to scream out and punch through the walls. *This.* This right here was exactly why I didn't want to come back. Every time I thought enough time had passed, I was brought back to when my whole life lay ahead of me. The best and worst, and most emotional times of my life took place on these tiny fake sets. Before I ruined it all and made myself a laughingstock, all my major life events happened here. First time I drove, season five. First time I kissed a girl, season three.

I couldn't take a deep breath in. I shouldn't have come back. I didn't want to feel any of this. I wanted to numb the overwhelming emotions.

I wanted a drink so bloody bad.

A soft sniffle caught my attention. My head snapped in the direction of the sound. It came from the set on the other side of the wall.

I silently walked to the connecting doorway of the soundstage and found one of the classroom sets. Another room that felt as familiar to me as a childhood home. I still dreamed about walking through these sets, always relieved to be back but understanding on some level that none of it was real.

Every previous thought vanished and narrowed down to the sight in front of me.

Kate.

She sat at a desk in the middle row, head facing the front of the room where editors would CGI in whatever curriculum we were learning in that scene. She sniffled again, causing my adrenaline to spike.

My fists balled. I would bet my life's savings that her tosser boyfriend was the cause. I tentatively made my way over to her, clearing my throat so as not to startle her.

She shot up out of the desk, hands clasped behind her back like I'd caught her stealing.

"Sorry. I know I shouldn't—" Her mouth fell open when she registered it was me.

Her face was puffy and her eyes bloodshot.

"Oh my god, Charles Downing," she said. As though saying my full name out loud made it real. She pressed her hands to her cheeks and quickly wiped away a tear.

"Call me Charlie. It's okay," I said. I backed away slightly, making myself seem as small as possible. "I came early to check out the sets too."

Her gaze flicked over me, and she blinked rapidly a few times before glancing around.

"It looks exactly the same," she said in soft wonder. One of her hands flounced out to the side. Then she looked back at me, and her brow furrowed. "Of course, you know that more than me. I, er, duh."

I chuckled and looked at the floor. I found it too hard to look directly at her and remember how to blink. That wouldn't freak her out at all—to stare unblinkingly at her face.

"It does look just like it." My voice was deep and raspy from lack of sleep. My Adam's apple felt too high in my throat. This was the first time she and I were ever having a conversation. Just us two. Not electronically. I cleared my throat again and said, "I was just thinking the same thing."

Her mouth parted and her eyes blinked over me. She had her glasses on today. I loved how the big round frames accentuated her doe eyes.

"Is it the same set?" she asked.

"No. We originally filmed on the Megamount set," I said.

"Oh, that's right." Her gaze went soft as she looked over my shoulder. "I forgot LexiFilm bought the rights to TF in 2015. I guess it would be silly to think it was the same after all this time."

I wiped my mouth to hide my smile. I loved her encyclopedic knowledge of all things TF.

I stepped forward so that one of the desks was between us. It looked so small. How had we ever been so young? "I didn't mean to intrude. I just thought I heard something."

Her cheeks reddened. "You aren't intruding. I'm the one who shouldn't be here."

I dismissed her worry with a quick shake of my head. I tentatively lifted a hand to point at her face. "What's wrong? Has something happened?"

Her eyes widened, and I recognized that my tone was far too familiar. I was a stranger to this woman. Or worse yet, a character.

"You were crying," I stated when she didn't speak right away. Like a caveman who just learned to talk.

"No. No. I'm fine," she insisted. "I'm just overly emotional being here. TF was a big part of my life."

I nodded. That could be true. But somehow, I doubted it, or at least it only felt partially true. Would Kate come here for comfort when something upset her like I had?

"Of course. It *was* your life. Like, you actually lived this. Well, not in space. Obviously." She snorted. "But this was your childhood. Is it weird being here?" I opened my mouth slowly, but she shook her head and went on. "You don't need to answer that. I should probably stop talking," she mumbled as she trailed off.

There were so many things I wanted to respond to. It was lonely being back here. It brought up so many feelings. I wanted to hug her. I wanted to comfort her. Worse yet, I longed for her to comfort me.

I hated seeing her so flustered, but I also found her incredibly adorable. She rambled and wandered through her sentences while speaking like she did in her letters. They were always stream of consciousness, like she was on the journey to discover what she wanted to say in real time. She could have pared down her words and deleted the rambles, but she never did. She would sooner write "ignore that" rather than go back and delete it. And I loved that about her. She didn't replay and overthink every thought and feeling in her head like I did. She didn't filter everything out until there were only grunts lefts.

I grunted in acknowledgment.

Case in point.

She fidgeted, glancing around, looking for a polite way to abscond. I had to respond better than I had last night.

"You seem upset." I scratched at my neck. "About something else."

Christ. That was too intrusive.

"Gosh, this is embarrassing. You found me here crying." She pointed to her face and her chin trembled. "Now I'm crying harder because I'm embarrassed, and I just keep messing things up with you."

My face must have contorted into something scary because she winced, and I had to force my eyebrows to relax.

"You didn't mess anything up," I growled out but that did little to convince her. "I was a shite last night. I'm sorry. It wasn't you. Just some ... thing I'm dealing with." I waved my hand as if to erase the whole thing. I looked up at her with my chin tilted down, repentant.

She drew in a soft breath and mouthed. "Oh."

"You don't have to talk about it," I said. "Uh, what's upsetting you. If you don't want." I cleared my throat. How did people communicate face-to-face like this? How did anything ever get accomplished? I couldn't look at her for more than a second at a time without my tongue drying up and sticking to the roof of my mouth.

"No. Gosh. Look at me. A mess in front of Charles Downing. Honestly, I'm fine."

Hearing my full name on her lips shut everything down inside me like a layer of ice on a windshield overnight. I would only ever be the celebrity to her.

The tension between us grew as thick as the ice forming over my features. She must have sensed it because she looked up at me tentatively. Her tongue flicked out to lick her lips. My jaw ground together so hard, a headache formed.

"I'm just a person," I grumbled and wished I hadn't. She tilted her head and looked abashed. I added, "I mean, I'm concerned when I see a person upset. Just like anybody else."

Her features softened, and her focus moved back to the desk. "My boyfriend and I ... had a fight," she admitted. "Then I came here and it just was all ... a lot."

"Do you need me to kill him?" I said it flatly and immediately.

Her head shot up, and her eyebrows were high behind her bangs.

My right cheek twitched. Her gaze moved over my face, and then slowly, the shock melted into a smile.

A breath whooshed out of her and she laughed. "You're joking. British humor."

No, I'm not. "Of course."

She laughed harder, and I watched her as long as I could. I soaked up every moment of it so I could picture it when I made her laugh in our letters. Until she looked up at me again. Finally, she took another deep breath, visibly more relaxed. I would absolutely threaten to kill her boyfriend every day if it made her laugh. It really wouldn't be a chore.

"I'll be okay. Thank you for asking." She smiled at me, and I couldn't look away.

There was that power again. Our gazes were their own electric current. Could she feel it too?

When I didn't speak, she traced a finger over the desk, between us breaking the unintentional staring contest. "Actually, it's good we met like this."

My fingertips went icy. Did she know? "Why's that?" I asked tightly.

"Apparently we're filming together today," she said.

I frowned. She flinched.

"What do you mean?" I asked.

"I—uh, just looked at the filming schedule for today. They're doing something a little different. They want me to interview you and vice versa, I guess? I don't know all the details."

No, this couldn't be happening. I couldn't be around her even more and not fuck this up somehow.

"Why you?"

She winced, trying to hide the hurt I'd unintentionally caused. Fuck. Again. This was exactly what I meant.

"I write—wrote—Um ... I'm a writer and I have written several stories about you. And the show." Her face flamed red. She pinched the area between her glasses. "Yeah, maybe this isn't the clever idea that they think it is. I have foot-in-mouthitis around you."

"I'm going to talk to the director," I said.

"Wait." Her hand shot out to stop me. She grabbed my arm

and we both stared at it. If I thought my blood was heated before just being close enough to smell her and see her individual lashes, her hand gripping my bicep was incendiary.

She dropped it. "I didn't mean to disrupt anything. I'm happy to do it, obviously. Thrilled. I just ... I feel like I keep messing up with you."

I wanted to bare my teeth and growl. She thought it was her fault? I was an embarrassing mess at interviews when I was pissed, and now I'm rubbish and too quiet being sober. *I* was the issue here. It wasn't her fault that I barely lasted five minutes during interviews. I wasn't fit for her company. She deserved more than this.

"It's not you," I ground out. "Excuse me."

I turned away sharply. I needed to figure out a way to fix this.

Kate

FOR THE SECOND TIME IN TWELVE HOURS, I STARED IN SHOCK AT the retreating form of Charles Downing. *Charlie*, he'd corrected. What had I said this time? He was much more volatile than the media made him out.

No, that wasn't fair.

We had been having a good conversation. He'd seemed genuinely concerned about me, albeit a bit sleepy and grumpy. I'd been trying not to look at him, but he was somehow so much better looking close up, even slightly puffy from just waking. Maybe more so. In slid an image of him rolling over and smiling sleepily on a pillow glowing with soft morning light...

I stood up abruptly and walked off the classroom set. I would go get coffee until it was my turn for hair and makeup in a few hours. My stomach was too knotted up to eat.

The fight last night had been brutal. Pete had already sent me several texts that started with apologies and then became more and more angry.

The one that I had just gotten before Charles, er Charlie, showed up had told me I was an embarrassment to TF and to writing.

Even though I knew he was just lashing out, it was a kick to the gut.

My first evening in LA had gone so poorly. I stretched the truth in my last email to make RC think I was glad to have come.

And I *was* glad. Mostly. I wanted RC to think his pushing me had benefited me. It had. I was still here for my writing, and Pete be damned.

And then Charlie found me.

I still couldn't wrap my mind around it. We'd had a conversation. And then ... What? He said it wasn't my fault he got upset but ... uh, nobody else was around.

I hated that I couldn't read him. I hated that I thought I even had the right to read him even more.

Back to square one. I would be professional. Distant. No more crying. No more being an overly emotional fangirl.

In the makeup chair, coffee in hand, I anxiously waited to learn what the plan was for today. I had little gel things under my eyes to help with the dark puffy circles from crying and curlers in my short hair. I looked absurd. I snapped a picture and emailed it to RC with the subject, "Am I beautiful yet?" I sent it without thinking and then cringed for a solid minute straight. How the hell was he supposed to answer that and still maintain the careful distance we'd built? Foot-in-mouthitis was worsening.

It's not you. Charlie's rich, deeply accented voice replayed in my head.

The guest in the makeup chair next to me—a woman who

read the books while battling cancer, saying they saved her life and taught her how to fight—and I chatted a little about how excited we were. I'd sat next to her and her husband last night at dinner and enjoyed their company. Her name was Kristen, and she was my mom's age, but the warmth that poured from this woman was nothing compared to the cold professional who raised me. She had that zest for life that I'd always envied.

I'd been debating if I should text Pete and ask him to back off when my ears perked at something my stylist was saying to the man next to her. Kristen's hairdresser was leaning closer to hear over the sound of the hair dryer.

"I guess he threw a fit and demanded to change his interview or something," she said.

Instantly, I knew they were talking about Charlie. The dread that Kristen's easy conversation had coaxed out of me returned in a dizzying flash.

"What a diva," the guy said. "Didn't he pull all sort of antics back in the day too?"

"Yeah, he was a mess. The director basically told him to get over it and that she wasn't redoing the shooting schedule because he didn't like who he was paired with."

I sucked in my lips. When I looked in the mirror, neither stylist seemed to notice my internal freak-out.

They snickered. I had been a little offended on behalf of Charlie at first but was humiliated to know how much he was against this pairing.

"What set him off? Is he still sober? I saw he was in rehab a few years back," the guy said.

I exchanged a look with Kristen next to me in the mirror. If the makeup artists were even remotely concerned about us hearing their gossip, they didn't show it.

"Who knows? The times I've worked with him, he's been nice." She shrugged and started taking out my curlers.

"Who was he supposed to work with?" the other asked.

I blew out a long breath and raised my hand. At this point, the situation couldn't get much more awkward.

They both looked at me and gasped. Kristen gave me a sympathetic smile.

"Shit. Sorry, babe," my stylist said.

I shrugged like *it happens*.

"What's the deal? You're a doll. I mean I don't know you, but you seem nice enough," my stylist asked.

"Thanks." I flushed. "Nothing happened. I just rub him the wrong way, I guess."

Or maybe all the stories I've written about him made him uncomfortable? Was he embarrassed? My stomach tightened with even more anxiety. It didn't seem prudent to mention my stories.

She made a tsking sound like it was hard to believe. "Actors are just ..." she started.

"Dicks." The other finished. "What? They are!" He flinched back as she smacked his shoulder and widened her eyes to the surroundings. "They live in a different world. It's very weird to witness."

"They're not all bad," my stylist defended. "But yeah, definitely a different planet." Then she pointed at the futuristic space station set around us. "Ha. I didn't even mean to do that."

They both cackled, and I looked to my chair partner and smiled. Some of the tension in my shoulders melted away. So, keeping track: RC told me actors are just people. But those who worked directly with actors all the time said they aren't normal. It must do a number on your perception of self to be catered to all the time. People either talked shit about you or idolized you. There didn't seem to be a middle ground.

Much like I had acted.

What if Charlie just wanted to be treated normally and I had freaked him out? I doubled down on my vow to just be chill around him. Whatever that meant.

Time to push thoughts of Charlie away and focus on why I was here. I was on the set for my favorite show ever, getting my hair and makeup professionally done.

Perspective, Kate!

A throat cleared, and we all looked in the mirror to find Charlie standing behind us. "Am I interrupting?" His tone was unreadable. His face a flat mask. I studied him in the mirror. He seemed slightly more refreshed than earlier, but his neck was flushed red like he'd been arguing with the director about how much he didn't want to work with me. I mean, just taking a guess.

"Kate?" He said my name and I fought a shiver.

"Oh. Me?" I said like a total idiot when I realized he'd been asking me.

The hairdressers had grown suddenly silent, like they hadn't just been talking shit about him.

"Um, I'm not sure," I said, looking in question at my hairdresser.

"We're just about done," she said with a polite smile.

"I need to talk to K—Miss Dubois."

I squeaked and prayed nobody heard it.

"I can take five?" my stylist asked.

He nodded, then cleared his throat. "Thank you. Yes. I would appreciate it."

"No prob, be back in a bit."

"We're done here too. We can give y'all some privacy," the other said, and Kristen shot me one final "good luck" look. All too soon, everyone scurried off, and Charlie and I were alone.

"Is everything okay?" I asked, hating how tense and weak my voice sounded.

He stood towering over me. I was basically face level with his crotch. I regretted thinking that the second it popped into my head. Because then, it was all I was aware of and I was just staring at the zipper of his dark pants, completely forgetting how to look anywhere else. Great. And then I was turning red.

Abort! Abort!

He caught my gaze, pointedly, very much right past his hip and definitely not on his crotch, and stepped back to sit in the chair next to me. His gaze moved over my face, and I became acutely aware of how ridiculous I looked with makeup and hair half finished. He didn't seem surprised to see me in this state, but then again, he must be familiar with the pre-filming regiment.

I wondered who should speak first. Definitely him. I wouldn't break the awkward silence just because every passing millisecond felt like a million years. I balled my hands fisted under the cape.

"What's up, Chuck?" I gasped at my verbal misstep as he winced. I had NOT thought that through. "Oh my god, did I just—"

He held up a hand. "I've heard it before."

"I didn't even mean—"

"It's okay."

"Foot-in-mouthitis strikes again!"

"Miss Dubois, honestly—"

"Just Kate is fine."

"Just Kate," he teased.

"Ha!" I opened my mouth to talk, but he rested his hands on my hands, gripping the sides of the chair.

"Kate," he said again, letting out a breath. The side of his mouth lifted to gift me with his infamous dimple. His jaw really was so square and handsome. Then my gaze flicked to where his large warm hands sat atop mine. He slowly pulled them back into his lap.

"I need to apologize for my behavior. Again," he said.

I don't know what I expected, but after a fraction of a second of surprise, I quickly waved him off. "It's fine."

"No. It's not." His gaze was unwavering as he said it. "Nobody deserves ..." He shook his head. "I acted like a complete wanker and *you* don't deserve that. You're here because of your work. And—" He glared at his hands, white-knuckled on his knees.

It was the most he'd ever spoken to me at once. I loved the lilting smoothness of his accent. I scrambled to process his words. "Is it something I'm doing? Maybe I could stop."

"No," he spat.

I flinched.

"Christ," he grumbled. He collected himself with a slow breath in and out. "It's not you. I mean it is. That is to say ..."

My insides churned. The muscles of his thick neck worked a swallow. Charlie Downing had fallen off the map since his stay in rehab was splashed all over the news. It only occurred to me now that maybe he wasn't standoffish or grumpy. He was just plain not good at talking to people without the social lubrication of alcohol or drugs. I bit my tongue to keep from talking for him. He just needed a minute to find his words and didn't need me to speak for him.

"You remind me of someone," he said finally.

"Me?" The surprise was evident in my high-pitched question.

His mouth remained a flat line, but a dimple appeared in his right cheek. It almost looked like he was trying not to smile. "Yes. You." The dimple disappeared and his gruff demeanor was back in place. "But it's certainly not your *fault*. I need to get my head out of my dupa. I'm sorry," he said.

"Oh." I reminded him of someone? *Who?* I wanted to shout. Was it the mystery person on the call? Maybe he really was with someone and it had managed to escape the tabloids. Though based on his reaction, it hadn't sounded like a positive association. So maybe an ex?

I sat up straighter, trying to get him to look me in the eyes again. I found myself fluttering under his focus. "I promise not to be anything like that awful person," I teased.

"They're not awful." He smiled softly before he quickly cleared his features. "They're just not mine."

On that note, he stood and left, leaving me absolutely speechless.

My hairdresser returned as soon as he walked away. "But he does have a fine body, doesn't he?"

I could only nod as she got back to work.

They're just not mine.

I stared at my reflection in the mirror for so long that the person looking back became unfamiliar. The volumized hair, lack of glasses, and fresh makeup added to the strange effect. Who on this planet could be special enough to have Charlie Downing so upset? And why did I find a piece of myself extremely jealous of them?

21

———————

DRAFT UNSENT

TO: KateDubois@geemail.com

FROM: TheRealFreddyStan4Life@geemail.com

SUBJECT: RE: Am I beautiful yet?

You are always beautiful.

Please don't waste any more tears on the sorry excuse for a man. You are too wonderful for that.

I really wasn't kidding when I said I would kill him.

Christ, if I send this, I'll end up in jail ...

———————

TO: KateDubois@geemail.com

FROM: TheRealFreddyStan4Life@geemail.com

SUBJECT: RE: Am I beautiful yet?

Love the look. Especially the weird jellyfish things under your eyes. Are you being tortured? Do you need help?

Good luck today.

Love,

RC

22

Charlie

I WAS SEATED FIRST ON SET. THE HAIR AND MAKEUP TEAM DIDN'T take long on me, and Kate was scheduled to be out any minute.

Things would be easier now. I apologized for being a grumpy bugger. We could move on. Just one interview. It would be fine. We were fine.

I checked my email but still hadn't heard from Kate since her photo from the makeup chair that made me grin and get my shit together earlier. She hadn't mentioned the fight with Pete, but that wasn't surprising. She rarely discussed their relationship. She also hadn't mentioned anything about her confrontation with Charlie, and, pathetically, I found that more troubling. I was prickling with the idea that she kept things from me. And then I berated myself for getting jealous of myself. I was the biggest bloody idiot on the planet.

This was why I needed to come clean if I was going to continue to talk to her. The secrets had to end. The lines were getting tangled.

And then what would happen? She'd storm off set. The gossips would sell our exchanges to the highest bidder.

Bloody hell. It was just one interview. We'd go our separate ways. She'd go back to her trashcan fire of a boyfriend, and I would stop the emails. I *would* get my feelings for her under control.

This internal dialogue felt oddly similar to the way I would justify having just one drink in the past. One drink that led to twenty that led to blacking out. I pushed away the familiar thoughts before they snaked into self-recrimination and guilt over the past. My therapist had taught me to catch many of those thoughts before I got stuck in a never-ending loop.

I'd signed my last reply "love." Since we did that now. She'd sent selfies before, usually goofy ones or her holding a book she wanted me to read, but I'd never asked for one. Saying "love" was absolutely a new threshold.

And as if the gods heard my thoughts, in she walked. I noticed that anytime she came near, I forgot how to breathe. I sucked in a steadying breath and forced myself into a relaxed position even though I wanted to bounce up and greet her like a golden retriever. Her hair was in its signature style but with more height, and her makeup was understated save a bright red pop of lipstick. Kate could be in any state of dress and still be the most captivating person in the room.

Her eyes found mine and stayed there as she crossed to join me. And that made me feel a thousand feet tall. When she finally had to look away so as not to trip on camera wires, I took the opportunity to study the simple black dress that clung alluringly to her hips. This was neither of the options she'd sent pictures of, and it felt like a gift to learn something new, something RC hadn't known.

"Hi," she said breathily as she sat down across from me in

the lounge area of the dormitory set. She gave a little wave of her fingers.

"Hi," I smiled back.

We stared at each other again. Did she notice how often we did that? Or did it only feel like a lot because every time our eyes met, I mentally hoarded the moment into a glass case in my mind for the future. *In case of emergency, break glass and remember you aren't so alone.*

"Flashcards. Phew." She held up the question prompts they gave us. "I'm not that quick on my feet."

"Doubtful," I mumbled.

"Huh?" She looked up from where she'd been squinting at the first card, holding it close to her face.

"Viviana," I called, and the PA was at my side in an instant. "Can you go ask wardrobe where Miss Dubois's glasses are?"

Viviana stepped away with a nod, speaking into the microphone at her neck.

"How did you know?" Kate raised an eyebrow.

"You had them earlier. Before makeup," I lied smooth as butter.

"Oh. Yeah. They didn't want me to wear them because of the glare."

"They'll figure it out. You need to be able to read. Unless they want the cards blocking your face the whole time," I said.

"Maybe it'll be better that way."

I frowned.

"I mean, it could be my schtick," she said. "Like Wilson from *Home Improvement*. Add to the mystique."

"Why would you want to hide?" I asked flatly.

Set crew moved around us, holding light meters next to our faces, then adjusting furniture to frame us better.

"Oh." Her mouth formed a perfect little heart shape every time she made that sound of surprise. "I don't. I mean—I'm not

ashamed but, you know, it makes some people uncomfortable."
She tucked her hair behind her ear.

"What does?" I asked. I leaned forward, elbows on knees so I
could hear her better with all the people moving around us.

She mirrored me and leaned forward too. "Um, my writing.
Some people think it's like cheating. Or not real writing. Because
the characters were created by someone else."

"They're wrong." She was close enough that I could smell
her sweet scent under whatever hair products they'd used on
her. "And probably jealous."

Her large brown eyes moved over my face, and she shrugged
with a quick smile. "Maybe. So many people think it's just about
sex, but it's not like that." She waved her hand, but the second
she registered what she'd said, a flush spread over her creamy
collarbone. "I mean, granted. There is a fair amount of it in a lot
of fan fiction. And sure, even in mine." She laughed nervously,
using the cards to fan her face. "Foot in mouth ..."

"Is that right? And who is it that you write about again?" I
asked, my voice low and rough in my tight throat.

Her eyes widened and her pupils blew out. Maybe I had
grumbled the words more clearly than I intended to. Maybe
they had sounded just a bit flirty.

I wanted to hear her say it. I wanted her to tell me about the
delicious scenes she wrote.

Then I realized I was being a dirty flirt and she had a
boyfriend. I was being the scoundrel who used to take home any
TF groupies who threw themselves at me. I would be better than
that, even if having her so close overloaded my rational brain.

"I—"

I saved her from answering. "There's nothing bad about love.
And writing love. Just because women tend to write the most of
it. It's misogyny."

She blinked.

"There could be horrific violence but the second a woman is shown in pleasure, then it's considered trash," I added.

Her mouth was hanging open again. "Y-yes." She was nodding emphatically. "That's exactly how I feel."

"Damn the patriarchy," I started, and we both finished. Her eyes widened at our synchronization, and we laughed.

Our bodies were leaning closer toward each other. I'd never been a breath away from her like this. It was a gift to be able to note the freckles that filters usually blurred. To be able to see how her lips moved as she spoke. The slight scrunch to her eyes as she thought. All the things I never get in an email.

I needed time to catalog every one of her emotions and how they looked passing over her features. To think, I could have been looking at her face this whole time.

Distantly, I was aware that the set around us had quieted. It must have been time to start filming, but I wasn't ready to break this connection. The time was going too fast. Soon she'd be an ocean away again. But wasn't that what I wanted? For everything to go back to the way things were?

I grossly underestimated what meeting Kate in person would do to my willpower.

"You have nothing to be ashamed of. You're a good writer," I whispered to only her.

I wanted Kate to feel confident going into our interview. She shouldn't disparage herself or downplay what she wrote. She was talented and she should own that.

Her mouth dropped open, and only years of training for interviews stopped me from flinching at my misstep.

"Wait. Have you—"

"Here are your glasses, Miss Dubois." Viviana handed over the glasses and Kate slid them on.

"Thank you." She was staring at me but thankfully, just then, the director, Sally, walked up.

"Okay, glad to see you two chatting," Sally said. "Keep it up, you know, read the cards. Keep it casual. Just a friendly conversation." She patted my shoulder and smiled at Kate.

"Sounds good," I said.

"And alternate. You ask one question and then Charlie," she instructed Kate. "Good luck," she said and strode back briskly to her chair.

Kate, who had been looking at me, mouth still hanging open, glanced up and scanned the groups of people around us with growing horror. With every second, her color drained as she realized just how many people would be watching our "casual" conversation.

"Kate," I said her name softly.

Her hands balled in her lap, the cards getting crushed. She sat ramrod straight, and the tiny pulse at the base of her slender neck thrummed out of control.

"Kate," I said her name again but sharper. This time she turned to me. "Hi."

She blinked, confused. "Hi?"

"It's a conversation. Just you and me."

She huffed. "That isn't exactly as helpful as you think it is."

I stiffened, feeling hurt. "Right."

"I just mean—"

I forced the rejection away. "It's okay. I know what you meant." I smiled my infamous dimpled grin, the one in all the magazines. "Then imagine that I'm your closest friend and pretend you're catching up with them."

Her gaze moved over my shoulder, and her mouth softened into a gentle smile. She took a deep breath and nodded, some of her color returning. I would give up the entirety of my royalties to know the person who just popped into her brain.

Please let it be RC.

I cleared my throat. "You got this."

After "action" was called, and after a few stumbling starts, Kate found her groove. She was adorable and charming. Unlike some interviews I'd endured, she actually listened to the answers to the questions she asked. She was quick on her feet and didn't make it obvious when she read from the prompts. Christ, she was a natural. More so than I ever was, even when I was still "Chubby Chucky."

My questions to her started basic enough: How old she was when she first started watching TF? What was her favorite episode? How had the show changed her life, and how did she get started writing fan fiction? I knew these all, of course, and just as in our emails, she was endearingly earnest and honest. The next set of prompted questions, however, were idiotic. The producers wanted me to ask about her fan fiction that focused primarily on my character as an adult. They wanted to create tension between us to help with ratings. Her beautiful blush would make every promo trailer if they had their way. But I wouldn't let them use her. She wouldn't want to talk about something so personal.

"Tell me about what you're working on now?" I asked smoothly when it was my turn.

"Oh. I just work at a small office—"

"No." I cut her off with a gentle smile to lessen the sting. "What are you writing now?"

She straightened and flicked a gaze to a producer off camera. She lifted her chin and took a steadying breath. "Well, I'm writing, or rather, have finished a novel."

That's my girl.

"Tell me about it." I held her gaze.

She stuttered, trying to find her words.

"Imagine I'm your friend, and you're giving me a pitch for your book in a lift. You only have four floors to go." I smiled at her.

Holding my gaze, she relaxed and beautifully explained the plot of the book I had already read. It was succinct and intriguing, and I even heard a few soft rumbles of interest around us. I was so fucking proud of her.

"Sounds interesting. I'll have to google what a space opera is," I teased.

She opened her mouth to say something and closed it. Her eyebrow raised. Another slip. I had to be more careful. Hopefully, she didn't get the reference to one of our earliest conversations.

"I can't wait to read it," I added while pretending to study the next question.

"Well, it's not published."

"Not yet." I smiled.

Color rushed to her cheeks and spread down her neck. She sucked in a smile and stared blankly at her cards, grinning ear to ear as she collected herself.

It was her turn to ask me a question. "Of the Intrepid Trio, who is most like their character?"

Out of reflex, I stiffened at the familiar question I must have been asked a hundred times over the years.

"Everyone would say me and Freddy Finks are one and the same, I'm sure," I answered flatly.

She frowned as her gaze moved over my face.

"That must be hard? To be conflated so often, since you're not the same person," she asked softly without looking at the cards.

I cleared my throat. If it was anybody else, I would have changed the subject or gotten grumpy. This wasn't her fault, and I couldn't *not* answer her. "It was very easy at first. I was a kid. I was Freddy," I said.

"And then?"

"Then it wasn't."

Her brows furrowed in concern. "What do you—"

I stood up too quickly. The microphone ripped out of my shirt, causing a loud static sound. I bumped into the boom mic hanging over us, sending feedback across the soundstage.

"I need to take five," I said.

I was such an overly emotional man-child. *This* was why I was drunk for so many interviews. I wanted to have this conversation with Kate, as my friend. Not as two people who only just met with strangers watching and cameras in our faces. It terrified me how badly I wanted something real with her. Something I couldn't have.

How the hell was I supposed to get through this?

I felt the crew around me freeze. More fodder for the rumor mill. I could run off stage and hide like my diva reputation warranted. But I'd already walked away from Kate twice. I was tired of being a coward around her. She was the bravest person I knew.

You make me brave. If she thought I made her brave, then I could be brave for her too.

Sally called for a lunch break. Kate was pointedly not looking at me.

"Kate?" She looked up when I said her name softly. "Would you like to join me for lunch?"

Her eyebrows bounced up. "Yes. Sure."

23

———

Kate

I WAS HAVING LUNCH WITH CHARLIE DOWNING. CHARLIE DOWNING was sitting across from me eating a salad. This was totally normal and not freaking me out at all.

RC was gonna lose his ever-loving mind when I told him about this. Poor RC, I hadn't caught up with him in hours. He was probably wondering what the hell I was doing.

I glanced at my phone. It was late enough in England that he might be getting ready for bed. No, he was a night owl. He probably was wondering where I was.

"Everything okay?" Charlie asked me, gesturing to my phone I had been staring at.

"Oh yeah. I was just wondering if I should check in with someone," I said. I turned my screen facedown so I wouldn't be distracted.

Weird. I felt weird. I didn't know if I wanted to tell RC about the *real* real Charlie. This was getting complicated.

"Your boyfriend, right?" he asked, looking up with his head

tilted down. It gave him the appearance of being smaller than he was, innocent and sweet. His question was gentle, but he watched me like whatever I said next mattered to him. Maybe that was just how he listened. Intensely.

Charlie always seemed so soft-spoken in interviews, it shouldn't surprise me now. But maybe part of me still half expected him to act more like the outgoing character he played on TV.

But Charlie Downing was so unexpected. In a good way. Like inviting me to lunch when I had thought he was about to storm off set.

His question settled in belatedly, distracted as I was. My boyfriend ...

Oh. *Oh my god.* Pete. I had not even remotely been thinking about him. A wave of guilt twisted my gut. Should I have been thinking about our breakup? Or the increasingly annoyed texts he'd been sending? No, I was genuinely more worried about RC. And if that wasn't a strong indication of my true feelings ...

"Actually." I cleared my throat and flicked a look up. "That fight I told you about. We broke up."

"Did you?" Charlie sat incredibly still. I couldn't read him at all.

"I promised myself I wouldn't talk about my personal life with you anymore and here we are." I gave him a shaky smile.

"Are you okay?" he asked, his brows knitted with concern.

"Yeah. I just think—" I shook my head and thankfully stopped another bout of overshare. "Yeah. I'm fine."

He scratched at his neck. "You can talk about it if you want."

He nodded and glanced around, looking fully uncomfortable now. Or maybe curious? He'd slipped on a hat and glasses before we walked to a small bistro off set. Now we sat under dangling wisteria that mostly blocked us from the other patrons.

Not that his fame mattered in LA. Pretty sure that was a reality TV star sitting a few tables away. And was that James Roe? I brought my focus back to Charlie.

"Meh. I've done plenty of blabbing today," I said.

"Not really. Not about anything real. That was just"—he thumbed behind him, presumably referring to the studio—"for television."

"Ah, I see how it is. You can give canned answers, but I have to share the juicy deets," I teased.

"Tit for tat?" he asked, leaning back and crossing his arms, almost in challenge.

Was Charlie really proposing we share actual details about our lives? Did normal people do this? I had no frame of reference anymore.

"Like the interview, only we pick the questions," I said, trying really hard to not think about the fact that this was happening.

"Deal," he said.

"Excellent." I mirrored his cocky posture. "I ask first," I added quickly. "Since I already showed you mine."

His square jaw clenched, and his eyes squinted as he watched me, like we were the final two players in a high-stakes round of poker. Finally, he tossed out his hands to the side as though he, Hollywood's most reclusive former child star, was a totally open book. "Shoot."

"Where do you live?" I asked. Then realized that was a little too personal. "Like, not your actual address. I swear I'm not going to show up and, break your leg or something. Just in what general area do you live?"

"Southwest England." He watched my face closely. I wondered if I had a piece of lettuce in my teeth.

"Not London?" I had assumed he had a place in the city.

He shook his head. "My turn." He drummed his fingertips on the table in thought. I sat hypnotized as his thick, deft fingers moved in a soft pattern. When he cleared his throat to speak, I blinked up at him. "Do you like living in Minnesota?" he asked.

I tilted my head. I hadn't remembered telling him that.

"It was on the bio sheet Sally gave me before we met," he said. The tips of his ears were red. Was he embarrassed that he remembered that detail? Because I had to say, I really, *really* liked that he knew anything about me at all.

I shrugged as I thought about the question. Did I? I liked the Twin Cities during the roughly three months it wasn't freezing. "I like parts of it. I didn't think I'd be there this long."

"Where would you live if you could pick anywhere?" He watched me as he took another bite, his jaw working.

"I have a friend in England. He sends me pictures from time to time. It looks mild where he is. I like to envision living in a tiny cottage somewhere." I closed my eyes to imagine it. "Me, writing away by a fireplace, with a little cup of tea. Surrounded by books. And snacks. Like a little hobbit."

When I opened my eyes again, Charlie swallowed his last bite audibly and stared at me. Unblinkingly. This time, I was absolutely sure there had to be something in my teeth.

I ran my tongue over my teeth. Had I misstepped?

"Hey, wait a minute," I said. He went still again, his eyes widening fractionally. He was watching me like ... like I don't *know*. Like I understood something about him that I could hold over him?

Had he already said more than he was comfortable sharing? Because he hadn't shared much. Also, he didn't seem uncomfortable in the same way I'd seen him in countless interviews. He seemed far more relaxed. Like how he had been on the phone call, I not-so-accidentally overheard. But there was an undefinable tension that I couldn't quite compute.

"That was two questions," I finished.

He let out a sharp breath and laughed good-naturedly before

pushing his plate away. "You caught me. You can ask two this time."

"Mwahaha! I'm drunk on power." I rubbed my hands together like an evil genius.

He coughed out a laugh. I swore if I could monetize GIFs of him with that smile and that gleam in his eyes, I would be set for life.

I tucked my hair behind my ears. "Why is it that you hate interviews so much?" I asked, feeling braver with his looseness.

It was no secret that he kept to himself and rarely left this home. Or that he hated giving interviews.

"Straight to the bone on that one, huh?" he said. He scraped a nail across the metal tabletop. "I'm rubbish at them, truth be told. Not like you, you were a bloody natural today."

"Sure, sure. Distract me with flattery," I joked through a blush. "Go on."

"I'm serious. You handled it all very well." He leaned forward, both our plates had been taken, and I didn't even remember anybody coming by.

"The cameras take some getting used to," I said. "But, surely, you're used to them by now?"

"True." He sighed and took off his hat to scrub at his short-cropped hair. I, professionally, took a moment to admire the hard work of his personal trainer. "I guess. I'm worried I'll flub it all up somehow. I'll say the wrong thing. Again."

"Again?" I asked.

"There were a lot of years, I'm sure you saw, where I was an absolute prat. But honestly people knew my temper and they worked me up. They would call me 'Chubby Chucky' or 'Freddy Stinks,' literally to my face. They were more cruel than high school bullies."

I shook my head. "How awful. You were a child."

"Yeah, I was." He frowned like it hadn't occurred to him. "I was just a kid for so much of it." His gaze went unfocused as he looked over my shoulder, a furrow in his brow. With a shake of his head, he brought himself back. "But I shouldn't have let them goad me. I can't even think about it. All the times I embarrassed Emma and Harrison." He winced. "I honestly hadn't even wanted to be a part of this reunion."

"Because you were worried about embarrassing your friends?" I asked.

He opened his mouth and then closed it again. After a moment, he said, "I guess, yeah. I hadn't thought about it like that. But I always feel like I'm one stupid move from being splashed all over the headlines again."

I couldn't believe how open he was with me. I felt incredibly honored to even be here with him, let alone see this genuine side that few did. I wondered if his own friends knew this.

"I suspect, and I hope I'm not crossing any lines, that your two best friends were there for you during the worst." When he nodded, I went on. "I don't think that that level of commitment goes away with just a little bit of foot-in-mouthitis. Not after all these years. I hope not or I'm in trouble." I widened my eyes comically.

He smiled so deep, both dimples appeared. Thank goodness I was sitting down because I would have been blasted across the room.

"I suppose you're right," he said.

"You wouldn't stop caring about them, just because they made a mistake or two, would you?" I asked.

"Never," he said adamantly. "Those two ... I can't really explain how ... It's always been the three of us." He stopped speaking and swallowed as he glanced away. When he looked back, he'd collected himself. "Okay, that definitely felt like more than two questions."

"You're right." I shrugged innocently.

"Well, since you know all my secrets, why don't you tell me about why you and Pete broke up?" he asked.

I stilled. Something about the way he phrased that. It felt so familiar. This whole conversation had a natural ease that two complete strangers shouldn't have. And yet ...

"Oh. Pete. We really weren't compatible. We weren't a good fit. I guess I was just lonely, and it felt like settling down was a natural progression. And he was there. And he seemed interested."

Charlie flinched visibly.

"Wow, that sounded far more pathetic out loud. Yeesh." I tried to joke it off, but he didn't smile.

"I think a lot of people stay in bad relationships for far worse reasons. Don't be so hard on yourself." He reached out and squeezed my hand. I was startlingly reactive to his touch. A small gesture shouldn't send chills down my arms. I wondered what would happen if I held on to him. Totally wouldn't be weird.

"Anyway." He gently pulled his arm back to his side of the table. "Thanks for going to lunch with me."

"Gosh, you sure owe me. What a chore," I said. We shared a smile. Look at me, just sharing smiles with my childhood celebrity crush like it ain't no thang.

"I was a grumpy bugger back there. These types of specials tend to go for what's going to get the greatest number of viewers. And unfortunately, they also seem to have a sixth sense about what I'm most, uh, sensitive about." He shifted in the seat. His large frame making the metal chair seem flimsy.

"I'm sorry," I said honestly.

"I prefer to keep interviews light and surface level."

"Totally," I said. "I'll follow your lead when we get back."

He cleared his throat again. "I like talking to you, uh, face-to-face, better anyway." He flicked a glance at me, gauging my reaction.

"Me too," I said and felt like my heart was three beats from growing wings and flapping out of my chest.

He let out a sigh. "So. In this life where you have your cozy cottage in England, what are you doing?" he asked. I could tell when the subject was being changed. I wouldn't push.

"I want to be a writer," I said.

He gave me a pointed look. "I don't know how to break this to you, but you are a writer."

I tilted my head and made a face. "A real writer."

"Explain." He leaned back and crossed his arms. His whole body took up so much space without ever feeling oppressive.

"Respected. Published," I said.

"Ah."

Somehow that felt like it wasn't what he wanted to hear.

"If I'm published, then I'll be taken seriously," I clarified.

"You've said that before," he said.

"Have I?"

He stilled and focused on his glass of water. "I mean, it seems like something you've said a lot. This idea that you need to be published to be considered a success."

I frowned. "I suppose. I feel like most people think of my fic as a silly hobby. When I'm published, it won't feel like I've wasted all this time."

"I don't think it's a waste if you enjoy it." He held my gaze. "It seems to have made an impact on a lot of people. It's what got you here."

"True," I said. I hoped I didn't sound ungrateful. The need to explain spilled out before I could stop. We were so far past overshare, we were basically seventh grade girl besties levels of close.

"When I was eighteen, the summer before college, my mother took me to the Met on a business trip to New York. We passed the *Joan of Arc* painting by Jules Bastien-Lepage and I was transfixed. The young girl stands out against the muted browns and greens of the background. Her haunted eyes pierced through to a truth that nobody else could see. And the longer I looked, the more detail I could see of the three angels in the background. A girl younger than me who changed the course of history. It was impossible to comprehend.

"My mother eventually joined me at my side when I hadn't moved on. She said, 'That's you.'

"I'd preened at her words. She almost never doled out compliments and the artist obviously held the subject in such high esteem. Then she added, 'A young woman with her head in the clouds and hearing voices, just like your stories.'" I couldn't quite meet Charlie's gaze. His hand was clenched on the table, just a few inches from mine. He didn't speak, so I went on.

"It hadn't been a compliment but a censure of the fan fiction that had been taking more and more of my time. I walked away from the painting and shortly after chose a 'safe' major in business instead of creative writing."

"I never knew that," he said, frowning to himself.

"How could you?" I shook off his pity. "But that's the moment I knew I was a joke to her."

"You're not a joke. You don't need a publishing contract to prove that." His tone was so serious I was forced to meet his intense gaze.

But he didn't know me; we were strangers. He couldn't understand all the looks of disapproval I'd gotten over the years.

"Thank you," I said. "Look at us. A couple of armchair therapists over here." I chuckled awkwardly and he smiled.

I'd just about worked up the nerve to ask if he had read my stories when he glanced at his phone and swore.

"We better get back. Sally wants to get a few more questions in." He put down an alarming amount of cash on the check that had also magically appeared.

"Oh, yeah." It was best not to ask; I would overanalyze his response to the point of driving myself mad. Plus, I wouldn't be able to make eye contact again. My blushes were already becoming an issue.

I checked my phone. There was another text from Pete.

You wasted no time, I see. I frowned, not understanding the message but felt a wave of anxiety.

"What's wrong?" Charlie asked as he put his hand on my lower back to lead me in the direction of the exit. I was still staring at my phone, dumbfounded.

"Nothing. Just a cryptic message from Pete."

His face transformed into a hard glare. "He's still messaging you."

"Yeah. But it's fine. He's harmless." *Just way more insecure than I thought.*

Charlie was quiet the rest of the walk. I started replaying our conversation, worried he was suffering from post-overshare regret.

Back on set, the director, Sally approached us.

"Have a second to chat?" she asked. Her smooth features gave nothing away. At her side, the assistant flicked looks between Charlie and me.

Charlie grunted with what I thought was a yes.

I ducked my head and made to leave.

"You too, Miss Dubois," she added.

I stopped in my retreat and turned to Charlie; surprise written all over my face.

"Of course," I said.

My heart began to race right along with my mind. I jumped to the worst conclusions. I was going to be asked to leave. I'd said or done something wrong. They hated the interview.

The director turned and headed for a back hallway, and I moved to follow her. As I passed Charlie, he briefly touched my arm. I stilled as he lowered his head to my ear.

"Don't worry," he said, his warm breath tickling my neck.

I swallowed and nodded. Whatever came next, at least he was here.

And it was strange to find that thought so reassuring.

24

Charlie

Kate and I were led to a back office. Sally excused her
assistant before closing the door after us.

I had assured Kate that everything would be okay, but I had
no idea if that was true. If the director wanted to yell at me for
starting lunch thirty minutes before schedule, she wouldn't
need Kate here for that.

Sally leaned against a desk covered in paperwork. She
nodded to the two chairs. Kate sat, but I stood behind her, hands
resting just behind her neck on the chair. It would be so easy to
lift my pointer finger and graze it along the column of her neck.

"And how was lunch?" Sally asked.

"Good," Kate answered brightly.

I looked up to see Sally watching me closely. "I take it
neither of you have been online."

"Christ," I swore, already taking out my phone.

"It's okay," Sally said. "Nothing we can't handle."

"What's wrong?" Kate asked, eyes wide, looking between the
two of us.

"It's nothing bad," Sally assured. "Some photos of you two on set have been leaked."

"And now from lunch," I added as I scanned posts trending with my name. "Shite. I didn't even see them. They're getting sneakier."

I sat down and pulled Kate's chair closer to me. Her arm brushed mine as she leaned over to look at my screen as I scrolled through.

"You're trending. #FreakyFreddy and #MysteryMistress," Sally said.

Kate's hand went to her mouth. She bent closer to pause my scrolling. The sweet scent of her shampoo wafted up to me. "They want to know who I am? Is this bad? Should we just tell them?" she asked.

"No," I snapped.

Kate looked up, hurt.

"I don't want them digging into your life," I explained. "You don't do anything. My team will take care of this."

Sally sighed. "Charlie, they're going to know who she is when the reunion airs. The more mystery you create, the more they're going to want to hound her."

"We need time to figure it out," I said, my brain already scrambling how to fix this. This wasn't Kate's fault. She didn't deserve to have her life imploded because she talked to me. It was impulsive to take her to lunch. I should have stuck to my plan of giving us as much space as possible. But somewhere in the last twenty-four hours my selfish subconscious decided to spend every possible moment with her while we had the time together.

And now this.

"It's only a matter of time before people put two and two together. Miss Dubois is online. She hasn't hidden anything."

There were pictures snagged of us from earlier today, when

she was in the makeup chair, heads together, her face open and soft as she listened to me. Then another on set during the first part of the interview, just before lunch. Kate was clearly staring at my mouth as I smiled widely, bodies angled toward each other.

Christ. Was that how I looked at her when we were together? I thought I had things under control. No wonder the gossips were so wound up.

"They think we're dating," Kate said, glancing briefly at me and then away.

She took the phone from my hand without seeming to notice the intimacy of the action. I tensed. A simple accidental click to my email and everything would be over. She clicked on a headline and read, "'Sparks fly on set? Sources on the set of the twentieth anniversary special of the classic television show, *TerraFormative*, have shared that former child star and known bad boy—'" Kate snorted. "Okay, well obviously this isn't even journalism."

I glanced up to see Sally smile at me, eyebrow raised.

Kate went on. "Yadda yadda. 'Heated exchanges with mysterious woman. If you ask this reporter, there is definite intensity between these two.' Then there are just a bunch of stupid GIFs." Kate sighed and locked the phone. Then she seemed to realize whose phone it was and handed it back to me. "Here. Sorry."

I grabbed it back, hiding a sigh of relief.

"This is good, kids," Sally said. "We can use this free publicity. People are hooked on you two. And when her background is revealed, fans will lose their minds. It's kind of romantic, don't you think?"

I refused to look at Kate but felt her study my profile.

"Sally," I said flatly. I refused to acknowledge the implications of us dating. "This isn't fair to Kate—Miss Dubois. She didn't ask for this. The press is relentless. You know this."

Kate's phone buzzed. When she pulled it out, the color drained from her cheeks.

"What is it?"

"It's just Pete. He's being crude." She let out a sigh and pulled her shoulders back. "Do we need to get back on set?" she asked and put away her phone with shaking hands.

"You can take a minute," I said.

"No. I'm okay. Really. Just feeling thankful I dodged a bullet," she teased but her anxiety made me furious. I felt helpless and unable to protect her.

"What's that?" Sally asked.

"Nothing," I snapped. "We should get back on set. Stay on schedule."

"Before you go," Sally said. "We're going to shift some things around. We can really take advantage of this."

I balled my fists to keep from yelling and stressing Kate out.

"Let's plan on having both of you on set all day the next few days, okay?" Sally asked.

Kate chewed her lip in thought. Our segment was scheduled to finish today. I could see her calculating what she would need to do to stay longer.

"She might have work," I said. "She was only supposed to be here two days."

"We'll pay for her time, obviously. I'll have contracts draw something up ASAP for you both. Miss Dubois, does that sound amenable?"

Kate hesitated.

This couldn't be happening. It was only supposed to be two days. I was supposed to see her and go back home. I'd already crossed so many lines I said I wouldn't. All of lunch had been like walking a tightrope. I was so afraid she'd figure everything out at least three times. More days with Kate meant more opportunities to muck all of this up. And yet I couldn't stay away from her.

"Oh, and I forgot to mention one thing." Sally waved her hand. "I have a good friend who's a literary agent. I let slip about your novel. He seems very interested in meeting with you. Maybe later this week? A call?"

Kate's eyes widened. She nodded numbly. Happily?

Sally glanced at her watch. "Look, I gotta go. You two discuss. I promise this is good. People were already looking forward to this reunion and now there's even more to be excited about." She looked between the both of us, clapped once, and pushed herself off the desk. "Miss Dubois, I'll set up that meeting with my friend."

Sally left, closing the door behind us to leave Kate and me together. Alone.

"You don't have to do it. The extra stuff." I turned toward her. "You signed a contract, I presume. They can't make you sign anything else."

"I-I actually don't mind." She shook her head, likely processing all the information that had just been thrown at her. The literary agent being mentioned oh so subtly was no coincidence. "This gives me an excuse to extend my trip. And an agent. I can't believe it." She pressed fingertips to her cheeks and shook her head, her excitement growing.

Then she flicked a gaze to me, and her hands dropped to her side. "You don't want to do it?"

After all that was shared at lunch, how could I explain that being around her was one of the hardest things I had to do?

I didn't want to do it. I didn't even want to be here. Not because of her, god no, but because I was only supposed to be in LA for two days. This was supposed to be quick and painless. I should have stuck with my initial rejection. And yet, I was weak. I had wanted to see her one time. How could I know things would get out of control so fast? How could I have known our chemistry would be so palpable?

I should have known. Looking at her now, the energy between us was obvious. Almost tangible.

I would stay. A few more days. Because when she looked up at me like that with hope swirling in those big dark eyes, I was hopeless.

"Bloody fucking hell," I swore.

Kate winced. "Is it so bad? I mean can't there be a press release or something to denounce the rumors?"

I forced myself to calm down and leaned on the desk, giving her plenty of space.

"It's not that. I don't care about the rumors." I looked up at her quickly and looked away. "It's that this is going to explode your life."

"I was planning on it to some degree when the special came out. I don't hide who I am. It's okay. If anything, it should help my writing."

"I know. You're so open," I added quickly so she wouldn't overthink that last slip of the tongue. "I'm mad because they did this on purpose."

Kate stepped forward, voice lowered. "Who?"

I gestured to the studio in general. "Whoever. The show runners, the producers, Sally. It doesn't matter. They wanted this leaked. These photos are from a closed set, *today*. It's not a coincidence."

The lines between her eyebrows deepened. "But why?"

"This is Hollywood." I pulled off my hat and squeezed the brim. "Everything is fake and contrived for money or exposure." I let out a defeated breath. God, I hated being back here. "I'm just sorry that you're getting mixed up in it. It's my fault."

Kate stepped closer. She needed to be walking away, running away from me. I wasn't stable around her. I gripped the desk behind me. Forcing myself to be as still as possible. I was drawn to her even when I promised myself I would stay away and look how that had gone already. I felt so ... drained.

"Listen. It's okay. I don't really care if they dig into my life. There's not even much to find. The sooner they realize it, the sooner they'll be over it." She rested a hand on my arm. This time when we both looked at it, she didn't take it away. "The great thing about instant-gratification culture is that everything is a flash in the pan. Trending hashtags are completely forgotten in twelve hours. It's sweet of you to be concerned, but it's truly not your fault in any possible way."

I blinked at her. I wished with my entire being that was true. The leak wasn't my fault, but would she even be here if not for me? I should tell her. Right now. Right here. The truth was on the tip of my tongue. I opened my mouth.

"But we should get to set. Filming waits for no one, or something like that," she said.

We were walking out the door and she stopped and shook her head. "A real agent? I mean, I dreamed, I thought maybe. I just can't believe it's really happening." She smiled at me with such unadulterated excitement that, for a moment, everything that brought us to this moment was worth staying a few more days.

———

IT WOULD BE RIDICULOUS TO POUT BECAUSE KATE HADN'T EMAILED me yet. I definitely wasn't pouting.

After recording the second half of the interview, I went to track down Emma and Harrison when Kate said she was going back to the hotel to rest. I wanted an excuse to stay with her. But she seemed so tired and in need of alone time.

I paced the lot, waiting for my friends, refreshing my email an embarrassing number of times. I couldn't sit still. If I pulled up my email one more time only to be disappointed, I might snap. I was worried about Kate. How would all this buzz impact her? How her thankfully now ex-boyfriend might respond to those baseless internet rumors.

I thought again of the picture of her looking at me. Maybe not completely baseless? No. I was hoping.

I decided to just head back to Harrison's without my friends and swim some laps or use his home gym. I couldn't stay at the studio anymore. It was the first time I'd itched for a drink today, and the longing took me by surprise. Being with Kate kept me in the moment, it had never even occurred to me until now.

I made my way to the front of the lot and stopped dead in my tracks.

Pete Klester was walking determinedly into the building I'd just exited. The building where Kate might still have been if she hadn't already left for the hotel.

I puffed myself up, arms crossed, and stepped directly in his path.

Pete stopped abruptly and he took me in.

"Oh. Great. You." He tried to inch around me.

"You're not going in there," I said, impressively calm, considering I felt like I could easily rip him limb from limb.

"You can't keep me from my girlfriend," he whined. His gross goatee was overgrown and there were dark bags under his eyes. He reeked of stale booze.

I kept my features impeccably unaffected. "Ex-girlfriend."

His face went instantly red. "You have no idea what you're talking about."

I flicked a glance up to find a security guard exiting his booth and heading toward us. I held up a finger subtly to keep him at bay as Pete tried to rush past me again.

"I have a pass. You can't stop me," he said.

"I absolutely can." I lifted my arm and he bounced off it.

"This is your fucking fault," he spat at me. "You know that? Ten seconds in her life and you've already ruined the only good thing she had going."

I really did *try* not to snort, but mistakes happened.

I raised an eyebrow looking down at him. He was a tiny little excuse for a person.

"She's created this whole fantasy about you. All her little stories."

His words filled me with rage, but I kept my mouth shut, flicking a glance to the guard watching our interaction closely. I suppose that was the only good thing about being back: I was easily recognized and had a lot of pull.

"You never deserved her." I shouldn't have said it. But I was human, sue me.

He shoved my shoulder. Without looking, I raised a hand to stop the security guard who jumped into action. Pete remained clueless. This was the moment I had dreamed of so many times since Kate announced she was dating him. I could knock him out with one punch, and he would have deserved it. But how would that impact Kate? How would that make her feel? I managed to swallow down my temper.

There was a substantial petty part of me that enjoyed seeing him this visibly upset.

"Fuck you," he spat. "She'll come back to me. You'll see."

It was getting harder to be the bigger person. It would be so easy to punch him in his weaselly little face. "I'm losing patience for this conversation."

His pinched face grew redder.

I looked around to make sure I didn't see any camera phones. I leaned forward, happy to see how he stumbled back. "You would never be enough for her," I said, even though I shouldn't have. I was past pissed off, but it was better to lose control of my tongue than my fist. "Not in a million years. You never understood the gift you had. And now it's too late."

"And who the fuck are you?"

His glare faltered as I slowly stepped into his space, looking down on him. "I'm the one who knows her best."

He stepped back, confused. "What the fuck ever. She'll never return your feelings. You think she wants to be part of this circus act?" He gestured around. "You think you could offer her anything? You're a pathetic washed-up child actor who can't even get his shit together."

I ground my jaw; my head throbbed from controlling my rage.

I gestured the guard over. "Yes, Mr. Downing?" he asked.

"Take this man's guest pass away. I don't want him anywhere near this set. Not even outside the gates." I kept my focus on Klester-Fuck as I spoke. I may not have much, but I did have some power left. "If you or any of the other guards see him again, call the police."

"Yes, sir." The guard tried to lead Pete to the exit, but he roughly shrugged him off.

I stepped in front of Pete one last time. "And if you ever talk to Kate again, I'll find out and I will make your life a living hell."

Pete was fighting back words, his lips white with the effort. He opened his mouth to say something and then closed it. Then he turned and stomped off, the guard following close behind until he was through the gate.

I stood there for several minutes collecting myself.

I wouldn't let his words sink in. I wouldn't let him have any power over me. He got so many things wrong in his temper tantrum. I didn't have any hopes of being with Kate. I would never be good enough for her. But at least I understood that.

Worried Pete would head to her hotel next, I headed over

there. I was already talking to security when I got the drunken email from Kate.

I turned from the security desk, heading for the exit to read her message in private when my attention was drawn to the bar. Kate immediately stuck out with her short bob and breathtaking beauty. Some man in a business suit was eyeing her up, and my feet moved in her direction before I could stop myself.

I would just make sure she was okay. Then I would leave.

TO: THEREALFREDDYSTAN4LIFE@GEEMAIL.COM
FROM: KateDubois@geemail.com
SUBJECT: Psssst
RC!
I'm drunk!
OMG, is it okay that I tell you that?
Of course it is.
But still. I feel weird about it. I neeeeever drink. So you know it's been A DAY.

ALSO. Sorry I have hardly messaged you since I got to LA. Let me tell you, it has been a whirlwind! I don't even know where to start. And also, it's getting harder to type. The screens on phones are really tiny. Thank duck for autocorrect. This probably wouldn't even be intelligible otherwise.

So, BIG news! The director of this special has a friend who's a literary agent. She said that he said that he might talk to me. CAN YOU IMAGINE? Has any of this made sense?

Well. I have other less good news too. Pete and I broke up. I think I've known for a while but it became abundantly clear last night. I don't know why I didn't tell you sooner. I guess I felt stoopid. Stoopid. No. That doesn't look right. You know what I mean.

So here I am at the bar *all by myself*. I'm okay. Really. I should probably have a glass of water.

I'm sorry I've been so MIA lately. I will make sure to catch you up on everything as soon as things stop blurring all around me.

Imma drink some water.

Love you,

Kate

26

Kate

Everything was happening so fast. So many ups and downs in twenty-four hours. I had needed to sit and process. With a cocktail. Even though I rarely drank, it felt appropriate.

I should probably be thinking about my breakup with Pete and his alarming texts, but in fact, I was rereading my last email to RC, wondering if I sounded obnoxious. I hadn't mentioned the time spent with Charlie Downing. Maybe because it still felt so unbelievable that I had an amazing lunch with him. But also, maybe because I felt weird talking to RC about it. Like I was cheating. And wasn't that ridiculous. My attraction to RC had been instant too, just like this, but not on a physical level. When I was around Charlie, my body was drawn to him. I found any excuse to touch him or lean into his space just to share the same air. At first, I told myself I was just projecting my lifetime crush. But after lunch today, there was no denying that we clicked. He was funny and modest, vulnerable, and open. He was a squishy little teddy bear wrapped up in muscles and grunts.

Was the chemistry as real to him too? I guess it didn't matter.

In just a few days, I would be home and maybe have a literary agent. I kicked my feet excitedly.

I sighed, refreshing my email, wondering if RC was still awake.

"What can I get you?" the bartender asked, causing me to look up. I was about to ask for water when I noticed a man at my side and realized the bartender had been addressing him. Goose bumps prickled down my neck.

I slapped my phone facedown. And straightened.

Charlie Downing was here. At my hotel. Standing close enough that his fancy cologne filled my senses as my cheeks warmed.

Had I willed Charlie Downing into appearing? Did I have superpowers? Was this really happening or just an alcohol-fueled daydream?

The bartender looked at Charlie expectantly, ready to take our drink orders. Definitely real. Heh. The *real* real Charlie was *really* really here. RC would like that.

"I'm okay. Just here to—" Charlie tilted his head toward me.

The bartender nodded, slapping the bar before walking away. I slowly turned on my stool to face him. I would just act cool and sober, and he would never know I was crushing so hard on him. "Hello. Mr. Downing. How are you this evening?"

"Hi, Kate." He grinned, head tilted. "I thought we were on a first-name basis at this point?"

I nodded but felt myself tipping. Charlie chuckled as he straightened me. I really wasn't that drunk, but I was beyond exhausted after the last two days.

"Must be these chairs," I explained. "They're wobbly. We should tell somebody so no one gets hurt."

"Doing okay?" he asked, and his hand remained on the back of my chair. I looked all the way up, up, up, and smiled at him. "Yup. I am A-OK."

"You seem a little drunk." He leaned in to whisper, his breath teasing my skin. I didn't shudder in pleasure, but I did feel goose bumps tickle down my neck.

I leaned in too, conspiratorially. "Maybe just a bittle luzzed." Wait, that wasn't right. I frowned, then tried again. "A. Little. Buzzed."

"Why don't you have some water?" he asked.

I shrugged. "I'm actually only on my second drink."

"Ah, a lightweight." He sat down next to me and spun me until my feet were on his stool, his own massive leg blocking me in. His head turned to scowl at someone, but when I followed his gaze, I only saw a man in a business suit, reading on his phone.

"I don't really drink often. Mostly, I'm exhausted. I hardly slept because, you know."

"Your row with Pete?"

"Yeah. And then before that, I was so worked up about coming here. Basically, I'm tired."

"I get that," he said.

I sat up and realized we were at a freaking bar. Bottles of liquid temptation all around. "You don't need to be here. I'm fine," I said.

"I don't mind the company," he said, making no move to go. When he held my gaze a fraction too long, he added, "I'm just waiting for Harrison and Emma to wrap up."

I shook my head. How was he so damn sweet? He might have said he was fine, but that didn't mean I felt comfortable drinking in front of him.

"Still. Let's go somewhere else. Coffee sounds good," I said.

We strolled to a coffee shop just up the street in silence. The activity melted away the last of my buzz. We'd talked endlessly at lunch, but my brain was all muddled up now with lusty hormones and guilt.

"Two dates in one day." I elbowed him playfully after he bought our coffee. "Not that these are dates. I mean, if you ask the internet they are ... for Pete's sake, Kate," I grumbled and then chuckled. "Not for *Pete's* sake at all, actually. Okay. I'm going to shut up now."

I couldn't even blame the drinks on that dorky verbal dump.

We made our way to a small table, and I did manage to keep my mouth shut. Charlie's lips tilted up in a soft smile as he asked, "Are you okay? Anymore messages from Needy Petey?"

I snorted at the apt nickname. "No. Not since that last one." I worried my lip. "He said he was coming to the set but I never saw him. Thank gawd. How embarrassing would that have been?" I shook my head.

"Does he still have your hotel key?" he asked with a frown.

"Not unless the front desk gives him one."

Charlie didn't like that answer. He grumbled something violent.

"You know I would have never pegged him as the clingy type. But ..." I flicked a look up to his face. "He started getting a little controlling. The more I think about it, the signs were there. I was just so eager to make it work. I think to prove my mother wrong. Blah. I know." I picked at the paper lining of my cup. "Ironically, it was my mother who warned me about controlling guys. She thought I should break up with him."

Charlie's eyebrows shot up.

"Yeah," I said, nodding at his surprise. "She said that I needed to put myself first and not let his life become more important than my own."

"I like your mum," he said in a deep tone.

"I'd like to say that she'd like you too, but honestly she isn't big on men, in general." I shrugged. "She's never been in any sort of relationship. I just assumed taking the opposite of her advice would be the smart thing to do. Alas, mothers sometimes know things."

I took a cautious sip of my coffee and felt its magic working. "But ultimately, that's exactly what started happening. I lost sight of what I really wanted so he could remain comfortable."

"Absolute wanker."

I chuckled at his dry humor as another thought occurred to me.

"Also!" I smacked the table and he startled. "Sorry. But listen, Pete hated my writing." I paused for dramatic effect. "He never said it outright, but he never finished anything I gave him. Saying he was too busy. He thought it was a joke. It embarrassed him."

Charlie sat very still. "The offer to kill him still stands," he said.

I threw my head back and laughed. "He just wasn't right for me. But gosh, it's like a weight off my shoulders."

"That's a good indication you've made the right choice."

I nodded, lost in thought for a minute. It was definitely the right choice. "Thank you for listening." I frowned. "What were you even doing at my hotel?"

He cleared his throat. "Just something for work."

"Oh really—"

"Well, who do we have here?" a woman asked as two shapes approached our table.

Emma Flynn and Harrison Evans. My eyes widened.

"Hello, Emma," Charlie said, standing to kiss her cheek. "Harrison." They hugged each other.

I sat blinking in shock. The shine of their presence had not worn off.

"Fancy meeting you here," Harrison said.

"I texted you," Charlie said dryly.

"Hello, Miss Dubois," Harrison said, oozing out the charm and leaning to hug me.

I awkwardly made my way to stand. "Call me Kate," I said, dumbfounded.

Emma leaned to Charlie and whispered, "You're growling," in his ear.

He unclenched his fists. "How was the rest of filming?" Charlie asked his two friends.

I crossed my arms before dropping them a second later. I was completely incapable of remembering how "natural" looked.

"It was lovely," Emma said, her gaze moving between Charlie and me. "You two are the buzz of the set."

I tucked my hair behind her ear.

"Quite the little tabloid scandal. You work fast, Charlie," Harrison said then winced when Emma elbowed him.

We chatted for a bit about the rest of their day, and I tried to hide a massive yawn behind my hand. "Sorry," I said when I felt all three of them looking at me. "I didn't sleep well and had a bit too much to drink. I broke up with my boyfriend." I frowned. "Sorry. Overshare. I mentioned the drinking too much?"

I sucked in my lips to keep from talking.

Emma's smile grew. "It's been a long few days for everyone." She looked to Charlie before asking, "Ready to head back to Harrison's?"

Charlie shifted from foot to foot, looking at me and then the other two. "Um."

"You always did have a way with words," Harrison said.

Emma rolled her eyes. "Unless?"

Was he hesitating because of me? "I'll be fine," I insisted, hoping I was understanding his hesitation. "I'm really fine. I promise."

Charlie looked down the street and glared. Seeming to make

a decision, he looked to the others. "Kate got some concerning messages from her ex. I don't want to leave her."

Pretty sure my jaw dropped to the ground. Based on Harrison and Emma's shared glance, I wasn't the only one surprised.

"Really, the hotel is only a block away," I said.

"But he might have a key still, no?" Charlie sounded firm.

"I—"

"No worries, mate. Lord knows Chateau de Evans has more than enough rooms. She could have a whole wing to herself," Harrison offered cheerfully.

"Good idea," Emma agreed.

"Is this really happening?" I whispered.

I stared at them all in wide-eyed disbelief.

"Kate?" Charlie tilted his head in question. "Would you be comfortable with that?"

"Would I be okay spending the night at Harrison Evan's house?" I asked.

"Well, to be fair it's more like a mansion," Harrison interjected.

"Mansion," I mumbled.

"Only if you feel comfortable," Charlie said. "There are plenty of rooms."

"With locking doors and private baths," Emma offered gently.

I stared at the Intrepid Trio and nodded numbly. "Uh, yeah. Let me just get my things."

"We'll go with you," Emma said, and Charlie nodded.

I squeaked a sound of assent as we made our way back to the hotel. Just me and my three childhood idols.

Okay, yeah. This was all totally normal. Wait until RC heard about this.

27

———————

DRAFT UNSENT

TO: KateDubois@geemail.com

FROM: TheRealFreddyStan4Life@geemail.com

SUBJECT: what the hell

Kate,

You are here. You are a door away, and there are beds everywhere. Not that I'm even ... I didn't mean ...

I cannot believe this is happening. I cannot believe how little self-control I have around you. I keep telling myself I will leave you alone, and then I do shite like this.

Christ, how am I supposed to sleep tonight knowing you are so close?

Sharing all these emails back and forth over the years, I feel like I've known you forever. When I'm around you, it's hard to pretend that I don't know everything about you. But I am a stranger to you. You've just met me, basically.

Fuck. I am so glad you left Pete. He was an absolute idiot to have you and lose you. But he never deserved to even speak your name. But Christ, you are single. You are one room over. I have to go say good night to you now.

Fuck.

Did you know you signed your last email "Love you"? What does that mean? How come you never mention me, Charlie, in the emails? Why am I feeling jealous of myself? What the bloody hell, Kate? I'm losing my mind. I don't know what the right thing to do is anymore. I want to be a person worthy of you, but every moment that passes, I'm more muddled up. And now we'll be together for the next two days. AND YOU ARE NEXT DOOR.

I'm not even making sense.

I can't send this—

———

TO: KateDubois@geemail.com
    FROM: TheRealFreddyStan4Life@geemail.com
    SUBJECT: Good night
    Kate,

Get some sleep. You will have plenty of time to tell me about all your adventures tomorrow.

    I'm sorry about Pete.
    Drink some water.
    Love,
    RC

28

Charlie

I knocked gently on the door to Kate's room.

"Come in," she called.

I took a steadying breath but still wasn't prepared for the sight of Kate in pajamas lying in bed. It was only the fact that she'd curled herself up in a little ball lying on her side with red-rimmed eyes, looking so small and helpless, that I was able to gather some self-awareness and push my desire aside. The initial energy radiating from her at the bar earlier seemed to have faded into maudlin sadness. It was far past midnight now, and she'd drowsed the entire ride to Harrison's house in the Hollywood Hills. *Mansion.* He'd offered her a tour, but I insisted she go straight to bed. The other two had left us alone in this one whole hall. I didn't want to know what Emma was thinking when she suggested an entire wing of privacy.

I stepped to the edge of Kate's bed. She looked so tiny, cocooned in the plush blanket. I was desperate to scoop her up and hold her.

"I've just come to check if you need anything before you go

to sleep," I said. I set down a glass of water and a blister pack of painkillers.

She shook her head. Tears balanced on the edge of her lids.

"Kate." My voice cracked. Her pain was unbearable. "What's wrong?"

Her lip trembled as she tried to smile on a shrug. "I don't know."

"Care to talk about it?"

She licked her lips and swallowed. "Yes. Maybe. I don't know. I'm anxious and sometimes that makes me a little weepy."

"Anxious?" I shifted back from the bed. "I don't expect—There's nothing ... If you want to lock the door." I retreated, dumbfounded and terrified I made her think she owed me *anything* for bringing her here.

"No. No. It's not you. I know you don't—" She frowned. "I just feel like I'm doing something wrong." She stared just past my shoulder.

"You're not doing anything wrong." Was the regret of her breakup settling in? She seemed so sure earlier, but she had been quite a bit more tipsy.

"I'm feeling really mixed up about things." She sniffled in a sigh.

"You don't have to figure it all out right now," I said softly. "All you have to do is sleep."

She looked at me with such relief I thought that I might get a bit weepy myself. "Okay."

"I'll let you go," I said.

"Don't go yet," she whispered.

She blinked up at me, long lashes damp with tears. Blood rushed through my veins at those three small words. I warred with myself. *God, please, yes*, I wanted to stay. But she was mixed up and vulnerable.

"I shouldn't—" I brushed my fingertips over the soft duvet. I didn't even remember stepping close to the bed again.

"I'm not looking for—" She glanced away, flushing. "The thing is. I think my heart belongs to someone else." She said it like she was just now understanding it to be true. That didn't help the thrumming of blood in my ears. "You are very pretty though," she added teasingly.

I huffed out a breath. "That's what they tell me."

I looked at my shoes. Her heart belonged to someone else. What a fucking punch in the gut.

There was no way she was still caught up on that wanker. My deepest hope had been that she thought of RC. But now, I wished I was the person on her mind. Here and now. The person she told everything to. But how could I ever be that for her when I kept so much of myself at bay. It wasn't fair to her.

Bloody hell, how had I managed to mess this all up?

When I continued to hesitate, she added, "I just don't want to be alone yet." She looked up at me with puppy dog eyes that would put Emma's to shame.

"I'll stay just for a bit. Until you fall asleep." My body was rigid with indecision. I could do this. I could comfort her and take nothing for myself.

She nodded and wiggled her way to the farthest edge of the bed and under the blankets. I kicked off my shoes and clicked the lights down. It was just bright enough that I could make her face out in the dim light once my eyes adjusted. I cautiously laid down next to her.

On top of the blankets.

Fully dressed.

She had the duvet pulled up just under her chin, lying on her side, making her glasses angle in a way that couldn't be comfortable. I mirrored her pose, our heads resting on pillows, hands curled loosely in front of us as we faced each other. There were several inches between us, room for a whole other person, but the intimacy was overwhelming.

We didn't speak for several minutes. Wheels were turning behind her tired eyes, but there was a strange comfort to the silence. This whole situation felt surreal. I continued to watch her as her gaze moved over my features, as though she was memorizing them. I had dreamed many scenarios of us together since we started talking, but this was a greater gift than I ever thought I'd get.

It was certainly more than I deserved.

She blinked slowly and yawned, hiding her face into the pillow as she did. When she turned back to me, there was a gentle smile on her lips. I smiled back, unable to help myself.

"I think I'm dreaming," she said, her voice whisper soft. "I'm going to wake up and I'll be back at work and none of this was real."

My smile dissolved. "This is real." *Us*. We were real. Kate and I were the only thing that felt solid to me. I wished I could say it.

"I'm so afraid that this will be one of my more elaborate daydreams. Maybe it would be better that way. To experience all this only to go back to real life ..." She sighed. "I don't know how I'm going to manage it."

I felt the same way. I had thought I might be lucky enough to just look at her, but now that I'd spent the whole day with her, there was no going back. It was such an undeserved and unexpected gift. At any moment, our time together could come to an abrupt end, and I wouldn't be able to handle it. Would I ever be able to breathe on my own again after breathing her air?

But she wasn't talking about us or me. And I had to get back to the safety of my home. Away from blowhards and suck-ups. Kate and I were real, but life here wasn't.

"The truth is," I said. "This whole world isn't what people think it's made out to be anyway."

"What world?"

"Hollywood. LA. Fame and celebrity. It has its perks and I'm grateful for everything I've been given. But once the shine wears off ..." I shrugged.

Her gaze moved to my mouth, and I licked my lips.

"Was it hard for you to come back to LA? I thought I had read something about you not wanting to do any more appearances," she asked, looking a little sheepish to admit to reading about me online.

"I hadn't planned on coming. I really want to be done with *TerraFormative.*" I looked up and held her gaze. "I'm very glad that I did."

"You didn't like it? Being on the show?" She swallowed and tucked herself deeper into the blankets.

She was so open. So lovely and sincere. I would be brave with her. Plus, I wanted her to know me. I had to take steps.

"Just the opposite," I said. My voice was low and rough. "It was my entire life. I haven't adjusted well. Since the show ended. It's rather embarrassing actually. After all these years, it's hard for me to be back here. It makes me a cranky bastard."

She smiled with the shake of her head. "You remind me so much of my friend."

My heart beat so strong my body vibrated the bed. It would give everything away.

Just tell her. Tell her now.

Her little brow furrowed. "Do you have anybody to talk to?"

"I, uh, like a therapist? Yeah."

"Good." She untucked herself to poke my shoulder. "But I meant like a friend. Somebody you're close to?"

I grabbed her finger and held it a moment too long. Her gaze flicked between mine. We were so close. So close. Lying on a bed. How the hell did I get here? What was wrong with me? I released her hand, and she tucked her arm back under the duvet.

"I have Harrison and Emma. We've remained close over the years," I said.

"That's good. Do they struggle too?" she asked.

"I don't get to talk to them as much as I'd like." It was so hard to admit this. Talking like this with Kate only reminded me that I was so lonely. "We only talk once a month. They're pretty busy."

"You miss them." It was more a statement than a question.

I nodded once as my neck grew warm.

I cleared my throat. "I have a close friend. One I talk to almost every day."

She hummed after another jaw-cracking yawn. "Is this the one I remind you of?" Her words soft with sleep.

I swallowed. My hands were fisted under the pillow. "Yes." It came out as a whisper.

"She means a lot to you, doesn't she?" She smiled, and her eyes slowly blinked closed.

"So. So. Much. More than anybody." It was difficult to speak with how tight my chest was.

"Oh. That's nice." She struggled to open her eyes, but they fluttered closed. "Sheslucky," she slurred, mostly asleep. Her breaths evened out even as she tried to fight the tide pulling her under.

I had to tell her. I couldn't go another moment. Perspiration prickled all over my body.

"Kate, I have to tell you something."

She made a soft hum in question.

"I should have told you from the very beginning."

Her breathing deepened. I reached out and pulled her glasses off her gently. She smiled and titled her head to help me. Such a familiar gesture, as though I'd always been taking care of her like this. My heart ached, thinking of what it might be like to get to take care of her all the time. What would a life like that look like for us?

She sighed deeply and snuggled more into her little ball of blankets as I set the glasses on the table near the water.

Be brave like her.

"It's me. I'm the real Charlie." There I said it. I put it out there.

"I know," she said.

I sat up on an elbow. "What?"

She slept deeply.

"Kate?"

Nothing.

What did that mean? Had she heard me? If she had heard me, she wouldn't have fallen asleep.

"Kate?" I tried again. Nothing. She was dead to the world.

I rolled onto my back and ran a hand over my face. "Bloody hell."

I lay there for a while blinking into the darkness. I barely managed to tell her once. Was I going to be able to tell her in the light of day?

If I let myself imagine a life together ... I couldn't. She deserved more than I could offer her. She deserved someone who told her the truth.

I could easily let myself fall asleep here. Pretend that I hadn't meant to. We could twist ourselves up in the sheets and wake up warm and wrapped around each other. If I rolled toward her in my sleep, if I let myself breathe in the back of her neck, it wouldn't be crossing a line then, would it? It would just be something that happened outside of my control. My arms around her waist, pressed up against her lovely full bottom. God, that pear-shaped body of hers.

I let out a long sigh before gently maneuvering out of the bed to disturb her as little as possible.

I clicked the lights all the way off and stepped silently out of the room. Gently, I locked the door and closed it without making a sound.

Emma stood in the hall when I turned around. I jumped.

"You're worse than Agata," I said.

She stood with her arms crossed and her chin nudged toward the door. "It's her, isn't it? Your American."

"Shh," I said and tugged her farther down the hall.

"Charlie. What the hell is going on?"

"Nothing. Nothing happened. I was just tucking her in."

"That's not what I mean. Is that her?" she repeated.

When we were a safe distance away in the den, I scratched my eyebrow and nodded.

She sighed out a curse. "I put it together just now. I don't know how I didn't figure it out sooner. You showed us her social media. I knew she looked familiar when we met her. And god, the way you look at her. It's so obvious." She tapped a foot, shaking her head at herself. "Did you set this up? Did you get her invited here?"

"No! God." I glanced back to the hallway. "She earned her place."

Her eyes flicked back and forth as her mind filtered thoughts. "That's what changed. When I was over at your place?" She scoffed with a shake of disbelief. "I wondered what caused the sudden change of heart."

I didn't need to answer. She knew now. She was putting all the pieces together.

"You didn't set any of this up?" she repeated.

"No." I cleared my throat. "Well, I got that wanker of a boyfriend a ticket so that she would actually come."

Emma's eyes widened.

"And I suggested the meet and greet. So she wouldn't be so nervous. But that was good for everyone."

"Jesus. Charlie. I've never seen you like this," she said.

"I've never felt like this," I said softly.

Her arms relaxed out to her side. "Oh. Christ. That's sweet." Then she seemed to remember herself and her scowl was back. "But still. This isn't okay. You have to tell her."

"I did tell her," I said defensively.

"Did you?"

"Technically."

"How did she react?" Emma's gaze grew concerned.

"She snored."

Her eyes rolled so hard her head went back. "This will blow up in your face."

"You don't think I know that? I'm a bloody mess." I slumped into one of the chairs.

"If she cares about you, it will be okay. I don't understand what you're so afraid of."

"I just don't want anything to change. I just need to get through the next few days and then get home," I repeated the same plan I'd told myself a thousand times.

But this time the lie tasted bitter.

29

Kate

My eyes shot open. The room was bright. The blankets luxurious. My heart raced like it had already been awake and went on a jog.

Where was I? A bedside table with water, my glasses, and medicine. Gaps filled in in rapid succession.

Leaving Pete. The show. The pictures online. More filming. The literary agent. It all slammed into me at once, causing the tension behind my eyes to tighten.

The hotel bar.

Charlie.

Harrison and Emma.

Charlie talking ... And ... something else. A secret? A confession?

Had I overshared?

I groaned and rolled my face into the pillow.

I'm the real Charlie.

I gasped and sat up so fast my head spun, and a wave of nausea sucker punched me. He'd said that.

I know.

But that couldn't mean what I thought. It couldn't be that RC was Charlie. But what else could it mean? Had he said it? Or was two vodka tonics enough to cause my overactive imagination to full-on spiral?

I stood up, hands outstretched like I could stop the world from spinning out around me.

"Focus," I told myself out loud.

Splashing water on my face in the bathroom like a man in an action movie, I stared at my reflection, water dripping down, and willed my memories to solidify.

I had imagined it. I was dreaming. We were talking. He was talking about the woman he loved. He was saying that he had to tell me something.

I groaned and pressed a fist to my forehead. What was real?

Here are facts that I know to be true about both Charlie and RC:

One, doesn't drink.

Two, lives in Southwest England.

Three, attended the funeral of his friend.

Four, has two best friends.

Five, there is a woman he wants but can't have ...

A tingling sensation traveled through me. Well, this was a compelling list.

This wasn't happening. I was contriving some fantasy to help deal with my growing feelings for Charlie. I had been bombarded with guilt last night coming here. Maybe a little because I was fresh from a breakup—though, to be honest, probably not as much as I should be.

What had kicked my conscience into overdrive was the idea that I had been betraying RC somehow. I had finally acknowledged my feelings for RC while simultaneously allowing my crush on Charlie to run wild. I had wanted him to stay last night.

Charlie. I had wanted him to kiss me, and I felt *bad* about it. Not that Charlie was even trying to sleep with me. An image of him lying across from me in bed flashed into my mind. He'd been so gentle with me. For being so large, he took such care not to jostle me. With his eyes narrowed in concern, he looked as though all my worries were his too.

I sighed loudly. I had it bad.

All these emotions conflated as my brain tried to excuse my having feelings for two different people. Tried to make up a reality where all the dreams I ever had could come true. My brain had always been good at finding pieces of facts and twisting them into a story that fit my narrative.

I just needed to breathe and calm down. Even if Charlie Downing was my RC, I couldn't just ask at this point. I needed him to tell me. He was obviously painfully private.

It had felt like a betrayal to RC as I spent the day getting to know Charlie. I had shared that story about my mother. Where had that even come from? But he was so easy to talk to. And Charlie had shared back. RC rarely entrusted me with stories from his own life. Or if he did, the stories were vague and laughed off. It shouldn't be so easy to spend time with Charlie already. But it was. A little voice in my brain continued to ask: Was that because I already knew him?

I drank some water and took the medicine. I needed to think. And that required a clear head.

"Oh god," I groaned, gripping my stomach.

My stories. All the stories I'd written. If this wasn't an elaborate fantasy, then Charlie had read all the fic I wrote about him. But ... RC reached out to me. He told me he loved them. The room spun.

Whispered voices drifted down the hall, and I stilled. I ran back to the bed and dove under the covers. There was a soft knock on the door.

"Kate?" Charlie called gently.

I stared straight ahead. How was I supposed to look at him? How could I even talk to him? I needed time to process.

If RC had been Charlie this whole time, I couldn't even contemplate the implications. It couldn't be true. Was this a joke? Had he been playing some sort of long con? But to what end?

No. Chances were he didn't want me to know who he really was. The drama from yesterday alone, after a few pictures, threw him into a state. He hated being in Hollywood. He didn't want to be back in this world. He didn't want the attention. I had to respect that.

I wouldn't freak out. If this wasn't some fantasy, there had to be a reason he waited to tell me. I would give him time to tell me on his own terms.

The knock came louder.

"Y-yes?" I said shakily, hopefully sounding sleep-addled to his ears.

"I'm sorry to wake you. But Sally called and they want us on set as soon as possible."

"Oh. Okay, be right out."

I would wait for him to tell me. Or I could just ask RC. Straight to the point. I couldn't infer too much from one sleepy conversation. I refused to be that person. But until I knew the truth ...

How the hell would I be able to look at him?

30

———

DRAFT UNSENT

TO: TheRealFreddyStan4Life@geemail.com
FROM: KateDubois@geemail.com
SUBJECT: Did I dream it?

Are you really him?

Please tell me now. I'm losing my mind. I feel like I could easily be imagining this all. Like I'm playing some horrible joke on myself.

I'm sure I heard your confession. But it could be just as likely that I only wanted to hear you say those words. Surely, you haven't been lying to me for almost two years. Fine. To be fair, you would argue that you hadn't actually lied about anything. But come on, let's call a spade a spade. You withheld some pretty crucial information from me. Do you not trust me?

Part of me feels like you kept the truth from me because you don't. Part of me is hurt. Part of me is confused and angry. Really angry. I don't know if I should confront you or just end the friendship? Both of those options suck. Both of those options mean everything changes and that scares me.

Tell me you're him.

I want it to be you so bad.

Please, just tell me the truth.

My feelings for you haven't changed in any way. But if I knew one way or the other, I wouldn't be feeling so damn conflicted about my attraction to Charlie. This is all so complicated. If you aren't him and I suggest it … I can't even think about how he'd react.

God, I cannot send this.

Kate

———

TO: THEREALFREDDYSTAN4LIFE@GEEMAIL.COM

    FROM: KateDubois@geemail.com

    SUBJECT: Are you around?

    RC,

I need to talk to you. I'm having a hard time, and I could really use a friendly face. Please. A video call?

I'm having feelings for somebody that maybe I shouldn't be. I need a friend to talk to.

    Love,

    Kate

———

TO: KATEDUBOIS@GEEMAIL.COM

    FROM: TheRealFreddyStan4Life@geemail.com

    SUBJECT: What's wrong?

    Kate,

You know you can talk to me about anything.

I made the mistake of saying no to a video call last time. I won't do it again. I'm just asking for a few more days.

I think also, if you are having feelings for somebody else,

then you should explore them. I know you and Pete just broke up, but the heart doesn't wait a magical number of days before it knows what it wants.

RC

31

Charlie

KATE WAS ACTING STRANGE. OH, SHE PRETENDED NORMALITY, BUT I thought myself a bit of an expert on Kate Dubois. She'd look at my temple or my jawline when I asked her a question. At first, I thought maybe I was projecting, but I was sure of it now that we were stuck in the back of a town car heading to the studio. Now that I'd experienced being the sole subject of her focus, I couldn't go back to anything else.

She emailed me, er, RC, this morning about feeling guilty for having feelings for someone. Did she think it was too soon after Pete? Or could it possibly be what I really wanted? That she'd seen the real me. Not Freddy Finks or the celebrity Charles Downing.

I told her to explore her feelings. Either that was the best move or completely idiotic, and once again, I ruined my chance with her.

Unfortunately, she didn't seem to remember the conversation from last night. If she had, wouldn't that have been the first thing she said to me? I had to tell her again. Everything had to come out. No more secrets.

There was no going back. We didn't have enough time. A few more days if that, and we'd be separated, and I'd be back in Devon. Which was absolutely still the plan.

I cleared my throat. We hadn't spoken much since we both hurried to shower and head out.

"Did you sleep okay?" I asked. My voice sounded too deep and raspy in the quiet ride.

Her eyes snapped to me and then away before darting back to the corner of my eye. "Yep. Just fine. You?"

"Not really," I mumbled.

"How come?"

Because I spent half the night wondering if you heard me and the other half wishing I hadn't left you alone in that bed.

"Time difference, probably."

I would remind her. Re-tell her. Put everything out there. I just didn't want to do it now and frazzle her before we started filming. She was already skittish enough.

A sharp turn caused her to slide across the smooth leather and into me. She looked up at me and blushed. "Sorry."

I swallowed. I needed to say something. Anything. Not about how kissable her lips looked. Or how I wished I could wrap my arms around her.

"And thanks again for, uh, taking care of me and letting me stay with you all," she added.

"Of course."

"I'll have to thank Emma and Harrison too. Are they already at the studio?"

I nodded.

Kate looked at her fingers twisting her lap.

"About that," I said. "It only makes sense if you keep staying with us. The show is asking you to extend your stay so ..." I was unsure how to finish. Had I really asked her to spend the rest of the trip with me? This was why I was not allowed to speak without thinking first.

The longer she hesitated, the more my doubt seeped in. What did she even know about me? I added, "Only if you feel comfortable. I don't want you to feel like you need to agree just because—"

"Because why?" She looked confused.

"Because I'm a celebrity. I don't want you to feel like you owe me something." Heat burned up my neck.

"That hadn't even crossed my mind."

"Oh. Good." *Way to announce you have a giant ego, you prat.* "Some people feel like they need to say what I want to hear," I clarified.

I winced at the implication that I wanted her to stay. It was true, of course. I wanted to soak up every minute of her time while we were on the same continent. "Not that it's what I want. I mean. It is what I want. If you want it." I blew out a breath. "I'm rubbish at talking to people." I leaned against the door, rubbing a hand over my mouth.

"I didn't think you were implying anything ... unseemly," she said and squeezed my arm until I turned back to her.

"What has you hesitating?" I asked.

"I can't imagine anyone else getting this VIP treatment." Kate worried her bottom lip, debating with herself. "There's probably a hundred reasons why I should argue that I can't accept."

I smiled down at her. "Well, then let's pretend you made all those arguments and in the end, you decided to stay. Pretend Emma insisted." I shrugged. "Knowing her, she probably will."

Kate let out a breath. "Okay. Well, in that case. I'm all out of excuses." She smiled up at me. "That's incredibly generous. Thank you. I still feel like I'm waiting to wake up."

I swallowed. She had remembered that part of the conversation.

I gently pinched her wrist. "Nope."

"Ouch." Before I could pull my hand away, she grabbed it out of reflex.

"That didn't hurt," I teased.

Her eyes widened. "You don't know that. I could have a low threshold for pain."

Her hand rested on top of mine. We both looked at it. I slowly turned it over and laced her fingers through mine. Her warm, soft fingers grasped me firmly, giving me strength. I could probably shot put a Volkswagen with all the adrenaline rushing through me. The delicate bones of her chest rose and fell. She looked at our clasped hands, a little furrow pinching her brow.

"Is this okay?" I asked.

When she looked back up at me, her gaze flickered between my eyes. "Yes," she said.

When I thought just seeing her would be enough, I had been a naive buffoon. It would never be enough to just be near her. But that was all I had for now and I would take it. A few days and then back to reality. I wouldn't waste any more time.

Of all people, Agata's menacing glare popped into my head at that moment. *You woo?* As RC, I had lost my chance with Kate when I wouldn't agree to a video call. I wouldn't make that same mistake again. But I wanted her to know me a little better. The version of me that existed outside the computer or the media's lens. I was just a man who was falling for her. A man who couldn't stop his feelings from growing exponentially with every moment spent together.

I told her, well, *RC* told her, that she should explore her feelings for this other person. There wouldn't be any doubt how I felt about her. I would reveal who I was. *Again*? But for now, I would woo her.

"Last night, you said your heart belonged to someone else." I swallowed and found my throat so tight I wasn't confident I could get the rest of the words out. "But I was wondering if maybe you'd like to get dinner tonight? As a date," I clarified. "I really like getting to know you, Kate Dubois."

Her jaw fell open. She blinked and her mouth snapped shut. After an eternity that lasted probably only two seconds, something shifted behind her gaze. A slow smile curled her lips. "I'll have my people call your people and we'll set something up."

I threw my head back and laughed. My Kate. Always keeping me on my toes. I lifted her hand to my mouth and kissed her knuckles.

————

Kate

I WAS HOLDING CHARLIE DOWNING'S HAND. I ASKED RC IF I should explore my feelings with another person and he told me to go for it. If RC wasn't Charlie, then I once and for all knew that RC was not romantically interested in me. And for the first time, the thought didn't crush my chest.

"So—" I hesitated. "What happens when we get to the studio?"

I squeezed our joined hands and raised them slightly in question. He took it as an opportunity to kiss my knuckles again. Thank goodness I was sitting down because the tingle at the back of my knees would have made me collapse.

He let out a long breath. "We do the bit. Or whatever it is they want us to. Then we have dinner." He ran his thumb back and forth over my overly sensitive skin. "This." He cleared his throat. "Means more to me than ... If people see, they will find a way to ruin it. I don't want it to be tainted. Let's keep this"—his hand squeezed mine—"for us. For now," he added.

I understood. I was a little relieved to have the decision made but also disappointed about more secrecy. I wasn't ashamed to walk in hand in hand with him. Obviously. But his request was probably for the best. I had just been with somebody else, and I was there for my writing. I didn't care what strangers thought, but I didn't want this new/old friendship with Charlie to get spoiled before it began.

"I understand," I said. I leaned forward and kissed his cheek.

I went to pull away, but he didn't let me. One strong hand held my neck, fingers tangled in my short hair, stopping my retreat.

"Kate," he said. His mouth hovered just in front of me.

"Charlie." I mimicked. Since we were hovering inches apart, saying each other's names.

I heard his swallow and watched as his eyes squinted in humor. "I'm very much looking forward to our date tonight."

What did that mean? What would our evening look like? And where would we go from there?

No. I wouldn't worry or obsess or come up with fantastical realities. Charlie was here now. He was looking at me. He brushed his thumb over my cheek and yet it warmed my entire body.

"Me too," I said, a little breathy.

The town car pulled through security and into the lot.

"We don't have to do any more filming. Ever been to Mexico?" He scrubbed a hand over his short-cropped hair, his knee tapping wildly as we got closer to set.

I laughed. "Charlie. We can't quit now," I said.

He grunted.

"I think it sounds fun," I said. I raised an eyebrow at him.

The soft flirty look melted from his face, and the mask I'd seen him wear in so many interviews was back into place. I hated seeing him shut down just to get through an event he hadn't wanted to be at. "Call me crazy, but it sounds like maybe you don't want to do it," I asked gently. "On account of the sudden interest in Mexico?"

"Canada sounds good too."

"Charlie?" I probed.

He groaned and, to my utter shock, pulled me onto his lap and buried his face in my neck.

"I don't want to." He sighed deeply against my hair, sending shivers down my arms.

I scratched my nails over his head, feeling bold by his obvious comfort in my touch. He shuddered as I said, "You can tell them no."

He pulled back. "Sally said there's a chance you could get an agent. I want you to get what you want."

His face was as serious as I've ever seen it. And it was pretty serious most of the time.

I felt a pang of dread. "You think if we don't do it, she won't set up the meeting?"

"I don't know. People are around here are ..." He paused to think of the words. *Poor Charlie.* He really was so jaded about Hollywood. He hated every moment of being here. And yet he said he was glad he came. "Manipulative," he finished. "But listen, my annoyance at being a circus act isn't worth you not getting a chance at an agent. I just want to make sure you're okay with everything."

"I'm fine. You don't have to worry about me." I really didn't mind but his discomfort was adding to my stage fright. We just needed to get through it. We would have each other's backs. It would be alright.

"Okay." He pulled me to him one more time to inhale my scent, as if it gave him strength. "Let's get this over with."

I cupped his cheek with his hand. "How bad can it be?"

32

———

Kate

OKAY, IT WASN'T GREAT.

I winced as the director thrust the uniform toward Charlie.

"Not a bloody chance," Charlie said, arms crossed and a scowl on his face.

"People would love to see the Intrepid Trio back in their training flight suits," Sally explained.

Behind her, a man from the costume department watched the exchange nervously.

"I don't care. I'm not putting that on. This is a hard line." Charlie was large and fierce. I could see now how people found him intimidating. Everything soft and sweet from our short drive over was gone, and the mask was back in place. The worst part was my inability to do anything. I wished I could lean forward and take his hand to offer the comfort he so badly needed. Even I had to admit, filming Harrison, Emma, and Charlie in their old flight school uniforms—made for *children*—was over-the-top cheesy. And maybe a little ick.

Sally let out a long-suffering sigh. "Fine. Fine. Harrison and

Emma didn't go for it either." She waved the man from costumes away. "Go to makeup. We're already behind schedule."

When she walked away, Charlie looked at me pointedly and nodded in the direction of a small alcove off the sound stage, between the sets. "'How bad could it be?' she asked." He raised an eyebrow at me, a hint of a smile tugging his lips.

"It wasn't *that* bad," I lied. I poked him in the ribs, and he grabbed my hand before it could retreat, just as he had in the car. Like whenever I touched him, he didn't want to end the connection. It was a theory I would have to investigate later as our day wore on.

He flicked a glance around then narrowed his eyes and leaned close to whisper in my ear. "Please tell me that wasn't something you wanted to see."

I guffawed loudly. "No. No offense but seeing you in the uniform you wore before puberty does not do it for me."

He looked into my eyes, studying me closely. There was something like insecurity in the knit of his brows.

"You know that I do *know* you're not Freddy Finks, right?" I placed a hand on the strong muscles of his shoulder and squeezed. "And I certainly do not have a crush on a fictional character."

Anymore.

He let out a breath like he'd actually been worried. Then my words registered, and his right dimple popped. "Are you saying you have a crush on me?" When he dropped that accent to a lower octave, I melted.

"I thought that was fairly obvious." I licked my lips.

His gaze moved over my face. He leaned over me, arm braced on the wall, my neck craning back just to look at him. Charlie's gaze was filled with a yearning that had to match my own. His head lowered to mine, like he was about to kiss me where anyone might see us even after we'd set boundaries in the car. Charlie wasn't ready for our relationship to be made public yet. A loud laugh between people passing nearby broke the hazy lust cementing us in place.

"We better get to makeup," I said, not moving.

His jaw flexed but he nodded and pushed off the wall. "Just a few hours," he said as though to rally himself.

"Just tug your ear like Carol Burnett if you get scared," I teased.

"And what will you do?" he asked.

"Whatever I need to." I winked and walked away like I was some saucy minx and not a nerdy writer from the Midwest. It pleased me to hear his soft groan as I sauntered away.

Less than an hour later, Emma, Harrison, and Charlie sat in deep chairs holding buzzers while I stood holding a long, thin seventies style microphone. Overnight, the designers had performed Hollywood magic. The set had been built to mimic the flight deck of the ship, *Homebound*, so that even their chairs looked like they'd been pulled straight from the original *Terra-Formative* set. Sleek screens displayed constellations and star clusters on the walls around us. Their chairs faced a small, raised dais in the center of the room where 3D maps of space were projected during each episode. I brushed down the goose bumps that prickled my arm in a moment of *How did I get here?*

I stood on the dais, the center of their focus. I would not cry happy tears in front of the cool kids.

"We're going to try something a little different today," Sally explained. Her stilettos clicked on the sparkling floor as she paced between us. "We're going to play a trivia game. Kate, you'll be the host, asking the Intrepid Trio plot questions about the *TerraFormative* universe." She turned to the actors, hand out. "And you three will buzz in fastest to say whether each plot point is 'fact or fan fiction.'"

I shot Charlie a look and he oh so subtly rolled his eyes.

Harrison shrugged and spun around in his chair once. Emma slid a competitive look to the guys.

After making sure our mics and lighting were right, we were off. Maybe because I'd spent the night at Harrison's home or because I'd been waiting to find out a potentially life-changing truth, whatever the reason, I was surprisingly collected during recording. If there was anything I knew it was *TerraFormative* trivia.

At first the questions were super obvious. Well, at least to me, as they centered mostly around TF canon and the stories I wrote. As I asked more questions, I grew more comfortable ad-libbing, much to my own surprise. Every time a wave of terror would crash over me at the reality of the situation—I was filming a game show with my former favorite childhood actors—I'd feel myself go shaky. But then one look to Charlie and his cheeky half smile and my nervousness would settle.

We worked through lunch to make up some of the delayed schedule. Sally liked to remind us all frequently how much every hour cost.

My heels were starting to hurt, and my throat was dry despite the constant replenishment of fancy bottled water. Still, I was having fun, and even Charlie seemed to be enjoying his time. The banter between the three of them was a gift to behold. Their bond, forged at age eleven, remained strong.

They were currently arguing about a frog supposedly "misplaced" on set.

"You put that in my trailer on purpose!" Emma yelled in mock outrage.

"I have no idea what you're talking about," Charlie said serenely. "Someone must have left the door open."

Harrison was laughing so hard, he had to dab tears from his eyes.

"Enough reminiscing, let's keep things moving, Miss Dubois," Sally said in the earpiece she insisted I wear.

"Okay, okay." I held up my arms. "Whether or not Charlie *definitely* hid that frog in your bed, we have to go on to the next question," I said loudly as they quieted. "Fact or fan fiction: Freddy Finks was once engaged to Nix, the cyborg from the destroyed planet Tacaps, to save her from being destroyed by Max Malachi's anti-tech family."

Emma buzzed before I even finished the question. "Fact!" she yelled.

"Incorrect," I said sympathetically.

Emma crossed her arms with a pout.

Charlie shot her a look of absolute disappointment and then glanced helplessly to Harrison. But Harrison had discovered the buttons on his chair's armrest actually worked and began to press them in delight, oblivious to the question. There was something admirable in Harrison's ability to take nothing too seriously. Charming, but also slightly infuriating.

Charlie obviously didn't want to answer another question correctly. He already had a hundred points more than the very grumpy Emma. If Harrison took nothing seriously, then Emma took everything very much to heart. But at least she tried. Harrison wasn't even on the board; he'd checked out several questions ago.

Eventually, Charlie gave in with a loud sigh and reluctantly hit his buzzer. "Fan fiction," he said slowly, holding my gaze.

I looked down at my flashcard to keep from blushing. That plot line had been pulled from one of my own stories. Many fics had been written about Freddy and Nix's coupling. Mine was the only one that featured a marriage of convenience to save Nix from Max's family of pure-human extremists set on ridding the universe of any humans who relied on technology to live.

"Correct. Ten points to you," I said.

"Yay," he deadpanned.

I forced myself to stop smiling as I read the explanation on the card. "In TF canon, Max's family did believe that human bloodlines needed to remain pure after the destruction of Earth. However, the opportunity for Freddy and Nix to explore their growing connection never came to fruition." I looked up from the card. "Tragically, if you ask me."

I was pleased to hear a few chuckles from the crew on set.

"Poor Chuck," Harrison said. "Unlucky in life and in fiction," he teased, and Charlie shot him "piss off" fingers.

"Uh, gentlemen, let's not forget this show has a PG rating," Sally's voice called out. In my earpiece so only I could hear what she said, "But keep this going. I wanna know what that was about. Ask Charlie if he's seeing anybody."

"Ha, no," I said loudly. The three actors all looked at me confused. I turned away slightly and whispered back, "I mean, I think it's best to focus on the fan fiction aspect."

I glanced to where Sally was watching me closely several yards away. "I know you think the fan fiction is what people want to hear about but that's just a fraction of it. You need to be flexible and roll with the punches. I thought you were serious about your future career as a writer, Kate?"

The threat was clear. If I wanted my meeting with the literary agent, then I needed to do what was being asked of me. Charlie had been right about the cold-blooded side to the business of Hollywood. All the fun I had been having flipped into anxious dread. Charlie's scowl was fierce as he looked between Sally and me. Apparently, we were not being as subtle as we thought we were.

"Charlie," I said. He watched me closely, an eyebrow already disapproving. I took a deep breath in to steady my voice. "You seem to have an extensive knowledge of the *TerraFormative* universe," I said.

I could ask him. I could ask him right here and now if he read my stories. It would be another clue to help me decide if he really was my secret pen pal.

He didn't say anything, only narrowed his eyes subtly. I realized that I hadn't actually asked him anything.

"A-are you a big reader? Have you ever read any TF fan fiction?" I asked tentatively.

"Good," Sally said in my ear. Her compliment made me feel slimy.

"I'm very familiar with the canon of the original books," he said tonelessly.

He hadn't answered the question directly but that denial was as clear as the truth. This was a detail he was not willing to share with random people. Shame washed over me.

I couldn't do this. I couldn't be another person in Charlie's life that caused him to put his shields up. I wanted to be a person that helped him to fully relax in his own skin. I told myself that if he wanted to tell me the truth, I would wait. My writing career was important, but being a decent human would always come first.

I nodded, feeling a blush burn up my cheeks. "Right." I cleared my throat. "Next question—"

"I forgot about that," Harrison said, sitting up excitedly and turning the chair toward Charlie, oblivious to the undertones of the situation. "You always had a book on set."

"Charlie always read between takes," Emma agreed.

"I mostly napped," Harrison said.

"We know," the other two said in unison.

"They had to reshoot several scenes because of your snores," Emma added.

Harrison shrugged. "Maybe that's why I'm still single."

Emma scoffed.

"Don't you know the Intrepid Trio is cursed in love? Just ask the media," Charlie said lightly but there was an edge to his voice.

"People are far too interested in our business." Emma shook her head.

I shot a look to Sally, who was watching the exchange closely.

"What business? They aren't wrong," Harrison mumbled. Then his head tilted as he recalled something. "No. Not all of us. Charlie had that American bird, remember? Hey, you never did say what happened with her."

Charlie was stock still. The world stopped spinning and time slowed down. Dead silence. The entire cast and crew held their breath with me. It was like Harrison had a sixth sense of the worst possible thing to say. Why was he just thinking of this now?

Emma's eyes widened to a comedic level. "She had a boyfriend. Remember?" she said through her teeth.

"That's right." Harrison snapped his fingers. "Shame, mate. You were quite hung up on her."

I sucked in my lips. Charlie remained surprisingly unreadable when he finally looked to me. I stared back at him, afraid to give any of my true feelings away.

It is you. Please let it be you.

He had to deny it. He hated people in his business. He hated publicity of any kind. I shouldn't have pushed or let myself be bullied into this line of questioning.

I watched Charlie with growing horror, wondering if I'd just undone the closeness we had tenuously built. I was about to change the subject again, when he slowly nodded his head once. A dimple appeared in his cheek. Then. THEN. He looked directly at me and responded to Harrison's statement, "That I was."

I chewed so hard on my lips and tried to bite back my smile.

It was as good as a confession, subtle to anybody but us. As much as one could be given in front of a room full of strangers. With camera phones.

My entire body must have been glowing from pure joy. "Well, let's get back to it, shall we?" I waved the cards in front of my face.

"Oof," Harrison said. "Bloody hell, Emma. What was that for?" Harrison rubbed at his ribcage. "Sorry I didn't know we weren't supposed to talk about her."

Emma covered her mouth with long, delicate, manicured fingers. Her mouth hardly moved as she whispered, "Read the room, Harrison."

Harrison's brows furrowed even more. I shot another look to Charlie, who continued to watch me unabashedly. I realized I was still fanning myself with the cards, unable to tear my gaze from his. Harrison's gaze flicked back and forth between the two of us.

"Wait," he said, straightening.

"Harrison," Emma warned, smile firmly fixed in place.

"I knew I recognized you!" Harrison stood, and my stomach plummeted.

"What's going on?" Sally said in my ear and then louder, "Anybody care to explain?"

"It's you. You're the American. I thought you looked familiar that first night. I can't believe I didn't put it together sooner," Harrison was shouting loud enough for costuming to take detailed notes.

"I-I—" I had no idea what to say.

It was confirmation he had talked to his friends about me. I was happy and terrified and anxious all at once. But no. The truth couldn't come out by accident. It wasn't fair to me or him.

"Cut!" Sally called and moved to the center of the soundstage.

I looked to Charlie, who remained impossibly still. This was all my fault. Charlie didn't want anybody in his business. I had to make this right. How could I make this right?

"Harrison. Sit down!" Emma said.

"But this is great news. She broke up with that wanker." Harrison threw an arm out to me.

Someone on set gasped, but I was too afraid to look anywhere but at the madness unfolding in front of me.

Charlie was on his feet now too. He looked around the set before coming back to me.

"Maybe we should continue with the questions?" I said loudly, holding up the cards. Not a single person acknowledged me.

"Harrison, maybe this isn't the best time?" Emma said.

Charlie stepped forward and put a hand on Harrison's shoulder. He lowered his voice. "Yes. It's her. Now shut your bloody mouth before this winds up online."

Harrison threw up his arms before mimicking zipping his lips. Charlie had just confirmed he was RC. He had just confirmed it to his best friend. I felt the world spinning too fast. I looked down at my shoes. I had never noticed how high I was off the ground? Humans were a terrible design. We could topple over so easily.

"Kate, are you okay?" Charlie tilted my head up with a gentle finger to my chin.

"I'm fine. I'm so sorry about this. Are you okay?" I asked, and he frowned.

"What in the hell is happening?" Sally asked again, growing impatient.

"It's nothing. It's a long story," Charlie explained.

Sally shoved her headset down. "Did you and Miss Dubois know each other before this special?"

"No," he snapped before looking at me. I looked back to my

shoes. The denial shouldn't hurt. He wasn't ready to tell the whole world. It wasn't anybody's business. It shouldn't hurt.

I squeezed my hands into fists. A hand brushed mine, and I was surprised to see Emma shooting me a sympathetic look from my side. Harrison came to stand at my other side, Charlie's two best friends flanking me.

"Miss Dubois?" Sally asked me.

I couldn't look at her. Or anybody. I just shook my head once, focusing on one of the screens that showed a slowly rotating star cluster.

"Christ," Charlie mumbled. "Kate." He was in front of me again. "I'm sorry, okay?"

I gave him a watery smile. I wasn't the actor here, but I did my best. "It's fine. I understand."

"No. You don't." He glanced up to Sally. "Yes. Kate and I are friends. And have been for some time. I read her stories online and I sent her a message to thank her because she's bloody brilliant."

The truth at last. Loud and clear. Little gasps and "aws" echoed from all around us. My hands were holding the cards in front of my face. Emma gasped at my side. Harrison whispered, "Fan fiction?" to himself. Sally's chin lifted. Her eyes narrowed as an understanding passed over her features.

Charlie turned back to me and grabbed my hands. "I'm sorry to have told you like this. I'm sorry it took me so bloody long."

I swallowed and tried not to sway.

He shrugged and gave me a sweet smile. "It's me. I'm your RC."

Your RC.

He held perfectly still, waiting for a reaction. Light clapping broke out but abruptly cut off when Charlie turned and glared. I couldn't believe he confirmed it. He didn't have to. I would have waited.

And yet, I was thrilled. I didn't think. I broke out from between his friends and jumped at him. He had just enough warning to catch me as I wrapped my arms around him.

"I know," I repeated from last night.

He coughed out a laugh before lowering his forehead to mine. He let out a long shaky breath, and I squeezed him tighter. I'm not sure how long we stayed like that.

When Emma cleared her throat, he slowly lowered me to the ground.

He shook his head but had half a smile on his face. Before he turned around, the smile fell, and the angry man was back. He glared as he looked at every person on set, from the catering crew to the gaffer. "And it's nobody's bloody business but ours."

Charlie

WELL, DAMN. THAT WASN'T HOW I WANTED KATE TO LEARN THE truth, and I certainly hadn't wanted all these bloody people around. I knew Sally would do something like this. She had been pushing Kate to more personal questions. I had seen the worry and doubt warring across Kate's features. It was an impossible position that Sally put her in. I should have never agreed to any of this.

I shot a glare at Sally, but she just crossed her arms and lifted her chin.

I felt a hand and turned to face Kate. The way she looked up at me, fighting a smile, eyes wide and gleaming. Okay, so that smile made all the drama worth it. When Kate jumped into my arms, nothing else mattered. I may have been upset at first, but now my fears felt so ungrounded. I wouldn't waste the time we had together.

"I had been hoping," she whispered just so I could hear.

My blood hummed at her soft confession. I leaned forward and whispered, "We have more to discuss. But first—"

I looked around the set and raised my voice loud and clear. "And if any of this ends up online or in the show, I will contact my lawyers." I focused on Sally. "Especially on the show. I mean it."

She threw up her hands, but there were mischievous wheels turning behind her eyes.

"That's a wrap," she yielded. In a lower tone, she said, "I think we got everything we needed."

I ground my jaw.

"Charlie, it's fine." Kate squeezed my arm.

"No. It's not. Someone on set is trying to use you for ratings and I won't stand for it." She frowned, and I realized I'd snapped at her. She nodded and stepped back. Emma threaded her arm through Kate's as she gave me a cautioning look.

"Fine, no worries," Sally said. She turned to leave, already talking into her headpiece again.

"Cheers. I'm starved," Harrison said, looking between the ladies and me. "I still can't believe I didn't make the connection sooner. How silly of me."

Emma stepped closer as the four of us made our way off set. Kate was slightly ahead, chatting with Harrison. Well, Harrison was chatting, and it made me nervous. He flicked an open smile back at me. There was a gleam in his eye that made me suspicious. Had he really been that bloody clueless, or did I owe him big-time for forcing my hand? Maybe I would be angry later, but for now, the world shone brighter, and even people weren't as annoying.

"Well, that was all very dramatic," Emma said quietly at my side.

"I don't trust Sally. I don't trust anybody on this set. They're trying to use Kate and it's pissing me off." We made our way out to where a car was waiting for us.

"Is it Kate you're worried about?" Emma asked.

"Of course," I said.

Outside, behind the lot, the town car waited for us, magically summoned.

Emma held my gaze. "Okay. Just be careful," she warned. "Kate's a grown woman. Remember that." Louder to Harrison and Kate, she said, "Should we go get dinner? I think Charlie's a bit hangry."

Kate snickered and I rolled my eyes.

"Kate and I have plans," I said.

"Do you?" Emma asked.

"You'll have plenty of time for that," Harrison said. "Come on, let's take Kate for a night on the town. Give her a little taste of the celebrity life."

"Oh yes!" Emma hopped excitedly.

I blinked at Harrison. It took all my effort not to growl *mine*.

"No. You guys don't have to do that," Kate said.

"We want to," Emma said. "If we leave it up to him, you'll just order takeaway and stay in all night."

Kate shrugged, mirroring my own thoughts that the suggestion sounded like an ideal night in.

"You two really are homebodies," Harrison grumbled.

"Listen, Charlie. This is a once-in-a-lifetime opportunity for Kate. Don't you want her to experience the fun side of fame?" I opened my mouth to object, and she held up a finger. "Don't, you grumpy arse. There are plenty of perks and don't you forget it."

"I don't even have anything to wear," Kate argued weakly. I could see her considering the glamor of it all.

Yes, I hated it, but she really did deserve to have some fun.

Emma clicked her tongue. "Well, you obviously don't need to

worry about that. I keep tons of stuff at Harrison's just for situations like this."

Kate's eyes widened in excitement at the prospect of seeing inside Emma's wardrobe. I had to give her this. After so long of keeping myself at bay, after a day of filming and her doing amazingly, she deserved to have a night to be free and have fun. And sure, there were some perks to fame that I hadn't exercised in a while.

"We'll be careful with the paps," Emma said to me, giving her famous pleading pout. "Let Kate have this."

"Fine." Emma clapped her hands and squeaked in excitement. I added, "I'm doing this for Kate. Not for you."

"Oh, I know," she said.

Kate's smile transformed into such a breathtaking sight I decided to do anything she ever asked of me. Then something seemed to click in her brain and she frowned. She stepped closer to me. Emma took the hint and dragged an oblivious Harrison into the waiting car.

"Are you sure you're going to be okay going out? What if I drink?" she asked.

I grinned at her and didn't stop myself from tucking hair behind her ear. "I'm often around people drinking."

"That's not what I asked," she said, holding my stare.

I grabbed her face with both hands. "I'll be okay. I want you to have fun."

"If you feel like you need a drink, squeeze my hand," she said seriously.

An excuse to touch Kate whenever I wanted? Looked like I would be very thirsty tonight.

"I thought I should tug my ear," I teased.

She frowned, considering. "Hmm, good point. You can do that."

I pulled her closer to me. "I like touching you. I think that's the better option."

She flushed and wrapped her arms around my middle. "Just practicing."

"Come on, you two. I'm starving," Harrison called from the back of the car.

As soon as we got back to Harrison's, Kate was whisked away from me.

"Go eat, Grumpy Gus. We'll meet you two down here at ten," Emma said.

Kate gave me a fake worried look before she allowed herself to be tugged away.

She looked so happy. There wasn't much I had to offer, but a night of luxury on the town was one of them. I would be by her side while I could and that was all that mattered.

"Oh, man, you have it so bad," Harrison said, slapping me on the shoulder. "Now let's feed you before you muck it up somehow."

33

―――――

Kate

I blinked in awe at the beautiful array of glorious fabrics in various styles and cuts that shimmered expensively in front of me.

"I feel like I should put on those little white gloves they use to handle the Declaration of Independence," I said.

"These are far more valuable than that silly little document," Emma teased, making her British accent more posh.

I gently lifted out a forest green mini dress with capped sleeves. I sighed and put it back.

"Emma. These are amazing—"

She lifted a hand to stop me. "If you're about to argue about how you can't accept this offer, I'm just going to ask that we skip to the part where I convince you anyway. The fact is, I would rather these be worn more than once. The designers I support are slightly better with their global footprint but still not great."

I smiled. RC had mentioned a best friend who was trying to always save the world. He also mentioned how pushy Emma could be, and now I was witnessing it firsthand.

"You sound like Charlie," I said. "But actually, I was going to say that this isn't a makeover montage in a movie. These hips are not going to magically fit in the dresses cut for your size zero, five-nine frame." I shook my head, laughing. "But thank you for your optimism."

"Oh." She frowned, thinking.

"And we won't even talk about those." I pointed to the row of shoes that I would never be able to walk in. Heels were one thing, but Emma's pointy stilettos reached heights I hadn't trained for.

She tapped her lips in thought, then shrugged. "Well, lucky for you, I do have the power to create a movie-style makeover."

"What?" I stared at her.

"I don't like to take advantage of my situation very often, but I have to admit there are definite perks." She brushed her hair off her shoulder, looking bashful. "Not to freak you out, but there is probably nothing you could ask for that I couldn't get for us in less than an hour."

"Anything?" I asked.

An hour later, as we snacked on street tacos, her room was descended upon by stylists, for clothes, hair, and makeup. Was it way too much? Probably. But it was so damn fun.

The personal stylist brought several dress options for my body type. We settled on an emerald-green satin dress with long sleeves and a neckline cut so low that wearing a bra was not an option. It pinched in high on my waist and flared out to cover my buxom booty. And maybe a tad too short.

"A strong breeze and everybody will know my waxing preferences," I said.

"Don't worry, doll, we have tape for that. We just want to give the illusion that flashing might occur at any moment," the stylist said.

Emma was dressed and ready, sipping a cocktail, as she

watched the stylist add a few finishing touches to my makeup. She looked otherworldly in a silver sparkling gown that seemed to be held together by only a few strands of Swarovski crystals. With her red waves cascading perfectly around her shoulders and her intense blue eyes, she reminded me of an ethereal elf from Tolkien. Really, how could any human be so gorgeous?

"Can you please tone it down or I won't be able to go out with you," I said, only half kidding.

"I can't turn it off. It's who I am," Emma teased. "Plus, this is how I get investors."

"I bet you could get anything with that body. Like, I know how sexist that sounds to my ears, but I still believe it's true."

"Not anything," she said quietly. She pushed off the wall and came to look me up and down before I could investigate that oddly cryptic last statement. "You have no idea how amazing your bottom is."

I flushed. "I really did *not* expect you to say that." I fought to keep my arms at my side and not cover my booty.

"It's true. I know many a people who have paid for an ass like this," the stylist said.

"I—" I literally had no idea what to say. "I always say that god over poured the mold downstairs and made up for it by taking some from up here." I gestured to my chest.

"No. You're fabulous." The stylists stood up and dusted off their pants. "This high empire waist makes you look tiny. And again, that booty. Very on trend. Congratulations."

"Uh, thank you." I glanced at my phone. It was well after ten. "Oh, we're late."

Emma waved me away. "They know I meant later. It's fine."

Once we were properly accessorized, the others cleared out, leaving Emma and me alone.

I glanced at her to find she was watching me like she was

preparing to deliver a lecture. "Are you going to threaten to shoot me if I hurt Charlie?"

She gasped. "Darling, how gauche. Only Americans threaten with guns."

I shrugged. "Fair."

But Emma cleared her throat and toyed with the hem of her skirt. "All I was going to say is that I'm glad that Charlie has someone to talk to. I worry about him out there all alone. And it seems like he's opened up to you quite a bit. That doesn't come easily for him."

My shoulders relaxed. "Yeah. It took me two years to get his real name."

Emma laughed but said, "You know, we've all been burned and none of us are quick to trust at this point. You must be a pretty good egg for him to do what he did today. I still can't believe it." She shook her head.

"Me neither."

"Fan fiction, huh? How long do you think Harrison and I have to wait before we can take the piss out of him?"

I contemplated. "Probably give it a week at least." We made our way to the door, but I hesitated. "I didn't mean for that to happen today. I wanted to wait until he was ready. I know you three have a lot of trauma from that show. I wasn't trying to rush him."

Emma's smile faltered. "Trauma. No." She shook her head adamantly. "Nothing ... nothing violent or anything like that ever happened when we were kids. We had many adults protecting us."

I shook my head. "No. No. I just mean ... There are different levels to trauma, you know? I'm not trying to use the term lightly but you three were thrust into something massive at a young age. I'm glad you were physically safe, but I can't imagine there was much in the way of protection against the non-physical effects. Fame has got to mess with anybody's head. And growing up on camera? It's hard enough, you know? I mean, I would imagine so."

I stopped rambling when I realized Emma's face had fallen.

"I'm sorry. I overstepped."

She shook her head to clear it. "I just never really thought about it like that. I've always just thought I should be grateful."

"I think you can be both. Grateful but maybe still recognize that it wasn't normal."

Emma watched me closely before she shook her head again. "I'm sorry. There's just nothing to be done for it. I have to hug you. I absolutely get it now."

She wrapped her arms around me. "Get what?" I laughed as we carefully hugged, not messing up any of the stylists' hard work.

"Oh, you'll see," she said ominously. She linked her arm through mine. "Let's head down, shall we?"

Only a half hour late, we made our way downstairs to Charlie and Harrison.

Charlie spotted me the second we entered the living room. He ran a hand over his face, his eyes moving all over me, never settling on one area.

He moved closer yet stopped a few inches in front of me.

"You look absolutely breathtaking," Charlie said.

"You look great too," I said, admiring his all-black fitted slacks and tight button-up shirt. The clothes molded to his sculpted form. "Nice pants," I teased. I wondered if he too remembered every conversation we'd ever exchanged. The reality that Charlie was my RC was starting to settle in, and between that and the glam look, I was flying high.

He made a low growling sound. "Maybe later," he said.

I bit my lip as Emma and Harrison made their way to the door. "Are we ready?" Emma asked, bright-eyed.

"Limo's here," Charlie said.

My jaw dropped.

"I heard you liked your last trip in one. Thought you better have at least one more," he said.

I smiled up at him in delight even as my heart clenched, remembering that our days were few. It wasn't clear how much more time Sally would need to film. It felt like we'd done more than enough to fulfill our contracted quota. At this point, I'd probably sign on for another month if it meant that I wouldn't have to leave Charlie. But I couldn't think about that now. I just wanted a night on the town with this gorgeous man and his two best friends.

———

THE PERKS OF CELEBRITY LIFE HAD NOT BEEN EXAGGERATED. THE limo was even nicer than the one that picked me up from the airport. I had gone from never being in a limo to discerning the qualities of different types. Yeesh, look at me quickly adapting to celebrity life. There was a bottle of champagne I'd only ever seen in rap videos waiting on a miniature sideboard when we got in. Without a word, Harrison handed the bottle to the grinning driver. "Cheers, mate. Bring that home to the fam as part of your tip."

After a luxurious but too short ride, the four of us were delivered to a secret back club entrance and directed straight to the VIP area. The club itself was unlike any place I'd ever seen: jam-packed with the world's most beautiful people, velvet couches, dazzling chandeliers, and servers who looked like they'd been pulled straight from the movies. Actually, they were probably trying to become actors considering where we were. We had a private room offset from the crowded dance floor, where we could watch the crowds, but they couldn't see us.

Several gorgeous men and women made eyes at Harrison, Emma, and Charlie as we made our way to the room, but nobody dared approach.

"What do you think?" Emma asked after an hour or so on the shared dance floor.

I had decided before we left that I wouldn't be drinking tonight. Not just for Charlie, but because I didn't want time to go even faster. I wanted to remember every detail. Okay, and to be fair, I still didn't feel great after the two drinks last night.

She sat next to me on a small couch, Harrison and Charlie across from us. Charlie sat with one strong leg crossed over his other knee. His muscular thighs were close to busting the seams of tight-tailored pants. He hadn't taken his eyes off me tonight, and it made me feel like I was the only woman in the world. Catching me ogling him, he tugged at his ear with a coy smile. I raised a teasing eyebrow at his call for help. I wanted nothing more than to cross the small table between us and straddle him.

"Earth to Kate?" Emma playfully shouldered me.

Oh yeah, she'd asked me something. I brought my focus back to her and blinked slowly. "I think I could get used to VIP treatment."

She laughed with an elegant toss of her hair.

"This is amazing," I added. "Thank you so much for bringing me."

I would never forget this night as long as I lived. I found myself trying to keep track of details and only realized later that I'd been subconsciously documenting everything to share with RC. The understanding hit me so hard that I almost felt dizzy. I wouldn't have to remember to tell him everything because the real Charlie was here at my side. Wouldn't it be amazing to never have to remember to tell him anything again because he was there to experience it with me?

Harrison squeezed in on the other side of Emma, and they

laughed loudly about something I couldn't quite make out over the thumping club music.

I was debating how to join Charlie, when my eyes drifted to the club beyond our room. Several shiny faces looked familiar, but I couldn't recall anyone in particular, up-and-comers on a few streaming shows that were taking off.

Then I saw someone I absolutely recognized. Wesley Cole. He'd played the bad boy Max Malachi in *TerraFormative* and had been a constant source of antagonism to the Intrepid Trio. I hadn't seen him in person yet, though he'd been listed on the call sheets. His recording schedule never synched up with ours. Maybe the "bad guys" were being filmed separately.

Wesley had also grown ridiculously handsome with the passing of time. Was that good luck by casting or another perk of money? At a young age, his black hair had developed distinctive silver streaks, becoming his most recognizable feature. His sharp jawline was covered with a hint of a five o'clock shadow and dark circles bruised the pale skin under his eyes. All that, combined with his thick dark brows, always made him appear hard-edged and unapproachable. A dastardly look which drove the fangirls crazy.

Wesley's eyes moved across the room as he laughed with a friend, as if sensing he was being watched. The moment his gaze landed on Emma, his dark eyebrows furrowed. His gaze raked up and down her body; the raw desire that passed over his features forced me to glance away. By the time I looked back, he'd smoothed his face back to neutral.

So maybe not all the rumors were fake and just for publicity.

I very casually tilted my head toward Emma. "Emma," I said as I nudged her.

She turned, smiling. "What is it?"

I leaned closer and had to all but yell to be heard over the club music. "Don't look. But I think Wesley Cole is over at that table and he's staring at you like—"

But the second I said his name, her head snapped right in the direction I told her not to look, but Wesley had already turned away.

"Or look directly at him." I sighed.

"Excuse me," Emma said, already pushing off the couch and moving toward him.

Wesley flicked an overly casual look in her direction, and the second he registered her advance, he glanced around as if to decide if he could still make a break for it.

"Uh-oh," Harrison said, taking a drink and watching the drama unfold.

"What's going on?" I asked.

"Long story," Charlie yelled.

"First loves," Harrison yelled at the same time.

"Why does she look so mad? And why does he look so scared?" I asked.

"I think you answered your own question," Charlie said.

"That's a story for another night." Harrison's easy expression slipped as he watched her approach Wesley.

"Should we go intercept?" Harrison called.

"There's no stopping Emma when she's on a mission," Charlie said.

Several onlookers watched as she stomped up to Wesley. She didn't even give him a chance to talk, she just dragged him away as he desperately looked around for help. But it was too late for him. Emma and Wesley disappeared around the corner. A second later, Charlie moved to the now unoccupied space left by Emma.

"Is she going to be okay?" I asked him.

The line of his mouth flattened. "They have a complicated history." He rubbed the area between his eyes. "I wish she'd just

—" He shook his head. His gaze roamed over my face, and a softness shifted his features. He reached a hand to cup my chin and really looked at me.

"Are you doing okay?" I rested my hand over his as I asked.

I wasn't sure what he was thinking, and I momentarily wished I could just email him to get a glimpse into his brain.

He nodded with a warm smile as his focus moved over me. "I'm just really glad you're here. I almost can't believe it."

I sighed and leaned back into his arms. "Me too."

Harrison melted into the crowd, leaving just us two in the private room.

"You tugged your ear, are you sure you're okay?" I asked. His arm went around my shoulder, his fingertips just dangling above the low-cut top of my dress. I grabbed his hand and held it to me.

"This is all I need," he said into my ear.

Around us, the nightclub was in full swing. People ground their hips together on the dance floor. Women and men with magazine-worthy bodies danced provocatively on pedestals around the club. The walls were filled with art and photos of naked women lounging seductively. I was eighty percent sure someone was being pleasured in the dark corner to our left, based on the way her head was thrown back and her panting chest.

Warmth spread through me as I became even more aware of Charlie's hot body pressed against mine. Every breath out tickled the short hairs of my neck. The whole atmosphere of the club grew hypnotically erotic.

"Have we shocked you?" His deep British accent in my ear rolled through my body like ice over a tongue.

I turned to find his face just a breath from mine. His light hazel gaze moved over my face bouncing from my lips back to my eyes. He thought that, didn't he? That I was just a pearl-clutching naive girl. Well, he forgot who he was dealing with.

Slowly, I spun to face him. The deep V of my dress was just under his nose. His eyes flicked there for a moment, hesitated, and then returned to watch me as I moved close. I went up on my knees as I slid my arms around his neck, pressing my chest into his shoulder.

Lips just brushing the shell of his ear, I said, "I thought you said you read all my writing?" I pulled back in time to watch the confusion on his face darken into understanding.

His pupils blacked out as his jaw slackened. I ran my lips up the column of his neck, breathing hot breath onto his skin before I gently bit on a strong muscle, flexed with tension. I arched my back, fully embracing this side of myself. It wasn't alcohol or the sensuous environment. In an alternate reality, if I'd ever come to a place like this with Pete, I would have never been so brazen. I never felt safe with Pete like I did with Charlie. I was free to be myself, in all the glorious—and albeit a little kinky—facets of myself.

After all, what were dark alcoves for if not to get a little freaky?

"Remember the story I wrote where Freddy and Nix had to go undercover at the sex club? They had to pretend to be a couple?" My wrists hooked behind his head, and my back arched so I could lean back and study him. "I seem to remember you specifically mentioning that one."

His throat worked a swallow as he blatantly stared at my cleavage on display at this angle. He looked back to me and nodded.

I leaned forward and worked my way onto his lap. I couldn't straddle him in this dress, lest I did intend to show the whole club those waxing preferences, so I sat sidesaddle and ran a hand over his strong, square jaw. His muscles clenched under my slow perusal.

His body was hot and hard, and if I wasn't totally mistaken, the arousing effects of the club currently pressed into my hip.

"I really enjoyed that story," he said roughly, tilting his hips up to adjust his pants, taking me with him. He was so strong, it was like I wasn't even there. He'd be able to toss me around. I could be rocked up and down on his lap and not have to do any of the work. The idea made me clench in anticipation.

"Remember the scene in the upstairs private rooms? Where he had to bend her over and—"

"Kate," he said gruffly. "I remember. Every word you ever wrote. Vividly."

The intensity of his words caught me off guard. My desire for him. The passion in his dark gaze, it was all too much.

"I thought of you," I said. "I'm sorry if that's weird. But so often when I wrote any of my newer stuff, the most intense scenes, I thought of you."

His brow furrowed.

"Not Charles the actor, *you*. RC," I clarified.

His head shot up, hands on my hips gripping. "You did? But—"

"I didn't need to know what you looked like." I dropped my forehead to his and closed my eyes. He'd always been so solid in my imagination, even before I saw his body. The feelings I had for him were personified in an amalgamation of people until he was just RC. Now, in his lap, it was difficult to picture the man from my imagination without seeing Charlie. It had always been Charlie. It would always be him.

"It's hard to explain, but it was you I thought of so often." I swallowed down the fear at the honesty. God, don't let him think I was a freak. "For me, this has been more than just emails for a while."

"It was more for me too." He rubbed his nose into my neck, sighing contently. "Before I even knew your name, I was already half mad for you."

What did this mean for us? Where would we go from here? Eventually, the party would be over, and I had to go back to real life. No more wasted time.

"Charlie? I know in the grand scheme we've only just met. But ... doesn't it feel much longer?"

He held my gaze and nodded. "I thought you knew. I thought you guessed, a dozen different times since we came to LA," he confessed shakily.

"How in the world would I ever make that connection?" Then I added, "To be fair, in my wildest dreams I hoped. But it seemed unfathomable."

"Same for me." He kissed my neck. "This feels like a dream for me too."

My head swam. I was too happy, too on fire with want for him. I didn't know what the future held, but I needed more than just holding his hand.

"Don't you think we should take advantage of this time together while we can?" I wiggled in his lap, not subtle in my meaning.

He dropped his head to my shoulder, and I felt more than heard his sharp exhale of breath as he nodded again.

His head continued to move across my shoulder, pushing the sleeve of my dress down with his teeth. The fabric was silky, was just barely covering my hard nipple, and the tape supplied by Emma and the team was doing its job. My whole body shivered at the feel of his tongue grazing the sensitive skin of my shoulder. One of my hands gripped his bicep as the other moved to the back of his head, gently encouraging his exploration.

Maybe this was too soon. Maybe being newly single should make me feel ashamed, but it was hard to feel wrong when everything with Charlie felt so right. There was a comfort in his presence that two years of talking every single day had built. My desire for this man felt more real than anything I'd ever experienced with Pete or any other boyfriend. It felt natural and pure. I wouldn't shame myself for finally chasing joy.

The slow heady beat of the bass, combined with his clean, masculine scent, made me feel like I was swimming through an erotic dream. Charlie sucked gently on the sensitive skin where my neck met my shoulder, not hard enough to leave a mark but enough to add fuel to my fire. My thighs squeezed together impatiently, and I sighed loudly, eliciting a groan from him.

"We really shouldn't be doing this here," he growled but made no effort to stop his hand from dropping to smooth over my bottom.

"Probably not," I said. "But I like it."

"Fuck." He growled and squeezed my ass before moving his hand to my knee. "There are so many things I want to do to you."

"VIP room, VIP privacy," I teased.

It was true though. We were removed from everyone, shrouded in darkness.

He looked at me then, reading my desire as his hand on my knee moved a little farther up. I licked my lips and adjusted to spread my legs. His nostrils flared and he moved his hand up higher. The music was loud, but his quick breaths were audible in the din.

I tilted my head and studied his lips as his fingers moved closer and closer to where my heat was building. He closed the distance, and his lips met mine.

I was kissing Charles Downing. Better yet, I was kissing my Charlie. This was a Charlie kiss. A little shy and softly exploratory but erotic as hell as he grazed my lips with his.

Gentle brushes back and forth shot electricity through every nerve of my body as his hand reached the apex of my thighs.

A single finger tentatively explored the wet fabric that separated him from me. He gasped hotly against my mouth when he found how turned on I was. How could I have ever doubted my own sexuality? I wasn't wrong; I was with the wrong person.

"Christ, Kate. You really do like it."

I was too overwhelmed to look at him. I wasn't ashamed to be so into this, not with him. His response told me there were no hard feelings on his end. Just hard.

I deepened our kiss, mouths opening to let his tongue enter me. He pulled me tighter against him, another finger flitted and teased up and down, and I fought to keep from writhing on his lap.

We were hidden, but I probably shouldn't draw too much attention to our room.

He tucked a finger under the fabric and moved it aside to explore unencumbered. His finger slipped around easily, and I gripped him harder, shuddering. Surely, I couldn't get off here, in public like this. It was indecent. And yet ...

My hips moved in rhythm with his fingers, until his thumb brushed against the spot that made me break our kiss with a gasp. My fingers gripped him so hard, they'd be sore later. His eyes didn't leave mine as he moved and explored to discover what I liked. I rode his hand in the middle of the club and I couldn't care less.

His chest was heaving up and down. His neck and shoulders were flexed in carefully contained control. From the outside, it would just look like I was staring at him, sitting on his lap. Nobody would be the wiser. Except maybe for the obvious ecstasy written all over my face.

I needed more. I wanted to ride his lap with nothing separating us. I wanted to ride *him* and feel him deep in me. I wanted to feel full of him.

"Charlie," I gasped his name as I clenched against his fingers, coming in a rush at the thoughts of him naked and pumping into me.

"Kate," he soothed as the pulses gentled. "Fuck. You're so beautiful when you come."

My cheeks burned like fire against his neck. His pulse hammered against me.

"I can't believe I did that," I panted.

This was what happened when I let this side of me loose. I wrote kinky stories people loved, and I had orgasms in nightclubs with a hundred people around.

There was something so freeing in that.

He carefully, subtly removed his fingers, smoothing my dress before bringing them to his mouth to suck them clean. "This is just the beginning."

My hand went to his lap and I cupped the outline of him. He was thick, long, and rock hard. He hissed and pivoted against my hand.

I looked past his shoulder across the club to see Emma heading toward our room, her brows furrowed. She grabbed a shot from a passing server and threw it back. I quickly shifted on Charlie to indicate we were about to lose our privacy.

"Can we go somewhere else?" Emma stood above us, arms crossed and eyes glossy.

I tried to stand up, but Charlie held me in place. "Give me a minute," he whispered in obvious discomfort. I winced for him.

"Are you okay?" I asked her.

I hoped my recent orgasm wasn't written all over my features, but she seemed lost in her own thoughts.

"Definitely." She sniffed and tossed her hair over her shoulder. By the time she looked at me again, a smile was fixed in place. "I've just had enough of this club."

Once composed, Charlie waved Harrison over.

"We can head home and put on comfy pants," Emma said, her voice slightly slurred.

"You don't have to sell me on that," Charlie said. "Is that okay with you?" he asked me. There was a look in his eyes that said our previous activities might need to be put on hold to take care of Emma.

"Of course." Tonight had been like a dream but it wasn't something I needed. More like something my older self would have been grateful to have experienced. But honestly, I was just as happy to get out of these heels.

"I'm sorry. If you guys want to stay, I can get a different car." She stumbled, reaching for her bag.

"Not a chance. We've got you." Harrison helped to steady her.

For just a moment, her smile faltered. I glanced away as she said to her best friend, "You were right. I should've just left well enough alone."

"He's an idiot," Charlie said. Emotion swelled in me for this sweet friendship.

My heart longed for such support. What it might be like to fully rely on someone you've known most of your life? I could only hope.

34

Kate

Charlie's hand threaded through mine, and my whole body pressed against his in the limo.

Harrison and Emma whispered to each other across from us. He spoke in a constant low rumble, and she responded with a quick nod or sniff. When she tried to speak up in a high-pitched "But I never—" Harrison's deep and soothing voice cut her off.

I let my head drift onto Charlie's shoulder, and the gentle rocking hum of the car made me drowsy.

Emma finally settled as Harrison pulled her in for a hug. She had her arms crossed, but her head rested on his shoulder. I felt the need to fill the silence of the car, the evening having taken a decidedly somber turn.

"Thank you again for letting me stay with you," I said to Harrison.

"Mi casa etcetera," he said lightly but with tired eyes.

"It's a beautiful home," Emma said and then looked up at him. "You don't stay there much. Such a waste."

"It's a lot of house for one guy," Harrison said, his smile not quite convincing. "Thought it would be filled with kids by now. Alas, I've managed to fill the empty space with all my Oscars."

Emma rolled her eyes but squeezed him tighter. He smiled brightly but it didn't negate the sadness in his eyes. He hid it well. Of the three of them, I'd assumed that he enjoyed fame and fortune the most. But the more I got to know the Intrepid Trio, the more it seemed their picture-perfect celebrity life wasn't all it was cracked up to be. I'd assumed that people whose lives were objectively a success would be the happiest. But it looked as though I had managed to romanticize even the most glamorized life.

This trip was a vacation from the realities of my world, but it wasn't sustainable. I needed to focus on getting published and being taken seriously as a writer. After all this, I would go home to an empty apartment and a stale career, if I wasn't careful.

Charlie lifted my hand to kiss my knuckles as though he read my mind.

"You know, I've only been there a few times, but your house always reminded me of George's." Emma sat up and turned to Harrison. "I can't believe I never told you that before."

"That's why I bought it. Reminded me of our summers at his house," Harrison said. His eyes went hazy with recalled memory.

"George Sedar, the author?" I asked.

"Yes," Harrison said. "All of us went to school on set during filming but during the summer holiday, we'd usually spend at least a few weeks at George's place. He treated us like just another one of his grandkids."

"Do you ever talk to them? The grandkids?" Emma asked Harrison. "You were good friends with one of the girls for a while, weren't you?"

"Not in many years," Harrison said tightly, the fuzziness in his focus sharpening into a glare.

"It's hard to believe those kids are our age. In my mind, they'll always be little," Emma said. "Like those perfect summer weeks have remained exactly the same in my memory."

Harrison cleared his throat and nodded.

"Then again, I hardly feel like I'm thirty-one," Emma said. Her spirits seemed to be lifting with the focus on their shared past.

"I feel the same," Charlie said gruffly. "Where the hell did my twenties go? Don't answer that."

"I'm still twenty-something. If anybody asks," Harrison joked.

"Sure, we definitely didn't all get hired at the same age of eleven," Emma teased.

Harrison shook his head. "Not me. I was ten. Technically."

"Is this your only home?" I asked, keeping the conversation light.

"I have a flat in London too," Harrison said.

"You don't need that posh place. It's tiny," Charlie said. "You know you can stay with me when you're there."

"Your hideaway hole isn't exactly convenient." Emma scoffed.

"The Vicarage," I said quietly, in surprise. I kept having these moments of dawning that RC *was* Charlie. Agata. This was the same man that begrudgingly adopted three awkward preteen chickens. Something clicked. He'd felt bad for the three chickens, older and unwanted anymore. He couldn't let them be separated. I looked up at him, and I was sure my adoration was written all over my face. This sweet, sweet man.

In the low light of the interior, his jaw was even more defined, his features at their most relaxed state. He was with his two best friends, and he was content. I wished this ease all the time for him, especially knowing how much he struggled just to come to California. Just to exist. He was so strong and compassionate and loving. So sensitive and fiercely loyal. So burdened by a past but trying to heal.

I squeezed him tighter.

Charlie smiled down at me, a little confused by my sudden affection. He turned back to the others. "You should all come and stay," he said it casually, so I didn't have time to register my surprise at the offer. But I knew this was important to him. To have his friends around more. Nobody even had time to answer because he quickly added, "Neither of you have met the kids."

"I'm sorry, who?" Emma asked, eyes wide.

"My chickens. Freddy, Adam, and Lucy."

"You have chickens?" Emma asked in shock.

"I'm an uncle?" Harrison asked, eyebrows high in delight.

Was it selfish to be happy to know a detail about his life that not even his best friends knew?

"I have a rooster too. Nugget," Charlie said. "Though he and Agata are still working through their differences."

"Seriously, who the bloody hell is Agata?" Harrison asked, and Emma and Charlie burst out laughing.

Not much later, we pulled up the long driveway to Harrison's absolutely breathtaking mansion tucked away in the Hollywood Hills. It was something out of a movie, or at least afforded by movies. When they said it reminded them of the house from their childhood, I'd expected something cozier. But this was several boxy levels, covered in floor-to-ceiling windows and lit up, warm and welcoming. I hardly remembered seeing the house in its entirety last night. I'd been so completely exhausted, and then we'd rushed to leave earlier. But now, I could fully take it all in.

The inside was just as luxurious. Sleek furniture. Granite and marble. State-of-the-art appliances. It was so far from above any home I'd ever been in. I wanted to ask if I should take off my shoes but that made me feel like a bumpkin. I followed their leads and left mine on. Emma went straight to the open kitchen, setting her clutch on a sleek counter.

From a massive refrigerator I thought was just a cabinet, she grabbed several bottles of Pellegrino and passed them out. I shifted uncomfortably, wishing I could toe out of these shoes. Every single item I could see was the height of luxury. Things I didn't even know could be fancy. The way the cabinets opened and closed. The smell of clean citrus that gently filled the air without overpowering. The perfectly controlled climate. My mother had always been successful. I was lucky to never want for anything growing up. But this was an entirely different level of wealth.

What was I even doing here? It felt like I'd been invited to a party at the cool kid's house, but I felt so out of place I just wanted to call my mom and go home because they were drinking and smoking cigarettes. A panic began to rise in my throat. How would I ever go back to reality?

I didn't want to think about tomorrow.

This magical evening was coming to an end, and I wasn't ready. Especially not on this heavy note.

"Ready for bed?" I asked Charlie.

In my periphery, Harrison and Emma exchanged a look. Charlie swallowed and held out a hand to me.

I gathered my courage. I wanted Charlie. I wanted this night with him. No time like the present. Reality could wait, it was never as fun as fantasy anyway.

Charlie

"This is breathtaking," Kate said.

She stood on the balcony off the bedroom, taking in the

bright lights of the city. R&B softly played over the surround speakers. The pool shimmered below, glowing blue in the darkness.

"I couldn't agree more." Her figure in that emerald-green dress had driven me wild all night. The deep tease of cleavage, the way it flowed over her voluptuous backside. A gentle wind blew her skirt, teasing a hint of upper thigh that my hand had caressed not long ago.

She glanced to me, finding me staring openly at her and not the view. She flushed and tucked her chin. Seemed the naughty vixen from the club had gone back into her shell. She smiled and turned back to the view, rubbing her palms up and down her arms.

I went to stand behind her and held on to the bar of the balcony, engulfing her in my natural heat. She shuddered lightly in the warmth.

"You looked beautiful tonight. You look beautiful all the time," I said, dropping a kiss on her neck. "I said that to you in an email I never sent."

She turned in my embrace and stepped up on tiptoes to wrap her arms around my neck. "Really? How many of these emails have you not sent? I'd like to see them if they're all that complimentary."

"I bet you would." It was another avoidance, another misstep of not answering. I hated it the second I said it.

Her smile fell as a tiny furrow formed between her brows.

"I feel like ..." she started and then shook her head, stopping.

"Talk to me, Kate." I smoothed that furrow before fixing her fringe back in place. She'd seemed distant since we came upstairs. Maybe she felt pressured after our foreplay in the club. Maybe she was tired of me never giving her a bloody straight answer?

She let out a breath. "I'm just feeling so many things.

Thrilled to be here. In shock that it's happening. Afraid for it to be over." She licked her lips and looked up at me hesitantly. "In some ways I feel like I know you intimately. But in other ways, you're a stranger to me. It's giving me whiplash a little."

I rubbed up and down her arms as she spoke. This sweet, complicated woman was supremely out of her element yet had rolled with all the punches. She'd been patient and kind and understanding with me despite all that I'd hidden from her. There was so much I still wanted to share with her, but the ticking clock of our time together was louder than my heartbeat.

"Kate. I know I've held back. But I want ...so much. Too much." I kissed her deeply. She kissed me back, soft and pliant, melting against me. Kate. My Kate, here in my arms. God, I hadn't realized just how bad I wanted this until it was happening. I hadn't even let myself hope this big.

If, in the past, I had used alcohol to numb myself from feeling, then being with Kate was the total opposite. She helped me feel everything. I forgot that living could be like this. I forgot that so many sounds and touches and smells could light me up and make me feel alive. So many years numbing myself. So many years living to avoid any feelings. Kate came into my life and my world exploded with passion and emotion and hope.

I broke the kiss just to look at her. To check that she was real. Watching Emma struggle with her feelings with Wesley tonight was another reminder to be thankful for what I had here and now.

She frowned in worry, and I feared my features were a little too intense.

"What is it?" she asked.

"Everything I said at the club is true. I-I've thought about you for so long. I dreamed about us for years." My voice caught as I spoke.

"Why didn't you tell me who you were sooner?" She lightly rubbed the back of my head.

I had changed over the last two years getting to know her. The complications of my fears didn't matter as much as the truth of her in my arms. It all boiled down to one thing.

"Scared," I said.

"I am too," she breathed.

It hardly seemed possible. Before I even knew her, she was bold and brave. She came to LA with no experience and absolutely excelled.

"You make me brave," I said. I put my hands on her full bottom and lifted her. I loved how the satin of her dress felt over the perfect roundness in my grip. She squealed and wrapped her legs around my waist.

"I do?"

"You're incredible." I carried her to the nearby bar top, resting there, so we were face-to-face.

"I don't feel that way. I feel very ordinary. I don't know where to go from here. I don't know how I'm supposed to go back to my simple life after this. Being published has been my dream for so long and now it feels closer than ever." She rubbed her thumbs into my shoulders, looking up at me tentatively. "And being here with you is more amazing than I ever let myself imagine."

"Kate," I said like an exhale.

My forehead dropped to hers.

"And as you know, I have a very vivid imagination," she finished.

Don't go.

Stay with me.

We can stay here in this moment forever.

But even as I thought about it, I didn't want it. I wanted her, but not this city or this imaginary break from real life.

"I want you to have everything you've ever dreamed of," I settled on.

"I'm not even sure what that is anymore." Her gaze moved over my face. "We don't have to worry about any of that tonight. There are so many other things we could be doing."

I exhaled sharply, trying to keep my composure. "We don't have to do anything."

"I think two years is plenty of time to decide I want this, thank you very much." She pressed a closed-mouth kiss to me. "Let's not waste the time we have. Plus, I'm dying to get out of this dress."

I groaned.

The time we had. This would end. After which, we'd go thousands of miles in different directions.

I let out a slow and shaky breath before I cupped the back of her head and brought her mouth to mine. I kissed her deeply until she melted into me. Until that tension was gone, and she pressed herself against me like she had in the club.

I broke our kiss to stare into her eyes. "Let's go to bed," I said.

She swallowed but let me help her hop down from the bar. She walked backward into the massive bedroom, never taking her eyes from me.

"This isn't going to be quick." I prowled toward her.

"Oh, no. My schedule is so packed," she said dryly.

"I've been fantasizing about this night for years. You're not getting any sleep."

She smirked and walked backward until her knees hit the bed, and she sat down on the edge. "You say that like a threat," she said with a breathy tremor to her voice.

"It's a promise."

35

Kate

Charlie walked away.

In the movie of my mind, sound effect tires screeched to a halt. *I'm sorry. What?*

"You're going the wrong direction," I said as he retreated to his closet to dig around in a drawer. There was no possible way I misread this situation.

"This is just the start of my plan," he said. He came back out and tossed a soft flannel shirt at me. "Here. Put that on."

I blinked. "Charlie, I thought less clothing was preferable here?"

He shook his head and turned around, holding his phone up with a goofy, excited smile.

"Uh," I said. "Listen, I'm pretty open-minded in the bedroom but with your fame, maybe pictures ..."

The bed shook with his return. He leaned over and put a finger over my mouth. "Kate. Trust me."

"Fine. But I'm changing in the bathroom."

He scowled.

"The first time you see me naked will not be changing into your pajamas, for crying out loud." I grabbed his top and stomped off to change quickly in the bathroom, grumbling to myself the whole time.

I was still cranky when I came back to stand by the bed.

"Don't be mad. Though you are quite cute when you jut that bottom lip out." He handed me the glasses I'd taken off while removing the tape from my boobs earlier. Boy, I thought this night would go very differently. I might need to sharpen my seduction skills.

I took my glasses and frowned in question.

Charlie climbed on the bed and leaned back against the headboard. His gaze lingered over my exposed legs. Freshly shaven for no reason, *apparently*. "Nuh-uh," I said and leaned down to cover my legs. "Don't even think about it now. You don't get to see me naked before I get a seductive strip tease out of you now. And it will be good; straight out of my fantasies."

He raised an eyebrow. "I always did love your imagination." He grinned with a shake of his head before he lifted an arm and gestured for me. "But for now, come here."

I blinked up at him. I'd really thought ...

"Come *here*," he repeated with a smile.

"When you said you were going to keep me up all night, I'm gonna be honest, I had something else in mind."

Begrudgingly, I did as told and scooted closer until my head rested on his chest. He wrapped me up, holding the phone where we could both see it.

He rumbled a deep "Hmm."

"What are you doing?" I asked.

At that exact moment, his phone lit up with an incoming call from "Tiny Polish Terror." I snorted, rather unladylike. Charlie's eyes widened in abject horror. "That was not part of the plan. It's

Agata," he said. "I have to get this." For all his huffing and puffing, Charlie clearly loved her.

I grinned at his tenderness for the woman and said, "Of course." At the same time, I pulled the covers up to hide, suddenly feeling very shy.

"What time is it there?" I asked from under the blanket. It was after two a.m. in LA.

"Morning. She's probably up feeding the chickens. She knows I'm always awake. Are—are you hiding?"

"No," I said. From my hiding place.

"Get out here. I want her to meet you." He pushed the blanket down as he answered the call.

My fuzzy head appeared in the corner of the screen, and I tried to pull away, but he tugged me right back in view. The only thing visible on our end was what I thought might be a shoulder? Maybe a chin? The phone shook so much it was hard to tell.

"Your cock is out of control," a woman's accented voice yelled.

"I assure you, it is not," Charlie said, with a glance to the blankets. "Though it's quite grumpy about it."

"Charlie!" I hissed.

He laughed. "Agata, love. We've talked about this. You have to move the camera up."

The hissy static of a shuffling phone was combined with quiet murmurs in a language I didn't understand. "Ugh, why you want to see this old face anyway?"

"You're the light of my life, Agata. I need to see you." Charlie, the dirty flirt.

"Oh, I see Mister Charlie is in a good mood. Mister funny man, haha." Agata frowned at the screen and then moved so close to the camera only the top of a white-blond eyebrow and forehead were visible. She gasped. "Pretty American?"

I tried to slide away and back under the covers, but Charlie held firm. "The prettiest," he confirmed. "This is Kate."

I cleared my throat. "Hi Mrs.—" and then froze, realizing I didn't know her full name.

"Wisniewski," Charlie whispered.

"Hi, Mrs. Wisniewski," I finished.

"You call me Agata. Oh, look at those big, beautiful eyes. Much prettier in person. Well, through screen. Good job, Charlie. Good boy. He woo?" In the camera, the splotch of red spread up my neck as she spoke my praises.

"I'm trying to woo, Agata," Charlie grumbled. "You're cock-blocking. Oof."

I elbowed him lightly. Well, I meant it to be lightly.

"I've never seen the woman gush so much in my life," Charlie mumbled.

I ignored him but said to Agata, "He woo."

"Good boy, Charlie."

He bent and kissed the top of my head. "I want you to meet the kids," he said to me.

"So soon?" With a hand to my chest, I did my best Jane Austen heroine impression. "What will they think of our compromising position, Duke of Chickenston?"

His eyes darkened and narrowed, but he didn't seem annoyed. "Let's circle back to that duke business later." Louder, he said, "Agata, put the kids on."

"Yeah, yeah, I go."

The next shot shakily showed three brownish-ginger hens fluffed up and quietly sitting in a wooden cubby surrounded by straw. Wait. Two hens and one hen butt.

"Ugh. Freddy, dear, you've got yourself turned around again," Charlie said with patient fondness.

I chuckled and saw Charlie looking adoringly at the screen.

Look at us, two cozy lovebirds video chatting with a bunch of chickens and a cranky housekeeper across the world.

"Ah!" Agata squealed, followed by a flurry of camera shaking, flying feathers, and squawks. The phone blurred before a loud thump and the movement on screen went still. A tilted view showed the retreating form of a screaming Agata running away at full speed. Little woman could move. A big black and brown rooster had its plumage fully puffed up, wings extended as it chased after the poor housekeeper.

"Nugget!" Charlie yelled at the rooster. "Not nice."

The rooster quickly gave up his chase and came back to the henhouse, where we still sat propped on the straw floor.

"Bad Nug!" Charlie yelled.

Rooster legs crossed in front of the phone.

"That wasn't very nice, Nugget," I said sweetly.

A red-eyed bird face popped up suddenly in front of the camera, filling the whole screen.

"Christ," Charlie jumped.

"Hello, handsome," I cooed.

Charlie frowned, glaring at the screen.

"I know you're just trying to protect your ladies, but you can't scare Agata like that. She feeds you, don't forget." I kept my voice soft and crooning as he tilted his head side to side in rapid movements, as though listening. "You're a good boy," I soothed.

"Christ, what are you doing to my cock?" Charlie groaned.

"You're just misunderstood, aren't you," I said, ignoring Charlie, though quite enjoying how "cock" sounded in his rich accent.

Nugget's feathers smoothed back down, and he pecked at the screen. "Good boy," I repeated more softly.

"My god, woman, you've made him love you."

"He's a good boy," I said.

Charlie ended the call. I blinked at him. "Why'd you do that? We were talking." I crossed my arms.

"I'm not about to become cuckolded by my own bloody cock." He lunged at me and kissed my neck until I was lost in a fit of giggles.

When the laughter stopped, we were kissing again. His heavy form weighing me down, making me feel so good. I arched against his hard length and moaned.

"Charlie," I whined.

He broke the kiss and pressed his forehead to mine, looking deep into my eyes. "Christ, I love hearing you say my name like that." He rubbed his hips into me. And I groaned at how hard he was. "But we aren't done yet. I really did have something I want to show you."

He sat back and pulled me to lean against him again. I huffed out a long breath and told my body to calm down.

He navigated to a folder in his photo albums that read *For Kate.*

"I had planned on telling you everything earlier. A long time ago." He shook his head and ended the train of thought. "There was so much to show you. Eventually, I'd hoped ... maybe one day." His eyes closed and he took a deep breath. "I've been taking pictures to show you."

I gasped softly as he scrolled to the very top of the album.

"I know if feels like I haven't told you everything, but I really do live a simple life. I just left out some of the details. You do know me better than everybody."

I smiled up at him.

"But. I still have some things I want to show you." He clicked to enlarge the first one. It was a modestly large brown brick country home complete with climbing vines and a turret. It was too big to be called a quaint little cottage and it was gorgeous. I gasped.

"That's the Vicarage?" I asked.

He nodded. "Just there, behind that little building—that's Agata's cottage by the way—is where I built the chicken coop you just got to experience."

"I can't believe it," I said.

He continued to the next picture.

"This is when you first walk in the front door. This whole floor needs loads of work," he said.

He continued on like that, picture after picture of each room. I adored every word from his mouth. My greedy eyes drank up every detail.

"It's all so beautiful," I said.

"It is. I love it," he said. "This is the kitchen. Agata doesn't let me in here much, but if I have tea with her, it's at this little table."

I nodded. My throat felt too tight to talk. I could picture it all so clearly now. All his daily routines were no longer a mystery.

"The kitchen needs the most renovating. All the appliances are ancient. I hear about the 'tiny fridge from Cold War' on a daily basis." I laughed at his attempt at a Polish accent.

He kissed my forehead and kept scrolling through, one photo after another, and all the missing pieces of him came together to form a clear picture.

"I can't wait to see the afters," I said. "When are you starting on the renovations?"

He frowned. "I'm not sure. I was just waiting to feel settled. Until I felt ready or ..." His gaze moved over my face. Sadness passed over his features before he quickly schooled them.

"What?"

"Nothing." He swiped to the next picture. "I love this room. You w—" He stopped abruptly. My heart skipped. I was desperate to know what he had been about to say, why was he still filtering his thoughts. But I knew this was a huge step for him and I wouldn't push. He cleared his throat, and there was a slight shake to his voice when he continued. "It would make a great office. There's a little fireplace and look here." He zoomed in on the next picture. "This is the view from that room. Look. You can see the sheep from the farm over the hill. That's Farmer John's land."

Tiny dots speckled rolling green hills. It was breathtakingly beautiful and picturesque. This was his home. This was his life. Longing tugged at my heart. I could almost envision myself curled up on a chair reading ...

"I love the sheep," he went on, "but I will be honest, on very warm days, if the wind blows just right, we have to close up the window because sheep are smelly little buggers."

I cackled and discreetly wiped a tear away. I had no idea why I was so emotional looking at these pictures. I longed for something I couldn't let it dream of. I saw myself writing in that office. I felt the warm breeze blow in through the window to ruffle my hair. It was such a detailed fantasy it felt more like a memory.

I couldn't even give that daydream the slightest bit of hope. This was the ultimate fantasy my little brain would latch on to and spin into something that would only ultimately break my heart.

"These pictures are less fun." He cleared his throat. "From the funeral. Ah, this was the private jet Emma and I took. I thought maybe you'd like to see it. I don't normally, uh, fly that way if I have to travel but it was last minute and everything." He scrolled through pictures of a luxurious plane and Emma smiling sadly at the camera. The next was a picture of him and his two best friends, away from everyone else, heads bents as they held on to each other. A tiny huddle of comfort. It caused another blur in my vision.

"There's not a lot from that trip," he said gruffly.

I hugged him so tightly that my arms shook. "God, I wish I could have been there with you."

His chest hitched before he said softly, "You were in some ways."

He sniffed and continued through a few more people I didn't recognize, and then he was back home and more pictures of his chickens.

"Lots of chicken pictures, Duke Chickenston," I teased lightly.

"I'm a proud papa," he said. "Look at those beautiful eggs they lay. Every day. It's impressive." He pointed to a basket of speckled eggs.

"Aw, is that sweet Freddy?" I asked when he stopped on a picture where a chicken was stuck in a crust of bread.

He nodded and kept swiping. "Sweet, little idiot."

Any disappointment I felt before I joined him in bed was long gone. Sex would have been amazing, but this was so much more special. This was making love in an entirely more intimate way. My chest tightened with overwhelming emotion.

As he swiped through one picture, I jumped. "Wait, go back!"

"I sent this one. Remember?"

"No, I know." I laughed and grabbed the phone from him. "But look. Did you know this when you sent it?" I zoomed in to show his chest in the reflection that had sent me spiraling.

Based on how the color drained from his face, he had no idea he'd done that. "Bloody hell," he whispered. "I swear I didn't know."

I handed his phone back and grinned. "I know. Man, Pete lost his mind over that one." I rolled my eyes.

"Did he see?" His face hardened.

"No. I found it later when I was studying it."

"Liked that, did ya?" Features softening, he chuckled warmly.

I hid my face into his chest and groaned. "I may have pulled it up from time to time."

"Oh really?" He was grinning cockily when I sat back to look at him.

He needed to know what it meant that he shared himself with me. I grabbed his warm hands in mine, setting down the phone momentarily.

"It's all so wonderful," I said. "Thank you."

"You're welcome." His throat moved on a thick swallow.

I lay back on my new favorite pillow in the world, his chest, with a contented sigh.

"Kate?" he asked. "I want you to come see it." His deep voice against my ear was a caress. His heart thumped against my cheek, and I felt him shift slightly to look at me.

"I want you to meet the kids and Agata. I—would you like that?" he asked, and his voice wobbled.

It was as though I'd stepped into a pool of sunshine on the first warm spring day.

I squeezed him so tightly that my body shook. "I can't wait."

TO: KateDubois@geemail.com
FROM: TheRealFreddyStan4Life@geemail.com
SUBJECT: Good night
Kate,

I have a confession. The most gorgeous woman just fell asleep in my arms. I hope that doesn't make you jealous. I had plans to let her seduce me, but my captivating conversation lulled her to sleep. What can I say? I'm a real Casanova.

I'm afraid to move, lest I disturb her. I'm still in the clothes I wore last night, don't worry.

Kate. You're here. I cannot believe I'm really holding you.

I'm sorry I didn't tell you everything sooner. Listening to you sleep is the most soothing sound I've ever heard. To think, if I hadn't been so scared, we could have ...

No matter that. We are here now. I'm glad I finally shared with you. I'm thankful for this time together. I'm sorry I waited this long.

Love,

Charlie. The *real* real Charlie.

PS: You just rubbed your sweet body up against mine. I better go to sleep before my hands start wandering ...

Charlie

KATE WAS WRAPPED AROUND MY CHEST, AND I DIDN'T HAVE TO leave. I could lie with her all night and watch her sleep. In a very normal, non-creepy way. I pulled off her glasses and set them on the side table, smoothing back the hair that snagged when I tugged them off.

She was so beautiful. The smooth line of her jaw leading down to her neck to a bare shoulder my oversized shirt had exposed. Her thick lashes and dark freckles. Her chest rising and falling in sleep. She trusted me enough to let me be this close to her.

Sharing those pictures slid in some final missing piece in my heart. I was deeply in love with Kate. I'd denied the truth to myself for far too long.

I wanted her to know everything about my sad little life. I had finally shared everything with her, and she'd been in awe as if the details were special to her.

How could I go back to Devon without her? There was

nothing else for me. I almost slipped up and said that I imagined that upstairs room as her writing office. I wasn't even sure how long I'd been imaging her in my life. Since our lunch together? Since our email exchanges started? My love for her felt brand new but also destined. Just started yet infinite. I was a fool to have lied to myself for so long. Why would I have saved all these photos to share with her if I hadn't already understood that on a core level?

She said she wanted the cozy cottage life. She would fit in perfectly. She said she wanted to visit but that wouldn't be enough.

At some point, I fell asleep because I woke up heated and hard. Fuzzy and not fully conscious, I couldn't help how my body reached for her even in sleep. I had pulled her back to my chest, and my free hand lay heavy on her hip even as she arched into my hard prick. I traced up and down her beautiful waist, down to her thigh, moving aside my shirt, and brushing her knickers. Tiny goose bumps formed on her skin under my palms. My eyes were still closed, so I could sense that the room was no longer completely dark, but I had no idea how early or late it was.

She sighed softly.

"Is this okay?" I asked, stilling my hand against her stomach.

"Yes," she breathed out. I nudged her ear with my nose, moving her hair to pepper soft kisses over her neck. She smelled delicious all warmed up with sleep.

She grabbed my hand and slid it under my shirt to her breast directing me to squeeze her. I grinned at her eagerness, gently rolling her nipple and coaxing moans out of her. My hand was large enough that I could reach around and hold both of her tits. I squeezed her whole body tight to mine, loving that every inch of her was touching me. I wanted to hold her tight to me, engulf her. She moaned, pressing herself even harder against my cock.

I finally blinked open my eyes to find the room was filled with soft morning light even though the clock told me it was barely past six a.m. We'd hardly slept. Kate quickly shimmied out of her knickers and snapped to sit upright. She pulled off her top and tossed it to the corner. She sat on her knees, unabashedly exposing herself to me.

She was glorious. My eyes couldn't decide where to look first. "Charlie?"

Her pert breasts were at attention, little pink nipples pebbled. Her gorgeous full hips curved wide with silken skin begging to be lavished. Christ, that arse. Even from this angle, it was mouthwatering. I wanted to flip her around and bury my face …

"Charlie!" She threw a pillow at me.

I shook my head. "Sorry. I think I blacked out." I reached out for her, bulging painfully hard against the dress trousers I still wore. "Not that I'm complaining, but what happened to a seductive strip tease first?" I asked.

"I can't risk it. No more interruptions. No more old friends popping up. Or intimidating mother figures calling."

"Or cockblockers," I added helpfully, still taking in the glorious view, arms extended to her, fingers grasping in the empty air.

She laughed. "Ugh. Yes. I'm morning horny and I need you now." She threw herself on top of me and wrapped her arms around my head so that one breast rubbed against my chin. I lost all conscious thought as I sucked her.

"Oh god, yes." She sighed.

I popped her out of my mouth to ask, "Morning horny?"

"You know, peak horny time. The evenings I'm too tired.

Midday I'm too busy. But mornings, I am full speed ahead, bright-eyed and bushy-tailed."

"I can see that." I sucked her other nipple and she moaned louder. I pulled back again, and she grumbled in annoyance. "What about last night? That was very late. And if I recall, you were very, very wet," I said in my deepest growl, remembering her slickness.

She shivered against me. "Good point. We might have to run some experiments."

"Different times of day," I agreed.

"Different positions."

I groaned and dropped my head between her breasts. "Christ, Kate. I have two years of fantasies built up. We will have plenty of data to sort through." I massaged her full bottom as I rubbed my head between her breasts.

"Thankfully, I'm a whiz with spreadsheets." I laughed as she gently pushed at my shoulders. "Stand up," she demanded.

I did as she asked, next to the bed.

She crawled on her knees toward me, and I miraculously managed not to grab her. I kept my hands fisted at my side, letting her do whatever she wanted.

Very, very slowly, she unbuttoned my shirt, focused thoroughly on her work. It took all my power to keep still. But she was a natural leader, it seemed.

"I could get used to being manhandled by a beautiful naked woman," I said.

"Just the one, I hope," she said lightly but ducked her head as her warm, delicate hands pushed the shirt off my shoulders before tossing it to join her own.

"Just the one," I agreed when she met my gaze.

Those same hands took their time running down my neck, and she arched up to bite a tendon in my neck.

"I love your neck," she said.

Her hands smoothed along my shoulders and down my chest.

"And all this," she went on. "You're beautiful."

I sucked in a breath as she brushed over my nipples. She looked up at me like a scientist notating a subject's reaction to stimulus.

"Is this for—the spreadsheet?" I asked roughly.

She raised an eyebrow. "Precisely. I don't see so well without my glasses, you know. I don't want to miss a single detail." She brushed a nipple again and I inhaled sharply. "Interesting."

"I'll get my revenge," I said.

She bent forward and gently kissed one pec and then the other, a tongue flicking over my hard nipple. I groaned.

"Oh. No. Whatever will I do?" Her hands continued to explore my abdomen. My core muscles flexed under her touch, slightly ticklish.

She scooted off the bed to walk behind me, exploring my shoulders and the muscles of my spine. She wrapped me in a hug from behind. Her warm, soft breasts pressed into me, and her breath brushed between my shoulder blades.

Still behind me, she reached around and brushed the top button of my trousers, and I flexed hard, a flood of heat rushing to my cock. I had never in all my life been so rock hard. I had never been explored like this. It was incredibly erotic but also felt tender and loving. Fuck, if I didn't feel cherished.

So long I had wanted her. So many nights I had fantasized about this exact moment.

"The way you touch me," I said on a gasp as her hands brushed over my bulge.

"There wasn't a day that I didn't think about you. Or wonder what you were up to." She shoved my trousers down. "My day wouldn't feel complete until I shared it with you."

I swallowed, emotion tightening my throat. "You consumed

my thoughts all the time," I said as she walked back to stand in front of me. "I couldn't wait to share the smallest detail of my day with you. You've been my go-to for so long." I cupped her cheek, and she leaned into my hand, closing her eyes for a moment. We stood almost completely exposed, and while our hands wouldn't stop reaching for each other, our gazes remained locked.

"Go-to?" she asked.

"The person in my life that I 'go-to' for the dumb shit. When I hear a really corny joke or Freddy gets stuck in a tree again. You know all those little details about my life so all I needed to do was just send one word and you'd get it," I explained. It didn't even scratch the surface of my feelings for her, but I hoped it conveyed what I meant.

"You're my go-to too." She shook her head. "Even when I was with—"

I growled.

"Sorry. Not a great time to bring him up, but that was probably a good indication that my heart wasn't fully invested with him."

I swallowed with difficulty. Her hand rested on my chest, and it was as though my heart tried to beat into her palm. "Your heart is invested now?" I asked on a whisper.

Her dark eyes held mine. "So completely, yes."

I let out a long shaking breath.

Could lovemaking be like this? Funny yet serious? Gentle and vulnerable?

She watched me closely, and I saw the moment she shifted from tenderness to desire. "There is still much of you I'd like to learn." I bulged obscenely from my briefs in case she had any doubts about how badly I wanted her. Her gaze remained locked on mine as she freed me, gauging my reaction as her soft hand ran the length of me, testing.

I mumbled something incoherent. I couldn't keep my hands patient anymore. I grabbed her bottom, squeezing roughly. Loving how she overfilled my palms. Christ, it was like she was custom-made for my deepest desires.

Then she dropped to her knees to continue her exploration. How could I be this lucky? How could any man deserve the attention she lavished me with? She scratched her nails up the back of my calves. She gripped my thighs. Squeezed tightly.

"I never knew I could like thighs this much. So strong," she murmured.

Her sweet exploration continued higher until, finally, she used both hands to stroke down my length. My cock jolted in her grip.

I threw back my head and groaned. She licked her way up, taking her time every single step of the way. I might need to sit down. I was going to fall over.

"Christ, Kate." My hands went for her hair. They twisted in her short locks as she grabbed my backside and took me fully in her mouth.

"Kate—I can't." I made the mistake of looking down at her as she worked me. Eyes watching me, hooded with desire, cheeks hallowing with suction, full lips gripping. "Ahh," I yelled and just barely stopped myself from coming without any warning.

I pulled back from her, popping out of her mouth audibly. Her eyes watered but she had a smug smirk on her face.

I was distantly aware that my chest was heaving uncontrollably, but she was just as gone. Her sweet lips were swollen and gleaming. Her chest flushed red as she sat back on her knees, panting. Her eyes wide and dark as they devoured every inch of me.

"My turn." I helped her to stand, wrapped my arm around her waist, and tumbled us into bed.

I brought her up to fit against me, positioned just as we were when we had awoken, her bottom to my hips. She slung one leg over my thigh, exposing more of herself. My hand lowered to tease her as she wiggled against me. My cock slid between her hot thighs.

I hissed out a breath. She was already so warm and wet. I could so easily slip into her and fuck her like this. Instead, I shifted us so I could lay her on her back. I spread her legs wide and laid on top of her. We kissed until she was gasping. Our bodies moved against each other like I was already inside her. I was close to coming again just from this hot, messy snogging.

I broke the kiss and lowered to hover on my forearms above her breasts. I licked one nipple and looked up at her. "Is this okay?"

Her brows knitted. "Yes." She'd barely gotten the word out and I took a nipple into my mouth. I sucked gently and palmed the other. She gasped and said, "Stop."

I froze, and every muscle of my body tensed. She leaned over with an "oomph" and reached for her glasses on the side table. She pushed them on and blew her fringe out of her face. "Okay. Continue."

I smiled and went about my work, splitting my efforts fairly between her breasts. Sweat prickled my back as I moved lower, continuing my kisses over her sweet soft abdomen. "Is this okay?" I asked, panting.

"Yes."

My hands roamed over her sides and hips. I growled and flipped her over onto her stomach. "Is this okay?"

"Uh, yes?" Her voice was as shaky as my body. Thank the lord I worked out so much. I was basically planking over her as I kissed between her shoulder blades and down her damp spine. She wiggled and shifted restlessly.

I sat up only to study her perfect backside. I loved her dainty shoulders that curved into her tight waist and gave way to that amazing bum. I tongued down her spine, tasting her sweet and salty skin.

I tugged her hips up to bring her onto her hands and knees. "Is this okay?"

"Yes," she whispered, a little shy.

I wanted to take her like this. I could so easily slip into her and fuck her into the bed, and I bet she would love every fucking second of it.

I would get there, but first ...

I pushed up and off the bed, to kneel on the floor next to it, and pulled her arched body toward me. On her hands and knees at my eye level, her most intimate parts on full gleaming display. My new favorite view in the entire universe. I kissed her full hips and ass. I bit gently on the ample flesh, and she gasped out. I continued to the area I wanted to explore the most, already swollen and ready with want. I blew out a soft stream of air before I repeated, "Is this okay?"

"Charlie." She growled out my name. "Just assume everything is a yes. From here out. I will tell you if it's not okay." She was half wild, her hands gripped the pillows, and her hips canted impatiently.

I chuckled and kissed her inner thighs to taunt her with touches as she had done to me. She lowered to her elbows, angling not so subtly for what we both wanted. Finally, I let myself taste her. A long, slow lick. We both groaned. She was delicious, and I was anxious to devour her, but I wanted her begging for it. I moved back again to brush my lips over her arse and nip at the sensitive skin where it met her thighs. She canted her hips up and whined.

"Shh," I said patiently. This wasn't an easy angle, but worth the payoff. I went back to lick down her soaking lips and flicked her clit again before retreating. I watched as she clenched at the air, desperate for more. I retreated again to massage her hips and thighs and lower back, occasionally brushing the most sensitive areas lightly.

"Charlie," she groaned.

Finally, I put her out of her misery. I quickly flipped her over, eliciting a shocked squeak from her, and put her thighs on my shoulders. It was fun to enjoy her juicy arse from her previous position, but it was time to get down to business.

I delved back into her sweet cunt without warning. Her gasp of surprise melted into a moan. I kissed and licked and devoured her. My hands continued to massage her full ass as her legs squeezed my head. She writhed out of control, slick with sweat and arousal. I whispered praises to her in between breaths. My whole body shook with exertion, but I had zero complaints. I inserted a curved finger and then another while she bucked, driving her even closer to the edge. Sweat covered my shaking body. I'd never wanted to make anybody come so hard. I sucked her clit into my mouth, tongue undulating as my fingers worked. She was all but crying out, feet digging into my back. Christ, I hoped she left bruises. I would wear them like bloody medals of honor. I didn't relent until her entire body tensed and she screamed out my name.

She collapsed back, legs and arms sprawled. "Bloody hell," she said in what I think was an attempt at a British accent.

I laughed as I came to her side on the bed. My muscles ached but I felt like a god.

"I've never—not like that—I didn't think I could. Was that first part, uh, from behind, a British thing?" she asked.

"Hmm." I kissed her shoulders and neck. "I must admit to a slight obsession with your backside."

"I think we can be amenable to that request," she said primly.

"Is that the 'royal we'?" I asked and she giggled.

"God save the queen," she said on a satisfied sigh.

I wrapped myself around her, knowing I was probably bruising her hip with how achingly hard I was.

She turned to me; her face close to mine. "Is this okay?" she asked with a teasing eyebrow and then kissed me.

I had been so wrong about my feelings for her. She was all I needed. I couldn't let anything take her away from me. I couldn't go another two years without touching her. I wouldn't manage a single day after this. How could I ever get enough of Kate?

————

Kate

MY HAND LOWERED TO GRASP HIS COCK. HE WAS HOT AND SO HARD when I squeezed, the flesh hardly gave at all. I rubbed my thumb over the tip, smearing precum.

He hissed.

"Is this okay?" I asked and stroked him slowly before cupping him below and gently teasing his balls.

"Let's just ... assume ..." He couldn't even finish mimicking my previous words because I moved my hand back to this shaft and stroked him faster. His eyes rolled back and he forgot what he was trying to say.

"Just wanted to be sure." I grinned as I moved on top of him. I continued to stroke as I straddled him. My other hand pulled out a condom from the drawer I tucked away earlier.

"Kate, we really don't have to—"

"Let's pretend you went through all your arguments on why we should wait, and I won." Then I stilled. "Unless you don't want to of course, that sounded a little ..."

His hips pivoted up. "I want to. Christ, yes. You won all arguments. The defense rests."

"No rest for the wicked," I said and shifted above him as he got the condom on. Watching him roll it on the incredible length of him made me shudder and clench in anticipation. He was so large and hard, but I had no doubt we would fit together just fine.

I leaned forward, bracing a hand on the headboard as I helped guide him.

"Ready?" he asked when he was just barely nudged at my entrance. His whole body was strained, the strong muscles of his neck and shoulders pulled tight.

I was more than ready. My body already tightened in anticipation to feel him deep within me. I didn't think I would be able to come again, but then, I would have never thought I could enjoy being eaten out from behind either. Or finger-banged in a club with people nearby. Miraculous orgasming, not just in fiction anymore. They really did exist, care of one Charlie Downing.

Now it was my turn to relieve some of this poor man's tension.

I answered by slowly lowering onto him. It was a long and luxurious journey. I dropped my forehead to his, and we clasped hands, sharing breaths and unbroken eye contact. When we were fully connected, we both sighed in breathy relief.

"You're amazing. You feel—" He threw his head back and rocked up with a grunt.

We released hands so I could run my nails down his chest and clench around him. He gripped my ass again. He really was quite partial to it.

Without warning, Charlie flipped me onto my back and began pumping into me. God, the feel of him using me. His hard body covering every inch of me. His strength and patience.

I laughed without meaning to, my head shaking side to side. He opened his eyes to study me, slightly worried. His muscles were rigid as he hesitated.

"This is funny?" he asked.

"No. I'm sorry. I'm just—This is so good." I arched up and groaned. "I think I'm punch-drunk on orgasms. But I really think I could come again."

He laughed and dropped his head to my shoulder. "Okay. Good." He ground out, intensely focused, "I can be amenable to that request." He glided almost all the way out just to snap back in, and we gasped. He gripped the headboard, strong biceps and triceps, all the 'ceps, taut with raw strength. He thrust into me faster and faster, abs flexing in waves as his body worked so hard. My ankles hooked around his back, sliding as they tried to hang on to those rock-hard, glistening muscles. Every single inch of this man was magnificent.

"This is unreal," I gasped out. "I'm so close."

His free hand slid down my chest, squeezing my breast before lowering to caress my clit.

Stars exploded behind my eyes. I stopped breathing, mouth open in a silent scream. He stopped rocking to let me pulse the rest of my orgasm on him. When I finally came back to my body, I sucked in a breath. I brought my hands to my sweaty hairline.

"I feel like I might cry." My lips trembled. "Oh my god, I really think I am crying." Then I started to laugh. "Now, I'm laughing. You broke me."

He moved again. "Kate," he rasped. The headboard creaked under his hand, and his body was coiled so tight bullets would bounce off him.

I stopped laughing. I brought him closer to me and rubbed his face tenderly.

He never broke eye contact as he set his pace for the final sprint to the end. We were lost to each other. To the sensation of being fully connected. Moments later, he took his turn and pulsed into me with a guttural shout.

Eventually, after several more slow pumps, he pulled out and collapsed next to me.

"I really didn't think I was going to last," he said, staring at the ceiling.

I turned on my side to watch him pant. I was hot and tender and in some euphoric state.

"Miraculous orgasming," I said, patting his chest once before I, too, collapsed back.

38

Charlie

I don't know when we fell back asleep, but we were rudely awakened by intense knocking at the door.

Kate and I both sat up and blinked dazedly at each other. What time was it? What day was it?

I'd passed out harder than ever after our life-altering sex. We'd barely cleaned up and made it back under the covers before sleep took us.

The knocking came again, more urgently. "Hey, guys, I'm really sorry to bother you, but you need to get up so we can talk," Emma said.

Kate looked at me worriedly. I squeezed her hand. "It will be okay," I said quietly. Louder, I called out, "Yeah. Hang on."

Kate and I quickly got dressed in a half-asleep rush. I told Kate it would be okay, but from Emma's tone, whatever she was here to discuss wouldn't be good. Things had been too perfect. For one glorious night, I had been with my two closest friends and the woman who meant everything to me. I knew from experience this was when life would find a way to ruin everything.

With effort, I caught the spiraling thoughts as best I could. *Be here and now*. I didn't know anything yet.

When Kate and I were decent, I opened the door to Harrison and Emma, both looking miserable.

"We waited as long as we could," Emma said, hands fidgeting on her phone.

"We didn't want to, uh, interrupt what sounded like the glorious union of two nations. Oomph." Emma elbowed Harrison as he spoke.

"Sally is blowing our phones up," Emma explained. "As are our agents and publicists."

Kate appeared at my side. She handed me my phone and was opening hers already. I had countless missed calls and texts.

"Christ. What is it?" My stomach cramped with the desire to numb whatever bad feelings were about to overwhelm me.

Kate grabbed my hand. "It's going to be okay," she said. "Whatever it is. There're no more secrets."

I nodded at her, but I couldn't shake the feeling that the carpet was about to be ripped out from underneath us.

"The internet discovered Kate's writing in connection to you. Her personal life is all over the internet," Emma explained.

Kate took in a sharp breath as my blood pressure skyrocketed.

"There are pictures of us leaving the club and I'm crying. They're making up all sorts of shite," Emma said in a rush. "Obviously, I don't care about me but ..." She looked at Kate with concern.

Harrison said, "There's video from the recording that was leaked. You admitting you knew her before. That you read her fan fiction and contacted her." His face was drawn and pale. "I'm bloody sorry, mate. I fucked it all up by blabbing."

I felt the floor fall out from under me. Or maybe *that* was the rug being pulled out.

"It's okay, Harrison. Honestly, they were bound to find out." Kate patted his hand, and he shook his head and flicked a worried look to me.

I saw red. "I bloody knew it. I knew someone on that set was fucking leaking to the press. Christ, it's probably Sally." I went back into the room to grab my phone to call her and spun back around when I realized I was still holding it.

"It's okay, Charlie—" Kate said.

"I'm going down there. They can't get away with this." I was furious. I couldn't even hear what the others were saying.

Emma was scrolling through her phone. "Honestly, it's not all bad. A lot of people think it's romantic. I mean it is a pretty sweet story when you think about it."

"Our lives are none of their bloody business," I snapped.

The other three flinched. "Sorry. I didn't mean to yell. I'm just—" I balled my fists, my phone digging into my palm, and then relaxed them with a slow breath. "I warned you she was up to some shite. I'm going down there to talk to her right now."

"Okay. Okay. Listen. Look at me. Take a breath." I followed Kate's instructions. "We'll go down there together, okay?" Kate put her hands on my face until I calmed down enough to focus on her.

"Yeah. Okay." I sniffed.

"We're coming too. I don't even know what's going on with shooting anyway, we were supposed to wrap yesterday," Emma said.

Harrison shoved his hands deep into his pockets. He kept flicking worried looks at me.

"Look, Harrison, I'm not mad at you. This isn't your fault. I just fucking knew. Nothing in this industry is real. It all gets tainted," I said, trying to keep my voice level.

Harrison chewed his lip and nodded but still looked morose.

I'd have to deal with him later, I couldn't worry about everything right now.

Kate stopped me again and put her hand on my chest. Only a little bit ago, those hands were providing me pleasure like I had never imagined, and now we were dealing with this.

"This is why I kept myself from you. This part of the world is toxic and ugly and you're too good for it," I said.

"If it's part of your life, I can handle it." I let out a breath at her words. She couldn't. She didn't understand. Everything I had been holding on to slipped out of my fingers. I was so scared. So worried I'd lose her now. I wanted to numb the whirling thoughts. Wanted to make my brain not jump to worse-case scenarios.

"I'm okay," Kate said. I frowned at her. "If you're worried about me, don't. Honestly. I don't care what the internet says. It's not real." She gestured to all around us. "All this, it's not real. You told me that, right? None of that stuff matters. But this?" She looped her fingers through mine. She watched me closely. "Right?"

"Of course it is. That's all that matters."

And I would do anything to protect it.

———

"Charles, this is an overreaction." Sally crossed her arms. "It's just gossip. Like we said before, it was all bound to come to the surface. You keep secrets, the press will sniff them out."

I ground my jaw. "They didn't have to sniff them out. It was handed to them on a bloody silver platter."

"I think he's just upset because of where these pictures came from," Kate hedged.

We were back in Sally's makeshift office. Emma and Harrison had been asked to wait outside when I stormed the metaphorical castle to speak to Sally. There was a security guard right outside the door, which only supported my theory that she was behind all this. Otherwise, why had she anticipated my reaction?

"I can ask around," Sally said with a shrug. Like it wouldn't matter anyway. Because it didn't matter. The damage was done.

"I can't believe this, Sally." I shot out of the chair and paced. Kate sat quietly, watching me with worry. "I didn't want to do this bloody special. Then you roped me and Kate into that utter bollocks with the game show and now this? What's your plan?"

Sally let out a long-suffering sigh. "Again, you're overreacting."

"Telling someone they're overreacting to a situation, doesn't bloody calm them down like you seem to think," I snapped.

She straightened, face hardening. "Nothing has happened that we weren't fully anticipating. Frankly, the buzz is fantastic. The internet thinks it's an epic love story."

"Oh yeah? How about the article that accused Kate of stealing me from Emma and that's why Emma was crying outside the club? Or the one that said Kate is sleeping with me just to get people to read her writing."

Kate winced beside me.

Sally rolled her eyes again. "There are always going to be bottom-dwelling 'reporters.'" She put air quotes around the last word. "They don't matter. What matters is the hive mind of the internet, and they're buzzing over you two. They love you! They think it's incredibly sweet."

"It's not their bloody—"

"Charlie," Kate snapped. She was standing at my side. "I don't care what they say about me. Are you hearing me when I say that? I'm okay."

I relaxed some as her words sank in, but she didn't understand. This was a ploy or something. I couldn't figure out the angle yet.

Sally gestured to Kate as though to prove her point. "If you could calm down, you could see that this is actually a great thing for your career. What's left of it," Sally added unnecessarily.

"I'm aware of my celebrity status, Sally. Thank you." I glared at her.

She didn't care. She looked to Kate. "Yours too."

Kate frowned with confusion.

"I was waiting to tell you. I have great news," Sally said. "The studio execs saw the taping of the gameshow and want to extend it into a series. They've already signed on for a full season. You and Kate as co-hosts, with a variety of celebrity guests. All *Terra-Formative* fans, of course. The internet loves you. The studio too." She extended her arms out when neither Kate nor I moved, like we missed the memo. "You've lucked out. Congratulations!"

"I'm not doing a bloody gameshow," I growled.

The punchline of the Intrepid Trio was relegated to B-list gigs. They wouldn't be happy until I was decked out in absurd costumes and spewing ridiculous puns. I was nothing but a laughingstock.

I looked to Kate. Could I do this for her? If this was what she wanted? I couldn't live another day in this toxic environment. I felt myself longing for home and comfort more than ever. I needed a bloody drink. Or to just get away. This was a bad idea and all the pressure built behind my eyes.

I needed to take Kate away from here and bring her to the Vicarage so we could hide from all of this.

Kate had gone pale. "I'm a writer. I-I don't want to be on TV," she said.

I slumped into the chair, relieved.

"This isn't who we are," I said.

Sally ignored me. "Kate. I know this seems overwhelming

but you're charming. People love you. This could catapult your career. I know you didn't come here to use Charles. I obviously don't believe those silly rumors either but when the universe throws an opportunity like this in your lap you pivot. You seize the day." Kate remained quiet as Sally spoke, wheels spinning behind the director's eyes. "Think of how fun it would be; the people you could meet. I saw the pictures of you in that gown last night. That could be your life."

A little frown formed between Kate's eyes, and her head shook softly from side to side. "I just want to be a writer."

"We would be there for comedic relief and you know it," I jumped in. "I already did my time in that role. I'm not doing it again. And Kate is a *writer*."

Sally smiled patiently. "We can accommodate that." She flicked her hand to the side. "I mean, maybe you can write some of the jokes and stuff? The trivia! Oh, you'd be so great at that! We'll figure it out."

The other shoe dropped.

"What about the agent?" My voice was a growl.

"What?" Sally looked to me like she'd forgotten I was there.

"You told her there was a literary agent interested in her writing."

Color rose up the director's neck. "I mean, yeah. I will check in with her."

"You said it was a him," I said.

Kate had gone completely still, with her fingers clasped tight in her lap.

"Was there every really an agent?" I asked, already knowing the answer.

"It's just business. You know how these things work, Charles." She held my gaze pointedly.

"I won't let Kate be used and manipulated. She doesn't deserve this."

Sally crossed her arms and tilted her head. "Like you haven't done anything to get what you wanted?" Sally looked pointedly from me to Kate.

"Don't," I warned. She was implying that I had anything to do with Kate being here. Kate had been invited on her own merit. But Sally would lie, cheat, and steal to get whatever she needed from us.

"Sometimes you have to do things to get the ball rolling. You of all people understand that."

Kate looked between us. Something dawned on her features, and she stood up abruptly.

"Kate. Wait," I said, reaching for her.

Kate stumbled back to the door. "I need to get some air."

She all but fell out of the office, and I chased after her.

"Charles, wait," Sally said.

I glanced at Kate's retreating form.

"This could be what saves your reputation," Sally said. "What's your plan? To hide out in the middle of nowhere forever? This could be good for you. Don't you want that?"

I shook my head. "I just want Kate," I said and turned to follow Kate.

This. This was exactly why I never left home. Never trusted anybody.

"I'll send you some paperwork," Sally called after me.

39

Kate

There was no literary agent.

It was a lie.

Was there anybody in the show who cared about my novel?

I stumbled outside, the bright California sun temporarily blinding me. I put a hand to my chest and tried to calm myself.

Charlie followed me out a moment later. That look she'd given him. *Things we do … it's just business.* A terrifying understanding dawned on me. Something I hadn't even considered. I bit back a sob.

"Was any of this real?" I asked him when he stepped in front of me, blocking the sun.

"Yes, of course. Kate. Look at me." He grabbed my hands. "You and I are real."

"I'm not talking about you and me," I snapped and regretted the hurt that flashed on his face. "My writing. I thought they brought me here because of my writing. Because of all the followers. Because it meant something." I gasped and bent over, and my hands went to my knees. "Oh my god. It was you. You told them to bring me here so you—you could meet me? See me?"

I felt sick and icy with dread. This couldn't be happening. My whole life upended in just a few short days. It was a dream. I had been so silly.

Charlie dropped to his knees in front of me. "Kate. No. Christ, no. I swear to god. I found out you were invited when you told me." He gripped my hands, shaking them until I looked at him. His eyes were wide and wild. "Your writing got you here," he said.

"Did it?" How could my voice sound so calm when my insides were rioting?

"Of course."

"I want to believe you," I said.

He rubbed his forehead across my knuckles. "Please believe me."

Our connection had been so deep and raw from the very first message. I wanted us to be real more than anything.

"I don't know this world. I feel so stupid. I've been lied to over and over." I coughed out a sob and pulled my hands away to wrap them around myself.

He stood up and pulled me into a hug, squeezing so tight. "You aren't stupid. And you should believe me. I would never—"

He cut himself off, and then I really felt the earth shift. I stepped out of his arms. "Don't finish that sentence with something we both know isn't true," I said.

His Adam's apple bobbed. "Kate. I would never do anything to hurt you. I was trying to protect you from all this. Why do you think I never told you who I was?" He turned away and kicked the stucco wall of the building. "Fuck. This was exactly what I didn't want you to experience. This seedy underbelly. You're so pure and good and look at what they're doing to us."

I pulled back, a tear overflowing from my eye. "I didn't care about the rumors, Charlie. I don't know how many times I have to say that. I didn't care because I knew you believed in me. I knew I was brought here for my writing." Another tear leaked out and I quickly wiped it away. "I don't know that anymore. I want to believe that but part of me from the very beginning felt this was all too good to be true." I was having a hard time breathing. "And ... I just wanted to be taken seriously as a writer. That was all I ever wanted. Now everything the internet is saying is true. I didn't get here because of my talent. I got here because of you. Your machinations." I glanced around and scoffed. "What am I even doing here?"

"You are a serious writer." His nostrils flared. "I don't know how many times I have to tell *you* that. You are here because of your work. I didn't do anything to get you ... here." That second of hesitation wasn't missed. The darkness that passed over his face.

I cupped a hand to my mouth. *No, no.*

"What? What did you do?" My strength was crumbling. I didn't know how much more I could take.

"It's not like that, okay?" He cupped his hands behind his head, staring up at the sky. He took a deep breath and let it out before he dropped his arms. "I only even came here because I heard you were coming. You told me, remember? I was just telling Emma that I didn't even want to come when I got your email."

"Yeah, but—" Something clicked. Some minor detail that never made sense to me until now. That added to the whole surreal feeling of everything being too good to be true. "But then I told you I couldn't come. That we couldn't afford it and Pete ... and then you told me to wait to decide." I hiccupped in understanding. "That was you. You arranged the hotel and the flight."

"Yes. So? That was just tangential stuff." He waved it away like it wasn't even a concern. Like he hadn't even manufactured this. Like he wasn't keeping yet another detail from me because *he* didn't deem it worthy of being shared.

"That's why Sally said that." I sounded cold. Distant. "What else have you done?"

"Kate, it doesn't matter," he growled.

"What. Else."

He tossed his arms out in defeat. "The meet and greet. I suggested it." His tone had gone flat too.

"Why?"

He looked at me with red-rimmed eyes. His clenched mouth twitched before he spoke. "You said you were nervous about meeting the cast. I wanted to help calm your nerves and I wanted to see you."

I sighed. "You understand how manipulative this is, right? I just did this. I just got out of a relationship where I was slowly being maneuvered and turned into somebody I wasn't."

"I'm nothing like him." His chest heaved. "I would never do that. Kate, I just wanted to see you. I told myself that I would just see you and then we would go our separate ways."

"You could have seen me any time!" I yelled, too high-pitched. A few people walking by shot me a look. I lowered my voice and stepped closer to him. The anger radiated off me. "I asked to see you. I told you I wanted to meet you and you told me no." My tears were flowing so fast I had to keep scrubbing them away. I couldn't believe this was happening. "You said no. And I told myself we would just be friends, that you weren't interested in me that way. So I put myself out there. I made myself move on from you."

"I know. I curse myself every day for leading you into that arsehole's arms."

I rubbed my hands over my face. "It's not even about Pete. It's not even about you."

He glared at the ground. "He's the one that probably leaked

everything to the press. After he came here and I banned him, he had something to prove, didn't he? Little bloody coward with his stupid fucking goatee."

I lifted my head up. "What?"

Understanding dawned on Charlie and his jaw worked. "Pete came here. He was threatening me and stalking you. I don't regret banning him. I did it for your safety."

"And you didn't tell me because?" I asked.

"I was going to and then you were drunk and we were talking. Not that I care that you were drunk. I just meant that I got sidetracked. I forgot to tell you. Fuck, I'm not explaining this well." He crossed his arms tightly.

My defenses were shutting down. I grew tired. "No. You didn't want to tell me. You were controlling the situation. From the very beginning. You never, not once, trusted me enough to put everything out there. You were scared." I stepped toward him, all fight leaving me. "I understand that you have a disease, Charlie. I really do. It makes you scared and white-knuckle grip what little control you have in a situation. But you cannot do that to me. You can't make me be the reason that you are here. It's too much pressure."

"Kate, I—"

I held up a hand. "I came to LA because you told me that my writing meant something to people. I thought the studio fought to get me here because I actually mattered. But it was a joke. It was me creating the ultimate fantasy and letting myself have it. I knew it." I laughed through my tears. "It was too good from the beginning. A literary agent?" I scoffed. "After one little interview. I'm so naive. My mother was right." I shuddered in a breath. "I let myself fall for this fairy tale. I let myself think life could really be like something from my stories. I don't belong here."

I started to walk away.

"Kate, please." His broken voice stopped me.

"Please what, Charlie? I don't want to fight with you." I couldn't look at him. My heart was breaking. For my friendship. For my hopes and dreams. It was like they were drying up and blowing away. "You are my best friend. My go-to person." My voice cracked, and I shuddered in a breath.

He stumbled back, fists clenched at his sides.

"You hate this world," I said. "You want to go home. That's all you've wanted since you got here. You aren't meant to be here, and neither am I. I have to go back to Minnesota and figure out what I'm doing now. I have things to sort out and you do too."

He stood stock still. Pain contorted his face. I knew I'd hurt him, but he hurt me too. My anger began to melt away into sadness. We weren't ending like this. I refused to lose what years of friendship had built up, but I had to make a new plan now. I still had Pete's stuff in my house. I had a job waiting for me. An unpublished manuscript to ...

I couldn't think about any of that right now.

I stepped up to him and wrapped my arms around his waist. His arms hung loosely at his sides. I let go and stepped back, smiling sadly, chin trembling.

"You need to go back home to the kids. To Agata and the Vicarage. You need to stay on track. I care for you, Charlie. More than you may ever know. But I will not be the reason you derail your life after you've worked so hard."

I walked away.

I was done with LA.

I was going home to reality.

"Kate," he gasped.

This time I didn't turn around.

———

Charlie

I stared at the various alcohol bottles in front of me. So many options. Cheap or top shelf? Straight up or mixed in a cocktail?

So many ways to obliterate your entire life in just a few pours.

Christ, I missed Kate so much already. She'd probably not even gotten to Harrison's house to pick up her stuff yet. I'd watched her go and then stumbled away from the studio and into this dank hole-in-the-wall. Just this morning, I'd held Kate in bed and explored her body thoroughly. How could it still be the same day when nothing when everything was wrong?

This early in the day, there was only me and a barfly. He ignored me, talking to the woman working behind the counter instead. I was glad for it. The bartender had glanced over to me several times. She said she'd be over to take my order in a minute, twenty minutes ago, when I first came in.

Kate herself said it had all been a fairy tale. Too good to be true. I was a few days of vacation for her, never meant to be more.

"Pfft," I said loudly.

She accused me of manipulating the situation for control. It wasn't about control. It was about protecting Kate. I had been right. She didn't see that now, but she would. This stuff with the media might blow over if I let her go now, but if we were together all the time, this would be her life every single day. She said she didn't mind, but it would never stop, not until she gave up on me and went back to a simple life. Nobody was worth the trouble.

Certainly not a reclusive recovering alcoholic.

Recovering for how long?

"She didn't understand I was protecting her," I said out loud, to myself.

The bartender sighed but still didn't come over. God, I was embarrassing even when sober.

There was one thing I hadn't considered when being with Kate. For as good as everything felt with her, the pain of not having her by my side was debilitating. I could have never come, could have never known how sweet and lovely she was in person. I wouldn't have known that the chemistry we felt in our communications was a thousand times more powerful in person. That connection was not something I'd ever had with any other person. What were the chances? It was miraculous. She was miraculous. I shouldn't have left Devon. I shouldn't have come to LA.

It would have been so much better for everyone.

Everything hurt. My whole body felt achy and feverish from the second she gave me the goodbye hug that felt as final as the series finale of TF. It was over. I might never be okay again.

It always astounded me how fast things could be taken away. How quickly everything turned to shite. You could lose a career in a few months. A home in a week. A sports car in one drive. And the most important person in the world in just fifteen minutes. I was familiar with instant loss. Everything gone in a flash and would take years to get back. As if the faster you lost it, the harder it would be to earn it back. It had taken me years to build myself up to where I was now. And that wasn't anything at all. I had a little house with a mean woman and some chickens.

My throat tightened unexpectedly at the thought of Lucy, Adam, and Freddy. Especially sweet, stupid Freddy.

I gripped my phone in my hand. Dropped my head to rest on it.

It wasn't nothing though, was it? My life in Devon was *something*. Maybe not to everyone, but to me.

I hated hurting this bad.

I hated the pity in my best friend's eyes when I told them

about my relapse. I hated how it made me see myself. Hated how I hurt the people who, for some bloody reason, gave any fucks about me at all. I hated that I always seemed to feel things deeper than other people.

I sighed.

I hated every bloody feeling, but I hated *not* feeling anything more.

With a deep, shaking breath in, I unlocked my phone and pressed call.

My sponsor answered right away.

"Hi. I need help. I can't do this alone," I said with a shaking voice.

"You're not alone," he said.

A loud sob wracked me as the pain flowed out of me along with my tears.

TO: THEREALFREDDYSTAN4LIFE@GEEMAIL.COM

FROM: KateDubois@geemail.com

SUBJECT: Home safe

Charlie,

It feels weird calling you that here and not RC.

Everything feels weird.

I've made it home safe. Sally reached out to me to try again to pitch the show. I declined. I just thought you should know.

I am worried about you. Please don't let our last conversation lead you to do something you might regret.

Please call your sponsor if you need to. Please call me if you need to.

I'm still here. I'm still Kate.

I miss you.

Love,

Kate

41

———

Kate

"I honestly wasn't sure you'd come back," Gail said. "I figured you'd get one taste of the limelight and throw away this dusty old job."

I snorted and reached into my desk. "Hardly." I handed her the tiny snow globe I got her from the airport on the way home.

I had taken a whole week off before returning to work. A week to miss Charlie. To miss RC. To not really miss Pete at all. He hadn't reached out since that last text. I didn't think he was the one who leaked my identity to the press, he's a bit too spineless for that. I did box up his stuff and ship it to him. I wasn't going to risk a face-to-face if I could help it. Work was likely to be awkward enough.

Gail sat on the edge of my desk. "I gotta say, you do not seem happy. Is it because it's hard to be back?"

"No, I'm fine." I shook my head, frowning. "I'm sorry. I am happy to be back." *Not really at all.*

She braced her hands on the desk. "Did something happen with the recording? I've been dying to hear all about it."

"No. It was good. I think they got what they wanted." I ground my jaw.

How could I even mention everything that happened in a quick catch-up conversation? I met the love of my life and his best friends. I rode in limos with celebrities, stayed at their incredible home, and then found out everything was a lie and that I was a laughingstock.

"Then what's going on?"

"Just a little bummed it's over I guess," I settled on.

"Imagine my surprise when I saw pictures of you with Emma Flynn, Harrison Evans, and Charlie Downing all over the internet."

I winced. I had completely blocked out all of that, maybe hoping on some level that if I just ignored it, it would go away.

"You looked stunning, by the way," she said. "And happy."

I let out a breath between puffed cheeks and looked at Gail. "I don't even feel like that person. It feels so far removed from reality. Like it was all some ... dream."

"I can't even imagine. Are you—do you want to take more time off? You can if you need to. Keep working on the book?"

My head snapped to her. "No. I—No. I'm fine. It's better to be here and stay busy. My apartment is just depressing."

"I heard about Pete. The whole office did. Can't say I'm especially tore up about that. I know it's my fault that you even considered him to begin with and I'm sorry. He ended up being just so intense. He's been miserable to be around since that trip. His boss sent him to Omaha on an unnecessary sales call just to get him out of our hair. You don't need to worry about him."

"Oh. Okay." That was good to know. "Thank you," I added.

But again, I hadn't even been thinking about Pete. I'd been thinking about the complete lack of emails from Charlie. I spent an embarrassing amount of time during the rest of my vacation reviewing the photos of us splattered all over the internet. We looked so happy. We *were* so happy. How had it only lasted a few days, and yet my entire perspective of what happiness meant had shifted?

And why hadn't he reached out? The only emails I received were the ones from Sally, futilely pushing a show that neither of us wanted to do. I missed Emma and Harrison too, though I didn't really have a right to. I would never see Emma again. Or Harrison. The trip was a break from reality. I tried to focus on being thankful for the experience, but now, when I listed what I was grateful for, it felt like empty mantras.

Why hadn't Charlie emailed me back? Was he okay?

I was still angry. I handled the fact that he'd kept his identity a secret okay but then to learn he'd been manipulating me behind the scenes ... It was like I now saw our whole relationship from a totally different point of view. And I didn't like the story it told.

I promised myself that after Pete, I wouldn't let a man derail me. Not that this felt the same, but it was still me losing sight of what I wanted. I didn't get an agent magically. That was just one route to accomplishing my dream. So what that it didn't work out?

I heard RC rally me.

Come on, woman, you're not giving up so easy, are you?

I needed time to myself. I needed to get my head on away from Pete or Charlie. Away from TF and Emma and Harrison.

Prior to them, prior to any of this, it had always been about the writing. No more distractions or fantasies. Time I focused on that.

———

Charlie

Agata was unusually quiet when I returned home the last week. We worked silently around each other. Occasionally, she'd sigh loudly, set down her rag, and turn to me like she was about to speak, but then she'd shake her head and get back to work. She didn't even yell at me. I almost wished that she would.

I was back in my bubble. I had escaped the garbage of Hollywood, but now the Vicarage felt too big. Too cold. Too lonely.

The chickens brought me some comfort. I went out to check on them, avoided being pecked, and collected their eggs. Running from Nugget was my new morning workout routine.

I responded to fan mail. There had been a surge since the stories from the reunion leaked. I didn't think too much about it. I replied as I always did and didn't comment on the questions about my relationship status.

I hadn't replied to Kate's last email. She said to let her know "if I needed her." Well, I was doing just fine.

Sally sent the paperwork for the show, but I hadn't even opened the contract. After Kate left, I explained to Sally that our segment was done, and we were going back home. Sally insisted that we both needed time to think about the offer and we'd come around. Sally really did live in la-la land if she thought Kate and I would ever agree to that show. I was never returning to LA. I was never leaving this estate again.

I existed. This had been the original plan, so why did I feel so bloody empty? Because I let myself have hope. I let myself hope that Kate would want to join me on my little island of self-pity and leave her entire life behind.

What had I expected? That Kate would just drop everything to come live with me? She essentially told me her writing was more important than anything. I should have just stuck to the plan. No. I should have never gone to LA. I should have never even sent her that bloody email to begin with.

So why was I here, sitting at my desk in the dark, debating

replying to Kate's email? She walked away first. She told me the celebrity lifestyle didn't matter, but the second shite hit the fan, she ran. Just like I always knew it would be.

The office curtains ripped open, pouring light into the office.

"Christ!" I jumped and hit my knee on the desk and then swore again at the pain.

"Too dark. You mope long enough. Now you eat." Agata glowered at me.

"I'm not moping," I said, definitely moping.

"Yes. I know this face. You come eat big lunch and you make plans and you feel better."

"Agata, I really don't—"

Agata snapped her head to me. "No. You listen. You cannot go on like this. You are young and healthy and strong and you are wasting away. My job is to help you. Now you come eat."

I blinked at the ferocity in her voice. But more surprising was the little shake to her voice and her watery eyes.

"I let you have a week of putzing about. Time to move. You are not living, Mister Charlie. You might as well be drinking if this is how you be. I have a job to do. Go eat. It smells like boy feets in here."

So I hadn't been eating. I hadn't been working out. I stuck to my sponsor calls and online AA meetings so I didn't completely spin out but that was it. I had, in fact, been putzing about thinking about Kate. Agata was right.

I pushed back from the desk with a sigh. Agata wiped furiously at the glass window.

"I'm sorry, Agata." I bent down and hugged the scary little woman. "I mope."

She sniffed and then hugged me back. "You big stupid man. You worry me."

"I'm sorry. I'll eat."

She pushed me away and swiped at her eye.

After a bowl of stew and crusty rolls, I did feel marginally better. Agata, who finished cleaning my office in record time, was back and busying herself in the kitchen while I ate. I suspected she was ensuring that I held up my end of the bargain.

"Delicious as always. Thank you, Agata."

She nodded once and turned before I could see her grin.

"You know what?" I said after I soaked up the last bits of lunch. I looked around the Vicarage. I was tired of saying I would start the renovations and never doing anything about it.

"Hmm?"

"I think it's time for you to get your kitchen," I said.

"Oh, thank god. I am this close to making you wash all the dishes."

42

———————

DRAFT UNSENT

TO: KateDubois@geemail.com
FROM: TheRealFreddyStan4Life@geemail.com
SUBJECT: I miss you
Kate,

Fuck. I miss you so much. I haven't stopped thinking about you. I miss talking to you every day. I miss feeling excited about a little icon in my inbox that means I have a message from you. I'm in constant agony. I don't even want to drink to numb myself. It feels better to suffer. I don't want to forget you, even if it hurts.

I can't forget the way you smell and taste. I can't forget the sounds you made when you came.

Please write me. Please tell me we haven't screwed this up ... that I haven't screwed this up.

I'm still so mad. I'm still so hurt. I just wanted to be enough for you, but this is the reality of my life and it's shite.

I love you so much.

I can't tell you like this.

———————

DRAFT UNSENT

> TO: TheRealFreddyStan4Life@geemail.com
> FROM: KateDubois@geemail.com
> SUBJECT: where are you?
> Charlie,

I'm worried about you. I'm mad at you, and I'm embarrassed, but I still care so much about you.

I hope you've made it home okay. I hope you and the kids and Agata are okay. I miss knowing every detail about your days. I thought you kept so much from me but you really did tell me almost everything. I miss our talks. I think of a hundred things a day I want to tell you. I miss you.

This isn't fair. The way things ended. It feels so unfinished. We need to talk. But I'm scared that there's no solution that doesn't end with us not talking anymore. I would give anything to go back to how it was, just to know that you're okay.

No. That's not true. Now that I've had you fully, I don't know that I can ever go back.

I think I'm in love with you. How can that be? If you're in love, isn't that enough? But I guess that's me misunderstanding how the world really works.

I am in love with you.

But I can't tell you like this ...

43

Charlie

"Don't let her in," I said to Agata.

"Charlie, I can hear you. Don't be a prat. Harrison has to use the loo too," Emma called through the door.

"Please let us in, mate," Harrison whined.

I wasn't mad at Emma and Harrison; I knew they didn't do anything to ruin my life. I bought it all on myself just fine, but I hadn't been ready to talk to them. I'd skipped the last two monthly calls and ignored the emails other than to say I was fine and assure them I wasn't drinking or using.

"Fine." I unlocked the door.

I growled and went back to the main hallway where I was expanding the dining area into the kitchen. I wasn't risking any of the historical architecture of the space, but the dingy dining area needed more light.

I grabbed the sledgehammer and bashed it through a non-load-bearing wall. I'd learned a lot about renovation and my home in the last weeks with the help of a paid professional who ensured I wouldn't bollocks things up too bad.

"Wow, it's looking really great around here," Emma said, walking into the room.

"Thanks." The wall crumbled with my next smash.

"Good to be getting this aggression out," Harrison said when he returned from the loo. "Are you still miffed with me, mate?"

"I never was." I hit the wall harder.

"Right," he said.

"Can we talk?" Emma asked.

"I'm not going," I said. I wiped my forehead with my forearm.

"I'm having déjà vu," Emma said. "We aren't even here to talk about the premiere."

"Well, we aren't going, if you aren't. It's the three amigos or not at all," Harrison said.

I flicked a disbelieving glance to him.

"Why do we even need a premiere for an anniversary special?" he added.

"The whole thing is a waste anyway," Emma said. "The cost of the theatre, the clothes and hair and makeup. It's all a lot."

I looked between them suspiciously.

"We really aren't here for that. We are here for you," she said seriously.

"We're worried about you, mate," Harrison said. "I know you've been hurting."

My chest constricted. So often, I worried that they only contacted me out of obligation or because of work. But these were my best friends. No matter what I did, they continued to show up. More people to whom I wasn't worthy of their devotion.

I shrugged and smacked the wall one last time but it didn't even make a dent. I sniffed.

"Cuppa?" I asked.

They nodded, and Agata yelled that she was already on it from the kitchen.

"I take it from this display of testosterone that you still haven't talked with Kate?" she asked.

"Nope." I set down the sledgehammer and gestured to the covered chairs in the next room.

"Have you checked in with her?" Harrison asked.

I stared blankly at him. "Obviously not."

"Why not just talk?" she asked.

"There's nothing to say." I sat down and wiped the dust from my forehead. "She said she didn't care about the rumors or the fame stuff and yet at the first sign of trouble she ran."

Emma and Harrison exchanged a look. "Well, that's not exactly what happened," Emma said.

Harrison remained awfully silent, studying his tapping foot.

It wasn't fair. She was hurt because she didn't think anybody would take her seriously. "I tried to tell her that Hollywood would do this," I said. "I warned her repeatedly."

"But it wasn't Sally or Hollywood. It was you," Harrison said. I shot him a look, but to his credit, he didn't back down. "Look, mate. You wanted to see her, I get that. But all she ever wanted was for you to just be honest with her. She thought you finally had been truthful about everything, only to learn you had a hand in getting her there. She didn't feel like she deserved to be there."

"She absolutely did. More than I bloody did. I told her that," I defended.

"Possibly. But your actions spoke louder," Emma said. "She felt manipulated."

"She said I controlled situations out of fear," I mumbled. "What bullocks."

"Yeah, you do," Emma agreed.

My head snapped up. "What?"

"It's why you're out here all alone." She gestured to the echoing house around us. "And that's fine. You're controlling and taking on more and more as you can. But you can't control your feelings. And certainly not Kate."

"I was just trying to protect her," I growled.

Agata set down the tea tray. "Oh, men always know what woman need. Heaven forbid they let us make choice for ourselves."

"You know, you never rolled your eyes before you met Emma," I growled as Agata retreated into the kitchen. "And I wasn't controlling her. Maybe the situation. A little," I growled and kicked dust off my boot. "It didn't matter. There was no future for us anyway."

"Because you're famous?" Emma asked. "Because I really didn't get the impression that she ever cared about that or the rumors."

"I agree. She seemed very levelheaded about it in fact," Harrison said.

"She has a lot of followers on her site. She probably has a mild understanding of it on some level," Emma guessed. "But if you are really into each other, I highly doubt it's an obstacle that can't be overcome."

"They'd never leave her alone. It would be like that forever. I couldn't ... I'm not enough to ..." I shook my head.

Emma frowned. "What's really going on, Charlie?"

I had to trust these two. I had to trust they were here because they cared. "You and Harrison, you've moved on. You've done great things. I feel like ... like I'm a recovering alcoholic who lives on a farm and does jack shite all day long."

"That's not true," Emma said.

"Oh yeah? I work out and play with my chickens. It feels like you guys have both had so much success since, and I—"

"Don't have anything to offer her?" Emma finished softly.

I shrugged. That was the sum of it. "She's just so bloody brilliant and brave. And god, so talented." I ran a hand over my face. "I get so overwhelmed leaving the Vicarage that I'm in danger of going on a binge at any moment. I don't act anymore." I gestured to Harrison. "I don't do shite to save the planet." I looked back to her. "I'm a lump."

"You weren't to Kate. The way she looked at you ..." Emma said.

"Me or my fame?"

"It's not about that with Kate," Harrison snapped. "Don't pretend that it ever was."

I sighed because I knew it was true. It was the excuse I used to push her away.

"You know her better than that," Harrison said. "Did she ever make any comments before you met her? About how you should be doing something more with your life?"

I shrugged, feeling more and more petulant.

"Does it seem like that's important to her, you having a career? Is that a deal breaker for her?" Emma asked.

"No. She didn't seem to care. It's just," my throat tightened, "embarrassing. I'm supposed to be a provider. I'm supposed to be producing something or having some big goal to impress her."

"Can I just say something?" Emma asked.

"As if you could be stopped," I mumbled.

"You keep saying you haven't worked. That you haven't done anything but screw up. But that's simply not true."

I felt the old fears tangling on my tongue. The things I never even confessed out loud. "I walked into that set as Freddy Finks when I was eleven years old. I didn't have to act or pretend. I was just the chubby funny kid. I had a perfect setup and then managed to screw up everything since it wrapped. I never had to be anything else. I don't even know where the line between Freddy and I stopped."

Harrison shook his head and so did Emma.

"I feel that way too, mate," Harrison said.

I looked up to him. "Really?"

"Yeah." He nodded like it was obvious. "We were kids. I wasn't some brilliant actor. Why do you think I do so much now? It's like ... like I need to prove that I'm something outside of Adam Abbott."

I rubbed at my clenched jaw. "I never knew that. You seemed so sure of who you are since we wrapped."

He shook his head. "Nah, mate. I struggle too."

"We all do," Emma said. She didn't mention her philanthropy, but I always suspected that was her way of making up for fame she didn't feel she deserved. "You know, when I was talking to Kate, she mentioned that what happened to us was a form of trauma. I never thought about it that way. I thought it was this thing I had to be forever grateful for. But it really was so hard on me. On all of us. We were kids, thrust into levels of fame that adults crack under."

"Maybe we should have talked about it more," Harrison said with a laugh.

I nodded, still a little in disbelief.

Emma said, "But, Charlie, you have worked hard. You started acting when you were so young."

"We were children and we were working a full-time job and going to school," Harrison said.

"It's a miracle we all managed to reach thirty, really," Emma said, trying for a joke.

"You two did. I drank through most of my twenties. I don't even remember most of my so-called best years," I said.

"The best years? Hardly. You're in the best shape of your life and your twenties are a shit show for everybody," he said.

"I embarrassed you. You were my two pillars in life and I was an embarrassment to you." I glared at my clasped hands. "I know I apologized during the program but it kills me that I ever hurt you."

"You never embarrassed us. We loved you and were concerned for you," Emma said.

"Never, mate," Harrison agreed.

"Then you worked to get sober, don't forget," Emma said. "Very few people can say that they've worked as hard as you. You worked hard at creating a refuge away from the fake Hollywood scene." Emma gestured to the Vicarage. "To be authentic. That's what this place is. And now you're fixing it up too."

My jaw unclenched.

"And even if all that wasn't true." Emma grabbed my hand. "What your output is, what you produce? It doesn't mean anything at the end of the day. It doesn't prove anything. It doesn't make you more worthy or less worthy of her love."

I looked at her. "You practice what you preach, Em?"

"Don't do that. Don't deflect and be a prick to me because you know I'm getting to something here."

Shame burned up my neck. "I'm sorry," I said.

"She's just saying, all you have to be for her is *you*. That's all you have ever needed to be," Harrison said. "That's all she wanted from you. These last two years showed that. You fell for her and she for you, over your letters alone. It's pretty powerful if you think about it that way. If ever you needed proof that you were more than the sum of your production, just look at that."

Could it be that easy? It felt like cheating. Like I couldn't possibly be worthy of Kate with such a meager existence.

"So long as you don't bugger it up with trying to control every situation," Emma said. "You have to trust her and yourself if you're going to be partners."

"You are a catch," Agata said, and we all looked up at her.

Once again, I hadn't even heard her arrival. Even Harrison seemed startled by her sudden appearance. "Big house. Big muscles. You just like your little chickies. Scared."

Harrison and Emma looked at me and then each other. Then we all broke out in laughter.

"I am a chicken," I sighed and sat back.

Harrison shrugged. "To be fair, being famous is shit sometimes. It is hard to know who cares and who is using you. But you know that's not her. You know that's not who she is. You're afraid to be found lacking. Have faith in her. Trust her. Maybe she has only ever needed someone who believed in her too. And you left her because you didn't think she could handle you. Give the woman more credit than that."

"Fuck," I said.

"Head in his dupa," Agata said with a smack of her towel against her hand.

"Indeed," Emma nodded.

———

Kate

I LOOKED AT THE SIGNED CONTRACT IN FRONT OF ME.

I thought I'd feel different. I thought the niggling doubt that I wasn't a real writer would magically dissolve away. Yet another way I built up my expectations.

"It's a very good standard first book offer," my mom said over the phone.

Turned out the leaked photos and coverage could help me get a literary agent. Maybe that was why the contract didn't make me feel better. It still didn't feel like *I* had done anything to deserve it.

"Good," I said. "You think I should sign it?"

"That's up to you. Not my industry, but it sounds like a good offer," she said in a tone I knew all too well. Thousands of hours of business calls as I listened nearby. "Especially on a first book."

"Okay," I said.

I don't know what I thought. Had I expected her to jump up and down in excitement?

"Kate. You don't seem pleased."

"No, it's not that. Gosh, I'm so grateful. And thanks for having your lawyer look it over too. She matches my agent's sentiments. I have wanted this for so long. I guess, I don't know ... I hoped it would feel different. Like *I'd* feel complete now."

I regretted opening up to my mother—I almost always did. Here was when she told me that's what I got for building castles out of nothing and romanticizing the future.

"Let me ask: do you feel like you don't deserve it? Like it will be taken away any second?" she asked.

I gaped. I pulled the phone away from my ear to make sure it was still her.

"Uh. Yes. It's like I lucked out. Like I only got the agent because of this burst of fame," I said.

"And the publisher who offered, they only read your book and made an offer for that same reason?" she asked.

"Maybe? I don't know." I pinched the area between my glasses.

"From a business standpoint, a publisher would not risk their investment on a flash of fame. The writing needs to be strong too."

"Okay?"

"I'm saying that your writing must have been good for you to get an offer. Not just the trending hashtag," she said simply.

"Oh." Was she complimenting me?

"But that feeling that it will all be taken away, that you are faking it, and somebody will notice any minute? That's normal. It's called imposter syndrome."

"I have heard of that. I didn't—" Other people may have it, but those people deserved what they had, not like me ... *oh.* Understanding settled over me.

"We all experience that," she said.

I snorted. "Except you."

"Yes. I do too," she said plainly. Factually. Like she hadn't just completely shocked me.

"You—*You* feel that way?"

"Of course. I'm surrounded by rich white guys rolling around in billionaire dollars," she said. "I'm convinced ninety percent of my job is just pretending I have any fucking clue what I'm doing."

"Whoa. Really? Mom, you're blowing my mind a little right now."

"Listen. The truth is you have to trust yourself. That's the only way to fight through. Tell yourself that you deserve to be there and the rest will work out. Even when the voice in your head tells you otherwise, just tell it to fuck off."

"I guess. I just feel like I don't deserve it though. Maybe I'm just wishing for things that can't happen." I carefully spoke the next words, "You always said I was flighty and had my head in the clouds."

"And if you ask anyone who works for me, I'm a career-obsessed frigid bitch. So?" She snorted. "Nobody's perfect. And honestly who defines the parameters for perfection anyway? Men? Pfft. What do they know?" She cackled at her own joke. "No, love, if I did say that, that you have your head in the clouds, I only meant that dreams just don't magically come true and that you have to be willing to put in the work for it."

"Oh."

"But listen, I *envy* that about you," she said. "Your creativity, your fanciful mind. That's what makes you so good at being a writer."

"You envy that?"

"Hell yes, I'm so technical. I see things very black and white. On or off. You are on another level. I'm proud of you."

I couldn't help the cough that escaped me. "You are?" I hated how young and insecure I sounded. I was standing in front of that painting again, waiting to be called a fool.

There was a beat of silence. "Kate, are you serious? Of course, I'm tremendously proud of you." She sighed. "Shit, I'm terrible at this stuff. You were invited to an international television program to talk about your writing. You obviously have made an impact on peoples' lives, far more than I ever have. People typically run when they see me coming. At least you bring joy and distraction from a shit world. And they obviously loved you. My intern showed me you were trending a few weeks back. You did that. Don't sell yourself short."

I sniffed, not quite able to find my voice.

"I'm sorry if I ever made you feel like you were a disappointment to me. That's simply not true," she added, her voice rough but still holding it together. Not like me. My chin trembled with the effort not to cry.

"Thanks, Mom." I let out a long slow breath.

"But listen, Kate, I'm proud of you. I always will be. But more importantly you should be proud of you. If writing is what makes you feel like you're contributing, if it fulfills you, then do it and fuck the rest. And don't give any shits about my opinion. I'm just another idiot trying to figure it all out."

"Good to know there's no age where we figure it all out. But thanks, Mom. For saying you're proud. I know it's not what I should care about but I do."

"Oh, honey." She made a soft sound. "The irony is that I was never made to feel good enough by your grandparents. They wanted a husband and babies for me. I guess there's no way of escaping our parents' expectations even if we try so hard not to. I'm so sorry I ever made you feel not enough. I'm clearly very bad at many things." Quickly she added, "Just don't tell anyone else that."

I laughed.

She sighed again. "What do I know? The older I get, the less I understand. I mean that in the best way. If writing brings you joy, then do that. What else is there? I'm a person who likes fixing broken businesses and scaring people. That's my joy."

"Someone has to enjoy it," I teased. A tension I didn't even know I was carrying melted out of me.

"I have never been good at interpersonal relationships. For you, I will try and I will be better. I won't come at you like I would a failing business. God, even saying that makes me realize how fucked up I've been. I'm so sorry, love. I love you just as you are. Find what brings you happy and just do that. What else is there, really? It's all gonna be over before we know it."

Charlie. And writing. It wasn't much. It was everything. It's what brought me joy.

It was time I became the heroine of my own story. I was living a literal dream come true, a fanfic come to life. I wouldn't lose this chance. What was the point of writing fantasies for other people if I didn't live my own?

"Thanks, Mom. So you'll be watching the show when it airs?"

"My intern already put it on the calendar."

44

TO: KateDubois@geemail.com
    FROM: TheRealRealCharlie@geemail.com
    SUBJECT: Hello, from a reader
Hello Miss Dubois,

My name is Charlie Downing. Yes, like the actor. Because I am him. It's likely impossible to believe, but I am going to be upfront about that right now to avoid any confusion.

I'm writing to let you know I've read your stories, even though I'm terrified to admit it because it makes me sound like a nutter. I think you are brilliant. I can't stop thinking about you.

You have changed my life.

Best,

Charlie Downing

TO: TheRealRealCharlie@geemail.com
    FROM: KateDubois@geemail.com
    SUBJECT: Nice to meet you
Hi Charlie,

Nice to meet you. I am *so glad* to hear from you. Thank you for your kind words and for reading my stories.

You can preorder my new fiction novel here. It's a space opera, have you heard of those?

I don't know near enough about you, please tell me more.

Kate

————

TO: KateDubois@geemail.com
FROM: TheRealRealCharlie@geemail.com
SUBJECT: CONGRATULATIONS!
Kate,

Bloody, brilliant! Congratulations! Perhaps this seems too forward, but I'm so proud of you. The world deserves to hear your stories. I hope it's everything you wanted.

Cheers,
Charlie

————

TO: TheRealRealCharlie@geemail.com
FROM: KateDubois@geemail.com
SUBJECT: Thank you
Charlie,

Thank you for your confidence. I am learning to embrace the fact that I have an actual book that is being published. Don't worry, I won't let my newfound celebrity go to my head.

I can't help but notice that you didn't fulfill my request for more personal information per my last email. Are you amenable to that request?

Yours,
Kate

———

TO: KateDubois@geemail.com
FROM: TheRealRealCharlie@geemail.com
SUBJECT: More info
Hello Kate,
I am very amenable to that request. I am amenable to any request you ever have of me.
Yours forever,
Charlie

———

TO: KateDubois@geemail.com
FROM: Emma.Flynn@geemail.com
CC: Harrison.Evans@geemail.com
SUBJECT: Is this Kate?
Hi Kate!
This is Emma Flynn, and I've included Harrison Evans too. He's sitting next to me as I write this. We were just wondering if you had a moment to talk? I've got an idea. Ugh, fine, *we* have an idea we'd like to talk to you about.
Can we chat face-to-face? I promise if you don't want to talk about Charlie, I understand. I would like to see you regardless. I miss you.
Xoxo,
Emma and Harrison
PS: Agata gave me your email. I hope that's okay. She is smitten with Harrison. (He didn't even know who she was for two years.)

———

TO: KateDubois@geemail.com

FROM: Harrison.Evans@geemail.com

CC: Emma.Flynn@geemail.com

SUBJECT: RE: Is this Kate?

Kate,

Emma greatly exaggerates my stupidity. I knew who Agata was, I just forgot that I knew who she was.

Listen, mate, we didn't get a chance to get to know each other much, but I would like to change that. And Emma will not stop singing your praises. Between her and Charlie, your ears must be constantly ringing. Charlie has his head too far up his dupa (Agata taught me that), but I think if we could just explain some things, it might help you make sense of him a bit. We'd love to see you.

Xoxo,

Harrison

———

TO: KateDubois@geemail.com

FROM: TheRealRealCharlie@geemail.com

SUBJECT: A request

Kate,

These emails back and forth these last few weeks have meant more to me than you could possibly know. Talking to you again is more than I ever dreamed of. I would be content just knowing you're happy.

The renovations have just about wrapped. There is just one room left, the one upstairs with the window facing Farmer John's. I'd like to make it into a library/office. I was hoping you could help me with a few last-minute details? I think the room needs a feminine touch, and yours is the opinion that matters most to me.

(Emma would make me build it out of composted newspapers or lord knows what else.) Have you received the fabric samples and paint swatches I've shipped? I know that it seems a bit out of nowhere, but it's really something that must be decided in person.

Also, I have one more request. And it's a big one. It's a bit last minute, but do you have any plans next week?

I have agreed to attend this premiere for a special I recorded a few months back (why they need a premiere for a show that's being streamed online, I do not understand).

I have a slot for a plus one. All flights and hotels included. (Separate room for you, of course.) I would really like to see you in person. I know I said email is enough, and it absolutely is, but if you are interested in meeting me, please let me know.

I will make the arrangements just in case.

Yours forever,

Charlie

———

TO: KateDubois@geemail.com

    FROM: TheRealRealCharlie@geemail.com

    SUBJECT: Just checking in

    Hello Kate,

It's been a day, and you haven't responded to my last message. Not to get all Needy Petey on you (too soon?), but have you given any more thought to the premiere?

I know LA is a circle of hell and things didn't end so well last time, but I swear, I'm better prepared now. I have tools to help me cope with leaving the house, and seeing you again would be a gift I don't deserve but would love, nonetheless.

No pressure either way.

I love these conversations, and I don't want them to end. I'm sorry for all the pain and hurt and confusion I ever caused you. The chickens don't fall far from the tree, or whatnot.

Yours forever,

Charlie

TO: KateDubois@geemail.com

FROM: TheRealRealCharlie@geemail.com

SUBJECT: Final check-in

Attachment: draftemails.pdf

Kate,

I promised myself I wouldn't bother you again if you didn't respond, but the premiere is today. I'm sitting in the room we shared at Harrison's, praying that there is still a chance you might make it.

Emma and Harrison are acting weird and it's making me anxious. I'm worried about being on the red carpet today, but I know even if I stumble and say something stupid, it will be okay.

I will be okay.

Also, I should have sent this weeks ago when we first reconnected, but I was waiting to tell you in person. Since it seems that may not be happening, I can no longer wait.

Please find attached every unsent email I ever wrote you. Time stamped and dated. This might help you understand the poor choices I have made in the past.

I was so afraid I'd never be enough for you.

Now, I'm afraid of never talking to you again.

Yours forever,

Charlie

45

Charlie

I STEPPED OUT OF THE LIMO TO AN EXPLOSION OF FLASHING LIGHTS and yelling. I gave my best Hollywood smile, despite the lingering sting of Kate's rejection. As I helped Emma out of the limo, the crowd went even wilder.

"Are you two dating again?"

"Whatever happened to Kate? Do you still talk?"

"Emma, how are you feeling about the divorce of Wesley Cole?"

A hundred questions were tossed at us, but I slipped on a casual smirk and waved as best I could without being blinded.

"Feels like the old days, huh?" she said as we situated the train of her dress.

"Yep," I said as I kissed her cheek ... just to rile them up.

"Hey, what about me?" Harrison asked as he stepped out of the car to join us.

"You need help with your dress?" I asked him. "Or need a kiss?"

"Double standards," he grumbled as he linked his arm through Emma's. I took her other arm.

"Here goes nothing," I said as we walked down the red carpet.

Eventually, we were separated to answer questions from various news outlets as we made our way toward the entrance of the TCL Chinese Theatre.

My nerves were settled. I was content in knowing that no matter what happened today, I couldn't screw up enough to lose the friendship of the two people closest to me. I knew that my entire identity was not wrapped up in TF. There was a freedom I had not expected to feel. My value was not defined by the character of Freddy Finks or TF, but it still held a huge place in my heart. And that was okay.

As I looked out into the screaming crowds and waved, as I thought of the fan mail I continued to still receive, I was content in knowing that this show meant so much to so many people. I was lucky to have been a part of it. I wouldn't have changed a thing.

Almost nothing.

Despite my best intentions, my head was on a swivel looking for Kate as I answered various reporter questions. I'd checked my email in the car on the way here. She'd still not responded. It wasn't like her, but I couldn't blame her. The two times she asked to see me face-to-face I didn't answer. I had so much making up to do. If it took another two years of emails, I would do it. If it took a lifetime of emails, I would eagerly take that challenge.

I braced myself for the next interview, one hand in my pocket and posed with my signature half smirk.

A pretty brunette thrust a microphone in my face. "Charlie! This is Nikki from StarzTV. Tell me, how was filming the anniversary special? Good to be back with the cast and crew?"

I loosened my shoulders and smiled. "It was an amazing experience. I'm lucky to be back in LA where it all started."

Her jaw dropped momentarily before she smoothly went on to the next question.

I spoke to my therapist about everything that Emma and Harrison had talked about when we last met. The anger. The feelings of insecurity and loss of identity. So many knots of tension that had been tying me down for so long, I didn't even know were there. There was no reason to be angry anymore. I could talk about how important TF was to me without feeling like a failure, without worrying that I hadn't deserved any of it.

I didn't have to hide anymore.

Not that I was planning on doing too much of this publicity shite. I still hated Hollywood and needed to get back to the next batch of chicks before they hatched.

Whatever the next question the reporter asked faded into the background.

I felt her arrival just as before. The change in the air was like a whisper telling me she was near.

I turned, and the crowd seemed to part just for me.

The shouts and flashes all faded away, and there was only her.

Kate.

She was beautiful. She stood by her car, nervously holding her clutch, chin lifted, shoulders back.

My beautiful, brave woman.

I walked toward her as the reporters lobbed questions I couldn't hear. Her gaze darted around the crowd before finding mine. Her eyes widened fractionally, and then she grinned ear to ear. My own smile would be captured and reposted all over the internet, and for once, I was grateful. I wanted to have this moment saved forever so that I would always remember the dizzying way my heart soared to see her again.

We took several steps to meet in the middle. There was only Kate. The chaos around us faded away.

"Hi," she said and then took a deep, steadying breath.

"Hi. You look beautiful. I'm so glad you're here." I tripped over my tongue to get the words out. I had so much to say and with no internal filter. Kate was *here*. And I was done holding myself back.

"I didn't think—I'm so glad you're here," I repeated. I grinned like a fool. My eyes couldn't find a place to settle between her gorgeous amethyst silk gown, her gleaming wide eyes, or her perfect beautiful smile.

"I wasn't sure I would come," she said and flicked a glance around us.

"Christ, I'm glad you did." I longed to reach for her but kept my arms locked at my sides. "I have so much I need to say. I sent you emails, did you see those?"

"I did. I read them all in the car on the way here." She looked up and took a breath. "I never knew. I have so much to say too. We will talk but, Charlie." She smiled, strained and fake. "There are about twenty cameras on us right now. And maybe a hundred camera phones. Maybe we should go inside?"

"I don't care." I stepped closer, until the tips of my shoes touched her gown. "I just care that you're here." My hands reached for her shoulders before I hesitated. "But if you want privacy?"

"That's never been the issue," she said, her gaze moving over my face.

"I know. I'm sorry. I have—" My arms reached for her. "Can I hug you?"

"Yes." Her cool, aloof features melted into a smile. "Actually, wait."

I was aware of the cameras again as I froze, arms half out, still not touching her.

"Just watch my makeup. And hair. And actually, Emma's stylist put this like shimmery lotion all over my arms. Honestly, if you touch me right now, I'll probably leave a Kate-shaped imprint on you."

I glanced to Emma and Harrison, who smiled knowingly at us. I looked back to Kate as she chewed her lip and then forced herself to stop.

"Kate. I don't care."

I scooped her into my arms. I lifted her off the ground. More wild camera flashes.

"Is this okay?" I asked.

"Yes. No. I'm totally ruining my whole look. Ah, I don't care." She held me tight around my neck.

Eventually, I gently lowered her to the ground, still holding on to her arms. A thousand cameras and gasps echoed all around us. I only had eyes for her.

"I've missed you so much," I said.

Her throat moved. "I've missed you too."

I stared at her like there was nobody else in the world. There really wasn't. Only my Kate.

"I've been such a fool. So scared," I said.

"It's scary. All this." Kate nodded. "I got a little lost myself. I-I thought I needed to prove something but—"

"You don't. Not with me. You're bloody brilliant." I cupped her face. "I love you, Kate. I wanted to tell you in some grand gesture. I've wanted to tell you since I first read your writing, since I first talked to you. I love you so much. I've been so scared I couldn't handle having so many feelings, but I'd rather feel everything with you, then the numbness of being alone."

"Seriously, my makeup." She rolled her eyes heavenward and fanned her face.

"Kate. Can I kiss you?" I asked.

She laughed and shook her head. "Is it always going to be like this?"

I shook my head, not understanding the question and a little worried.

"Just assume the answer is yes from here out unless I say otherwise—Oomph."

She'd barely finished speaking when I pulled her up to me again. Damn the hair and makeup, I'd fix it for her.

I kissed her to the sound of applause.

We only stopped when our reunion became a little too much tongue for network television.

Kate looked down with her palms pressed to her cheeks. "Thank God for Emma's smudge-proof lipstick."

I lifted her chin to examine the damage. "You're perfect."

"Hardly. But I'm yours. If you'll have me." She shrugged simply as though there was any doubt.

"Kate," I breathed out her name and dropped my forehead to hers. "You don't even understand. It's me that should be begging you for forgiveness."

"I just want you." She fanned her face again, risking a look around. "You've made quite the scene."

"I don't care. About any of them. I'll do the bloody interviews. I'll do anything. I'm not afraid or ashamed anymore. I thought I could never be enough for you. I thought I was a fuckup with nothing to offer you."

"All you ever needed to be was yourself. I just wanted all of you." She shrugged one shoulder. "I know, I'm selfish like that."

"You will have everything. I am yours for the taking," I said.

She wiggled her eyebrows. "Is that right?

"Ahem," Emma said loudly at my side. "Hi. Yes. This is all very dramatic, but the show is about to start," Emma said around a camera smile.

Harrison was grinning ear to ear. He gestured between the two of us. "We helped. Just so you know. We made this happen. Let the record show, that your best mate, Harrison, had a plan to save the day."

"Really, Harrison, read the room." Emma smacked his chest. "*They* made this happen." She looked fondly between Kate and me. "We were just a little behind-the-scenes movie magic."

I grabbed Kate's hand and smiled down at her. "Magic," I said.

"A million to one chance that we would ever meet," Kate said.

"Nah," I said, shaking my head. "I would have found my way to you one way or another."

"Come on, let's get in there." She squeezed my hand tight with a fond smile. "Let's hope we don't run into Sally. I may have a few choice words for her."

"Oh, Angry Kate is one of my favorites."

———

Kate

"I'm just going to address the elephant in the room," Harrison said.

Charlie was seated to my left, an arm slung over my shoulder. He hadn't stopped touching me in some manner since we reunited at the premiere. Not that I complained.

"Since when are you even aware of elephants?" Emma teased. "Usually they have to be sitting on your chest for you to notice and even then, you'd just ask if anyone smelled peanuts."

We were sitting in Harrison's highly landscaped backyard, enjoying the temperate California weather trying to come down from the adrenaline high of the night's event. We'd changed out of our fancy yet confining clothes and now lounged in the padded couches surrounding his firepit.

"I will have you know that I'm always aware of the tension in any room. I just don't have the compulsion to stick my nose in other peoples' business." Harrison stuck his tongue out at Emma, who rolled her eyes. "Or try and fix it."

Charlie looked at him skeptically as he played with my fingers in his lap. "Okay, out with it," he said to Harrison.

"The special. The interview segment between you and Kate." He gestured to Charlie and me.

I was thankful for the darkness that surrounded us. Outside the soft flames from the fire, my blush was well-hidden.

"What about them? Kate did a fabulous job," Charlie said, a little too casually.

"You did too," I said, wrapping myself around his arm. In theory, at least.

"The tension. It was palpable!" Harrison shouted dramatically as ever.

Emma laughed. "He's not wrong."

Charlie and I exchanged a heated glance.

"Ah, yep. That's the one. The look that risked a fire on set. Had we been there when you guys were filming it wouldn't have taken me nearly so long to put two and two together. I can't believe we missed it," Harrison said.

"Nobody but you missed it, Harrison. It was literally so palpable, the tabloids felt it," Emma said.

"This means all's well between you two again?" Harrison went on. "You can simply thank me. That'll be enough, but if you insist on flowers, I'll take a bouquet of poppies. I'm quite partial to the orange ones."

"Thank you, Harrison, for bringing Charlie and I back together. Thank you. Again. For the hundredth time," I said.

Emma rolled her eyes. "Please. He was just there. I made the plans to get everyone to LA. I contacted Kate's work—"

"Gail was incredibly surprised to get an email from *the* Emma Flynn. She told everyone who would listen," I interjected.

"And what exactly did you do, Harrison?" Emma asked, chin lifted haughtily.

"I was moral support. The cheerleader. I set the morale." He waved his hand through the air. "Ah, anyway, we're all together again and that's what matters."

"True," I said.

"Did you two find your on-screen chemistry as obvious as we did?" Emma asked coyly.

"I certainly remember feeling drawn to Kate the moment we met," Charlie said to me. "Well, before that. From her very first story I read, I felt a connection to her."

"Same. From the very first message. I don't normally reply right away, but it was almost a compulsion to respond to your email," I told him.

"I never read fan fiction about myself. Despite what the internet says. Something about your work jumped off the screen. It was like it was being brought to my attention. Destiny."

My heart swelled hearing him talk so openly. I was sitting here holding Charlie Downing's hand, chatting with my childhood idols, and it all felt perfectly natural. Like I was one of their friends.

"It was meant to be," I said.

He brushed his thumb over my cheek and lowered his head to lightly kiss me.

"Aw, that's so sweet," Emma said. "But once again, I will ask, what did you think of the interview together? I can't help but notice your avoiding the question."

Charlie let out a highly annoyed sigh. "Just say what you want to say, Emma," Charlie said.

I hid my face in his arm.

"I saw you two sneak out. Right in the middle of it! It was only a two-hour special. You couldn't wait?" Emma pointed as she laughed at us.

"Wait, they did?" Harrison turned to us. "You guys left?"

"Oh, yeah, Harrison. You're the most observant," Emma teased.

I still had my face hidden in Charlie's warm, strong bicep.

"Kate and I had important things to discuss that couldn't wait," he said.

"Right. Talking." She clicked her tongue with a *tsk*. "The two of you have no shame."

"We *were* just talking," I said indignantly yet in a tone far too high-pitched to be believed.

It was true. We couldn't wait. Charlie had pulled me away almost as soon as the premiere started. He told me how sorry he was for all our time apart, for the unspoken truths and machinations on his end. I understood his fear and shared my own. The last few weeks, we'd been communicating again. It was wonderful to have him back in my life all day, every day in our emails—except for the bit where I went off the map. I wouldn't have been able to keep my surprise visit from him and it had all been a whirlwind. And our big conversation had to happen in person.

"I needed to apologize to Kate. I couldn't wait any longer," Charlie said.

"I had to say some sorrys of my own," I added.

"Hmm, two hours is a long time to apologize," Emma teased.

Of course, we totally did end up making out and getting each other off, but that was neither here nor there. I cleared my throat.

Charlie spoke up. "That's a lot coming from you, Emma. I saw you and Wesley—"

"You saw nothing," she said primly.

Harrison looked between his two best friends, dumbfounded. "Was I the only one that actually watched the special? It was quite good."

We all laughed, and I cuddled deeper into Charlie, feeling more relaxed than ever.

"I do have a home theatre. We could watch it," Harrison offered.

The rest of us agreed it was a good idea but made no move to go. From the crackle of the fire to the cozy blankets that surrounded us to the pleasant, teasing conversation, there was something so perfect about this moment that none of us wanted to ruin it by moving.

"I have to admit, I enjoy this house much more with you all here," Harrison said. "I don't have to head to Albuquerque to start filming until next week. We should all stay. Like the good old days. We could swim and watch movies. I'll get that awful blue Kool-Aid and bags of microwave popcorn just like when we were kids."

I smiled at Harrison. His excitement reminded me so much of his younger self, the one I'd seen in film and early interviews. I hadn't realized how absent his authentic joy had been until just this moment.

"I can't be in this city right now." Emma swallowed and looked to the side. "It's difficult to be this close to Wesley. Sorry, Harrison. If he wasn't right bloody next door."

"Ah. Yes." Harrison's easy smile twitched. "I completely understand."

I felt a pinch of guilt. He seemed so crestfallen now. "I have to get back to finish up some stuff in Minneapolis. I'm training a new person to replace me," I explained with sympathy.

"How's he doing, by the way?" Charlie asked me.

"He's good. Smart. Listens. Gail likes him even though she acts like she'll be lost without me."

"You have that effect on people," he said.

"What about you?" Harrison asked Charlie hopefully.

"Sorry, Harrison. I need to get back to the chickens. I'm going to be a grandpapa soon," Charlie said proudly. "There are some other last-minute fixes I need to finish in the house too."

Harrison let out a sigh, shoulders sagging. "Well, at least we have this last night together."

Charlie looked at Harrison. "This isn't the end of the show, Harrison. More like," he tilted his head in thought. "A season finale with a great cliff hanger."

Charlie smiled, looking more hopeful.

"Next season will be even better," Emma promised, squeezing his knee.

Emotion swelled in my chest. This did feel like the beginning of something wonderful.

I spoke quietly to just Charlie when Emma and Harrison started discussing his next film. "You know, I never got back to you about those samples you sent me. I was making last-minute preparations to come out here."

"You're welcome again," Harrison cut in from the other side, despite our hushed conversation. "Ow," he said, and Emma whispered something sharply.

Charlie turned so that he blocked Emma and Harrison, focusing only on me. "That's true," Charlie said carefully, his gaze moving over my face.

"The thing with color samples and choosing fabrics is, I really can't get a feel for how they'll look without knowing the room's natural lighting." I fought to keep from fidgeting.

A grin tugged Charlie's mouth. "Definitely best to be done in person."

"So, maybe, when my lease is up this summer, I should plan

a quick trip out there? I haven't even met the chickens in person."

"Well, the thing is," he said, and my heart stuttered. "It's quite a lot of decision making. And if you're already planning on flying all that way across the pond, you'll probably plan to stay for a bit longer than just a quick trip."

"Hmm, is that so?" Warmth spread through me.

He swallowed. "Maybe just until forever?" His voice cracked.

My mouth parted.

"You don't have to answer right now," he said. "Take the rest of the summer to think about it. I know it's far away and your career is just taking off."

I opened my mouth.

"I don't expect you to drop your entire life to go live with some stranger from the internet—"

I held up a finger to his mouth to stop his anxious rambling. "Charles," I said firmly, and he frowned. "My Charlie. RC. My *real* real Charlie. Chuck. All of you. Whatever name you go by, you are my go-to person. And have been for some time."

"You are mine too." He pulled me close and squeezed me tight.

"And the fact of the matter is, I'm almost done with the next draft of my book. The publisher will need it by fall. You'll probably have to read through some things. There are some particular scenes that I might need your help staging," I said, biting my lip.

He cleared his throat. "I'm very amenable to that request. In any way I can help."

"Good. Because I have some ... plot holes, we might have to ... *fill* as soon as tonight."

He laughed with the shake of his head. "Kate," he growled, face inches from mine.

"And as far as your request for me to come stay at the Vicarage?" I asked.

He waited, still as ever.

I leaned in, mouth parting to kiss him. Just before our lips met, I said, "I'll have my people call your people and we'll set something up."

46

———

A Year or So Later
Charlie

AFTER FEEDING ALL THE CHICKENS, THE GOATS, AND THE LAMB that wandered over from next door, I showered to change into a pair of nice trousers and a clean jumper and checked in with Agata.

"It's ready." She shoved a plate of cake across the counter. "You eat a piece too." She poked my stomach. "Good to see meat on your bones."

I gave her a pointed look before gathering the tray of tea and cake and made my way upstairs to Kate's office.

I gently knocked on the door but got no response. The sounds of mad typing indicated she was deep in her zone. I quietly pushed open the door. Kate had her headphones on and was humming as her fingers blurred over her keyboard. The sun shone through the window, blowing a soft breeze through the French doors and stirring the hairs around the base of her neck. Thankfully, the smell of sheep was not blowing this way today. On his little perch, just outside her second-story window,

Nugget sat, dutifully keeping an eye on both Kate and all his hens.

"Traitorous bastard," I whispered and glared at him.

I set down the piece of cake and cup of tea. She didn't notice me. Her brows were creased, and her eyes were watering. She sniffled and looked out the window. She stared for a moment, hands paused in their work. Sunlight streamed into the room, swirling dust motes, before kissing her long, lovely neck. I would not disturb her by grabbing her and snogging the breath out of her. As much as I wanted to. It was almost just as enjoyable to watch her in her element. Almost. She wiped a tear from her eye and returned to writing. I moved to the chair, content to wait until she reached a good pausing point. For several more minutes, she typed before she sat back with a sigh, taking off her headphones. She sniffed and then startled when she spotted me in the chair in the corner.

"Hi." She flushed. "How long have you been here?"

I shrugged. "Just a few."

"Everything okay?" She blinked as though coming fully back to herself.

I stood and went to her. "Everything is fine. I didn't mean to interrupt you. I brought sustenance to keep you going."

"You didn't interrupt. Your timing is perfect. I just finished an intense chapter." Her eyes welled. "I think this book is going to be something good."

"I know it will be great." I reached out my hands and pulled her to stand.

She glanced to her desk and spotted her treats. "What's this for? I thought we weren't celebrating my birthday until we met up with Harrison and Emma later?"

"This isn't birthday cake. It's 'anniversary of meeting' cake."

Her face melted into a soft smile, and I pulled her into a hug.

We held each other and rocked to the hardly audible sounds coming from her headphones.

"I'm so glad you had a pity party and googled yourself four years ago today," she said against my chest.

"I should have never told you that."

"I know all your secrets."

"You sure do." I lifted her chin to look into her eyes. "Finding you online was the best thing that ever happened to me. You've changed my whole life, Kate Dubois."

"I never thought my real life would be better than any fantasy," she said.

"Now that is a compliment. Your imagination is one of the things I love most about you."

I squeezed her tight to me. My body felt as though it could barely contain the happiness overflowing within. Every day I loved her more. Every detail I learned about her was more precious than the next. I loved everything about her, and I would spend the rest of my life making her feel cherished and special.

"Even when I mentally check out for days at time?" she asked with a teasing smile.

"Of course. My body needs a break occasionally," I teased.

She rolled her eyes.

"I love the way your mind works," I said seriously. "I wouldn't change a single thing about it."

"I understand that now." She snuggled closer. "I always thought there was something broken in the way my mind works but it's part of who I am. I'm proud of myself." She said it as though she was still testing how the words felt on her tongue. "I'm proud of you too. And this beautiful home you've built for us."

I sighed contentedly, still holding her close when I remembered the other news.

"Speaking of, your mum called," I said. "She's coming to visit the Vicarage next month."

"Again?" She blinked up at me in surprise.

"What can I say? She loves me." I cocked a grin.

"She really does." She shook her head in disbelief. "And I don't think you realize how weird that is. No offense."

I shrugged. "She's protective of you but she knows that you are the most important person in my life. I would do anything to make you happy and make your dreams come true."

"You make me so happy." Kate kissed my cheek as I held her tight. "But I think it has more to do with the grand-chickens. And Agata. I think they started a club."

"They're definitely up to something," I said.

I broke the hug and grabbed a forkful of cake. "Here. Try this. Agata made it special for you." I fed her the bite and watched her eyes close in ecstasy.

"Mmm." When she opened her eyes again, they sparkled with mischief. She glanced at the cake, her computer, out the window, and back to me.

"What?" I asked.

"I'm pretty sure I manifested this. This scene exactly." She shook her head with a laugh. "Only," she bit her lip, assessing me, "you weren't wearing a shirt."

"That is an easily remedied problem." I grinned at her.

She laughed before resting her head on my chest. "Sometimes, I still feel like I'm dreaming."

"If you are, then we're sharing the same dream and I never want to wake up."

"I love you." She squeezed me tighter.

"I love you too, Kate. I will love you forever if you let me."

"I'm amenable to that request," she said, and I heard the smile in her voice.

After a minute, my hands began to roam of their own accord.

I cupped her backside and asked, "So, you had a fantasy of me bringing you cake?"

She nodded. "Long before I even met you."

I raised an eyebrow. "I've gotten myself a kinky little wench."

She laughed and bit her lip. "Oh, but you've known that for a while now," she said coyly.

"Tell me." I brushed the hair off her neck to kiss it. "What happened next in this daydream of yours? I would really like to make that happen for you."

She gave explicit instructions of just how we would spend our time until we had to get ready for our dinner.

I made very good on that fantasy, just as I would on any other Kate could possibly imagine, until forever.

———

Interested in a bonus scene AND a deleted epilogue that didn't make the cut? Sign up for my mailing list and read it now! FIND IT HERE!

Curious about what is going on between Emma and her former co-star Wesley Cole? Read on for a sneak peek.

Check out Better Date Than Never, *now available!*

*Find all my books at **pipersheldon.com***

Sign up for my newsletter so you don't miss any important release news!

SNEAK PEEK

Curious about what happened between Emma and Wesley that night at the LA club? Read on for an exclusive sneak peek at book two in the Unlucky in Love series, BETTER DATE THAN NEVER. Find out more information at pipersheldon.com.

BETTER DATE THAN NEVER

Emma

Several weeks ago

The four gin and tonics weren't what propelled me forward off the couch of the LA club and toward Wesley Cole. Or at least not the *only* thing.

After a tumultuous day of filming the twentieth anniversary special of *Terraformative*, the four of us, Charlie and Kate, Harrison, and I, unanimously decided to go out on the town and share a small slice of celebrity privilege. Most of the time, being dubbed the Golden Girl of the Intrepid Trio was a sort of pressure that sat heavier on my shoulders with every passing year. Not that I would ever admit that. I was eternally grateful for the empire of Emma Flynn I'd built after our years on TF. Still, this life of always being "on" exhausted me, and nights like this were few and far between.

I just wanted to unwind, in somewhat anonymity—or at least what anonymity VIP room status could buy— with my two best friends and Kate, who was quickly becoming a new favorite person.

Kate had subtly pointed out Wesley talking at the bar. As always, my fingertips went tingly at the sight of him, and I had to clamp down long-tampered belly-fizzies. He was still so bloody handsome. My body still thrilled at the sight of him. And how had he reacted to seeing me? He pretended not to. The second our gazes met across the packed room, he looked away as if he hadn't seen me. I pushed down the familiar hurt of rejection and focused instead on the *audacity*.

Oh, the prat!

I stood with a lift of my chin, only slightly unsteady. The calls of the others in my party trying to reel me back in went ignored.

The absolute gall of Wesley Cole. He infamously dismissed me on a press junket. He told Sally, the director, that he wouldn't film any scenes with me. Sally had wanted us to have a segment together to appease the huge portion of the TF fanbase that pushed for our character's—Max and Lucy—coupling, but his agent said he'd only do the special if we never filmed at the same time.

Hot shame burned through me as I recalled Sally's pitiful face. It was like being pummeled back in time to my insecure sixteen-year-old self with a painful crush that everybody knew about. We *had* been friends when we filmed TF together. Sure, he kept it secret and pretended I didn't exist when anybody else was around. That had probably been the first red flag. We had been much more than friends for one intense night before he promptly sent me back to London. Yep. Another red flag.

Then he married someone else—the biggest red flag of all.

What could I say? We were teenagers, and he was my first love, but now I was much older, wiser, and world-weary. All the hurt and shame were packed up tightly and shoved to the back of my brain.

Until the moment I saw him again.

So here in the dark of the bar, the desire for answers *and* the gin and tonics motivated my steps.

I'd been accused of being strong-willed and highly persuasive, that I wouldn't stop until I got what I wanted, and I wanted the truth as to why Wesley ended our friendship without a single look back. It was time to put the past behind me once and for all. Maybe then it wouldn't hurt so bad every time I saw him on the cover of a magazine or online.

As soon as he spotted me crossing the bar through the throng of dancers and toward him, he tried to make a break for it. Despite the thumping music and disorientating flashing lights, I caught the arm of his suit coat and dragged him toward the back of the club to somewhere quieter.

Too late, Buster.

"What are you doing?" he asked in his deep voice, flat with an American accent.

When I first came from England to LA as a child, I always thought he sounded so glamorous. It had deepened to a rich baritone long ago, sending chills as it rumbled down my neck.

"I just want to talk," I said, but my defensiveness sounded sharp and breathy.

He stumbled slightly out of my grasp and straightened. Glancing around, he carded his fingers through his black hair with that flash of white streaked above his brow. His signature look got him roles playing dastardly, morally ambiguous men. He sighed, letting his shoulders down.

"Fine. Outside," he said.

He walked away without another word.

"I'll just follow you then," I said sarcastically, following his hasty retreat. He went out a side exit to the private entrance where a car waited and strode confidently toward the black sedan with every intention of sliding into the back seat. I gasped and ran (carefully in my very high heels, mind you) to put myself between him and the car.

"Are you actually running from me?" I scoffed, arms crossed. He stopped before careening into me.

He froze just as his hand grabbed for the door handle. His shoulders tensed almost to his ears. He loomed over me even though I was a few inches shy of six feet.

"Had to give it a shot." His gaze moved up and down the top half of my body, now unavoidable. The silver slip of my satin gown left very little to the imagination.

He closed his eyes and took a steadying breath. Because apparently, being near me was just that difficult. When his eyes opened again, they were sharp and glaring down at me, those famous dark eyebrows scrunched. He was *just* close enough to smell the hint of alcohol under the rich notes of his luxury cologne. His suit, as always, was exquisitely cut to his refined figure but slightly disheveled, and his collar was open right in my line of sight.

"Don't I deserve an explanation at least?" I asked.

His eyes flicked back and forth between mine before his usual unreadable features slid into place. He'd perfected this aloof look since we left the show, and now it was the only thing he wore. I couldn't help but think of it as a mask of indifference —as though twenty years of history didn't stand between us. "An explanation?" he asked.

"You're avoiding me," I pointed out, slightly breathless at his proximity. His scent. His warmth.

I might have rushed into this. Damn those drinks.

His jaw clenched, and I could have sworn he swayed slightly toward me before pushing himself on one arm farther away from the car while still caging me in. "We've agreed in the past that it's not a good idea for us to drink together," he said quietly.

I narrowed my eyes. "You're purposely being obtuse. You know I don't mean tonight. I'm referring to the past few days. Sally told me that you specifically requested not to film with me."

Wesley leaned over to speak to the driver. His chest brushed against mine, igniting the skin under the sheer material of this barely-there dress.

"Just give me a few." His voice vibrated through me as he spoke to the driver.

The window closed, and it was just us two in the quiet back alley. Only the occasional yell and the thumping bass escaped through the building walls.

He straightened but didn't make a move to uncage me. "Sally only wants drama for viewers."

I thought of the recent antics the director concocted for Charlie and Kate. He wasn't wrong, but it was more than that. "You can't pin that on Sally." My hurt was making me reckless. "You really can't even stand to be around me?"

He closed his eyes, nostrils flared before schooling them again. "Go back inside. If you still want to talk tomorrow ..." He ran a hand over his face, avoiding me. Lying. "We can try to meet up. But we shouldn't be talking right now."

His eyes had a glassy, unfocused sheen. I wrapped my arms tighter around myself. The LA night wasn't cold, but this dress was thin, and the crystals in my straps kept sending chills down my back.

At least I could blame the crystals.

It had always been like this for me, this allure to his stoic, self-contained persona. Maybe because his mask slipped at times, revealing a glimpse of a man I wanted to know more about, but only for me. It made me feel special and understood but equally as confused every time he took it away. No matter what my brain warned me, there was no denying the physical attraction. My body was a dirty betrayer. It made me question everything. Had he felt something close to this heat that night all those years ago when we gave each other our virginities? Something that seemed so silly now when it had been so huge, so important when we were eighteen. Had he felt anything for me back then? Or was I simply a box to check?

"You can't even look at me," I whispered, the words sounding hollow.

He glared at the ground. "Go back inside."

"No." If he would just look at me. Just stare into my eyes and remember who I was, what we were to each other. Not these past few years of resentment and silence. "Tell me why you can't even stand to be near me. We were ... friends." To my utter horror, my voice cracked.

His hands on either side of me balled into fists.

"I'm going through some stuff," he said, deep and fierce. His gaze focused on my neck. My collar. My chin. "The last thing I need is to have the media take *this* and run with it."

"This?" I asked with a hard swallow.

"Us." He looked around as if somebody might pop out from the back alley to snap a picture. Honestly, it wouldn't be that surprising. He added, "You know how they are with Max and Lucy."

Max and Lucy. Definitely not Emsley — our would-be celebrity couple name, given to us by fans ravenous for us to get together.

"Right," I said coldly, blinking.

His eyes hardened as they finally met mine. "Jesus, Ems. Did it occur to you that maybe this isn't about you?" he growled, the mask slipping.

I flinched like he'd shoved the words at me, swaying slightly.

I hated his sharp tone, but I hated more how hearing his nickname for me made me want to reach out and pull him against me. How it made me want to turn back the clock to a simpler time. Before all the flags turned red.

He sighed and softened his words as he stepped closer yet. "I'm getting a divorce."

The revelation sent a thrill of elation through me before I was quickly overcome by remorse and compassion for a man in obvious pain. His gaze shuttered, and I could see now, outside of my initial reaction to him, that he wasn't doing well. Those glassy eyes had bruises under them, and his usually meticulous appearance presented minor signs of upset. It wouldn't have meant much on anybody else, but with Wesley, strands of loose hair meant constant fussing, and a shadow of a beard meant neglect. None of these were typical for the son of Hollywood's biggest dynasty.

"I had heard a rumor," I fumbled for words as the shift in topic threw me off.

Not that I ever felt fully in control of my faculties around Wesley.

His gaze moved over my face. "Do you have any idea how humiliating that is? My wife is dating her director. My parents are ... Everything is a mess." He tugged at his hair again, looking away.

"I-I'm sorry. I thought—" A fresh wave of sympathy and regret for pursuing him so doggedly soured my stomach. I couldn't leave well enough alone, could I?

"The last thing I need is a media circus off the rumors of us from a show that's twenty years old. I wish people would just leave it alone. Every time I start to move forward—" He cut himself off, sucking in his lips with a glare.

It hadn't been about me. He was going through hell, and I'd projected so much meaning into it.

When he wasn't even thinking of me at all.

I had built up this reunion between us when I'd not even crossed his mind.

That hurt so much more than I wanted to admit.

"Wesley, I didn't know."

"You couldn't know." He let out a breath. "Look. I'm sorry I got upset. I promise this isn't anything you did. I just want to get through the next few days, then get back home and deal with my life falling apart. I'm sorry if you thought—"

"No. Stop. I'm sorry." I couldn't meet his gaze now. I couldn't stand to think how he might finish that sentence. I saw myself from his point of view again. The pitiful little girl from his past who couldn't let things go.

I swallowed down the hurt and shame.

"Please stop apologizing. It's all just ... complicated," he settled on.

"I'm sure." I chewed my lip in indecision. I felt myself about to do something stupid when I had already determined that pursuing him out here was a mistake. "I *am* sorry about Natasha. She always seemed so lovely."

He shrugged so defeatedly that I couldn't stop the bad idea. I reached forward to wrap my arms around him. Even as I squeezed his stiff shoulders, my rational mind screamed, *will we never learn?!*

I had been about to release him—and put him out of this extended misery—when he sighed the tension out from his body. His breath tickled down my neck as his arms looped behind my back, returning the hug with ferocity.

"Ems," he said softly.

God, hearing him say my name like that and feeling it rumble through me with our bodies pressed this close. It was the man who I remembered that nobody else ever seemed to see. It was too much. It was not enough.

Wesley was right. We really shouldn't be together when drinking. Every cell in my body felt lit up like Nakatomi Tower at the end of *Die Hard*. My stomach tightened with nerves and the hope that we would both just let ourselves make a stupid mistake. Consequences be damned.

We'd allowed ourselves one night before. When we were both eighteen and about to leave for the real world. We'd been friends forever, even if we weren't open about it, and that night we finally gave in. But everything had changed after that.

I leaned back to break the embrace and give my brain thinking space. My brain *really* needed thinking space. As I tried to step back, his warm, calloused hands smoothed down my shoulders to grab my elbows, stopping my retreat.

His gaze dropped to study where we were still pressed together, his thumbs moving over the sensitive skin of my inner elbow. That look in his eyes. I would have given my entire net worth to know what was playing through his mind.

He was still married. I was the Golden Girl. I should go since we both drank too much. It wasn't about me. Rational thoughts tried to make their way to my tongue, but my brain had gone offline. It put an out of office sign in the window and stomped off, sighing about not getting paid enough for this.

My body was in control now.

I should have just let him be. Why couldn't I quit him even after all these years?

He leaned ever closer. His lips were close enough that his breath mingled with mine.

It would be so easy. I could just lean in. Give in. Be someone else. Do something for me for once.

Yet ...

"I should go in," I whispered as hot tears began to burn the back of my eyes.

He stilled in his descent to my mouth. "You should."

We held each other's gaze, waiting for the other to end this moment.

Neither of us moved.

I brought my hand up and placed it on his cheek. The stubble tickled as he closed his eyes and nuzzled into me.

"I hope ..." What? What did I hope? "I hope things get better," I said.

He nodded against my palm. I rose onto my tiptoes and pressed a kiss to his other cheek. I lingered a moment too long, letting myself pretend for just an instant that we were two people sharing a friendly kiss. Not a married man going through something awful and not the Golden Girl balancing on the edge of a career-ending freak-out.

He was hurt, lonely, and drunk. He didn't want Emma Flynn. He wanted a warm companion. I needed to guard myself against these long-buried feelings. I couldn't let myself fall back into this pattern. I'd moved on and made a difference in the world. I owed it to the people who relied on me to remember that I was more than just my physical wants.

People counted on me.

With a sigh, I stepped out from the comfortable warmth of his embrace.

His head dropped, jaw tense, glaring where I had just been. He let me go without another word. We both knew that way led to nothing but regret.

I went back into the club, fighting stupid tears for a life that could never be. Letting go of a future I could never have. I *would* move on from Wesley Cole once and for all.

ACKNOWLEDGMENTS

Stranger Than Fan Fiction will be my ninth published work and I can honestly say the process of writing each of these novels/novellas has never been the same twice. This book in particular felt like a gift. I shot up out of sleep like I'd been zapped and proceeded to run to the computer where I wrote out notes for four straight hours in the middle of the night. The words and ideas tumbled out of me faster than I could type them. From beginning to right now this has been a passion project and often reminded me just how much I love story-telling of all kinds and the raw zeal of fandoms. Sometimes we need to escape into a fictional world and there is something magical about that.

As always, there are dozens of people I would like to thank and if you are reading this, just know I appreciate you.

To J.R., for letting me talk this one through on so many of our walks and sorry you had to learn more about the world of Dramione than you probably ever needed to know. Also, sorry about all the sleepless nights I couldn't shut off my brain, but hey, we are used to it at this point <3

To Tracy, as always thank you for reading it a hundred times to help smooth out the bumps and thanks for letting me crash your vacay as a mini retreat to get ALL THE WORDS.

To Ellie, for listening to me spew this book idea at you very early on and being just as excited about it as I was and reminding me of that fact when I started to freak out.

To Karla, for introducing me to Dramione. This is ALL YOUR FAULT and I mean that in the best way.

To Brooke, for being so damn excited about this with me and being my earliest reader.

To Nora, for all the things. You know what you've done.

To Lynsey, for reminding me that I always do this and that despite what my brain tells me, it'll all be okay.

To Pipe's Peeps, my Facebook reader group is seriously just the best.

To all my friends and family who not only put up with me, but also encourage and support me.

To the writers of fan fiction who pour so much of their hearts and time into creating amazing stories for NO OTHER reason than they love doing it. I am in awe of you. Thank you for inspiring this book. I would list the ones I particularly loved by name but there's a spreadsheet involved and not enough page space.

And thank you, for reading.

ABOUT THE AUTHOR

Piper Sheldon writes Contemporary Romance and Paranormal Romance. Her books are a little funny, a lotta romantic, and with just a little twist of something more. She lives with her husband, daughter, and elderly dog at home in the desert Southwest. She finds writing about herself in the third person an extreme sport in awkwardness.

Sign up for her newsletter here!
  http://pipersheldon.com/newsletter

If you are a Piper Sheldon fan, join her Facebook reader group to get all this insider info!
  Pipe's Peeps (Piper Sheldon Reader Group)

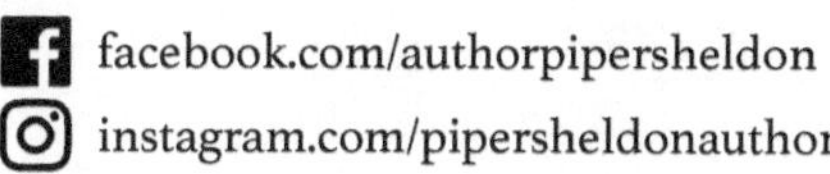

ALSO BY PIPER SHELDON

Unlucky in Love Series - Contemporary Celebrity Romance

Stranger Than Fan Fiction

Better Date Than Never

Down For the Word Count

Slippery Slopes Series - Small town, Romantic Comedy

All Downhill From Here

All Joking Aside

The Unseen Series - Paranormal Romance

The Unseen

The Untouched

Cozy Creek Collection - Small Town Romance, collaborative series

Fall Shook Up

Smartypants Romance

The Scorned Women's Society - Small Town Romance

My Bare Lady

The Treble With Men

The One That I Want

Hopelessly Devoted

It Takes a Woman

The Teacher's Lounge - Small Town Romance, collaborative series

Band Together

You can find all of Piper's books at pipersheldon.com or on her author page on Amazon.